THE INCOMPLETE

C000162337

BEN FACCINI grew up in rural France, ʋ
lived in Paris, London and Italy. His first novel was *The Water-Dreamer*
(Flamingo, 2002).

From the reviews of *The Incomplete Husband*:

'*The Incomplete Husband* lives up to its intriguing title – seemingly gentle, the novel turns out to have a bracing message about sleep-walking through life.' **Janet Davey**

'Giacomo's patient, quiet adoration of Elena; Elena's disturbed tie to her late husband and needy, clingy love for her son; Marco's exciting, challenging relationship with his girlfriend – these are the stories of what it means to love and be loved. All the characters bar Marco are immigrants. Deportation and violent protest form part of the backdrop to the story, but they stay in the background. Faccini doesn't feel the need directly to address issues of immigration such as inclusion or racism. He is more interested in exploring psychological aspects of one of France's major contemporary issues. Faccini moves across this emotional territory with fluent ease, weaving a common theme through each character. All must discover their place, what it takes to belong and the many trials of love.' ***Observer***

'*The Incomplete Husband* is moving and troubling and beautifully unresolved. It is elegiac but robust, full of missed moments, clashing mentalities, yearning for understanding and untimely complexities of consciousness. The observations are remarkable, clinical and empathetic at once. It's lovely.' **Emma Richler**

From the reviews of *The Water-Breather*:

'Totally original and mesmerising… Faccini is a brilliant writer and not a sentence in this wonderful book seems out of place.' ***Literary Review***

'Like Esther Freud, Ben Faccini has the rare gift of creating a world we can relate to from a child's perspective. He depicts minutely observed detail in a larger landscape, both emotional and physical… a book with an exotic atmosphere which lingers.' **Raffaella Barker**

'A remarkable novel about a family under pressure… rich, vivid, moving' *Guardian*

'Faccini's clean style and lack of mawkishness make for a convincing portrayal of the workings of a child's mind, and a truthful and affecting read. An assured debut.' *Daily Mail*

'A beautifully written, haunting meditation on innocence.' *TLS*

'A strange expedition into the border zone between love and anguish, a brilliant and poetic intermingling of memories and dreams.' **Lisa St Aubin de Teran**

'Ben Faccini does an excellent job of a very difficult thing, writing from the perspective of an eight year old – intelligent, observant, but still in the throes of magical thinking, and feeling responsible to keep further terrible things from happening.' *Observer*

'A startlingly assured debut. Ben Faccini captures the confusion of loss from a child's perspective and creates a story that is both life-affirming and funny. In the heat of the French countryside, we face a family's grief for a happiness they cannot restore, and one boy's obsession with trying.' *Irish News*

'This is a magical, beautifully written book and, as with the best of such books, I felt changed by it.' *New Books*

'Faccini captures the tics of a disturbed childhood in a vivid, dreamlike stream… This is life-affirming literature, uplifting, moving and executed with rare panache.' *Good Book Guide*

The Incomplete Husband

BEN FACCINI

Portobello
BOOKS

First published by Portobello Books Ltd 2007
This paperback edition published 2008

Portobello Books Ltd
Twelve Addison Avenue
London W11 4QR, UK

A CIP catalogue record is available from the British Library

9 8 7 6 5 4 3 2 1

ISBN 978 1 84627 082 6

www.portobellobooks.com

Designed by Richard Marston

Typeset in Garamond MT by
Avon DataSet Ltd, Bidford on Avon, Warwickshire

Printed in Great Britain

To my beloved Emily

Weep not for him who is dead,
nor grieve for him,
but weep bitterly for him who goes away,
for he shall return no more
to see his native land.

Jeremiah 22:10

PART ONE

Varanelle, Provincia di Parma,
Apennines, Italy, 1964

'Elena.'

'Yes.'

'What are you looking at?'

'Nothing.'

'You've been sitting there for hours.'

Teresa hoisted herself onto the windowsill next to her sister. Steep fields, bordered by forests, stretched up the mountains in front of them, their distant slopes scarred by landslides, streaked with cascades. Rows of dim peaks, dark with the stain of melted snow disappeared into the clouds.

'It's cold,' Elena said. She closed the shutters. A web of fading light spread across the walls behind her. The young women got into bed, pulling their blanket loose, and tucked it round themselves.

'Have you heard about that man?' Teresa asked.

'What man?'

'The one from Friuli who works at the sawmill?'

Elena turned to the wall. 'No.'

'He spends his nights walking, across the fields, up and down the mountains. He never sleeps.' Teresa gave the blanket a sharp jerk in her direction. 'That's what he does every night, goes up and down the mountains, searching for food, roots, berries, mushrooms, anything he can find. Someone from the village caught him drinking from the river on all fours, like a dog, lapping at the water. I saw him in the cemetery, perched on a tombstone, taking in the sun. He looked straight through me.'

They lay side by side in the growing darkness. Elena smoothed the hem of her nightdress and pushed her hair away from her forehead. She scratched her ankle, shifting from side to side.

'What's wrong?'

'Nothing.' Elena inched the blanket towards her.

'You're fidgeting.'

'I'm not.'

'You are.'

2

Elena stood listening to her sister's breathing, doing up the last of the buttons on her dress. She ran past her parents' room and out of the door to the nearest patch of oaks. She crouched to regain her breath. She looked back at the farmhouse, straining to see in the half-light, then sprinted on. A string of pale rocks appeared in the shadows, tracing a path up the mountainside. Hard crests of earth, left by the tyres of the trucks from the sawmill, dug into the soles of her shoes.

She reached a high bank and slithered down it, steadying herself on branches and stumps. Scents of cut wood, sawdust and resin spiced the air. She skirted round a pile of felled tree trunks and came to the entrance of the mill. The gates were bound by a chain. A padlock hung from it. She banged it to announce her arrival. A call, similar to that of a cat, miaowed through the woods as a reply. She was cold. She examined the ends of her shoes plastered with mud and dead leaves. She tapped them against a stone. She heard the scurrying of an animal in the bushes and a car travelling out of the village. Its brakes screeched at intervals down the road. 'Are you here?' she said.

She listened, her breathing the only sound. She banged the padlock, like a gong. 'Are you here?' she called in a louder voice. There was no answer.

She hopped from foot to foot to keep warm. A gust of wind in the trees startled her. She backed away, hurrying downhill again, through the woods, to the farmhouse. Branches whipped at her chest, her ankles stung with the scratches of brambles and saplings. She was halted by a mass of nettles. She retraced her steps until she found the stone track to the village. She ran along it, faster and faster, shivering and sweating at the same time. The path sped beneath her, downwards.

'Hey! Where are you off to?' A voice jumped out in front of her.

She shrieked and covered her face.

'It's me.'

'What… what are you doing here?'

'Going to the sawmill to meet you, of course,' Riccardo laughed.

'I'm… I…' she grabbed his arm and fell against him, copying his laughter.

He seemed even taller, his jaw larger. He guided her back up the path, towards the sawmill. Each time she stumbled, he gripped her hand and brought it to his lips, kissing each knuckle.

'Sorry I was late,' he said, stopping to light a cigarette, sucking until it glowed.

'You've been seen. My sister Teresa told me. They know you come up here.'

They were at the entrance to the sawmill. They walked round the fenced-off area. Machines and saws were tidied away beneath a metallic hangar. The roof jutted out at a sharp angle. Planks were roughly stacked. A smattering of woodchips covered the ground next to a rusting bicycle. Again Elena felt his lips on her hands.

'We're going to have to be careful,' she said. She opened his jacket and hid from the wind, his waistcoat buttons on her cheek.

'Sssh, don't worry.' Riccardo undid the knot holding her hair, feeling the down of her temples and nape.

'No, really,' she said, arching her spine. 'You don't know what people are like in this village.'

They walked round the sawmill in an unhurried embrace. He pointed to the edge of a workshop.

'That's where your father stands, there, by that box, barking orders at us all day.'

'And you?'

'I work there, cutting planks,' he said, indicating another covered area.

'What else do you do?'

'That's it!' His laughter smelt of tobacco. 'We talk, of course, when your father's not around.'

'What about?' She was shaking again. She burrowed further into his jacket.

'This and that, *diverse cose*, you know, rubbish really – why the cinema in town closed, where to buy trousers, how to repair a moped, that kind of stuff.' Elena looked up at his face, knocking his chin with the crown of her head. The whiteness of his teeth was startling. 'We all agree on one thing,' he said.

'What's that?'

'You.'

'Me!'

'Sure, the foreman's daughter, you're well-known round here.'

'Ah, come off it. Stop it.' She let go of Riccardo.

'No, seriously, we talk about you, how there's no-one like you for miles, the way you walk and run, how you laugh, your eyes, that kind of thing, that hair of yours, as black as crow feathers, that's what they say.'

'But I've never even spoken to most of them.'

6

'Ah, but they're watching you. They don't know what happens in that shuttered-up house where you live, but they've all dreamed of breaking in, I can tell you. I thought I was the only one who knew the path you take to town, or where you stop to wade into the river and throw stones, but I'm not. Do you think I like that? Each time I followed you I was sure I was being followed too. It took me months to get the chance to see you on my own.' As he said this, he took a long strand of her hair and brought it to his face and breathed in. 'They wouldn't believe it if they saw me now.'

'Who?'

'The guys I work with.'

'You haven't said anything to them have you?' Elena said, retreating. 'Please, Riccardo, don't.'

'Of course I haven't.' He ran a finger across one of her eyebrows and then back again, touching a mole by the top of her ear.

'You mustn't tell anyone,' she said. 'I can't even imagine what my father would do if he knew.'

'He's right to worry,' Riccardo said. 'Myself, I'd keep you locked up.'

'Is that what they say too?'

'Not really.'

'They do, don't they?'

'They speak dialect all the time, I don't always get it.'

Elena poked him in the stomach. 'You do, you know exactly what they say.'

'It's just village stuff.'

'Such as?'

'It's nothing.'

'Go on.'

'Well… if you insist. They say that your father drinks, and thinks he's better than anyone else because he's some little smug foreman, and

7

he's fattened your mother up like a goose, so fat she can barely leave the house. She even sits on your father's money at night, like an egg, to make it grow. And nothing is good enough for their precious daughters, that kind of talk.'

'Oh,' Elena swallowed uncomfortably. 'I see.' She took a few steps before turning to him. 'They say things about you too, you know.'

'I'm sure, I've heard it all before, one village is like any other.'

'But they say such stupid things.'

'Doesn't bother me.' Riccardo took her hand. He bent forward, breaking into a smile, the heat of his breath on her face. 'It's because we're happier than they are. Let them talk. Who cares?' He kissed her ears. The sound reverberated inside her head. 'Leave with me. We'll get out this place,' he said, leading her along the fence.

'Don't play with me.' She nudged him in the ribs.

'I'm serious. Do you think I'm going to cut wood for the rest of my life?' He looked at her. 'I told you, I've got nothing to go back home to. The barn where we kept our cattle burnt down, most of my possessions and the cows went with it. I've got nothing, there's no trace of me left back in Friuli.' He gripped her waist. 'Elena, don't you see? We could get out of here. Why not, the two of us, we could just go? Don't you ever think about that?'

'I do, of course… I…'

'I don't want to have the life my parents had. Do you? When my mother died a few months ago I couldn't get to the funeral, the railway tracks were blocked with snow. But the first person I saw on the way back here, the only person, was you, alone, walking straight towards me. What does that mean?'

'It…'

'I tell you what it means, that there's nothing for us here. We belong together. We should be off, starting something new. My brother, Giacomo, is going to sell our house and find work in Paris, and I have

8

a cousin in Argentina.' He cupped her chin. 'The world is ours, Elena,' he shouted. 'Ours. Imagine Paris or Buenos Aires. Which do you choose?'

'Lots of old people here have cousins in England and America, all over the place, Australia too, but we're different in our family, no-one has ever left.'

'So?'

'It frightens me, terrifies me.'

'What does?'

'All that,' she waved her arm towards the mountains, implying the valleys beyond, 'the world, all those places.'

'Ah, come on, what's wrong with you! The Russians have just sent some woman into space, did you not see her picture in the paper? Valentina something. She span round the earth several times.'

'Part of me wants to leave, sometimes, but then the idea of it is too much, I just can't imagine it, all those places and people.' She turned away from him. 'I've never been further than Parma,' she said. 'Bet you never realized that?' She hid her embarrassment, resting her head inside the folds of his jacket again. They came to the outer perimeter of the sawmill. It gave way to a pit filled with dead leaves. The light on the trees was growing brighter. 'I'd better get back.'

'Don't go,' Riccardo said. 'You've only just arrived.'

'My sister talked about you, I told you. She might wake, anyone could.'

They walked downhill. Within sight of the farmhouse, she held him, in a tighter embrace. 'I don't want to leave you,' she said. She clung to his wrists. A copse of trees shielded them from the house.

'Stay with me.'

'I can't.' She began moving away.

'See you tomorrow,' he said. 'At the sawmill.'

She nodded and disappeared round the back of the house,

9

knocking a spade over in the yard. A muffled squawking came from the chicken pen.

Elena folded her clothes and crept into bed. Her sister didn't stir. Carefully she pulled the cover up over her shoulders and laid her head on the pillow. The holes and cracks in the shutters were turning a different colour. There seemed to be more of them than before, as if new pieces of wood had fallen from the shutters in the night, a loose lattice sprinkling the room with the day's new light. Elena counted the holes twice, then again, and watched how the flickering of their dots joined up on the walls of the room.

'What's wrong with you?' Teresa complained sleepily, wiping the sheet between them. 'You're covered in sweat.'

3

Riccardo observed Elena from the side of the track. He whistled to catch her attention, protecting his eyes from the sun with his hand. She looked up and beckoned him to join her. As he approached, she noticed his face was covered in a layer of sawdust, on his eyebrows and hair, stuck to the stubble of his cheeks.

'You're mad. My father was here five minutes ago.'

'I want to see you in the daylight. All these months of meeting at night are getting to me.'

'I don't think he'll be back for a while.'

Riccardo pulled her towards him. She held his chin in her hands and blew across his forehead. She licked the bridge of his nose, curling her tongue round the contours of his mouth, and spat wood shavings onto the ground. He fingered the straps of her dress, flicking them off her shoulders.

'Not here,' she said. 'We can't.'

He kissed her neck and she jumped, wriggling and itching, as sawdust fell from his hair down the front of her dress. She stamped one foot, then the other, brushing her chest. He ran behind her, lifting the hem of her dress.

'Wait!' she said, 'not yet.' She raced ahead, guarding her midriff and rear from his repeated lunges.

'Oh Elena! Elena!' he sung.

'Sssh, keep your voice down!'

'What about behind there?' he said, pointing at an abandoned hay cart.

'It's in the sun, and in full view!'

'Or there?' He edged her towards a tree, its branches bowed and looped. 'It's shaded.'

'Someone might see us.'

'Over there's perfect,' he indicated a barn in the distance.

'No, Carlo Zanelli is in and out of that place all day, he's the nosiest of them all.'

They linked hands and headed further up the slope. The grass grew thick, its tips heavy with whiskered seeds.

'There?' Riccardo said, gesturing to an overgrown orchard.

'No.'

'I can't wait for us to get out of this shithole, *paesello di merda*,' he sighed. 'You should have seen our house in Friuli, no-one bothered us there. We didn't have a thing, but we were as free as birds.'

'Patience, my love, we'll leave as soon as we can.'

He guided her over a boulder, pushing her gently onwards. 'Have you told your father yet?'

Elena took a left fork in the path. Rounded clumps of grass carved out uneven steps. They hopped from one to the other. 'I started to, the other day, but I didn't dare carry on. I need more time.' She avoided a hole in the earth and saw a beetle on her left shoe.

'Are you going to rot in this place for him?'

'It's not like that.'

'He's a miserable bastard. How can you defend him?'

'He's my father. You only have a brother left. It's different.'

'So what? Your father's an idiot. You know what he does most days?'

'What?'

'He counts planks and tree trunks. How about that for a life?'

'It won't be easy leaving my mother and sister behind with him.'

'Why, what does he do to them?'

Elena didn't reply.

'Well, he's a grumpy old sod, and he has a neck as thick as a bull. How come you're so beautiful?' He snuffled, flaring his nostrils wildly, scraping his legs backwards. With his hands above his head as horns, he charged at Elena. 'One log,' he grunted, 'two logs, three logs, four logs...' She jumped out of the way, swatting his head. A different valley came into view. The farmhouse had shrunk, the chicken shed and wood stack merged with the main building. The window of her bedroom became a dot and then disappeared.

Riccardo stopped Elena and took a knife from his jacket.

'What are you doing?'

He pinched the hair hanging in front of her eyes. 'I just want to cut these tiny bits.'

'Hold on!' She crossed her arms over her head.

'They annoy me, they get in the way. I can't see your eyes properly.' He smiled, and she let her arms fall. He cut a few strands with his blade.

She patted her hair for signs of gaps. They carried on walking, pulling each other up the hillside. She was sure she could feel a breeze against her forehead where there had been none before.

'When I was buying the bread in Bardi,' she said. 'I met a woman who'd lived in Argentina years ago. She said you can travel for days and not meet a soul, only feel the sun on your skin.'

'And the weight of your money in your pocket!' Riccardo grinned.

'I've read some of that book on Argentina you gave me. I don't think I'll be that good at it, but I guess I should learn some Spanish. You've got to know a bit to sell copper pipes, haven't you?'

'We won't be helping my cousin for long. We can do better than pipes.'

'Like what?'

'Anything. You can do anything in Argentina, that's what my cousin told me when he wrote. As soon as Giacomo sends the money from the house sale, and I've worked a bit here, we can set up anything we want.'

'Like what?'

'How about a restaurant?'

'Whatever you want.'

'Steaks and sausages, roasts. We could have a meat place. That would be good.'

'But I don't know how to cook those things.'

'How about a garage?' Riccardo lit a cigarette.

'A garage?'

'Yeah, why not?'

'Beds?' Elena said.

'What?'

'Yes, you're good with wood. The most comfortable beds in the world! "Riccardo and Elena's Beds." That sounds great, doesn't it? Each one individually made, expertly carved, with sturdy feet, and small steps to climb up. And niches to keep your shoes, a ledge for a clock, shelves for your clothes, a place for snacks or cigarettes in the middle of the night, a mirror to look at yourself in the morning.'

'We could invent something,' Riccardo said.

'Such as?'

'I don't know, something no-one's ever imagined, ever.' He smiled. 'Give me some time to think about it!'

'Candles, I've always loved candles. We could make them, all shapes and sizes, different colours, for churches, houses, parties, whatever…'

'A chicken farm. Chickens are easy to rear. We could have thousands of them, all breeds, for eating, laying eggs.'

'A shop that sells just birds. That's it. The world's most beautiful birds all in one shop. Think of the feathers. It would be great for our children.'

'No, a shop's a bad idea. I'd go mad with all those customers sniffing round you.' He grabbed her shoulders. 'A woman like you can't serve behind a counter.' He pushed at the front of her dress, forcing his hand downwards.

'Let go,' she said, tapping him.

'Ah, go on,' Riccardo yanked at her dress again. 'Just for me, you can't stop me now.'

'You're going to have to wait a little longer.' Elena broke away from him.

'Let me have a look, please, please, ELLeeeennNA, please. You're even more amazing in the sunlight, you are.'

He held her face like a chalice. He studied every aspect of it, the sweat forming on her top lip, the thick eyelashes that beat against the tips of his fingers, the darkness of her pupils, the skin of her tanned cheeks, as shining as new wood. He spun her round and plunged his hand back down her dress. He followed the dips of her collarbones with his thumb, tugging the lapels further apart.

'Riccardo, will you stop that.' She chased ahead, laughing.

'Come on,' he shouted, overtaking her. 'Let's find some shade.'

They walked, hand in hand again, to the edge of the forest that spread in the direction of Monte Barigazzo. The road to Parma dropped into the valley, dipping in and out of the woods below. Cars came and went in slow procession. The ground grew steeper. A humid smell of undergrowth hit them. Rustles in the leaves heralded their arrival. Birds burst from the mesh of bushes.

'Listen,' Elena said, standing still. 'I heard something.'

'What?'

'That noise? What was it? It sounded like someone behind us.'

'Come, get a move on.'

'No, sssh, wait.'

Riccardo carried on walking, but Elena stayed, studying the trees and broken trunks. She picked up a stone and lobbed it into a heap of dead leaves, waiting for a response. There was no movement. She peered into the branches.

'Come!' Riccardo called. 'There's a stream.'

They clambered down to a trickle of water as it leaked its way through the forest. They sidestepped ferns and rocks, sliding along narrow broken banks, finally walking barefoot through the water itself, carrying their shoes. Cords of ivy, tassels of branches draped down in a patchy, broken ceiling. They came to a bend in the stream and the water became deeper and wider. A pool had formed between mossy rocks. Next to it was an undisturbed hollow in the ground, bounded by thickets, where the grass grew tall, an empty bed of green.

'This deep bit is freezing.' Elena shivered, skimming the pool with her foot.

'I'm going to swim,' Riccardo said.

He took off his shirt and his trousers. By the edge of the stream, he pulled off his underpants and gasped as he slid into the water. He ducked under the surface, re-emerging with his arms raised, exhilarated, spouting water from his mouth. He tore a piece of moss from the stone next to him and dabbed his chest dry, rubbing it against his armpits and stomach.

Elena sat on a rock, forcing herself not to look at Riccardo. For weeks it had been her he was trying to undress, not himself. He had never been this bold. She stared at the water against the base of the rock, its ripples no diversion from the agitation in her stomach. She busied herself, shakily cleaning her nails with a stick end. Riccardo got out of the water and stood over her, his wet knees leaning into her back, sticking to the fabric of her dress. She jabbed the stick into the edges of her cuticles and dragged it across her nails, scraping the dirt away. Drips of icy water fell from him onto her shoulders. She didn't flinch. Riccardo reached down and pulled her up. He led her to the thick patch of grass by the stream.

He undressed her, and lowered her onto the ground as the afternoon sun forced her to shut her eyes. He pressed himself down on her, his feet pushing into the soft earth. The sun burned at her closed eyelids. She gripped the blades of grass round her, the green and yellow of fallen leaves spreading over her bare thighs. When she finally got up, a spray of sun dots danced before her. Fearing she might faint, she knelt and saw two deep footholds beneath her, grooves of mud cut by the repetitive movement of Riccardo against her.

He swam again, before hauling himself onto the rock to lie in the sun. Elena studied the cluster of trees that encircled them, and there in the humid shade, ahead of them, she saw her sister Teresa, with her mass of curly hair, the lit-up, enquiring eyes of an animal at night. Elena sat frozen, unable to speak. Riccardo rolled over lazily, his head on her stomach, and touched her belly button. He followed her gaze towards the trees and noticed Teresa, staring, motionless.

'Oi!' Riccardo screeched, 'piss off, *via, via!*'

Teresa turned and scampered, crashing through the dead leaves.

'Catch her,' Elena yelled, 'catch her.'

Riccardo battled with his trousers, grabbed his shirt and shoes and began to run. Elena lurched behind him, a new soreness accompanying every movement. Teresa darted over fallen branches and under trees, her yellow skirt a taunting rag sucked through the bushes. She was soon well ahead of them and vanished. As they reached the edge of the forest, they saw she had already joined the path to the village. Carlo Zanelli came out of his barn and Teresa slowed down, turning nonchalantly to look at them behind her.

'What are we going to do?' Elena put a hand over her mouth.

Riccardo stopped running. 'She won't say anything. Tell them we were swimming. She wouldn't dare say anything.'

'She will. I know she will.'

'She's only fifteen, they won't believe her.'

'They will,' Elena said. She bent over and retched.

4

Elena sat on the kitchen floor, picking at the loose tiles, easing them out of their crumbling surrounds. The ticking of the wooden clock filled the room. Her mother and sister watched her from outside, their faces squashed up against the window, nostrils and yawning mouths clouding the glass with their breath. Gusts of shouting came from the backyard. The kitchen door opened.

'I can explain,' Elena said. 'We…'

'Don't say anything.'

Her father turned to the stone sink and poured water from a jug into his hands, splashing it across his face and beard. He drank from his palms, staring at the wall.

'We…'

'Don't say anything, I said.'

Elena saw her mother and Teresa slip behind the wood stack, their heads poking out intermittently to listen. Her father stood in front of her. Drops of water were caught in his beard, held intact by the tight black and grey curls. The end of his nose was wet and shiny. He wound her hair round his fist. 'What happened here?'

'Where?'

'Your hair, you've cut it.'

'I…'

'Why did you do that? You know I can't stand it.'

'Ouch!' She winced as her father tightened his grip on her hair, forcing her to stand. He twisted it so far that her head was tilted upwards, her scalp burning.

'I don't want to know how you and the Friulano met. He had the nerve to try and explain…'

'We were swimming…'

'I said I don't want to know!' He let go of his daughter's hair and she fell, shunting backwards across the tiles on her shins.

Teresa and her mother came out from behind the wood stack. They approached the window again, wrinkling their noses and narrowing their eyes. Their lips were thick and fleshy, like slugs on the glass. Elena's father thumped his fists against his thighs.

'I thought you were different, Elena, you of all people.' He reached for her hair, stroking it, twirling each strand. He stared at its blackness on the pitted skin of his palm, dividing the hairs between his fingers, spreading them out like a fan. 'A barefooted stranger, a shepherd from a mountain no-one's ever heard of, is that what you want?' he asked. 'I can hear them already, behind my back at the mill. You should have seen him when he arrived, a worthless stray, all skin and bones. We all avoided him. He used to drink from the river. Did you know that? Yes, like a dog. He'd dig up roots too, pick berries off the bushes. And he likes to sit on tombs sunning himself I'm told, jumping from one to the other, making fun of the dead. What do you make of a man like that?'

'That's not true.'

'He has ideas too,' he sneered, his voice rising, 'fancy talk about Argentina. There's work to be had in Italy nowadays, in Milan and Turin and all those places, but I suppose he doesn't know that, doesn't know much.'

'He's going to get a lot of money soon. His brother is selling their house back home. It was a farm, like here. He'll use that to set up something in Argentina. He has so many plans.'

'He's welcome to Argentina, or America, wherever they'll have him.'

'I want to go with him… I… I love him.'

Her father retreated to the sink and held the rim of the water jug. He stood for a long while in the same position, then the back of his bald head moved almost imperceptibly.

'Papa,' she said, seeing him cry. She put a hand on his shoulder. He shook it off violently.

'Get away from me!'

Elena turned and ran, breaking out of a low window into the fields. Her father stormed through the house behind her and out into the courtyard, kicking his way through the chickens and farm tools. The sound of his shouting increased as he cornered her mother and sister behind the wood stack. Teresa's screeches filled the courtyard. Her mother never cried out.

꙳

Elena walked round the cars parked in the village square and saw her father, in the distance, outside the farmhouse. She watched as he cleared dead leaves from in front of the door and closed it. A hand rearranged the hem of her wedding dress and she was drawn back into the church through a gathering of people. She made for the side chapel

19

where the flagstones were covered in mounds of wax, dripped and splattered in a circle.

Riccardo came towards her. 'They're all waiting for us.'

'I thought my father would come.' She held his arm.

'Don't think about that, not now. We're better off without him.'

'Your brother didn't come either.'

'I decided not to invite him in the end. He's in Paris anyway. He got more for the sale of the house than he says, I'm sure of it. It's not possible, it doesn't seem right the amount he sent.'

'What are we to do?'

'We can use the room behind the kitchen for the time being, your mother said, till we find a place of our own.'

'My father agreed to that?' Elena looked at the crucifix above the altar with gratitude.

'We should get going. They're all outside.' Elena let go of Riccardo and placed a candle in an iron holder. 'Come on,' he urged, flicking open his lighter to reveal a small blue flame. He lit the candle's wick.

'You go,' she said, joining her hands in prayer. She stayed and watched the flame struggle, but, hearing Riccardo walking back towards the door, decided to run after him. 'I'm so happy,' she said ecstatically into his ear and threw herself at him. He picked her up and swung her round till her feet knocked over a chair.

The earth turned wet, cold and dry again, hardened by the sun, split by the cold. Month after month, over the first year and a half of her marriage, Elena returned to the rock pool. By the stream, she removed the tiny strands of grass that had started to grow in the gashed mud and pulled at the weeds that ventured there. She touched the parallel gouges in the earth, running her fingertips over their ridges as if they were indelible traces on her, part of her body.

In the room behind the kitchen, Riccardo covered the walls with photographs cut from his book on Argentina: the city of Parana, the Pampas, the beaches of Mar del Plata, the Iguazu Falls, the glaciers of the Tierra del Fuego, the boulevards of Buenos Aires alight with brightly coloured traffic. At night, holding each other, Elena and Riccardo travelled the length and breadth of Argentina, from wall to wall, inspecting each picture in turn. In the background of the Mar del Plata photograph was a distant, lone figure, a woman in a bikini, and in another a small house which they decorated and named as their own, over there, across the seas. Every conversation brought new plans, a bakery, a postcard shop, a laundrette – and flamboyant, outlandish fantasies they entertained as in a game, a ranch with enough bulls to fill a valley, a vineyard that carried on for miles, even a dancehall with ornate mirrors on every wall.

6

'Your father's cheating me on my wages,' Riccardo complained to Elena as the seasons went by. 'He wants to make our life impossible. We should go to Paris and find Giacomo. I'll get the rest of the money I'm owed. That'll give us what we need to get to Argentina. We're wasting our time here.'

'But, you have a job already, we're happy,' Elena consoled him. 'I know things with my father are still strained, but I want to patch them up before…'

'Forget about him, and this place, please. You can't be so frightened of everything all the time. Stop worrying and hiding away.' Riccardo held her gently, enveloping her with his arms. 'Paris, imagine Paris, come on, think about it! Our first stop en route to Argentina…'

'You're right,' she said, clasping his jacket.

'Look,' he said, turning to the picture of the Mar del Plata from the wall. He held it to her face, running his fingers over the expanses of water, pretending to dip in and out of the waves.

All Elena could see was the tiny, remote woman in her bikini, dwarfed by the ocean. How, she wondered, could someone stand so alone, and naked, a speck at the edge of the world?

Elena started to feel sick while trying to read the street signs in the photo of Buenos Aires. She put it down to another failed attempt at talking to her father, but as she spent the day waiting for Riccardo, a series of vomiting fits took hold of her. By the time he had come home from the mill, she was sure she was pregnant. Her cousin Rosa confirmed the symptoms.

'Pregnant?' Riccardo looked at her in astonishment, stubbing out a cigarette.

'Yes.'

He sat on the bed, stood, sat down again. 'That's amazing. Are you sure?'

'As much as I can be.'

He hugged her. 'That's amazing,' he repeated. But, in the mirror, she thought she saw his eyes dim a little, in a way she hadn't seen before.

'What's wrong?'

'Nothing,' he said. He walked across the room and looked out of the window.

'No, something's up.'

'Well, we were going to leave though, weren't we?' he said, pointing at the photographs on the wall. He kissed her on the back of the neck. 'Promise me that we're still going to.'

'Of course,' she said. 'It'll be fine. We still can.'

Riccardo lay on the bed and closed his eyes. Elena waited by the door, disconcerted, not knowing what to do, unwilling to disturb him.

She felt her queasiness return. Her husband appeared to be sleeping, but then he stirred. She saw him lift up a hand and motion for her to come to the bed. With his eyes shut, he felt for her knee and rubbed it.

'Should I prepare some food?' Elena suggested. 'Wouldn't you like that? Don't you want to wash?'

There was no reply. Elena unbuttoned his shirt and kissed his ribs. There were wood chippings stuck to his chest.

Riccardo was already up when she woke. Elena found him dressed and clean-shaven.

'Aren't you late for the mill?'

'Not today.'

She sat up with great effort.

'What do you mean?'

'I didn't sleep a wink. I have a new plan. I'm going to head off to Paris like I said, as soon as possible, the money we have already should get me a ticket.'

'What do you mean?'

'I'll get what I'm owed from Giacomo, work for a while at his factory and go to Argentina with the extra bit I've made. I'll get everything sorted there and be back in time for the birth. Then we'll leave for good, the three of us, together. It's the only way. It makes sense.'

'I'm coming with you.'

'You're in no state to go anywhere.'

'I'm not ill, this stage passes.'

'If I stay here, we'll never make the money we need, and we'll be stuck in this village for ever, and with a child too. We haven't got enough for two tickets, let alone three.'

'You can't go,' she said. 'I won't cope. I know I won't.'

'I'm not saying it's going to be easy, but we have to try, don't we?' He looked at her. 'I won't be long, my love. Giacomo will have to help

23

me, he's that kind of a brother. He can't refuse me my money now that I have a child on the way.'

Elena stared at the floor. 'What am I going to do?'

'Perhaps you're imagining it anyway, and you can come to Paris with me. The doctor might say there's nothing there.'

'I've never felt like this before, Rosa was the same...'

'You in there, whoever you are, you've gone and screwed up our plans,' Riccardo said, pointing at his wife's belly, prodding her skin. He placed his mouth on her belly and blew softly. A warm, hollow noise like a failed note from an instrument escaped from his lips.

'I'll try and see the doctor this week,' Elena said, 'before you go.' She pulled the blanket over her face, remembering how, as a child, she had seen a man pack for his son's journey to America, tying up each box with string.

PART TWO

Varanelle, 1969

7

'Elena!' The young men shouted from the path to the sawmill. 'Come over here, come on.'

She dug at the weeds between the vegetables, tugged and severed encroaching roots. She cleared stones, throwing them into piles at the end of each planted row. The yells and whistles continued.

'Elena, Elena, why don't you bend over and pick up your spade again? Let's have a proper look at you!'

She turned towards the farmhouse and saw her mother heaving herself up the hill gesticulating, Marco trailing behind. Her son, she presumed, was asking for her, but her mother seemed angry. Elena banged the mud from the vegetables and hurried to meet them.

'What have you done now?' her mother panted and wheezed, pulling on Marco's arm to quieten his cries. 'What got into you Elena?'

'What?'

'Don't play the fool with me,' she said. Her forehead and neck were streaming from the effort of her walk uphill. 'Money has been taken from the sawmill, a bundle of wages.'

'Wages?'

'That's what I said.'

'When?'

'You went up there yesterday evening. Carlo Zanelli saw you, and your sister.'

'I was going for a walk.'

27

'You think your father's going to believe that? He's beside himself.'

'But…'

'He'll get the sack for this. Everything will be taken away from us.'

'I wouldn't steal, why would I do that?'

'To send money to Argentina, you said Riccardo needed more yourself the other day, to buy the house and pay for his ticket back.'

'He has a job for that, how could you think that? It could have been one of the men.'

'They don't know where your father keeps the money. Only you and Teresa know.'

'That's ridiculous, anyone could find it if they searched.'

Her mother let out a sigh. She looked at her daughter, scrutinizing her. She ran a plump, mottled hand through her greying hair, pulling at a knot. 'You'd better leave,' she said.

'Leave?'

'Get out of here. Your father's been drinking.'

'I haven't done anything. Why should I go, Mamma? You know I haven't done anything, don't you?' She grabbed her mother's wrist and shook it. 'Don't you?'

The two women looked down to see Marco crying, face down in the grass, his dark hair quivering as he punched the ground.

'Keep away from your father,' her mother said, softening her voice. 'He mustn't know I saw you.'

Elena began hurrying, her son in her arms.

'Where are we going?'

'I don't know, away from here.' She continued to run, sticking to the path round the back of the village, along the cemetery wall. 'We'll have our photo taken for Papa, or something, how about that?' She looked round her several times as they left Varanelle behind.

'Why photo,' Marco sung in a piercing voice. 'Why?'

'Because, my love, because.'

When the castle of Bardi came into view above them, Elena stopped by the half-dried bed of a river and cleaned her face in the water. She battled to stay calm. Marco picked up a pebble and flung it into the current. 'Not today,' she said, 'no splashes.' Marco tossed a larger stone into the shallow water by her feet. 'No, no, we need a perfect photo,' she said. 'The last one we sent to Argentina wasn't good.'

'Wasn't good?' the boy repeated, reaching for a third stone.

'Because you were sitting. I want you to stand this time. Do you understand? So your father can see how big you've grown. You'll be three in a few months.' To prove her point she stretched his arms out as far as she could and measured his hands against hers. She dipped her handkerchief in the water and wiped it across his face, scratching at dirt on the side of his nose with her nail. He blinked, blinded by the midday brightness and the reflections of the river. She noticed that he had a reddish scab on his forehead, and that his eyes seemed too big for his face.

The photographic studio was on the street leading to the castle. The owner took them through to a room with blacked-out windows. 'What will it be this time, Signora Carlevaris? Same background?'

'Yes, but the boy must stand.'

The photographer opened a wardrobe and offered her a selection of clothes to wear. He withdrew to the corridor as she dressed, but she felt his eyes behind the door.

'Hold still,' he said, as they posed in front of the camera. Marco was wearing a jacket from the bottom of the cupboard. It had silver buttons down the front and deep embroidered pockets. The photographer reached for Elena's collar. She pushed him away.

'Bit of a shame to cover yourself up like that,' he leered.

She resumed her position. Marco fiddled with his buttons, pulling the thread.

'Wait,' she insisted, pointing to the corner of the room. 'Bring us that block of wood.' The photographer placed it under Marco's feet and adjusted the height of the lens.

They hid behind the chicken shed when they got to the house. Elena slipped past the windows, holding Marco to her chest. Two empty bottles were on the kitchen table. The radio was on, but nobody in the house. She found her room turned upside down, her clothes in every corner. The mattress had been hauled from the bed and the photographs of Argentina ripped from the walls. Shreds of Riccardo's letters and postcards were strewn across the tiles. She reread snippets as she pieced the bits together, postcards of Buenos Aires, torn images of a city still awaiting her. One half of a postcard spoke of Riccardo's job in a garage and details about Argentinian immigration papers, another about a house he had visited in the district of San Telmo, the walls painted with exotic birds, as if expecting them. In yet another, he announced a possible return from Argentina that had been put off each time for various reasons. Two months earlier, he had written that he would shortly be in Italy, travelling again via his brother Giacomo in Paris.

And, only three days previously, an elderly neighbour, Silvana Fontani, had hobbled to the farm to say she had seen a man who looked like her husband down in Bardi. She had rushed to change clothes and spruce up the boy, then nothing. The old woman had been seeing things and she had felt furious at having fallen for her faulty vision. Even Marco, picking up on what he thought was a game, had joined in, pretending he had seen a man behind the farm. Elena had hurled insults in the direction of the old woman's house all night, remembering too late that the eighty year old was a *vedova bianca,* a white widow left long ago by a husband who had emigrated to Canada, never to return.

She found her school atlas under the bed. She had taken to sticking pins on its open pages for each stage of Riccardo's journey. When she had tipped the pin inserted into Varanelle backwards across the page, she had been able to reach Paris. Under a tile by the cupboard, she was relieved to find that the money Giacomo had sent her from Paris on Riccardo's behalf was still there. She dusted the dirt from each note.

'What are you doing?' Teresa said, leaning against the doorway, her curls held up in a bright knotted headscarf.

'Look what's happened to my things…'

'Papa will find you. He's out to get you.'

'I haven't done anything wrong!'

'Go to Rosa's house, she'll put you up, she's expecting you.'

'I haven't done anything.'

'You don't understand how angry he is. Get out of here.'

'Damn him!' Elena yelled, punching the air with her fists. 'How can he treat me like this?' She snatched up a few things, sweeping Marco into her arms, and barged past her sister.

8

It was to Rosa's house, three weeks later, that Teresa brought a new letter for Elena. It had arrived in the morning from France. Her sister and Rosa crowded round her in anticipation as she held it.

'What does he say? Is he in Paris?'

'When is he coming?'

Elena made straight for the front door, the unopened envelope in her hands. 'Keep an eye on Marco,' she shouted.

She vanished into the trees, up past the sawmill, to the steep paths and tracks she knew well, passages to sheltered harbours where everything was as before. Despite her excitement, she resisted the temptation of opening the envelope until she reached the rock pool.

She had waited so long and now she sensed Riccardo was announcing his return, to see Marco for the first time, to start where they had left off. All the questions and painful postponing she had endured over the last three years or so seemed irrelevant as she held the new letter. What did it matter that he had taken so long, now he was going to be with her again? Paris, she guessed, wasn't more than two or three days' travel away. She was finally going to leave Varanelle, with him. She walked through the trees, over the dryness of the cracked summer ground. The stream sneaked its way under a succession of rocks and she followed its course till she came to the pool and the grassy dip, their former, rounded bed, and she lay amongst the trees, alone with Riccardo. She tore at the sides of the envelope.

Instead of the usual postcard or scruffy letter full of crossed-out mistakes, she found two pieces of crisp paper. One was typed, square and official, in a foreign language that looked like French. She tried to read it, some words seemed similar. Her husband's name was mentioned several times. There was a date at the top: 17 July 1969. Attached to it was a handwritten letter, this time in Italian, from Giacomo. The handwriting was thin and slanted, limited to a neat square in the middle of the page. It explained that Riccardo had been killed in an accident at the Paris factory where he had briefly sought employment after his recent return from Argentina. Riccardo, her brother-in-law wrote, had wanted to make a last bit of money before fetching her and the boy. Arrangements, Giacomo added, could be made for a funeral in France or the body could be repatriated. The factory would come up with the necessary finances in both cases. If there was no rapid reply to the letter, Riccardo would be buried in a cemetery, in Clichy, on the outskirts of Paris.

Elena held the letter. She unfolded and folded it, held it in front of her, read without reading, unable to move. A gap in the trees enclosed the peaks of far-off mountains, heads of rock, the forests below as lifeless as singed hair. She tried to stand, but there was no strength in her legs. Stones cut into her back through the grass.

When she did eventually walk back to the village, she had to stop from time to time, clutching her stomach. Her parents' house was empty. In the back room, she found her photo of Riccardo in the pile of torn postcards. She removed it from the frame that had protected it from her father's onslaught and fell onto the bed, shuddering, holding the print against her face. Her skin was damp with cold sweat and the photograph left a smeared and watery imprint across her cheek. She stared out of the window and saw herself as a detached strip of bark, a widow of twenty-six settling on the forest floor, her future dissolving into the earth. She opened the cupboard that contained her dowry – tablecloths, blankets and a copper saucepan. She removed each item, one by one, and placed them in a bag.

'Well,' Rosa said as she arrived back at her house, 'what did he say?' Marco circled round them, trying to catch his mother's sleeve. 'So, what's he up to?' Rosa asked again. 'You were ages. You can't keep us guessing like this.'

Elena gathered the things that belonged to her and the child. She found Marco's spoon and washed it in the sink. She unhooked a cardigan from the back of the door.

'Elena, tell me, when is he coming for you?' her cousin demanded.
'I...'
'What's happened?'
Her mouth was dry. She stopped halfway up the stairs to her room.
'He's in Paris. He's waiting for us.'

PART THREE

Paris

9

'Clische, Cliscee.'

'What?'

'Cleeche.'

'*Quoi*? Don't understand.'

Elena extracted Giacomo's letter from her bag and pointed at the address.

'Ah, Clichy,' the taxi driver said.

Marco sat on the back seat and watched as they crossed the bridges and avenues of Paris. Every time Elena stole a look through the car window, she felt assailed by a feeling that Riccardo had been almost within reach, but at the same time far from anything she understood, even the images of Argentina she had invented in her head. She closed her eyes, shutting out the tightly packed buildings, the hooting cars and people scurrying from every angle, just as she had done during the whole terrorizing journey from Varanelle, as if it had been happening to someone else, against her will. Marco pushed and butted to get comfortable on her lap and they drew up outside a factory. The brick building was two floors high and stretched the length of the compound. Sand and gravel littered the yard. To the front was an office with glass windows and trucks parked alongside it. Elena lugged her bag from the taxi towards the office with Marco on her hip. She waited at the reception, was waved from one desk to another. She held up her photo of Riccardo with the discoloured background and a manager

37

came out of nowhere, his head inclined to the side in a display of sympathy. 'We didn't realize you were coming.' He led Elena to a room, pointed at a chair and vanished.

She fell onto the hard seat. She studied the palms of her hand branded with a red furrow from the weight of her bag. The manager returned with a glass of water for her and a toy car for Marco. The boy smacked it along the thick carpet. Through a side window, she saw machines and forklift trucks carting bricks and building materials, slabs of concrete, terracotta tiles. Further on, rows of men were assembling pipes and machinery. The door opened. A thin, brown-haired man with a limp came towards her. He looked like a boy still, a pale, meek face with familiar hooded eyes. It was Giacomo Carlevaris, her brother-in-law. He shook Elena's hand before embracing her.

'I'm sorry,' he said. 'I'm so sorry.'

She drank her water and trickled some into the child's mouth. She bit the edge of the glass so as not to cry.

'I'm afraid I couldn't stop them from carrying out the funeral, *mi dispiace*. That's the way things are done here.'

She bowed her head.

'A lot of people came.'

Getting to Paris for the funeral had been her only aim. A man at Parma station had promised to send Giacomo a telegram for her, to warn him of their arrival. Marco dropped his toy and nudged it back and forth with his foot.

'The priest is going to say a special prayer for him tonight.' He beckoned to his nephew, bending down to stroke his head. The boy eyed him curiously and then his mother. 'Don't expect much from the factory, but take what you can.' Giacomo said. 'They're bound to give you some compensation. I'll help you.' He pulled a ring from his finger and passed it to Elena. 'Here, you should have this.'

She held Riccardo's wedding ring, rolled it in her palm until it fell flat. She placed it on her finger next to her own ring, two bands of an identical circle connecting. She fished her flask of scent out of her bag. She sprayed it over herself, then the chair and the child's neck. Riccardo, Riccardo, she recited, Riccardo.

The cemetery was a short distance from the factory. Between tilted headstones and crooked tombs, Elena saw the mound of fresh earth, surrounded by stones. She laid the wreath of flowers she had bought in a shop nearby. Marco rushed ahead fiddling with loose plaques, knocking vases over. Giacomo stumbled after the child, arms open, tidying up the scattered objects as best he could, calling his nephew insistently. A wooden cross had been placed in the newly dug ground with the inscription: Riccardo Carlevaris 1941–69. She straightened it by banging the base into the earth with the side of her fist. She could hear Marco laughing and Giacomo chasing alongside, out of breath. She got down on her knees. She wanted to dig until she reached the coffin, to kiss Riccardo's sleeping mouth, talk into his closed eyes. She turned to see Marco toss a pile of dead flowers into the air. Her presence in the cemetery was as unreal as the rest of the city. Why wouldn't Marco stop laughing? She blocked her ears and heard the hard ramming of her heart in her throat.

From the cemetery, Giacomo ushered them onto a bus to the house he shared with five other Italian workers. They begrudgingly cleared out a room for the newcomers at the side of the rundown building. It had floorboards with powdery corners eaten by woodworm, and glass jars on the window sills where cigarette stubs had disintegrated into brown sludge. Elena unrolled a coat onto the bed as both pillow and blanket. Giacomo brought her bread and cheese, bottles of water and sweets for the child. He laid the food out for her on a cloth on the floor.

'When did Riccardo arrive in Paris?' she asked as soon as he stood up to leave the room.

'Nearly a month ago.'

'Why didn't he come straight home to me?' she said, wrenching the words out of her. 'Why? He never saw the boy. He never saw me.'

Giacomo knelt down beside her, rearranged the cloth and brushed the breadcrumbs towards a corner. 'He lost a lot of money in Argentina, he never wanted you to know. He was ashamed. A conman swindled him over the house.' Elena said nothing. She too started to pick at the crumbs. 'He had to earn some of that money back. He was going to surprise you with three tickets for Argentina. He was only going to stay here a couple of weeks.'

Elena absorbed the news and, again, she had a vision of herself digging at the earth in the cemetery and prising open Riccardo's coffin, touching his dead mouth.

'All I wanted was him, that's all I've been waiting for these last three years. I wouldn't have cared about the tickets,' she said, 'or the money. Who cares about tickets now?'

'He did,' Giacomo said. 'He was very proud.'

'Yes,' she agreed, as if to herself. 'He was very proud.'

When she was alone with Marco, Elena took out Riccardo's photograph and placed it next to their bed. Was this battered picture all she had to talk to from now on? She pulled at it, smoothing the image, but still his face didn't move. Through the windows, Elena heard cars and people sweep past in a continual onslaught. She wept to the foreign rumble of the traffic and the distant railway line.

With the men at work, Elena kept her mind busy by cooking the evening meal. She cut off bits of meat for Marco, sliced bread and peeled fruit from the basket in the kitchen. She hunted too, from room to room, through the various cupboards, removing lids, throwing open boxes and bags. She found acrid heaps of soiled socks, unwashed stained shirts and, under one mattress, a pornographic magazine with a notched cover. There was a bed in the far corner of Giacomo's room. Was it here, she wondered, that Riccardo had slept? She felt the blankets and scoured the sheets. Underneath the bed was a fruit crate filled with clothes. A pair of immaculately polished black shoes lay balanced on top, the stamp of a Buenos Aires shop printed inside the leather.

She unfolded each item of clothing she found: shirts, vest, trousers, socks and underpants. She held the vest and brought it to her nose, breathing in. She took the underpants and ran her hands through them, turning them inside out, smoothing the front, pressing them against her face. She took off her clothes and picked out a white shirt. Respecting the delicate creases, she opened up the cuffs and collars like stiff flower buds and placed it on her shoulders. She felt for her husband's fingers as she did up the buttons, handling each one as carefully as china. She took a pair of trousers, stood and pulled them on. She tightened their slackness round her waist, zipping up the front. She slipped on the shoes. Behind the door she saw the jacket Riccardo had worn to leave Italy. She brought it to her mouth and inhaled desperately, sucking its fabric. The odour of its cloth seeped into her as she placed it on her shoulders. Marco came into the room and watched her. She unfolded another shirt and fitted it over his head. The empty ends of the sleeves dangled on the floor in front of him. The collars reached the top of his ears. She took her son by the arm and they shuffled about the apartment, the boy treading on his cuffs, her oversized trousers held up with one hand.

When Elena did leave the house, it was to accompany Giacomo to a park where Marco could play. Her brother-in-law chased Marco in and out of bushes, carried him on his shoulders, did up his shoelaces and swung him along straight gravelled paths. A sickening dizziness would rise up inside her as she sat observing them, and she felt as if she were sliding down the side of a mountain, leaving Varanelle at the summit, further and further away from her, unreachable. She had attempted to explain to the boy, on many occasions, that Riccardo had died, yet she sensed he was continually confusing his uncle with the father he had been waiting for since birth. Marco never asked about Italy, Teresa, or her parents, and it hurt to see that the absence of her family meant little to him. Yet he only wanted to eat when she ate, and when she woke at night he woke too and rolled over to be next to her, his breath lulling her to sleep.

One of the occupants of the house, a squat man from a town near Rome, forced his way into Elena's room one night.

'We're all awake thinking of you,' he said. 'Can't you hear us stirring in our beds?'

'Leave me alone!' she said.

'We can't sleep. Why are you hiding yourself away?'

She gathered the sheets round her waist.

'Come on,' the man insisted.

'Go away!'

'It's not nice to think of you so lonely.' He brushed her shoulder and removed his shirt. An odour of stale sweat and plaster broke into the room. 'Come on, how long has it been?'

It was only when Elena threatened to scream that the man got up and slammed the door behind him. She never mentioned the incident to anyone, but Giacomo, as though he had heard, suggested they move to new premises while the question of her compensation money was resolved.

'You have to be strong,' he comforted her regularly, 'until I sort this out for you.'

10

'I'll carry that,' Giacomo shouted, hauling a canvas bag onto his shoulders. Elena struggled behind with a cardboard box. Marco leapt between them, up the stairs, towards a flat in the suburb of Aubervilliers. It had a couple of rooms and a basic kitchen in the hallway.

'It'll do,' Giacomo said, surveying the rooms. He slipped off down the stairs, returning with a mattress and left for work.

Elena went inside to find Marco dripping the rest of her scent flask onto the floorboards. She gave him a broom instead and set about cleaning and organizing the flat. She scraped the remains of burnt food off the gas cooker with a knife, scrubbing the tiles behind. Under the sink, she uncovered a stash of yellowing magazines held together by tape. She cut out a picture to cover a damp patch on the kitchen wall. It depicted a round-faced Russian, in a hat, sitting on a scooter, an inert black hen hanging from the handlebars by its feet. Above this, Elena added the only photo of Argentina she had salvaged from her parents' home: the Mar del Plata with the bikini woman on the beach. Her face was a dot, but Elena thought she could now see that her eyes were closed with fright, the ocean grey and limitless.

Giacomo had left a bag by the door in his haste. She circled round it a couple of times, before bending down to pick through it. She unearthed her brother-in-law's passport and learned that he was born, like Riccardo, in Pieria, above Tolmezzo, in the mountains of Friuli, on the fringes of Northern Italy. He was three years younger than her, five years younger than Riccardo. His eyes were marked as blue, even though they had struck her more as green. He had been abroad since the age of eighteen. There was money in the side pocket, a large wad of it. Was he not saving up to return home, she wondered, like so many others? In her few weeks in Paris, she had never seen him go out for a drink or meet up with friends. He had preferred to keep her up late on several nights, telling her about his and Riccardo's childhood in Friuli, and she had laughed as he slipped into his unintelligible dialect, asking him to repeat certain words again. She had found herself picturing her dead husband as a boy, the house in Pieria where they were born, their parents – missing links she had always longed for.

There was a small, elegant cardboard box in Giacomo's bag, held together by green ribbons. She shook it and attempted to peer inside, but she could see and hear nothing more than crinkled tissue paper. Between the sheets of a book were loose pages of drawings of trees and human forms alternated with hastily written words. Each was marked with a date on the back. She removed one, a shadowy pattern of oval eyes on stalks, with hooked eyelashes that spread towards a flame. She studied the weak connections between the pencil marks and, the more she observed them, the less she understood.

At the bottom of the bag, she came across Riccardo's factory pass in a rough plastic cover. He was clean-shaven, coarse dark hair swept back, jaw jutting forward, a prominent nose. Only the determination in the hooded brown eyes was recognizable. Beneath it was another photograph. It was of her, taken a few weeks before her husband's departure. Teresa had spent hours combing and disentangling her hair. Round her shoulders was the shawl she had worn for their wedding. She had packed the photograph herself between Riccardo's clothes. She scrabbled around with increased urgency. She rifled through papers and documents, making sure to put each sheet back where she had found it. She discovered a letter from the factory with her husband's name marked in bolder type. There was a number that clearly indicated a sum of money. She read each sentence not understanding. A few snippets, however, more or less matched the Italian. She was sure she had identified the words for 'machine' and 'death'. She let herself out of the flat. She read and reread the letter, sentence by sentence, overcome by consternation. Something was being decided behind her back, she was sure. Was Giacomo planning to siphon off the factory money before giving it to her? Was he set on cheating her? His kindness and constant attention all of a sudden made more sense. She tried to breathe. The stench from the communal latrine on the landing below clung to the stairwell. Slithers of peeling paint, so fine they resembled blades, stuck out from the walls.

There was an old lady in the flat next to theirs – an Armenian, they had been told by the owner of the building. As Elena read the letter once more, the door opposite opened and the Armenian woman came out, hidden under a mop of ropy white hair clogged with grips. Elena smiled, but the woman looked straight through her, as if her greeting belonged to a life she had long since left. After a while, the flush and swinging chain of the latrine burst into action. A hole of water sucked and churned at the landing below, along with the sound of resistant mucous and gummy food being dislodged. The Armenian woman reappeared, adjusting her tights, and heaved herself up the stairs. Marco dashed out on hearing the noise and waved at the woman as she reached her front door, bent over and oblivious to his enthusiastic gestures. The boy went back into the flat. Elena heard him hurling the marbles he had found at the walls. Giacomo was taking his time. Why, she kicked herself, had she ever trusted this unknown brother? She tried to remember the times Riccardo had spoken about him in detail. She could only think of a few.

Marco was asleep when Giacomo returned and Elena felt her head was about to spill open.

'What's this?' she said the moment he walked through the door.

She brandished the letter at him. He took it from her and she wondered, despite her distress, if his facade of placidity and innocent doodling would break.

'I'm requesting a compensation deal for both of us,' he said, translating sketchily, pointing at particular words. 'That's what the head of the union told me to do.'

'Why are they giving you money?'

'I was involved in the accident too.'

'You?'

'I moved in time, but I still got hit by the bricks.'

He rolled up his right trouser leg to reveal a wound with scabs of varying reds, and stitches from his ankle up to his knee.

'The doctors say it'll clear.'

Elena felt she might vomit at the unexpected sight of his gashed, unhealed leg, as if she were seeing her husband's own wounds, his blood-stained corpse.

'It's nothing, of course, compared to what happened to Riccardo,' he said, noticing the anguish on her face.

She opened the window, but the fresh air she was seeking was polluted with the acrid smell of pavements and gutters.

'What did happen to him?' she asked.

'You know, *lo sai…*'

'No-one told me exactly.'

'It's…'

'Tell me.'

'I told you before.'

'You didn't. The machinery was faulty, that's what you said.'

'Yes, that's what we're arguing in the compensation.'

'And?'

'Well…'

'I need to know.'

They had avoided talking about the accident in detail. As Giacomo described the sound of the pulley on the truck tipping, wire snapping and bricks falling through their net, the noise was repeated in her head, the echo of Riccardo's death still resounding through Paris, hammering at the door.

'He wasn't able to move in time. The bricks crushed and buried him.' Giacomo hesitated, before carrying on. 'His arms and legs were broken, and his stomach squashed, but his face was intact.' He looked at her. 'Elena,' he said softly, 'his face was completely unharmed, just a layer of dust on his lips.'

He took her in his arms.

She pushed herself into his chest. She knocked her head against him repeatedly. 'I miss him so much.'

She went to the kitchen and returned with a cloth, soap and bowl of water. She offered to dress Giacomo's wound properly. She pulled off his shoe and sock. She cupped her hands round his ankle and worked her way up his leg with the cloth. The pointed crusts of his scabs pricked her palms through the sodden fabric.

'Trust me to sort this out,' he said to her again.

His toes, she thought, were as small as a child's.

11

They talked at night, in the damp kitchen in Aubervilliers, to the sucking and juddering of the latrine cistern, to the sound of peeled paint falling onto the wooden floors.

'Why didn't your cousin in Argentina help Riccardo,' Elena quizzed him, 'the one with the copper piping business?' She rummaged in her bag and passed Giacomo a piece of paper. 'See, look here, I still have his address.'

'I don't think he has money himself.'

'What's he doing in Argentina then?'

'Just because you're over there doesn't make it any easier.'

47

'That's not what Riccardo said.'

'I know.'

They sat with the table between them. Elena scraped her nails along the wood, working crusts of cooked food away.

'He had so many plans,' she said. 'We were even going to start a restaurant.'

'Really?'

'Didn't he tell you?'

'No.'

'Oh, well, yes, that was one of his big things, or a shop.'

'He wasn't short of ideas,' Giacomo laughed. 'He would have them while scratching his nose, do you remember?' He put his finger on the bridge of his nose and rubbed it up and down, frowning. 'Like that, that's how he got his ideas.'

'No he didn't. I never saw him do that.'

'Of course you did, when he was thinking,' he looked at her face, before backing down. 'Maybe you're right, maybe I'm imagining it.' He tapped the table, and searched, like her, for marks to scrape away. 'And your family?' he asked. 'What did they say to your plans?'

'He never told you?'

'Told me what?'

'About them, what happened?'

'A bit.'

'My father hated your brother, you know that?'

'Yes.'

'He would have hated anyone, but he particularly loathed Riccardo. He wasn't like most fathers I suppose. He took me out of school and only taught me the things he wanted to. He used to prepare my food too, and check the bedroom for mice every night. He'd get on all fours and rattle around under the bed with a broom.' She blew on her hands. 'He swore the mice would run out with the noise. He'd pretend to

48

stamp on them as they rushed about the room. He always looked like he was dancing.'

'Did he ever get one?'

'No, they never came out!' Elena tipped her chair back and blew on her hands again. 'It's cold in here, isn't it?'

'We don't have to talk about him.' Giacomo said, noticing her awkwardness.

'He'd also comb my hair every evening, with his fingers, for hours on end.' She spread out her hands and raked the table, as if she were stroking a cat, 'like this.' She looked down, as if asking to bring the subject to a close. 'I never told Riccardo that.'

Giacomo stood up and went into the kitchen. He brought back a loaf and some pâté. He sliced the bread and spread pâté onto it. He handed her a piece and ate one himself.

'You know,' he said, in a lively voice, 'I'm not sure how I could survive without this pâté now! You can't get this in Tolmezzo.'

'Don't you miss home?'

'Home?'

'Friuli.'

'That's not home. You stay here a few weeks and all that vanishes, I tell you. I couldn't go back now.'

'What are you going to do then?' she asked.

'Stay here, probably.'

'Are you serious?'

'Yes, why?'

'This place,' she whispered. 'It's so…'

'What?' He leaned close to her to catch her reply.

'It makes you feel lost, it's so unsafe, everyone is out to get you, and confuse you.'

'You should have been here last year. Did you hear about the May riots?'

'No.'

'We had all the students up in arms, demonstrations everywhere, barricades and police on the streets, cars on fire.'

'Exactly, why would anyone stay here?'

'Well, you wouldn't believe how many Italians there are here. I once looked at some of the Italian names in the Paris telephone directory, at the post office. There were thousands of entries for Bruni, Rossi and Marini, and all that. I didn't even get a chance to look at the Marseille or Lyons books, and think how many of them don't have phones.'

Elena raised her eyebrows, unable to contain her laughter.

'It's true. Some very famous Frenchmen are actually Italian,' he said.

'Like?'

'The singer Georges Brassens.'

'Never heard of him.'

'Gambetta?'

'Doesn't mean anything to me.

'Yves Montand, Emile Zola?'

'Never heard of them. You're not doing very well,' she smiled.

'Yves Montand, come on, you must know who he is. He's that actor, really famous. He was in love with Marilyn Monroe...'

'Sorry,' she laughed.

'Well most people here know who they are.'

'Yes, but if you want to be successful you go to Argentina, or America, don't you?' Elena pointed out. 'That's what Riccardo said. People like Rudolph Valentino and Frank Sinatra, everyone's heard of them. Don't tell me their families stopped in Paris on their way to America?' She took a slice of bread and layered it with pâté. She bit into it, wiping her mouth with her sleeve. 'I think Marco and I should head off there when the money comes through, if I can pluck up the courage. There are some old people from Varanelle in Buffalo, they should help us.'

'It's not that simple. Look at what happened to Riccardo, he was swindled, left with nothing. You can lose everything by taking risks.'

The mention of her husband's misfortune jolted Elena. She picked out the inside of her bread and squeezed it into a soft ball, pressing it between her thumb and forefinger until it hardened. She rolled it along the table and squashed it flat.

'I'm sorry, that came out wrong.'

Elena took another piece of bread and pulled off the crust. She dragged it across the top of the pâté and ate it slowly.

'Riccardo never told me much about you,' she said.

'We hadn't seen each other for a while.'

'He was angry about the money you still owed him.'

'I gave him more than his share. It was hardly worth anything that house, that's what I discovered. You should have seen the place. It was barely enough to keep out the wind and rain. He didn't believe me; I think he understood in the end.'

'Who knows?'

Elena picked at the bread and stared at the wall.

'We talked about you, quite often,' Giacomo said.

'You did?'

'You're exactly the way he described. And just like in his photo.' Elena chewed her bread, trying to swallow. 'He loved you so much.' She covered her mouth and turned from him, still attempting to swallow. 'He'd often say, "Elena would like that," or, "that's the kind of thing Elena does."' Giacomo shifted his chair and turned to the window. The upper part of its frame was rotten with damp, the sill warped in the middle. From the courtyard below came the noise of someone emptying metal bins. 'No-one, he used to say to me, not even in the whole of Argentina, or Paris, could match the beauty he'd found in the tiny village of Varanelle.'

'Ah, come off it, don't be ridiculous,' she said, waving him away. 'He never said anything like that.'

'He did.' Giacomo breathed in. 'He really did.'

She stood and hurried from the room. The sound of plates being stacked came from the kitchen, and the brisk scrape of a knife.

Giacomo's leg injury meant he could no longer work the factory's heavy machinery. He transferred to a section of the plant that produced tiles and set about learning to make pots on the side, after shifts. One evening, he handed Elena a piece of unglazed clay with the middle scooped out, a brittle rim circling it.

'I made this,' he said.

'Oh.'

'You like it?'

'What will you do with it?'

'It's a bowl.' He placed it on the kitchen shelf where it wobbled unevenly. 'I need to sand the bottom.' He scratched underneath. 'It's my first ever bowl.'

'Will you make more?' Elena asked.

'I hope so. Someone at the factory told me about a pottery in the South, not far from the sea, in the Camargue. It'll be for sale in a few months, for next to nothing. It might be worth investigating if I learn fast.'

'A pottery?' Elena yawned, entering her bedroom. 'Are you sure?'

Giacomo filled his room with sketches of bowls, each more intricate and detailed than the last. Over months, the apartment became home to various new pots and vases, their rounded shapes and blotchy glazes lining the shelves. A Noah's Ark over-spilling with clay animals appeared for Marco. It became his prized possession and the boy could barely wait for the chance to play with it each morning. Long-necked sheep, stout cows and misshapen horses grazed on the scratched wooden floor.

Ten months after her arrival in Paris, the factory offered to give Elena the equivalent of her husband's month of employment. Giacomo was awarded an extra six months' salary. A tenuous promise was made to look into the possibility of further funds for Elena. Giacomo took her to the factory to protest. More documents were passed over for them to sign. An administrator explained they would have to be represented by a lawyer to contest the proposal, and his fees would be prohibitive. They spoke to the union representative. The fact that both of them were foreign complicated matters.

Elena retreated to her bedroom, while Giacomo took Marco to the park. She unhooked Riccardo's jacket from the back of the door. She sucked the thick cloth, filling her mouth with the dust of places she had never seen.

12

'Let's go out,' Giacomo announced, in a determined effort to dispel the atmosphere in the flat. 'I saw a place in Montmartre where we could eat.' Without waiting for a reply, he went into his room and returned with a cardboard box tied together with green ribbons. 'You should have this,' he said to Elena. 'I never knew when the right time to give it to you was. I didn't want to upset you.' He pushed it towards her. 'It was going to be Riccardo's present to you when he came to fetch you.'

She recognized the box from her searches round the flat. She placed it on her lap without a word. She undid the ribbons and lifted the lid. Inside, in the layers of crinkled tissue paper she had heard when shaking the box, was a pale silk scarf with circles of red flowers. Beneath it, also wrapped in paper, was a wooden train with a carriage for Marco. She pulled each piece of tissue paper out of the box, waving it in the air to check for more items, or a note. There was nothing.

Without seeking Giacomo's opinion, or expecting any comment, she tied the scarf round her neck and picked up her coat. 'You should have given it to me earlier,' she said as they left the flat. Marco skipped after them, the wooden train held high above his head.

'To us,' Giacomo said, forcing a smile out of Elena in the café. He raised his glass. 'I can't bear to see you so upset any more.'

Elena lifted her glass. 'To him,' she answered. 'To Riccardo!' She craned her neck sideways to view the menu chalked up on a lopsided blackboard. 'Can't understand a word of it,' she said. 'I've never been to a café before. What are we supposed to do?'

'Only my second visit. I'll try and tell you what the board says.'

She looked at him. 'We will get more money from the factory, won't we?'

'*Certo*, don't worry, I've got some now anyway and I can earn more. We can share it. *Cassoulet*, do you like *cassoulet*? It's a kind of stew, I think. Maybe I'm wrong.'

'I can't take your money,' she said. 'We'll manage with the factory again, won't we?'

'What are you going to eat?'

'Please tell me what you think about the factory?'

'You must eat, it's good for you. It'll build up your strength. What about crab?'

'Crab. No, never had it.'

'*Andouillette*? It's a type of sausage I think.'

'Sorry,' Elena said, standing. 'I have to see what Marco is up to. Order for me.'

She took a piece of bread from the table and made for a side room

54

with a sloping glass roof. Marco was playing amongst the flowerpots with his train. She passed him the bread. He snatched it, chewed it, assessed its quality and then dashed back to his games, stripping petals from the flowers as he went. 'Careful!' Elena said. She looked around her to see if anyone had noticed.

To the right of her was a door. She pushed it open and peered into a tiny room. There was a strong-smelling latrine in the ground, two grooved ceramic footholds either side. She shut the door and saw a mirror on the wall as she turned. She switched on the light next to it. She almost didn't recognize herself. Her face seemed to be that of someone else altogether. As if to confirm that impression, she pulled her hair over her face and looked back at the mirror, a curtain of blackness veiling her features. She then tied her hair back and studied her face, patting the skin under her eyes. She ran water over her wrists in the basin. A hard lump of soap was stuck to a chink in the enamel. She poked at it, pushing it into the plug. The coldness of the water reminded her of mountain streams, and an instantly associated craving to throw stones into a rushing current. This isn't where I'm meant to be, she thought, this isn't me. Opening the door again, she looked round the corner at Giacomo sitting alone at the table. And him, she wondered, is this where he is meant to be? Two plates of food had arrived, yet her brother-in-law was scribbling with a pen on the paper napkins. That's how he was, she thought, lost in a kind of permanent trance, dreaming. He noticed the smallest things and picked up on tiny details. He had a sort of enchantment with the world. He talked of possibilities she had never dreamt of, imagining colourful, childlike endings to her half-formulated ideas. Maybe that's why Marco was so fond of him, and his uncle of him.

His nose, from this angle, Elena observed, was similar to Riccardo's, less straight perhaps, his hair different, an unusual brown that was darker at the back of his head. His accent, his way of speaking, though, was like Riccardo's, and she had caught herself, on many occasions, shutting her eyes, just hoping to lose herself for a few seconds in a happier past. Marco slammed his wooden train into the back of her shoe. She smiled at his face staring up at her. He, alone, seemed familiar in all this, something she was still part of. They belonged to each other, the two of them. They only had each other. The rest was just disorder, confusion. She reached down to Marco and held him tight to her chest, squeezing his body with all her might. The boy tried to extricate himself and get his train. She held him tighter, kissing his forehead and neck. He broke free from her and spun the train back towards the flowerpots.

'Come and get some food if you want,' she said. He shook his head and she saw that his mouth was still full of bread, a tacky white paste on his tongue. She tightened her scarf and puffed it up at the front, between the lapels of her dress, in the manner of the women she had seen on the streets of Paris. The silk was smoother than any fabric she had ever felt before, the flowers of the design mere wisps, thin tails of red.

She went back to the dining area. There were more people seated at the tables. They looked up, their eyes following her to her seat.

'You…' Giacomo beamed, before checking himself. 'You look… very nice.'

He pulled the table towards him so she could sit down. Elena ate her bread. The bread in Paris, at least, was good. It was about the only thing she could confidently buy on her own, at the bottom of the street, without getting confused by the streams of traffic, the grating language of the passers-by. She could even count out the exact money at the baker's and enjoyed seeing Marco point excitedly at the bundles of fresh, long loaves in the baskets.

Leaving the café, they walked up some steep steps with Marco slouched, asleep, over Giacomo's shoulders. The boy's sleek hair and thick black eyelashes made his face look more like that of a small, curled animal than of a boy. Elena laid her coat across him.

'I'd like to show you something,' Giacomo said. They carried on up some cobbled streets. They reached a wide open space. 'Look, it's a real vineyard. Imagine, here, on a hill in Paris.'

Elena leaned over the wall. 'I feel like I've seen it before.'

'You have. I sent a postcard of it to you, with the money that first time, as Riccardo asked, when he left for Argentina.'

'Oh,' Elena nodded, recalling the postcard she'd had in Varanelle. 'Shame Marco is asleep. We'll have to bring him here another day.'

'We came here last Sunday. He loved it.'

She turned to her brother-in-law, unsure of what to say other than: 'Shouldn't we be going back?'

In the cramped hallway of the flat, Giacomo promised to show Elena more of Paris the next day.

'Why,' she said, 'are you being so kind to us? We'd be totally lost without you.'

'It's a pleasure.'

'But we can't keep on using your money,' she insisted. 'I won't be able to pay you back until the factory decides to help.'

'Don't worry about that.' He carried Marco to his bed and laid him fully-clothed on top of the covers.

'I hope my cooking is some thanks for your generosity…'

'Ah, stop it!'

'Maybe, when the time comes,' she said, emboldened. 'You might be kind enough to take us to Argentina, or America, when I hear back from those people in Buffalo. We'll be as little bother as possible I promise. I could never do that kind of journey on my own.'

'Whatever,' he said, a despondent look on his face.

'Of course, I understand, you have your own life to get on with,' she said, seeing his response. 'You have other plans.'

'What are you talking about? It's not that.' Giacomo looked up. His eyes darted round the room.

'It's too much to ask. We're a burden on you, aren't we?'

'I didn't have a life before you came along,' he murmured. 'I didn't have anything.' He hesitantly touched her shoulder. 'For the first time things make sense, thanks to you. I don't want you to leave.'

'Don't be silly.'

'No, really, I've never been as happy as tonight, opposite you at the café.' He took her hand and gripped it clumsily. Before she could react, he lunged, in an inept movement, and kissed her on the lips, pressing himself against her.

'What are you doing, Giacomo, no.'

She turned for the door, but he took her hand again. 'Believe me, Elena, you've got to believe me. I have never felt like this, ever, about anyone. I love you. You are all I've ever wanted.'

'But…'

'I love you, I'm saying I love you. Please believe me.'

'You…'

'I couldn't bear to be apart from you.'

Elena didn't answer and he reached for strands of her hair, bringing them to his mouth. He breathed in. 'Please,' he repeated, 'please. You're too beautiful.' He guided her towards the next-door room and his bed. As he took off her clothes, she thought back to the lump of soap in the basin at the café, and how her image in the mirror had meant nothing to her, as if she were no longer herself.

Where she had expected the same heat as Riccardo's hands and the heavy bones of his body, Elena felt lightness like feathers, unversed touches as virginal and quiet as a draught across her skin. She shut her eyes, kept them closed. She retreated into her memories, to the shape of her husband's body, to his scent, to the inflections of a voice that sounded like his. She searched for the feel of the sun on her face, grass against her back, for something familiar in the texture of the blanket. In the distance, she could hear a high-pitched noise and it became the sound of the stream, the sawmill at home pounding the warm air. The roughness of the blanket spread around her in prickly, dry weeds, the grit of sawdust. The noise of the mill grew more and more insistent in her head. She sat up with a start, opened her eyes. Marco was crying.

She rushed to her room. The boy was trying to say something, disoriented, still in his clothes. She gathered him up in her arms. He thrashed about on her lap. Without thinking, she thrust a naked bosom into his mouth even though she had stopped breastfeeding months before. He bit and wriggled, spat out the breast she was forcing on him. She rocked him, faster and faster. 'Hush, sssh, I'm here, my darling.' He flipped and bucked, nudging at her stomach with his head, trying to get comfortable. She patted his hair and held him close to her skin. 'Quiet now, go to sleep, sssh.' Marco nuzzled deeper into Elena's stomach and fell asleep again. Hunched over him, she felt a sharp pain in her right nipple, swollen and stiffened from his unproductive biting. The door behind her had opened. It was cold. Her back was freezing.

She saw Giacomo behind her. 'Come,' he whispered, 'please.'

She clung to Marco, shielding her uncovered body with his. Through the open door, she could see Giacomo had made a nest with the pillows and sheets of his bed. The child was breathing peacefully. She tightened her grip on him and he woke again, sitting bolt upright. 'Mamma,' he screeched. He stared quizzically at his uncle, then his mother. Giacomo waited for Marco's eyes to close again, peeking round the door, hiding himself. The boy stayed resolutely awake.

'You'd better go,' Elena said, looking down at the worn parquet, 'just go, please, *vai*, quick.'

Giacomo turned and slipped back into his room, thin and angular, the gauche nudity of unresolved adolescence.

13

Elena pushed open the heavy doors of St Eustache Church beside the marketplace at Les Halles. She dragged Marco towards the pews. They had wandered aimlessly all day, propelled on by her fears and guilt. They had hurried across squares and sat hidden in parks, under symmetrical trees mutilated to match the grid patterns of the city, sneaking a look at forbidding shop windows, not understanding. Elena's back ached from carrying her exhausted son. In the church, she sat in front of a burning forest of candles. From time to time, she gazed at the cross over the altar.

How had she the audacity to come into a church? Even dressed in layers of clothes, she felt as if she were still naked, lying with Giacomo. She had feasted on Riccardo's death, toasted him with wine in the café and then given herself to Giacomo in exchange for his help and money. Wasn't that what whores did? Her father had been right about her. Marco had woken and looked at them with such stupor that she could not banish his expression from her. Even now, when she looked at him, she could no longer see his child's face, but an adult grimace of disgust, a scar she had etched with her betrayal. She fished around in her purse for a coin and posted it into the metal box beneath the candles. She pulled one from the pile and lit it.

'Can I hold it?' Marco asked, butting into her bag, '*Posso, posso?*'

'It's for me.'

'Go on, please.'

'I have to do this alone, my love. I'm sorry.'

'No. Give it to me!' Marco yelled, 'I want it!'

'Keep your voice down.'

'I want it. I want it.'

Elena gave the candle to Marco and buried her face in her hands.

She knelt, lifting her skirt, pushing her naked knees against the cold floor. A steady drip of wax fell from the candle onto Marco's shoes, solidifying in a lump on the leather. The church at Varanelle could have fitted ten times into this vast building. She felt she was in the belly of a whale-like creature, an immense beast held together by bones of arches, carrying her towards certain punishment. A priest walked past. She snatched the candle from Marco and stuck it into a free holder. She held a finger above the flame, her skin heating until it burned and darkened. She walked to the exit, beckoning the boy to follow. On the other side of the door was Paris, endless, deafening. She and her child were nothing out there, no-one, driftwood on an inhospitable sea, an offence to God. She looked back at her burning candle before closing the door, sucking her finger. She resolved to stick to her decision of the morning. She would ask Giacomo to leave the flat. She would not see him again.

14

Elena watched her brother-in-law pack his things. Marco chased after his uncle, badgering him with questions.

'Where are you going? Why are you leaving? Why, why?'

Giacomo didn't reply and his lack of response made Elena apologize more than she wanted to. 'I'm sorry, you've been unbelievably kind to us, but I can't see what else to do.' His face was stiff. His red eyes avoided her. 'It was the wrong thing to do.' He dropped his bag against the door and returned to the bedroom to fetch his coat. 'I can't give you what you're looking for, I'm sorry, I can't,' she continued, following him. 'You need someone who can give you a proper life, a fresh start. I have to think of the boy and Riccardo.'

Elena stood in the hallway, the walls echoing with the abrupt closing of the front door behind Giacomo. She entered his abandoned bedroom. It had become like a garden in autumn, the floorboards littered with leaves of paper, pen drawings, dozens of them completed that day, perplexingly ornate, knotted labyrinths without exit, each with a precise date neatly written beneath. Miniature wooden sculptures dug out with a penknife hung from the walls, faces without features, hands asking to be touched. The only thing on the bed was a drawing. It was of an enclosed vineyard, like the one at Montmartre, and there were three slender figures, light as tightrope walkers, perched on the taut metal wires over the vines.

It was raining, a sharp, slapping ring against the dirty panes. Elena thought of the mountain mist in Varanelle, of rain boring holes into the packed earth of Riccardo's grave, of drops rolling on Marco's hair. She wrapped the sleeve of Riccardo's jacket round her fist. She tugged at it until it cut the circulation in her hand and strangled a white band across her flesh. She opened the window. Rain splashed onto the ledge. She clasped her knees and knew she couldn't shut this off. She had held the threads of her life together so far, but now she could no longer see a way out. She cried unrestrained tears, shutting the bedroom door to prevent Marco from seeing. She craved more tears, tears to help her understand how the life she had embarked upon with Riccardo had ended like this, how everything had fallen apart without ever beginning. She swallowed and her whole body ached with a longing for escape, as if that were its only function. She had no idea whether a month's wages would even buy her and the boy a ticket to America. Why hadn't the people in Buffalo replied to her? What would she do over there anyway? She had never wanted to leave Varanelle without Riccardo, and now that she had left, her leaving led nowhere.

She remembered how she had spent the night before Riccardo's departure awake and how nothing had been any clearer in the morning. Her thinking only ever made her more confused and frightened, uncertain of what she wanted or how she could achieve it. All she ever had were fears that drove her round in circles, a terrifying reel inside her head. She thought of how her mother cried and wiped her eyes with the back of her large hands, absorbent skin like paper, and the permanently closed shutters, the twilight of the house in Varanelle. The rain pummelled the windowsill. She wiped her eyes against her knees and watched people take cover along the boulevard below, lifting their jackets to protect themselves. Others were huddled in doorways, waiting patiently in the entrances of shops. The gutters were full, the surface of the pavements rotating with circular sheets of water. She picked at the parquet, sliding her hand along the wood, expecting splinters to cut into her. She screamed, loud enough for Marco to rush in. He watched as she lay on the bed. She pulled him onto her chest, burying her face in the thickness of his dark hair. She kissed him, her lips wet with tears. 'My Marco,' she said, 'my Marco.'

That evening a young Italian knocked on the door of the flat and gave Elena an envelope. Inside was a wad of money, and a note, 'for the boy, from Giacomo.' She placed the money in a tin in the cupboard, determined not to use it.

15

Elena chipped into the money in the tin. Her efforts at finding work reached an impasse after a month. An Italian restaurant offered to give her an ironing job on the agreement that she took the tablecloths and napkins home. When she explained she didn't have an iron or the space in her lodgings they lost interest. A brasserie was keen to employ her in their kitchens, but they wouldn't allow Marco to stay on the premises with her.

She requested an appointment at the Italian embassy. She missed her allotted time by taking Marco outside when he grew restless, but was finally ushered into a room with gaudy cornicing. She was met by a stern woman with an asymmetrical face, dressed in a tight jacket, two jangling silver bracelets on her wrist. She found the woman hard to understand, her overly precise and formal phrases nearly as incomprehensible as the French that surrounded her. She was reminded of her teacher in Varanelle who had battled to cut out her use of dialect before her father had removed her from school.

She had prepared the papers: the first letter from the factory, Riccardo's photo and Marco's birth certificate. She handed them over.

'I've been in contact with the factory,' the woman said.

'Thank you.'

'What have you been doing since your husband died?'

'*Sono stata*, I… Sorry, what do you mean?'

'Have you been living in Paris?'

'Yes.'

'On your husband's one month of wages? Isn't that what they gave you?'

'No. I've had other money…'

'Other money?'

'Well, my brother-in-law…'

'Giacomo Carlevaris? The one who used to work at the factory?'

'He still does.'

'Not according to the factory. They say he left three weeks ago.'

There was a moment's silence.

'Well, anyway, the factory report here,' the woman readjusted the folder on the table, 'says your husband probably didn't handle the machinery correctly. He had no experience of such machines, he hadn't been there long enough. I don't see what we can do in that case, and now your brother-in-law has left. They employ quite a few Italians, we can't afford to irritate them.'

The knock of the two bracelets chimed like a bell. Elena drew Marco closer to her.

'I also ought to warn you,' the woman pointed out, 'that if you intend to work illegally as a maid or waitress, you could easily get into trouble. We don't need that at the embassy, we have enough problems as it is.'

'I…'

'The law is very strict here. You need papers to work, to live here. It's not like… where do you come from?'

'Varanelle.'

'Where?'

'Varanelle, about eighty kilometres from Parma, near Bardi.'

'Ah yes, well it's very different here from up in the mountains.'

The candle burn on Elena's finger was beginning to heal, yet she dug the side of her nail into it, puncturing the skin. She pressed and squeezed the cut till she could feel a wetness oozing onto her palm.

'As I said, there's nothing more we can achieve this end really.' The woman checked the clock on the wall. 'So, what are you going to do?'

'I'll be leaving soon.'

Elena began gathering up her papers, stuffing them into her envelope.

'Back home?'

'No, I intend to go to Buffalo, America.'

'America?'

'Yes.'

'What on earth for?'

'To work, start a new life with my son, aren't we, Marco?' She sealed the envelope.

The bracelets snapped together. 'Young lady, I don't know where you get your naive ideas from, or what clichés you've been fed, but times have changed, trust me, Italians aren't going to America now.

This is 1971. What's wrong with Italy anyway?' She looked at Elena. 'You might think you're very pretty, but I can guarantee you they won't be waiting at the American customs desk with a Hollywood contract or a wad of dollars.' She almost smiled, and it wasn't obvious if it was to herself or Elena.

Elena pulled Marco away from the table. She muttered a goodbye and left, crossing a hallway with tall windows and a monumental staircase.

'Not that way!' an official shouted after them. They carried on until they found a way out.

It was night by the time they reached the door of the apartment in Aubervilliers. A man was squatting in front of the entrance, an overcoat wrapped around him. 'Papa! Papa!' Marco exclaimed, hurling himself up the steps. Giacomo lifted the boy up, hugging and whirling him through the air. Marco pulled on the door handle impatiently. 'Open it, open it.' No sooner had Elena turned the key than Marco grabbed Giacomo by the sleeve, yanking him inside the flat, towards the games they used to play. Within a few minutes, Elena could hear the two of them banging their clay animals across the floorboards into the Noah's Ark, imitating the noise of each creature. The boy's whoops of delight were matched by his uncle's excited imitation of horses neighing and cows mooing.

Elena placed the envelope with the factory's correspondence on the shelf in the kitchen. Giacomo found her there.

'I wanted to bring you something,' he said. He delved into his breast pocket and gave her a delicate clay pot. Round its rim were bony, knuckled branches with lifelike insects, the sides pierced with holes the shape of eyes.

'I'm getting better, don't you think?'

'What's it for?' she asked.

'Whatever you want, nothing really. I have something else for you,' he added. He produced a notepad. Inside were loose sheets of paper. They were portraits of her, sketches and doodles, her body transformed into the shape of an elegant animal, her detailed face resting on the neck of a bird, or the leaf of a plant, its stem an elaborate staircase through banks of clouds. In the top corner of each paper was a bee or a fly, sometimes a planet and a balloon, with Marco's features, held down by the thinnest of strings.

'I have to put him to bed now,' she said, slipping off to the next-door room.

She returned to find Giacomo sorting Marco's toys into a neat pile.

'I'll get you a bigger box for these,' he told her.

Elena had kept some fried courgettes from the evening before on the windowsill. She removed the plate on top of the dish, poured oil over them, and broke a loaf of bread into pieces.

'I can't stop thinking about you,' Giacomo said. 'This last month, every day, every minute. If I hadn't done those drawings of you I'd have gone mad.'

'More bread?' she asked.

'I can't help it.'

'What good does that do us?'

'I can help you. Stop worrying about money, you can share mine, have it all if you want.'

'It's not your money I want.'

'I love you, Elena, I know I love you, I'm sure of it.'

'You're not for me, you're, you're… you're my husband's brother, for goodness' sake.' She shook her head. 'What's wrong with you?'

'I loved you from the moment we met.'

Elena banged her hands against her hips. She knew she was about to start crying again. She flicked a courgette end with her fork, dragging it back and forth across a circle of oil on her plate. Giacomo stretched out a hand to touch her.

'Get me away from here,' she begged. 'Please, just take us away.'

PART FOUR

Aigues-Mortes, Camargue,
South of France, 1974

16

The Carlevaris pottery was the first stop on the school bus route out of Aigues-Mortes in the direction of Saintes Maries de la Mer, and, every afternoon of term time, Elena stood waiting for the vehicle to appear. The land behind her bristled with monumental pots, stone and wood figures, spreading from the parking lot into the patches of dead lawn, coiling round the house down to the road. There were stretched birds too deformed to fly, broken beaks jabbing at the ground, and colossal ragged women running with gaping mouths, naked travellers with faces of shoes, fountains without hope of water, bottomless urns, columns of chipped rock.

By the time the school bus came to a halt in the car park, Elena had loaded up a wheelbarrow with trestles, a plank, parasol and several boxes of pots. Marco walked down the aisle and jumped off. The doors snapped shut and a sea of inquisitive children's faces popped up behind the windows to see Marco being embraced by his mother, her adoring strokes and hugs enveloped by flying shards of broken clay and exhaust fumes as the bus pulled away.

Mother and son set off with their wheelbarrow, lugging their wares along the tarmac towards Aigues-Mortes and the crossroads to Saint Laurent d'Aigouze. They set up their trestle table in a lay-by, placed their pots and bowls in a neat display, a board with 'Pottery for Sale' propped up further down the road. According to the season, Elena added bags of cherries from the garden, aubergines, tomatoes and grapes which she washed and arranged in rows.

'You don't have to hang around for the bus every afternoon, I can make my own way to the house,' Marco said, putting up the parasol. 'No other mothers do.'

'But I don't see you all day.'

'I...'

Their exchange was cut short by the arrival of a car throwing up spirals of dust. A young couple wandered over towards them. They inspected the goods on display.

'How much for this?' the man asked picking up a blue plate.

'Thirty francs.'

'And this?' the woman said, twiddling a bowl in her fingers.

'Twenty.'

The couple discussed amongst themselves. Elena gave Marco a friendly poke in the back, urging him to intervene.

'*Puis-je vous montrer ce petit dépliant?*' Marco said, brandishing a printed flyer. Elena followed her son attentively, studying the couple's reaction. The boy had rehearsed the speech many times, and his teachers at school had corrected the leaflet. 'Everything you see here,' Marco proclaimed, 'comes from the Carlevaris Pottery further up the road. If you'd like to see the full range of our products, there is a map to show you how to get there. We're open every day, except weekends, from nine till six. We have discounts on many items.'

Elena and Giacomo had identified all the garden centres and public parks in the Camargue and beyond, proposing their services with Marco as spokesman. Beside a municipal swimming pool near Lunel, they threaded a copper pipe through a stone tortoise till the water dribbled out of its mouth again. In Arles, they covered the walls of a hotel terrace with fifty cicada candlesticks. On the outskirts of

Sommières, they fixed terracotta cow heads onto the facade of a house overlooking the river.

At weekends, they packed the van and drove to markets and golf courses or to the shaded, irrigated grounds of villas and chateaux. They installed their pots, created mosaics, or secured a Roman amphora in the middle of a fountain. Some owners invited them in for a drink and chat. Other clients pointed them down tracks, delegating instructions to maids and housekeepers who watched them unload their materials without lending a hand. In the rear of the van was a rack filled with Giacomo's latest wood sculptures: fish elongated by walking-stick legs, newts with spooned tongues, eyeless cats with tails that curled like ropes on the floor.

'Please, please, forget those weird things, nobody's going to buy them,' Elena said every time she saw them. 'Let's stick to pots.'

Yet a wealthy Dutchwoman outside Nîmes, bleached hair pulled back against a leathery face, regularly asked to see Giacomo's work. At the end of her gravel drive, where a clump of oleanders dropped blistered flowers on the ground, she lined up each sculpture in the sun before striding forward and rubbing the sides of an embossed creature, impossible and curved.

'I'll take this one,' she smiled decisively. 'It's as if it has always belonged here.'

Driving home, with the new cheque slotted in the ashtray, Giacomo dispelled Elena's doubts with little swerves of joy across the road. 'These sculptures will be the making of us. Just you wait!'

17

'Don't budge a centimetre, whatever you do, don't move,' Giacomo said as he circled round Elena. He sharpened his pencil and scattered the shavings on the stony ground. Marco prowled behind him, jumping up, from time to time, to get a look at the drawing pad.

'Enough!' Elena begged. 'I'm getting cramp!'

'One minute. Don't move, just don't move!'

Giacomo clambered up onto the elevated rock where Elena lay. He placed sprigs of juniper under her arms and jagged leaves in the sides of her shoes.

'Stop it,' she screeched, 'it tickles.'

Giacomo moved to the edge of the rock to resume his drawing. The valley in front of him gave way to a dry, deserted landscape of olive trees and clusters of prickly pears.

'Don't move,' he said. 'Please.'

He returned to Elena and switched the leaves from shoe to shoe, but a sudden, hot gust of wind blew them away, taking hold of her coal-coloured hair, weaving and ruffling it into the air like rich plumage. He pulled a piece of garden string from his pocket and wound it round the strands covering Elena's face. It too was carried away by the wind.

'Damn,' Giacomo said, fighting the unruly hair, pushing it behind her ears, trying to twist it into a bun at the back of her head. New wisps flew into Elena's mouth as she laughed. She spat them out.

'That's it. I'm getting up,' she said.

'No, you can't, I haven't finished.'

'I have to.'

Giacomo rushed to scrawl something down. He ended with a flurry and ripped the page from the pad. Marco scrambled up the rock. Elena stood, brushing the juniper from her armpits. Both of them crowded round Giacomo, eager to see what he had drawn.

The sketch bore no apparent connection to Elena's pose. The paper was a jumble of nondescript, hazy strokes punctured by the sharp lead of the pencil, an unworkable human figure that defied anatomy and reason. When Giacomo explained that the eye never reproduced what the brain wanted, and a fine drawn line could never be a substitute for the tactile emotion of sculpture, Elena threw up her arms letting out howls of laughter. She grabbed Giacomo and they jumped off the rock together, holding hands.

'What if I really did look like that?' she said.

She contorted her body to match the drawing, pulling a face at Marco, before toppling into a bush with a squeal. Marco joined her on the ground, writhing awkwardly, tucking his legs behind his back, grimacing wildly like a clown.

'Wasn't it more like this?' he asked, his head upside down.

With the sound of laughter behind him, Giacomo opened up the boot of the van and lifted out the picnic. Over the brow of the hill was a path to an ancient dolmen. It was the perfect secluded spot, he said. They ate with the food spread out on a blanket. When Marco disappeared inside the delicately balanced rocks of the dolmen, Elena ran to haul him out.

'I don't want you going in there,' she said. She peered inside and shivered at the cold darkness.

'Please, can't I just have a look?' Marco asked. 'I'm not going far.'

'No, my love.' Elena held onto Marco. 'Stay right here, next to me. Who knows what's in there, snakes or scorpions, that kind of thing. The boulders could collapse any moment too.'

'I don't think so. That thing has been there for thousands of years,' Giacomo said.

'Can I go into the wood then?' Marco asked.

'No, don't go anywhere. You can get a toy out of the van if you want to.'

Elena steered her son towards the shade of an ilex tree and they fanned themselves with anything they could find. Taking swigs from a shared water bottle, they listened to the far-off hiss of the Camargue reeds and the song that Elena began to sing, her eyes tightly shut against the heat.

'Isn't this beautiful?' Giacomo said. He pointed to the woodlands and foothills of the Cevennes beyond. 'I've never seen anything like it.'

Elena pulled at a dead blade of grass from the dusty ground. She dug her hands into the powder of the earth, and let it filter through her fingers. She took a tomato from the picnic bowl and threw it at a nearby clump of prickly pears. Instead of impaling on one of the spikes, it bounced and split in two. Within minutes, ants had swarmed over it, blackening its leaking flesh, unaware of her crouching beside them, watching.

Returning from a trip for Marco's eighth birthday, touring the cloisters of St Trophime in Arles, Giacomo asked Elena to marry him in half-whispers and smiles.

'Will you?' he asked, 'please.'

She held an unlit candle, thin slithers of wax peeling onto her hands from her repeated scratching. She looked for Marco at the rear of the church.

'Will you?' Giacomo asked again, offering her a box of matches. He struck one and held it in front of her.

Before she could answer, or absorb his question, he sought out a priest in the sacristy.

'Are you regular worshippers?' the prelate asked. 'Do you live in Arles?'

Giacomo explained, keeping details to a minimum, but it was details that the priest wanted. 'Is this your child? Have you both been married before?'

Elena got lost between the French of the priest's enquiries and the contradictory prayers clashing in her head. Using the need to buy Marco a birthday present as an excuse, she left the church with her son and disappeared into the crowds of the main square. They squeezed through tourists and shoppers, following the raised umbrella of a tour guide. They were met by closed ranks of backs, heads turned to the facade of the church, cameras snapping from every angle. They got lost in the muddle of visitors, the shouted descriptions of the buildings, dissonant speeches and languages rebounding off each other. Elena spotted an opening between two backpackers and pushed forward. Unable to get past, she retreated, gripping Marco as tightly as she could. 'Excuse me,' she said, but no-one heard. 'Excuse me!' A hand finally touched her on the shoulder and she turned, with relief, to discover Giacomo behind her, waiting to take them home.

Undaunted by the administrative paperwork the priest had hinted at, Giacomo organized the marriage in Aigues-Mortes. A delivery man from a neighbouring pottery, and another colleague Elena had never met, a kiln technician from Nîmes, acted as witnesses. In the church, Elena took off Riccardo's ring and placed it on Giacomo's finger. She felt the comfort of knowing that he was standing in for his dead brother, two husbands, one surname – a new facet to the same life.

18

To display their range of garden pots, kitchenware, sculptures and vases, Giacomo and Elena borrowed money to convert a barn next to the pottery into a showroom. A tract of land was fenced off behind it to stack up plinths and equipment, and an apartment built on the second floor. At night, the rush of trucks on the road knocked the shuddering pots against each other, the rough scraping of clay on clay.

'Look,' Giacomo enjoyed telling his nephew, as they stacked up driftwood to carve, 'inside each of these is something beautiful, a new life waiting to be born, an egg about to hatch, and no-one, not even us, knows what it's going to look like. Imagine that!'

'But that looks like a rabbit already,' Marco said animatedly. 'And that piece over there could be a loaf of bread, or a whale. That one could be a sitting child.'

'Sure,' Giacomo said, turning the wood round in his hands. 'Like the dust clouds we were watching the other day, you can see them as anything you like.'

'Now, come off it both of you,' Elena said, coming into the pottery. She patted them on the head. 'You won't get anywhere with these games.' She fished Marco's homework out of his satchel. 'Here, let's stick to this.'

Elena observed, enthralled, as her son completed each lesson, his writing as self-assured as print. She lamented her own lack of education listening to him reading out poems and history books, not daring to interrupt for the explanations of the French that she craved. She could not believe that such alien sounds could spring from her son so easily, her own flesh and blood. She kept her French speaking to a minimum, getting words mixed up with Italian, stressing things in the wrong place, throwing in phrases she mistakenly thought she had picked up. Every time she expressed herself in French, it seemed she was being forced to speak with a mouth full of chalk, pursing her lips into unnatural shapes. She found herself unable to draw in the air she needed and she worried she would suffocate mid-sentence if she carried on.

Marco, though, understood what she meant and rescued her from unknown or badly enunciated words. He alone, in fact, could ward off the outside world with his irreproachable pronunciation, create a barrier between her and harm. It was he who spoke to town hall officials about local council matters, who rang operators to query bills and bank details, who spent hours deciphering orders and letters from suppliers. At the markets in Arles or Nîmes, Elena relied on her son to pay for the vegetables and meat, to accompany her on local buses and trains. In shops, he disputed prices, wrote out cheques, and foiled the rapacious charlatans that she imagined to be everywhere.

'When you're a foreigner,' she explained to Marco, 'nothing comes free.'

What the customers wanted, Elena decided, were practical items. She designed loo-brush holders the colour of the sea, soap dishes on the backs of pot-bellied frogs, key rings with bulls' horns as hooks, storks and white Camargue horses with perforated heads for pepper and salt. She came up with suggestions for statuettes to place on graves, bowed figurines that held plaques saying 'to our beloved grandfather', 'Grandma, you're in our hearts', in lettering of weeping olive branches or white doves. Giacomo reluctantly produced these, and more: batches of ashtrays, candlesticks, orange and lemon presses, bottle coolers, window boxes, souvenir plates, bowls of painted fruit, piggybanks, letterboxes, Renaissance-style cherubs, napkin rings with a variety of Christian names. All these, Elena was sure, would be successful with the tourists. From a home design magazine, she copied ideas for kitchen tiles with seahorses and starfish, to which she added her own concept of oysters and mermaids. She imported plaster replicas of Michelangelo's David from Italy and sold the whole batch within a month by lining them up along the road.

She sent off orders for more plaster Davids to Italy, and along with them, she posted a letter to her family in Varanelle. She had toyed with finding a way of sending postcards of places from around the world: Buenos Aires, Rio de Janeiro, Toronto and Washington, to show her father how successful she had become, but the letter she sent was placatory and honest. She informed her family of Riccardo's death and of her new marriage to Giacomo. She wrote about Marco and the pottery. The reconciliation that she longed for, and the accompanying invitation to visit, never came. Instead, her sister Teresa wrote that the mention of her name was still forbidden, and that her mother had stopped crying. Her sister enclosed photos of herself, her husband and a baby, snaps of holidays with Italian backgrounds Elena fought to forget.

19

After they made love, Elena locked herself in the bathroom and left Giacomo alone to the sound of the bath filling behind the wall. The taps churned, the steam puffed out of the keyhole into the dark and the door remained firmly shut as Elena lay on the ground, both legs stretched up the wall. She had once heard a woman in Varanelle claim this was the surest way to get pregnant and, for half an hour before climbing into the bath, Elena stayed still with her back on the tiled floor, toes aimed at the ceiling, willing Giacomo's seed downwards into her upturned womb. She had been to the hospital twice, undergone tests, as had Giacomo. Each time, they had been assured there was nothing wrong. All that was needed was to keep calm.

In the bath she did stay calm, and immobile, the water turning cold, the soap dissolving into plumes of sunken fog. By the time she had been startled from semi-sleep by the belch of the dislodged plug, the skin on her fingers and toes had puckered and turned flaky white. She remained in the bath a while longer though, letting her body float down with the draining water, till her thighs were stuck to the enamel of the tub, till the last of the water forked into threads and disappeared into the plughole. She brushed her teeth and ran the hot tap, streaking a finger across the mirror to see her face.

She came out of the bathroom, to the impatient swishing of the sheets around Giacomo. She inched herself into bed beside him. She buried her head in the pillow and the mattress soaked up new scents of soap and shampoo. She heard Giacomo bite the sleeve of his pyjamas, an almost inaudible grinding of teeth. He touched her shoulder. She knew he wanted to talk, yet her response was to shut her eyes and draw the blanket over their bodies.

Often, in fact, she had to turn her face from Giacomo until she was no longer looking at anything but the paleness of the sheets. When he kissed her, she sensed him seeking beyond her lips, a reassurance on her breath, but she could offer him little but a distant reminder of their mountains, a distorted language they both knew. She battled against this deadness inside her, the weight of his flesh and love on her, the numbness of her hands. The kisses were the hardest. She avoided his mouth, the feel of his tongue on her teeth. She offered him her hair instead. He worked it through his fingers, lacing and loosening it over her shoulders till she became a marionette pulled up on worn strings of hair, waiting for him to talk, to talk like Riccardo.

And so, listening to the accented voice that breathed life into her, detached from the movements of her body, as if her mouth were someone else's, as if she were walking without being aware of it, Elena filled her mind with scripts of her own making, inviting her memories of Riccardo to join her. Behind closed eyes, she opened her mouth and looked for the coarse hair on his chest, the score of his scarred skin, the streaks of sawdust damp with sweat. She gripped the thin back enveloping her, the smooth chin brushing her neck, and turned Giacomo's childlike cheeks into Riccardo's face, thick with stubble, conjuring up noises and smells. At night, for brief moments, Riccardo reclaimed his brother's place, and Elena made love to him with her unburied sorrow, begging for absolution for her betrayal.

Giacomo, she feared, often guessed her devices and she could feel him staring deep into the well of secrecy inside her, into her womb as it echoed with his stabbing attempts at fatherhood.

A truck thundered past Elena as she stood in front of the pottery, shaking the plastic bags of strawberries hooked to the sides of the wheelbarrow. A further truck came, filled with workers heading home from the salt fields. They caught sight of Elena and rose in unison to wave as they sped round the corner. She looked at her watch. She had been waiting for an hour by the roadside, perhaps more – the school bus had never been this late. Grasshoppers and cicadas chattered from the tall grass on the other side of the road. A long-haired man on a bicycle pedalled slowly alongside the sculptures, checking each one as he went. A vehicle appeared and for a few seconds she thought it was the top of the bus. She walked back to the pottery, leaving the wheelbarrow in the sun.

'Giacomo,' she said. 'The bus still isn't here.'

He peered up from the wheel. 'Did Marco tell you he'd be late?'

'He said nothing.'

She looked through the windows behind her, back towards the road.

'Will you call the school?'

Giacomo cleaned his hands on the sides of his trousers and picked up the phone. There was no reply.

'It'll be fine, you mustn't worry.'

Elena returned outside, to the wheelbarrow, and pushed it towards the shade of a tree. She felt the strawberries inside their bags and put one in her mouth. It was hot, a plastic taste behind the sweetness, and she spat it onto the ground. She wiped the dust that was forming on the top plates and bowls. She noticed a crack at the base of one. It broke as she lifted it out. She flicked the bits into the ditch by the car park. The glaze held the sunlight until a cloud came. A car hurtled round the bend, then another. She looked at her watch. This had never happened. The bus was always on time. She returned to the pottery. She insisted Giacomo call the school once more. There was no reply.

'It'll be shut now,' he said. 'It's nearly six…'

She went back to the side of the road. Each car that came into view seemed momentarily to be a bus. She needed to sit, she felt unbalanced. A stinging feeling at the end of her fingers was growing into a wave of alarm, rising through her body. She pinched the skin of her forehead, shutting her eyes. She rubbed her temples, curling her hair round her fingers. She opened her eyes to watch the empty road. Gusts of wind, straight off the sea, were sweeping across the rice fields opposite, like an invisible comb twisting and curving the shoots of green. She felt it would only take a stronger gust to knock her over. She studied her watch. She stood. 'Marco,' she shouted. 'Where are you? Where are you?' She ran to the showroom, throwing the door open.

'Something's happened. I know it. He can't just be late. He's never done this.'

'There has to be a reason, it's OK. The school must have kept them late, that's all. He's thirteen now…'

'No, it's not right, it's just not right!' She searched through the paperwork by the till. 'Isn't there another number? We have to do something! Let's call the police? Do something! We have to do something!'

Giacomo held her by the shoulders and caressed her face. 'Elena, calm down, please, he'll be here in a minute.'

'Who knows what's happened?' She pulled at her hair, biting her hand so as not to scream.

Giacomo tried to sit her down, but she wanted to stay at the roadside. She unloaded the wheelbarrow, piling the plates into an uncertain column, the bowls one on top of the other. She watched, without moving, as they fell and broke. The wheels of the bus slammed to a halt on the car park, spraying small stones and clay at her feet.

Elena rushed forward as the bus doors opened. 'Where have you been?' She threw herself at her son and saw twenty faces squashed against the windows of the bus above her, wide-eyed and grinning, banging against the glass.

'What happened?' Elena held and kissed her son's face. 'I was so worried…'

'We went on a school trip, to Marseille.'

'Why didn't you tell me?'

'Because you never let me go anywhere.'

Elena led Marco to his bedroom.

'We need to say a prayer. *Ti prego Signore.*'

'Please Lord…' Marco repeated.

'Please Lord, bless the soul of my father…'

'Stay on your knees with me, my love, don't get up.'

'Please Lord, bless the soul of my father and…'

Elena took the framed photo of Riccardo from the shelf, disturbing the fish in the aquarium beside it, unsettling the turtledoves in their cage above. She held it in front of her son's face.

'Give him a kiss. Thank him for protecting you today.'

Marco kissed the glass. He looked at the threadbare edges and shallow, discoloured folds dividing his father's face into four, then up at the fish in the aquarium and the birds perched on the top of their nest box. Elena placed the photo back on the shelf.

'You know,' she said, smiling, tucking Marco's duvet in at the corners, 'the older you get the more you look like him, apart from the eyelashes, of course, his were shorter, much shorter.' She pinched his cheek, plumped the pillow and switched off the night light on the floor.

'I want the light on.'

'You won't sleep properly.'

'I will. Anyway Papa's coming to tell me a story.'

'His name is Giacomo, not Papa. How many times do I have to tell you that?'

'Sorry.'

'What story anyway?'

'I don't know, whatever, he makes them up for me.'

'What about?'

'Anything.'

'Has he told you what he and your father got up to as boys in those mountains?'

'No, I…'

'He should. I think you'd like it.' She began closing the door. 'Have you fed your fish?'

'Yes.'

'And the birds.'

'Yup.'

'Mamma.'

'*Sì*, what?'

'Don't wake me up tonight.'

'Well, come and get me then if you have a nightmare.'

'I'll be fine.'

'I'll be the one having nightmares with what you put me through today. I thought I was going to be sick waiting for that bus.' For a moment, some of the panic of the afternoon returned to her face.

'We only went to Marseille!'

'I don't like it. I don't like you going off like that. It's dangerous. Who knows…'

'It's fine.'

'You need to sleep now.' She looked at him. 'Goodnight angel. I'll

85

bring you some water in a minute.' She closed the door. 'Giacomo,' she called down to the showroom.

The sound of footsteps on the stairs was followed by two voices mumbling at length outside on the landing. Giacomo entered Marco's bedroom. His clothes were white with clay powder. He sat at the end of the bed.

He took a letter from his top pocket. 'Can you check this? It's for the town hall in Aigues-Mortes. I don't want to get it wrong.'

Marco read the letter. His uncle pulled a stack of grimy postcards from another pocket. He laid them out on the duvet. They were of canyons in America, rock formations in the Dolomites, a Greek vase from the British Museum, a Bolivian in traditional costume, a painting by Van Gogh. As they discussed each one, Elena walked back in with a glass of mineral water for Marco.

'Giacomo, you promised!' she said, seeing the postcards on the bed.

'I wanted to show him these, please.'

'You agreed to tell him about Friuli. Please don't fill his head with more strange ideas.'

'He needs to see all this beauty,' he said, gathering up the cards.

'Beauty?' Elena placed the glass of water on the bedside table.

'Yes,' he mumbled bashfully.

'And what do you know about that?' she half-laughed.

'I…'

'Giacomo,' she said, turning to Marco and raising her eyes to heaven. 'Do you think our families survived for centuries up their mountains, messing around with sculptures and beauty?'

'They…'

'No. I'll tell you what they did. They worked the land, cut trees, employed their common sense, and stuck to what they knew.' She gestured to Giacomo to follow her out onto the landing. She shut the door behind them. 'Listen,' she said, 'Riccardo would not have wanted you bewildering his son with all these fantasies, I'm sure of that, quite sure. The boy needs to keep his feet on the ground, understand about practical things, a career, money, and all that.'

'He's full of imagination, can't you see that? He likes these things.'

'Allow me to decide what he needs.'

'But Riccardo loved dreaming, imagining things too. He was so good at that.'

'No,' Elena cut in. 'He had ideas, but he always thought them through, unlike some.'

'But he was always pushing for new discoveries and travels. He never took no for an answer, did he? Why do you think he went to Argentina?' Giacomo said. 'He hated conventions, didn't he, you know that as well as me. He wanted a different life, not to be chained up. I think Marco…'

'Are you telling me what my child needs or what my own husband was like? I was the one married to him!' Elena pulled back to the edge of the stairs. She clasped the top banister for support, but her hands were trembling. 'Don't you go telling me what he was like or what he would have wanted, don't do that to me, do you hear me, don't ever do that!'

Giacomo shuffled the postcards, superimposing images on top of each other, Van Gogh, the Bolivian, the Dolomites, under and over, again and again. He stopped at the picture of the Greek vase from the British Museum. Between two dancing women, stood a centaur, its front legs raised. He looked at Elena, her eyes were fixed on the stairwell. She began walking down, her shoes scraping each step.

Giacomo went back to Marco's room, to find the boy dipping his fingers into his aquarium, chasing one of the fish back and forth. His eyes were red.

'You mustn't worry about your mother and I having our little differences you know.' He winked at Marco, waving the cards. 'I'll show you these another day. I think you should get some sleep now.'

'Why does she get like that?' Marco asked. 'It's because I was late from school, isn't it? I thought we'd be home at the usual time. I didn't mean to upset her.'

'You should have told me, next time I'll deal with it.' Giacomo said.

'She won't let me out of her sight now. She's going to go into one of her moods.'

'Come here,' he said, trying to hug the boy, but he escaped onto the bed. 'Tell me a story please, and not about Friuli.'

'Oh I think you'd like it. Your mother's right. You know it's a pretty magical place.'

'Magical?' Marco repeated, dubious.

'Well, kind of,' Giacomo said, pausing to think. 'I mean your grand-mother used to say there were strange beasts that had the power to transform themselves into humans.'

'Why did she say that?'

'To scare us, so we wouldn't stray too far from the house.'

'Did it work?'

'No! Your father was always wandering off. The beasts lived in caves covered in writing and symbols no-one had ever deciphered, so you can imagine, we spent days and days searching. They were said to be in the very entrails of the earth.'

'And?'

'Well, that's it, I'm afraid.'

'That's not much of a story. Is that what Mamma was making all that fuss about?'

'I know. Sorry,' he smiled. He got up to leave, circled round the room, hesitated by the door. 'Well, actually,' Giacomo added, sitting back down, 'now that I come to think of it, we did find a cave once.

88

Well, not really a cave, more like an underground chamber in the rocks. It can't have been longer than fifteen metres or so, but it was huge to us, I was only five at the time, maybe six.'

'What happened?'

'Your father told me to go down and have a look with him and when I turned round he'd gone, just vanished. Then I heard him shouting for help, and I began to panic and ran towards his cries, but there was no-one there.'

'And then what?'

'I heard a blood-chilling scream,' Giacomo said dramatically.

'Ah, come off it.'

'No, I did. I grabbed a stone to defend myself.'

'And?'

'I saw this horrific creature standing in front of me. It had fur on its head and horns. Its face was as white as bone and covered in leaves, its arms were sharp sticks.'

'What?'

'I ran, I can tell you I ran so fast and I shrieked like I've never shrieked. I sped down the mountainside with the creature after me. Every time I turned, it got closer and closer, and I thought I was going to pass out with fear, but when it got nearer I saw that it was wearing your father's trousers.'

'It was him!'

'Yes. He'd found a ram's skull and put it on his head, under some old wool, and just picked off a few branches from a tree.'

'Why did he do such a thing to you? Did you fight? You must have fought after that?'

Giacomo stood to leave again. 'It's night-time now, sleep well.'

'Well, did you fight?' Marco insisted.

'No, no, course not.' Giacomo bent down to flick off the light on the floor.

'Leave it on, please.'

Marco heard doors shutting, the television being switched off. He got up and took a pot of fish food from the shelf and scattered flakes inside the aquarium. The goldfish came up to eat and he studied their mouths trawling and swallowing the coloured food. Without knowing why, he whipped a hand into the water and chased the biggest fish. It spun round, looking for an escape from his fingers, its lighter underbelly flashing as it turned. He caught it and dropped it onto his desk. It flipped and twisted across the wood, mouth gasping. Bending over, he strained to see if he could hear a noise from its gills. There was nothing. It writhed and jerked its tail a little more before becoming still. He dropped it back into the aquarium. It sunk to the bottom, onto the gravel, and lay there, immobile. He banged the sides, frantic. He found it difficult to breathe himself, his chest restricting. He wanted to cry again. He knocked the aquarium, splashing water over the edges. The fish stirred, regaining strength, opening its mouth. He got back into bed. The turtledoves scuffled nervously in their cage. He pulled the duvet over his head. Cars passed on the road, thundering trucks, the rubbing of clay against clay.

Marco woke to find his mother standing over him. Her nightdress was filled with light like a lampshade, the contours of her thighs and legs dark underneath.

'You were talking,' she said. 'Was it that nightmare again?'

'Mmm, what? I wasn't talking.'

'I heard you from our room.'

Marco sat up and rubbed his eyes before collapsing back onto the pillow. 'I was asleep, Mamma,' he moaned. 'I was really asleep. I wasn't talking.'

'You were. It's OK I'm with you now my darling.'

She lifted the duvet and lay down on the bed.

'Budge up,' she whispered, easing in alongside Marco. She lifted his pyjama top and placed her hands on his bare back. 'You feel very hot.' She rubbed her hands down to the base of his spine then massaged his shoulders. 'Are you OK, my love?'

'I was asleep.'

'Let me feel your forehead.'

'Please, I'm...'

'No, come here.' She placed her palm against her son's brow. 'I think you have a fever. You're boiling.'

'I'm fine.'

'Marco,' she said, clutching him. 'Look at me.' She unbuttoned the top of his pyjama and felt his chest, touching and patting his stomach. 'Is that sore? Are you ill?'

'No.'

She switched off the bedside light. They both lay back on the narrow bed, without a word. Marco reached and scratched his knee. Elena wriggled left and right to get comfortable. 'You always smell so nice,' she said. 'I'd recognize your smell anywhere. Do you know that?'

'I can't sleep with the light off.'

She stroked his face. 'You're going to have to start shaving soon,' she said, running a finger over his top lip. 'I can't believe it.'

'Mamma, I'm tired.' Marco pulled the pillow towards him. 'I can't sleep if the light's not on.'

'You shouldn't need it at your age.'

'Please, I want it on.'

'You were having a nightmare, weren't you?'

'No.'

Elena turned the light on and lay back in bed.

'I've been thinking,' she said, turning round and kissing him on the neck. 'I want you to learn to make pots too. You'll be better than him, I'm sure.'

'Who?'

'Giacomo, of course, he's not coming up with anything new, and if you're to take over this business one day…'

'But…'

'You can do it after school, when you've finished your homework.'

She lifted her head and waited for a reaction from Marco. There wasn't one. She felt for the glass of water on the bedside table and drank a sip. She poured some into her hand and wiped Marco's forehead.

'Why did you have a nightmare again?'

'I didn't.'

'Well, what about that one two weeks ago, the one with the burglar? That's all you told me. You screamed a lot. Remember how I came rushing in here?'

'So?'

'Tell me what happened.'

'I can't remember.'

'Yes, you can, come on sweetheart; it's all right to have nightmares. I might be able to understand, in case it happens again.'

'It's while everyone's asleep,' Marco said, staring at the ceiling. 'I can hear a noise and I go down to the showroom.' He looked sideways at his mother. 'I'm standing there and I realize that there's a man outside.' He paused. 'I know there's a man outside and, for some reason, I go and unlock the door for him. Then I run and hide behind the till and wait. It's in the early hours of the morning. From my hiding place, I see the man come in and take all the pots, statues, sculptures, all the bowls and plates. I know he can see me. He even looks at me from time to time. As he leaves he tries to say something, but he doesn't, although he knows my name. When he's gone and nothing is left on the shelves I race upstairs and get back into bed and I can't sleep at all, because I feel bad about letting him in.'

'I see,' Elena said, pulling the duvet further towards her.

'Why does it happen?'

'Don't know, but it doesn't matter.'

'What does it mean?'

'No idea. Does he look like anyone you know, this burglar?' she asked, smoothing the sheet beneath her.

Marco peered up at the picture of his father above them, blurred and watery in his frame.

'Sometimes,' he whispered. 'Not always.'

'It's just your imagination working overtime. Come here.' She hauled Marco further onto the pillow. Her hair tickled his cheek, the vinegary and gritty smell of blackness. They lay still, their arms down their sides, listening to each other's breathing.

'I have nightmares too, you know,' she said.

'You do?'

'Often.

'Like what?'

'I'm standing in the courtyard, at the farm in Varanelle, and there's a deafening silence, the most terrible silence in my ears, like it's the weather, the silence is like bad weather pushing down on the earth, filling the clouds, all around me, and I know that behind the village, on the other side of the mountain, is noise, but I can't hear it, and I know I'll never hear it again.' Elena turned to the wall. 'Do you remember the house?' she asked Marco in a soft voice.

'No.'

'Nothing?'

'No.'

She sat up, covering her eyes from the night light, her fingers tightly shut.

'Mamma, what's wrong?'

Marco lifted the hair away from his mother's face and saw tears on her cheeks. He gathered the strands together behind her and pulled gently. He combed her hair with his nails, tightening and straightening as he went, stroking the crown of her head. She continued to shake her head, but eventually lay down again, pulling Marco's hand onto her chest.

'I love you so much, Marco, you're all I've got,' she said, 'do you understand that? All I have in the world.'

Unable to find space next to his mother, Marco stretched out upside down. Her feet stuck out of the bottom of the duvet next to him. He could see a mole on the arch of her left foot, a small scar on the dark skin of her thigh and, further away, on the shelf, his fish swimming around their tank in search of food. Was it possible, he wondered, that they never slept?

2 1

With every passing year, the Carlevaris family eagerly awaited the foreigners who crowded the Camargue in the summer. Whether they came to the pottery deliberately, or stumbled across it on their way to find petrol or campsites, Elena made the most of their presence. 'Marco,' she said mid-May, 'it's time to change the prices,' and she swept round the showroom, labels in hand, adding on extra francs. She concealed the proceeds of the sales in her bra, fearful of leaving them in the till at night. When she handed the money to Giacomo over supper, Marco noticed that his uncle always turned to feel for the heat of her skin on each banknote as he hid them in the breadbin.

The summer also brought what Giacomo termed his 'connoisseurs'. They were foreigners with an eye for detail, amateurs of unusual sculpture and pottery. They arrived towards the end of July, as the needles from the pine trees and the dead wings of cicadas dried in little heaps inside the garden pots. They were wealthy travellers from

European capitals, Parisians, Londoners, Romans, or visitors from places as far away as South Africa and America. If Giacomo was lucky, they departed from the pottery, the top-heavy limbs of one of his sculptures poking through a car sunroof in a final farewell.

It amazed Elena how the map of the world unfolded each time Marco talked to foreign visitors. He stood mesmerized, absorbing their words, watching the facial expressions that accompanied gestures, hanging onto every intonation. The passing Scandinavian tourists sought oven dishes, the English wanted solid mugs that fitted into dishwashers and the French were always keen to know the purpose of every item. The Germans bought the most bowls but spurned the plates. Occasionally, Italians driving from the Atlantic coast of France, or Spain, stopped for ashtrays and saucers. When Elena heard Italians speaking, she spoke louder herself, luring them into long-anticipated conversations. It struck her, though, that these exchanges rarely ended in any significant sales, and she was left thinking that she should always allow Italians round the showroom first, and then talk.

Growing numbers of Japanese tourists also came to the Camargue – people who, unlike other nationalities, were exclusively interested in Giacomo's thin-necked vases. While Elena took to bowing when they entered, a rapid bending of the back with a criss-crossing curtsy of the legs, Marco proffered hesitant Japanese phrases about glazes and kiln heats to the delight of the customers.

22

'Centre the clay, that's it, nearly.' Giacomo stood behind Marco at the potting wheel. 'No, keep your hands moving upwards. That's it, you're there, no, no, steady now.' The vertical tower of wet clay imploded and spun onto the floor.

'Let's start again. Centre it.'

'I don't want to do this any more.'

'No, you have to try once more,' Elena said from the sidelines. 'Please, my love, go on.'

'It's impossible,' Marco sighed.

'That's it, keep it going, easy, gently, gently, don't force it, that's it, you're doing well, wait,' Giacomo said. The tower of clay flew off again and hit the corner of a display cabinet.

'I'm not doing this any more,' Marco said. He washed his hands at the sink and left the room.

'What are we going to do?' Elena asked Giacomo.

'He'll be fine, we just have to be patient. He's a teenager, he has other things to think about. He'll get the hang of it one day.'

'How? We're in real trouble if he doesn't. We can't rely on you.'

'It'll be fine.'

'No, it won't. Only five people have been in here this morning and not one has bought anything.'

'It's like that some days.'

'It's not just some days. There's not enough to buy. We have to think of something. Other potteries round here are doing fine.'

Elena walked up the stairs. She stopped on the landing. She could hear music coming from Marco's room.

'You mustn't give up with the pottery,' she said, letting herself in, uninvited. She saw her son sitting by his bed with his cassette player on. 'Shouldn't you be revising for your exams?' she asked.

'Listen to this.' He stood up and rewound the cassette. 'It's a song by Yves Montand called *"Nuit de Camargue"*. Strange isn't it? Do you think he composed it here?'

Elena listened. The song spoke of two lovers coming together as pink flamingos flew by, the hand of a man on a woman's moonstone-white breast. She waved dismissively.

'What's the point of that?'

'It's a song.'

'But why make people sad?'

'It's not sad.'

'It is.'

Elena looked at her son's desk. It was covered in books he had bought in a second-hand bookshop in Nîmes, mostly biographies. She had seen many of them already in the kitchen. Marco read them without bothering to look up, after supper, while she watched television. She read the titles on the covers: *Saladin, Averroës, Elizabeth I of England, Chairman Mao, Cavour, Buffalo Bill, Napoleon, Nasser, Baden-Powell, Toussaint L'Ouverture, Madame de Pompadour.*

'What are all these about?'

'People's lives.'

'Are they all dead?'

'Yes.'

'I see.'

'I want to get the train into Nîmes again, Mamma. Could I have some more money for books?

'If you have another go at the potting wheel,' Elena said as calmly as she could. 'I'd prefer it if you revised anyway. Why do you keep on going into Nîmes? You've got your baccalaureate in four months. We want you working here as soon as possible after that.'

'What's the point...' Marco began to say, then he corrected himself at the sight of his mother's pained grimace.

By the bed, Elena saw tidy pillars of Teach-Yourself Berlitz cassettes. Her son's room was frequently filled with the sound of foreign languages being repeated in an overly precise, clear voice. Marco listened to American and British music too, and transcribed it, filling huge sheets of paper, replaying the pronunciation of certain words, looking others up in the dictionary. She noticed how easily, unlike her, several options for a word came to him, a host of choices, multiple possibilities for each sentence. When talking to customers in the showroom, if he said 'plate' in English, he could turn to another and say *assiette* in French, or *piatto* in Italian, *plato* in Spanish or *teller* in German. So it went with scores of other words and expressions. A multitude of tongues had flowered in her son's mouth.

She picked up a French/Basque dictionary.

'Isn't this going a bit far?' she asked, smiling at him in spite of herself.

Next to the dictionary were more books: the exploits of American pioneers, an illustrated guide to the Middle East, the new 1986 book of statistics, a history of the Nile.

'And all this? Is it useful?'

'Of course. I'm going to be the best-read potter in the world.'

'What's this?' she asked, picking up the torn-out page of a school book with a telephone number next to the name Mathilde.

'The number of a friend.'

'You shouldn't rip pages from books. Even I know that.'

PART FIVE

Aigues-Mortes, 1990

23

A teacher from Marco's former *lycée* found him in Nîmes late one day. Not wanting to stop and chat, Marco waved and turned down the road to the coliseum. Monsieur Deslandes sprinted after him, short of breath.

'Hey, wait!' he panted, until Marco was forced to stop.

'What are you up to these days?'

'I… I'm buying some things for work,' Marco said, opening the plastic bag he was carrying to reveal some paper rolls for the cash till, labels and marker pens. 'I'm redoing the pricing at the pottery.'

Monsieur Deslandes looked at him aghast. 'And your university studies in Montpellier?'

'I gave all that up over two years ago, there was too much to do at the pottery.'

'But, Marco, you were the brightest pupil we'd had in years.'

'Well, who knows, maybe one day I'll go back to Montpellier,' he shrugged. 'I'm trying to save the pottery from bankruptcy at the moment.' He swung the plastic bag awkwardly from one hand to the other. 'I'd better be going.'

'No, no, forget Montpellier. It's too provincial for you. You must go to Paris.'

'Paris?'

'Of course'

'I can't.'

'Why?'

'I can't. It's too complicated.'

'You must, Marco, I have good contacts, I can help, look at your friend from school, Rémy Albertin, he's happy in Paris. Get in touch with him.'

'I haven't spoken to him in years.'

'You should.'

'I…'

'Listen, I'll pop by the pottery tomorrow with some forms.'

'No, don't, please don't.'

'I'm serious…'

Marco made to set off again, but Monsieur Deslandes caught his arm. 'Here,' he said, pulling a pen from his pocket and jotting down a number on a torn piece of cigarette packet. 'Call me, please. You can't go on working at that pottery.'

They sat through many silent meals, Marco reading and Giacomo doodling loosely geometrical shapes, as Elena took every dish away to the sink the moment it was finished.

'We should employ someone,' Marco suggested one evening, placing the last month's accounts on the table.

'Are you crazy?' Elena said.

'We couldn't possibly afford to pay anyone,' Giacomo added.

'Depends who we employ.'

'No way.'

'Give it some thought,' Marco tried again, turning to his mother. 'If we found the right person, they'd come up with sellable products fast, and that would cover the cost of paying them. We have all the equipment.'

'The good ones have their own potteries already.'

'That's true,' Giacomo said.

'Can I not look into it?' Marco asked. 'Please, let's just consider it. I mean, my work isn't making a great difference, let's face it. I've been going for over two years now.'

'I think we're coping just fine on our own,' Giacomo said. 'People will come round to our pots and sculptures, we're just a bit different, more stylish perhaps.'

'Stylish?' Elena said with a huff. 'I'm surprised your sculptures haven't caused a crash yet, the way the cars slow down to have a look at those women you've put along the road.'

'You'll see, people will come round to them.'

'How long have you been saying that? They're weird, I'm telling you,' Elena said. 'We should import more from Italy.'

'It doesn't even cover the costs.' Marco waved the accounts. 'Let me look around for someone. I'll call a few people, there's no harm in trying.'

'I'm not happy about it,' Giacomo complained. He jangled the keys in his pocket. 'I'm going to lock up downstairs.'

'I'll come with you,' Marco said.

The two men stood in the courtyard in front of the showroom. A truck shot past and shook the sculptures, swaying the reeds in the marshes, rattling the night air.

'I'm sorry to bring up these matters,' Marco said, 'but we can't go on like this. I wasn't criticizing you.'

'I don't want to work with anyone but you. I'm not interested in some stranger nosing around our pottery, interfering in our affairs.'

'But I'm useless.'

'You're not, you'll learn.'

'I won't.'

'Of course you will.'

'Neither of you is facing the facts. I'm no good. This whole place is going to go under if we're not careful.'

'You tell your mother to push my sculptures instead of hiding them. They would sell if she let them.'

'Listen, all you need to do is go into Nîmes, or Montpellier, and see what the shops and potteries are doing, you'll find out pretty fast. We're not keeping up.'

Giacomo swung the key round his little finger, 'I'm not convinced another person is the answer.'

'Papa,' Marco said, all of a sudden, tensing, 'I actually wanted to talk to you about something else.'

'What?'

'I want to carry on with my studies.'

'Didn't I tell you not to give up Montpellier? You could have continued part-time.'

'No, this is different.'

'Why?'

'Remember that teacher of mine, Monsieur Deslandes.'

'What about him?'

'He's going to help me find a place at university, to study translating and interpreting. That's what I want to do.'

'That sounds much more up your street.'

'Yes, I really want to do it.'

'So what's the problem?'

'The best course isn't here.'

'Where is it?'

'Paris.'

Giacomo looked at him. 'Paris?'

'I want to go. It's time I did something for myself. I'm sorry. I feel so trapped here.'

Giacomo took the key and rammed it into the showroom door. He fiddled with the lock, lifted the handle and pushed his shoulder against the frame. 'Damn door,' he muttered.

'Will you help me?' Marco asked, standing behind him.

The key clicked in the door and Giacomo turned it. 'Have you told your mother?'

'No.'

'When will you tell her?'

'I don't know.'

'I'm not sure how well she'll take it. You'll have to tread carefully.'

'Why do you think I've put it off for so long? I know it's going to hurt her. I don't want her to go into one of her moods.'

'She's been a bit better recently, don't you think? She still never talks to me about anything, or goes anywhere, but she hasn't been too bad,' Giacomo said.

Marco studied his uncle's face. 'Will you make sure she's all right,' he whispered. 'For me?'

Giacomo fingered the hem of his jacket, digging invisible circles into the wool.

'Haven't I always done that?'

'Yes, of course you have, more than anyone. We wouldn't be anywhere without you.' He touched Giacomo's shoulder. 'I am worried about her though.'

'I'm always worried about her. I think we both spend a lot of time worrying.'

'She won't even go out alone, unless it's to Aigues-Mortes,' Marco said. 'She wasn't always like that, was she?'

'She was. I still don't understand it. Sometimes it feels like she's got used to this place, and then she hates it all over again. She's so capable and beautiful. It's her insecurity, that's what it is, it gets in the way of everything, once she decides something that's it, she gets too frightened to change.'

'You have to insist,' Marco said. 'Take her places.'

'I do, it's not easy. She'll listen to you. I can't badger her too much.

Giacomo shoved the showroom key back into his pocket. He stood in front of the locked door and checked it again, leaning against it. 'You never know who could get in here at night.'

'Papa.

'Yes.'

'You do you understand why I'm leaving, don't you?'

Giacomo backed away. 'I understand,' he said. 'Yes, I understand. You must go, for your own sake.' He turned towards the parking lot.

'Where are you going?' Marco called after him.

'I need to walk.'

Marco placed an advert in a trade magazine for an assistant potter. He interviewed several candidates, choosing a forty-four-year-old Moroccan from Quissac named Djamel. He had worked in a commercial pottery in Anduze and seemed capable of coming up with sellable items for the tourists. He was taken on without delay, with Elena's reluctant blessing. Marco recruited a young Algerian woman called Nassima at the same time, to take over the cleaning of the house and showroom for a few hours a week. His mother, it was decided, would devote her energies to marketing Djamel's new production. Elena expected Marco to join her in this sales drive, charging him with rewriting and sending off new publicity leaflets for the printers. Instead of new leaflets however, letters arrived from Paris.

'What are all these?' Elena asked, stacking up the envelopes for her son in the showroom.

He picked them up one by one. His mother was waiting for an answer. 'Well?'

'I'm thinking of carrying on with my studies.'

She took the top letter from the pile and studied it. 'Why didn't you tell me?'

'I was going to.'

'I suppose we're going to have to find a second car again to get you to Montpellier.'

'I'm not going to Montpellier… I'm going to Paris.'

24

The week preceding his departure to Paris, Marco returned from Arles to find his turtledoves flying free in his bedroom. His mother, he could see, had been in his room. His papers had been disturbed, the sheets of the bed thrown back, and the surface of the aquarium was thick with flakes of fish food. Elena was nowhere to be found. Marco checked the garden, peered onto the balcony and then made for the marshes along the canal. He shouted and whistled. Not finding her, he ran a full circle behind the pottery, towards Aigues-Mortes and the crossroads on the way to Saint Laurent d'Aigouze, and trailed his way back home.

There was still no sign of Elena by five in the evening. Giacomo told Marco to wait at the pottery while he took out the van. He stopped by rice fields and drove down tracks, listened for noises. He scoured the empty stretches of water, skirting the pockets of reeds that sapped the horizon, searching. All he saw were herons lifting off into the sky, flights of egrets, horses and bulls as they emerged from the tall grasses. He drove to Saint Laurent d'Aigouze, walked up to the church and settled down on the front step. The main square was empty save for the odd car; occasionally a child on a bicycle appeared out of a garage door and rode a few metres before returning inside. A bull ring had been set up down one side of the square. Giacomo got back in the van and drove off.

Elena walked on the road towards Aigues-Mortes and the Saint-Antoine gate. The rampart walls of the city spread out on either side of it, punctuated by further monumental gates in a perfect rectangle, sealing in the houses and straight streets of the town. She went into a postcard shop and swivelled the display stand. Photographs of the Camargue, flamingos, men on horseback, black bulls being herded into the water, whirled past in a confusion of colours. The rotating images came to an abrupt halt, as a large, ruddy-faced tourist slammed her fist into the display stand and spun it the other way. A picture of a man carrying the statue of a saint into the sea shot round and round. Elena made for another shop stacked with children's fishing nets, buckets and spades for the beach. The place was crammed with people, mostly families, queuing to pay. This is what they needed to make the pottery work, she thought, children's paraphernalia, toys and souvenirs of the area. She hooked out a key-ring in the shape of the town's dungeon, the Tour de Constance. There was a shiny plastic portrait on it, of Marie Durand, the Protestant heroine who had been imprisoned there for twenty-seven years. The woman had left the engraved word 'resist' on the wall of her cell. Marco had told her about it once and she still didn't know what to make of it – nothing good, she suspected. Elena rang a porcelain bell decorated with a band of gypsies and their caravan. She would ask Djamel to come and have a look. There were definitely things to copy.

She wandered to the Church of Notre Dame des Sablons. It was locked, earlier than usual. She checked the time on her watch. She had wanted to light a candle. She tried the door again, gave up, and walked back down the pedestrian street. She decided, at the entrance to the Tour de Constance, to pay for a ticket up onto the fortification walls. It was nearing closing time, but she could still see the odd person above her, high up, foreign visitors in loose sun hats dodging each other on the rampart walkway. She squeezed past clusters of tourists and reached the top. She made for the nearest tower, over the main entrance to the town. From there she crossed above the Porte Saint-

Antoine to the Porte de la Villeneuve. She sat down on the warm stone between two battlements. An arrow slit at her feet was filled with cigarette ends. In front of her lay open-air salt fields. Salt was raked into vast flat-topped mounds each side of the fields. Spreading out of Aigues-Mortes, the Camargue radiated its broken, rusted greenery and rooftops. She spotted a shack in the distance that marked the point where the road turned towards the pottery. Blasts of noise drummed at her head, rising from the sea, from the marshes, out of the earth.

She got up and carried on, buffeted by the wind. The smell of salt clung to the stone. She could taste it on her tongue, feel it thickening and coating her hair. She stopped to let a man pass. His bulky camera struck her back. She held onto a metal rail. She felt giddy, trembling, a fit of vertigo threatening to overwhelm her. The ridge of the wall narrowed before her eyes. She held her head high, a trapeze artist on a tightrope of battlements that heaved, ridged and shifted beneath her feet. She began to feel queasy, the same bleak constriction of the stomach that had started to plague her since Marco announced his departure. What was she doing up here on these ramparts? The veins in her head tightened and throbbed. Her stomach felt as if it were foaming inside. A fine bed of sand and salt crunched under her soles. Her shoes butted against a raised stone. She again clung to the railing next to her. Worn-down, polished stones from centuries of military patrols, and now tourists, offered her a way, but she couldn't walk. Someone was shouting at her to hurry. They were locking up for the night. More shouts followed. She was still far from the exit. She got going again, the stone walkway her only path. She tried to swallow her anxiety with new determined strides. She passed through further gates, the Porte des Moulins, the Tour des Bourguignons, in and out of damp chambers and hidden rooms. She could see the exit in the distance. The railway ran below her on the other side of the wall. She arrived back at the starting point and went down the steps, past the ticket office.

She found a café with no customers, back on the pedestrian street, a few tables out on the pavement. She ordered a fruit juice. She had never sat alone in a bar before. Passers-by were looking at her, or so she imagined. That's how it had felt in Paris when she first arrived, as if she had been unclothed in the streets, scrutinized and out-of-place, constantly different. Marco's leaving, she knew, was going to suck the earth from under her again, wrenching her only anchor from her hands. Darkness had been waiting for her to stumble all these years. She hadn't beaten it, only staved it off, and watched it circle round her, waiting. She drank her juice. The waiter asked if she wanted something else. Nothing, she thanked him, waving her hand, nothing.

A group of children ran past screeching. Why had she never dared leave this place? She could have gone with Marco years before while there was still time, before she remarried, but she hadn't. Instead she had tried to love Giacomo and believe in his pottery, his choice of life, hoping that they would conceive a child together. Work, and Marco, had been her shelter, a double barricade against the future, but now? The pottery made no money and Marco was leaving. What would be required of her: to face Giacomo and this place on her own? It still seemed unbelievable to her, at times, that she had ever left Varanelle and travelled to Paris, as in a dream. Riccardo had often teased her for not wanting to leave home, of being so frightened of everything, but now that she had ventured into this outside world, she was finally facing the predicament she had dreaded all along – to be alone, completely alone. She could only think of a few nights Marco had spent away from her in twenty-two years. Paris, of all the places he wanted to live, Paris! The very word in her mind was synonymous with death. She called the waiter over and paid for her drink. She dropped her empty juice can in the bin behind her. She wandered in the direction of the pottery. The marshes along the canal sat stagnant, their water concealed deep inside them. She breathed in the heated airlessness. The grasses mocked her from the sides of the road, shaking their spiky heads. A heron flew overhead, its dangly legs kicking at the sky. She saw a van approaching her fast, swerving.

'Elena, what were you doing?' Giacomo said, winding down his window. 'We've been looking for you everywhere.'

He ran out and guided her to the open door. She said nothing as she climbed into the seat. They drove back to the pottery and parked. Elena had never learned to drive and she regretted it now as everything in her wanted to start up the vehicle again and smash it into a tree or the sculptures, over and over, until there was nothing left. As she entered the kitchen, she stumbled into a bag of Marco's books on the floor, neatly packed and ready to go.

Giacomo's headlights illuminated the pottery, yellow beams shooting through the slats of Marco's shutters. He had managed to catch one of his two doves, teasing it from underneath the bed. It sat in its cage, still terrified from its chase round the room, wings beating swiftly at the bars. The other bird burst from the top of the cupboard and swooped into the centre of the room. It perched on his desk lamp, its feet sliding and slipping on the metal. Marco looked through the shutters and watched Giacomo holding his mother by the shoulders, leading her indoors. She was bent double as though in pain. There was a knock at the door.

'Don't worry. Your mother is back,' Giacomo whispered. 'Try and get some sleep, you've got a long day ahead of you tomorrow.'

Elena slipped from her room. She entered the kitchen and switched on the light. She saw on the clock that it was shortly before three in the morning. She picked at the plate of food Giacomo had left her in the fridge, but gave up after a few mouthfuls. She pulled a chair up to the table. Moths banged at the windowpane, trying to get in. Next to the telephone was her latest shopping list, defaced around the edges by one of Giacomo's doodles. She straightened the paper out. She had watched him on the phone absentmindedly covering bits of paper with lines and figures, bars and more bars to cross them out, dreaming shapes and creatures. This was a design for a bowl that had then been worn down by the circular movement of the biro, turned into a pattern full of hidden scraping sounds, scrawled into a round. The ink stains had leaked outwards in layers, like the marks of ten eager fingers, smearing and scratching. She visualized Giacomo's nails, filled with paint, pulled across her skin, leaving no trace, like their unfruitful lovemaking. The paper stirred in the draught from the door. An intricate lettering lay before her, stitching its secret motifs. Giacomo had inadvertently left her a message, she knew, a silent inconsolable sentence she would only understand when it was too late, when Marco had gone. She carried the paper to the bin, scrunched it into a ball and threw it inside. Scraps of food, she hoped, would pile up on it and smother its meaning in refuse and grime.

Elena went to Marco's room. The door was locked. She shook it. There was no reply. She gripped the handle and pumped it up and down, pushing against the wood.

Marco sat up. The sideways, bright eye of a bird glinted from the top of the desk lamp. The door handle shook again.

'Let me in,' Elena said. 'Let me in, please.'

Her son clasped the sides of the bed bringing his knees up to his chin, curled in a ball.

'Let me in.'

There was no reply.

'Marco, you can't do this. You can't leave me, you can't!'

Elena slid down onto the cold tiles of the corridor. Her inter-mittent shoves against the door filled their sleepless night.

PART SIX

Paris, 1991

25

Marco rented an apartment in the north of Paris, beyond Montmartre, down the hill from the back of the Sacré Coeur Basilica, on boulevard Ornano. It was made up of two rooms covered in tired blue wallpaper. In the corner of one room was a mattress, the other had two chairs and shelves down the far wall. Next to the bathroom was a kitchen, more of a walk-in cupboard with a fridge and a couple of hobs.

Even if the top-floor flat faced the wrong way, as Marco realized the moment he walked in, behind Montmartre, behind Paris, it didn't matter. By climbing onto the table in the kitchen and peering out of the air vent, there was still a diagonal view in miniature of some of the city, framed in the crusted-up holes of the metal grid. The greening bronze statues on the roofs of the churches and train stations were so small they only became human forms and horses by squinting, or remembering. Marco preferred the scenes at the front of the flat, towards the outskirts, where the skyscrapers divided the night into stacked-up cubes of light, traffic flowing red round the circular roads below. He would sit there, with the windows pushed open onto the darkness, reading the adverts on top of the buildings. If he leaned out far enough, he could catch the odd word rising up off the street, snatched fragments of unknown lives. He felt it was a disjointed eavesdropping not unlike that of the pigeons that gawked at him through the window.

The boulevard opened up into Porte de Clignancourt at one end. Then it was gone, fanning out into bridges and roads over, onto, under, the *périphérique* ring road. At weekends, a flea market spilled into the streets. From the nearest phone booth to his flat, Marco talked about Montmartre to Elena and Giacomo. His mother made no acknowledgement of his new accommodation in case she was deemed to be giving it her approval. His uncle's voice cracked excitedly down the line as he recalled the names of the artists who had lived in Montmartre. Marco had only really seen cartoonists who drew portraits around the Sacré Coeur, pursuing hassled tourists down the road yelling '*un beau dessin*, portrait, nice portrait, for you thirty francs, just thirty francs.' He had observed a cartoonist one afternoon drawing a woman in front of a crowd of sniggering tourists. The woman had no idea why they were laughing until she stood to look. She had been drawn in bright colours with grotesque stringy nipples, like melted cheese, hanging down to her toes. Her humiliated mouth was warped by a pair of baggy grimacing lips the shape of buttocks.

There was a video shop below the apartment. Throughout the night, Marco could hear the sound of cassettes being pushed through the door. If he couldn't sleep, and that was often, he would wait for the thwack of the post box and go to the window, trying to guess what each departing customer looked like. They were never the faces he expected, elderly men, well-dressed women, sometimes adolescents on bicycles, at three in the morning, five even. He would try and put the name of a film to each person, confident that, sometimes, he was probably right.

He rented a video player himself. In the shop he stacked up tapes in the crook of his arm, overwhelmed by the abundance of films he had never seen or heard of.

'Are you a member?' the woman asked coldly at the counter.

'I want to become one.'

'You want to take out that many?' she said, pointing a finger at his unsteady tower of videotapes.

'Yup.'

'Four's the limit.'

'Ah, you see, Madame, I was hoping we could come to some kind of arrangement. I live two doors down and I'm going to get through these pretty fast.'

'So?'

'I could pay half price on the ones I bring back within half an hour or something like that. If I watch a bit of each one, then don't like it, I want to be able to move onto the next, without having to pay in full.'

'That's not the rules. We're open till eleven. You can come back for the rest when you've finished the first lot.'

She went back to her catalogue, turning the pages deliberately slowly.

Marco walked down the aisles, returning the extra cassettes to their places. He turned to see the shop assistant studying his every gesture, as if he were about to set the place on fire. He plucked up the courage to face her again.

'You know, I like fast-forwarding.'

'So do I.'

'Really? Then you know what I mean: if it's rubbish I'll speed to the end and bring it back immediately.' He waited for some reaction. There was none. He spotted a hidden shelf below the counter containing original-language films. He scanned the English and Italian titles, amazed.

'Actually, I've changed my mind. I'm going to take some of these instead.'

The shelf was packed with old American Westerns, Italian and Japanese dramas, British comedies. He pulled out three Fellini films and a more recent one, *Time of the Gypsies* by Emir Kusturica. He filled in the membership form and rushed up to his flat. He played the *Time of the Gypsies* twice, in quick succession, mostly because of the music. He had never heard anything so moving. After the second viewing, he rearranged the sparse items of furniture in his two rooms and found the papers for his university registration. He reset the video to play the opening title song and read through the details of his course.

With only a few days to go until the university term started, he was, he thought, like a child again. He had never felt so light or so full of expectation. A year previously, he had more or less resigned himself to becoming a potter, expecting that his life, like his mother's, would drift into regret and disappointment, his chances passing and fading. Now, however, he was at the beginning of something new; a possible reinvention of himself.

Marco had a telephone line installed. The telephone directory he received, with its international prefixes at the front, tempted him into making up numbers. He rang people in countries as far apart as Australia, Jamaica and Turkey. He got through to an elderly man in Cairo who informed him in faultless, overly polite French that he had dialled incorrectly. The number for the pottery, with the prefix for India, led to a food shop in Delhi. A woman in Peru worried he was her son ringing from Spain. Marco didn't know how the cabling system worked, but holding the receiver he imagined the telephone wires of the world connected to him, his own line the first string of a vast net hauling in languages and voices from the other side of the planet.

In the back of a newspaper supplement, he discovered pictures of a heavy-bosomed woman advertising a chat line. He dialled the number. He waited to hear a woman's inviting 'hello,' and then put the phone down. Her voice settled into him, and to clear the sound of it, he played his BBC and Berlitz language tapes full volume. He went over the phrases being spoken, rewinding and rewinding, stopping for an inflection or change in cadence, pausing for an intonation. He repeated foreign accents until they merged with him, until he reined in his vowels, syllables, doubts and yearnings, twisting and transforming his mouth so he could have been anyone other than himself.

It wasn't long before Marco ran out of money. He found himself having to seek part-time work in a photographer's studio on nearby rue Ordener, to supplement the monthly allowance sent to him, in secret, by Giacomo. He dealt with customer complaints and acted as a general dogsbody. He wanted to learn to operate the printing machines. His skill, however, was in calming difficult customers with tact and flattery, something he found easy, earning the esteem of his colleagues who shirked the task. When alone in the shop, he flicked through the packs of photos awaiting collection. He discovered shots of parties, weddings and birthdays. None of it interested him. He was drawn instead to photos of holidays, bustling foreign cities, different climates and landscapes. He tried to guess which country the images were taken in, deciphering road signs, studying the vegetation, car number plates, churches and lakes, people in costumes or masks. He found a hazy portrait of a man in Turkey, the Bosphorus behind him. He bore an uncanny resemblance to him, thick black hair and large eyes in a slender face. The shirt was too fuzzy to see, but, even that, he thought, he could have worn.

Approaching customers as they paid, he would say in a courteous voice, 'Sorry for bothering you, but where have you been? I loved your photos.'

'Oh, thank you. I was in Romania.'

'What's it like?'

'The towns aren't great, the countryside is like here twenty or thirty years ago, so beautiful, and unspoilt.'

And to other customers:

'Excuse me, but have you been in Japan?'

'Yes.'

'I thought so. Your photographs are fantastic.'

'Do you know it?'

'Oh no. I guessed.'

'You must go, if you get the chance, totally bewildering, and the food is out of this world. Start in Kyoto or Nara, somewhere small, not Tokyo, that would be my advice.'

Other customers went to great lengths to discuss each photo, glad, at last, to have someone to relate their exploits to. The more experienced photographers sorted their shots on the counter, dropping duds on the floor. Marco's recompense, at the end of the day, was to sweep them into his rucksack. At home he arranged them on his table: landscapes blurred by moving cars, seas floating with frothy rubbish, portraits revealing the tops of sunburnt heads, partially exposed shots from the end of film rolls, ripped orange sunsets with wisps of hair glued to the sky, perfect frames where stains obscured the view of a castle. As with the languages multiplying in his head, Marco fought to connect these flawed images of the world into a repaired geography of his own making, an invented backdrop for his new life.

Marco bought second-hand guidebooks to add to his photos. At the flea markets in Clignancourt and Montreuil, he found guides to places as different as Tahiti and Bolivia. He read them all, from cover to cover, knew how to catch a bus in Hungary from Budapest out to Lake Balaton, how to view the Victoria Falls from both sides of the Zambian/Zimbabwean border, the transport links between Hokkaido and Tokyo in Japan. He loved the phrase chapters at the back of each book: 'Where is the Post Office please,' 'Do you sell train tickets,' and 'Is this the way to the national museum?' In a guidebook to Algeria, he looked up Nassima's region and studied the map, imagining the route she had taken to get to France. He enjoyed the cavernous FNAC bookshop in Les Halles where no-one bothered him. He could sit in the carpeted aisles for hours and glide through pristine, up-to-date guidebooks. He read about Ghana and Lithuania, wildlife in Slovenia, mountains in China, ethnic groups in Cameroon.

In a book on Argentina, he observed a man dancing between tables of dining women, his face obscured by a chandelier. At the back was the photo of a vineyard in Mendoza creeping down a hill towards a river. Often it was past midday when Marco had finished reading, only then realizing he had missed his lectures.

26

The corridors of the Sorbonne were tunnels of noise. The crowds in front of the noticeboards pulled at posters and printed timetables, pricked the soles of their trainers on fallen drawing pins. In the foray of scarves, hats and hoods, Marco located his fellow students on the course. Two of the young people, he had seen from the list, were French of Italian origin: a girl with brown curls, Sylvie Castellini, and another named Catherine Masi. Others had Russian or German-sounding names, some with more of an Arabic ring. During lectures, he observed these students with a mixture of envy and wonder, admiring their seemingly unquestioned presence in Paris. They appeared, like everyone else, always to have lived in the city, to have tamed its hidden rules. In comparison he was an outsider, a single floating unit, unknown to others. He only knew of a water-logged world hemmed in by marshes and ancient ramparts. It was as if the people around him were living a life he wasn't yet allowed to take part in, that he, alone, was caught in a rehearsal, a preparatory performance. In the cafés surrounding the Sorbonne, Marco listened to the routine

Parisian worlds the students described, worlds that he, a good five years older than most of his fellow students, could never confess to be just discovering. Lectures, readings and conversations swept him from revelation to revelation, further from the restrictions of the Camargue, into a wider awareness. He understood that his life, up to that point, had merely breathed out its time at the pottery, with no-one to see him, his youth wasted and concealed. He was stumbling from a extended sleep, fighting his way out of the bed that had kept him trapped in its sheets for too long.

He met up with his old school friend, Rémy. He had graduated two years previously and worked for an advertising agency. Rémy introduced Marco to people and places, but his reminiscences about their *lycée* days and Aigues-Mortes were too cumbersome. Marco invited Sylvie Castellini out instead. After weeks of seeing each other, she complained about the endless exhibitions he took her to, the concerts and films. On a rainy afternoon walk in the gardens at Versailles she stopped him from kissing her with the question: 'What interest am I to you really?' He had more luck with Catherine Masi. Their relationship lasted more than nine months. It ended with another question. 'What,' Catherine asked Marco, 'is there to be in such a rush about?'

So Marco walked alone. He walked across Paris, into the city and out the other side. It wasn't that he didn't like the Metro system, or the buses, it was just that he couldn't get enough of the city, grasp and taste his exploration of it, without walking, scouring every street. He developed favourite routes. One, from Austerlitz station, often took him through the Jardin des Plantes. There, he scaled the discoloured steps to the greenhouses and peered through the glass at the plants growing inside, tall cacti pushed against the panes, ferns and flowers forming competing walls of unnaturally tight green. From the gardens, he descended to the banks of the Seine where barges were moored. Music blared out of them, young people lolling off the edges, beers lined up. He listened to the water eating at the grubby edges of the stone banks, murky algae covering the steps into the river. Homeless men kept their rucksacks hooked on iron moorings. Sleeping bags stirred, and empty wine bottles lay on their sides. Marco had to keep going, finding new sights, happening upon the unfamiliar spectacles of a city still teeming with infinite possibilities.

Marco, at other times, found himself on the edges of the city, at Porte d'Italie or Porte des Lilas. He paced down avenues towards the *périphérique*, under it and over it. Did Paris really end and suburbs just begin? Wasn't it all Paris, Paris spreading, driving its tarmac and buildings into the ground everywhere, deeper and further? He cut through side streets, heading for what looked like parks, churches or interesting buildings. Without realizing it, he found himself in Clichy. His mother had asked him to visit his father's grave and verify it was being maintained. He had put off going. He hovered at the gate. He had always avoided cemeteries, unsure of what attitude to adopt when stepping over the dead. He forced himself down a path between the tombs. His mother had described the spot to him, in the furthest alley towards the trees. He examined carved angels, stretched with lichen, crosses, gilded names on headstones, dates multiplying and dividing across rows of graves. He had brought nothing to put on the tomb. He bent down and picked up a stone. He turned in the direction of where he reckoned the tomb might be. What could he promise with this stone in his hand? He felt nothing but awkwardness at his absence of emotion. He made for the gate again. As he left the cemetery, he dropped the stone from his pocket onto the road.

He ordered a coffee at the nearest café and read the pages of a newspaper left on his table. An elderly man was seated near to him. He tried to catch Marco's attention, to exchange a few words. Marco read the paper and held it high to shield his face, wishing as he read each new line that he had never sat down. The man's gaze behind the newspaper became uncomfortable. Marco didn't want to be singled out. He was reminded of his childhood and the times when his school visited an old people's home in Arles. Everyone would be paired off with a white-haired invalid hunched over in their chair, shrivelled up in their bed. He would sit on the folded disinfectant-smelling blankets and have nothing to say, absolutely nothing, just a wish to cry, not about the sadness in the old faces, or even the measly smiles he managed to coax out of them, but because he could not differentiate himself from their ageing silence. He got up, left some coins on the café table and began to run, faster and faster, shedding his solitude with every new street.

Marco had promised to visit Aigues-Mortes periodically and not done so. His mother left repeated messages on his answerphone. They were either like the laments of a moribund patient requesting his presence, or friendly boasts about the money Djamel was making for them at the pottery. In both cases, the aim of the call was to entice him back home. Marco made a point of ringing his mother most evenings and, before he knew it, she took to waiting up at night, insisting she couldn't sleep without hearing his voice. Subsequent visits to the Camargue, during university holidays, calmed her demands for a while and, although she no longer ended each telephone call by asking when he was next coming home, he could feel the unspoken words at the other end of the line.

When his final university year came to an end, Marco bought himself a tank and four terrapins from a pet shop in Les Halles to mark the event. It was only when he got home that he wondered about the sense of his purchase, and put his rashness down to the stress of his exams. He numbered the animals one to four. Unlike the fish of his childhood, he found it hard to distinguish one from another. He put the tank on the table by the window, and watched them knocking at the sides with their blunt mouths, mounting each other clumsily like building blocks, assembling loose towers of themselves before falling back into the water. As a child, he had dreamed of constructing the perfect aquarium. He had imagined it like an old TV set or even a converted washing machine. There was a whole world to create inside a tank, ruined castles to swim in and out of, hidden shells, plastic scuba-divers, palm trees. He had once pictured a tank full of Giacomo's sculptures in miniature, and rainbow fish darting under their craning protuberances and archways.

27

A professor from the Sorbonne urged Marco to contact the UNESCO headquarters in the seventh arrondissement, behind the Eiffel Tower. They were often in need of freelancers and he would recommend him personally. Marco made an appointment to meet a Uruguayan by the name of Raul Leccese from the translation sector. Dressed in his only suit, Marco waited at the reception for permission to enter the building. He was directed by a security guard towards the lift which he took to the first floor. The building was divided into three long linoleum-covered corridors, each differentiated by a colour. It was only on his third attempt, walking down a yellow corridor, that he found the office and knocked.

'Monsieur Leccese?'

'*Entrez, entrez,*' the man boomed enthusiastically.

'Marco Carlevaris, I made an appointment.'

'Yes, I was expecting you, always nice to see young faces in here.'

Raul Leccese was seated behind a box-shaped desk, its surface a heap of files, in-trays and out-trays.

'So, *questo cognome, Carlevaris*,' he said, breaking into Italian, 'this surname of yours, where's that from?'

'Friuli.'

'Ah, Friuli... surprised I speak Italian? My grandparents were from Puglia. Have you been?'

'I'm sorry, I haven't.'

'It's wonderful,' he exclaimed, standing to emphasize the point, 'make sure you go next time you're in Italy.' He read a piece of paper. '*Bon*,' he said, swapping back to French, adjusting his glasses. 'This letter of yours, it's very flattering, very flattering indeed.'

'Thank you.'

'Don't thank me. Thank your professor.'

Without intending to, Marco gave a rather overblown assessment of his qualifications and examination results, and the possible PhD that his professors were encouraging him to pursue.

'It's most unlikely that you'll get a permanent position here, I have to warn you,' Leccese interrupted.

'Well, I...'

'Oh, don't worry, you were absolutely right to contact me. We often need extra translators at conference times, there's far too much for the in-house translators to deal with. You wouldn't believe the number of reports we have to do!'

'Thank you.'

'It's no skin off my back if you're good enough. Now, what is it that you do, English and Spanish into French? I hope you know that Italian isn't one of the official UN working languages?' He selected a couple of test translations. 'You'll find an empty desk next door, you can work there.' He began laughing to himself. 'Don't pay any attention to the banging from the cupboard, that'll be my assistant wanting a coffee break.'

After his meeting, Marco wandered round the building, listening to the staff speaking in myriad languages, stealing a glance at the vast amphitheatre with its United Nations insignia. He went up to the café on the top level, bought himself a coffee, and looked at the grandiose views across the Paris rooftops. In the entrance hall, he read the vacancy announcements, scrutinizing the possibilities of appointments in distant countries, places he only knew about from guidebooks, capitals of countries in the furthest corners of the globe. As he read about a vacancy in Antananarivo, he remembered a photo he had of a Madagascan tree, bloated in the middle like a digesting snake, and people on bicycles, the road a dusty red.

Marco received a call from Raul Leccese three weeks later. He was called in for another meeting.

'Your translations,' the Uruguayan said, 'are impressive. Your professor was right. Now, as I said, there isn't that much here at the moment, but would you be interested in an internship for a few months?'

'An internship?'

'Yes. It could lead to proper work, though that isn't the official line and I can't guarantee anything. You could even do the odd paid translation for me in the meantime.' He paused, 'we can generally find ways of getting round the administrative barriers.'

'Well, thank you.'

'I've thought of a colleague in the education sector. She's organiz-ing a big conference on the movement of peoples across the globe. It's to have various strands, things aren't yet clear as usual, education, human rights, economics, environment and culture; a thematic mess if you ask me.'

'How interesting!'

'You think so?' Leccese hooted with laughter. 'Good on you! I think you're perfect for the job then.'

Marco was sent up to the fourth floor. He walked past notice-boards pinned with conference posters, papers with bold logos, display cabinets full of thick textbooks. A tidily dressed Egyptian woman in her fifties, Amani Sedeq, was waiting for him. She was friendly, but guarded.

'I can't promise you much in terms of clarity at this stage,' she said to Marco without any introduction, leading him to her office. 'There are still conflicting views on how this conference is going to develop. You know: internal politics and all that.' She went over to a box full of publications of all kinds, school textbooks and audio cassettes. 'So far, we have interviews from various countries that might be helpful to establish the background. They're interviews with foreigners living in France, a survey on living conditions amongst Mexicans in the US, Asians in Britain, Turks in Germany, that kind of thing.' She fished out a box. 'These are the French-speaking ones, Algerians, Moroccans, West Africans. I've had a quick listen, there's a lot of waffle, mostly unusable. There are some interviews by a Malian association documenting immigrant life in Paris and France. They look the most promising.' She held up a smaller box of tapes. 'I think these are the ones.'

'Should I transcribe them?'

'Absolutely. Someone else can do the Spanish stuff, the English and all that.' She sipped a cup of coffee on her desk. 'Would you like some?' she asked absently.

'No, thank you.'

She passed Marco a wad of papers. 'You can also lend me a hand writing invitation letters.' She rifled through a bookshelf, retrieving a slim paperback document. 'This is the official UN correspondence guide or whatever they call it. It tells you how to address people and their official titles and all that.' She passed it to Marco. He looked at the growing pile in his hand. 'You might start with the Malian cassettes at home,' she smiled dryly, 'if you're feeling brave, before the others.' She pointed at the crate of tapes and documents in the corner. 'We need to sort out the forms for your internship too.' She went back to her desk. 'I have a British colleague, Laura Roseborough. She's organizing this with us in the Social Sciences Sector. I think you should meet her. She works in the other building.' She dialled a number on her phone. 'She'll help you understand what we need.'

Marco hadn't been expecting anyone in particular, but when a tall, lively blonde walked in with an assortment of dossiers under her arm, he stood up quickly. He introduced himself and, as soon as she started asking him questions, he became tongue-tied and tense. She watched as he rushed to write in his notepad. He wasn't writing anything precise, gibberish in fact, made-up words to divert the attention. His first words for the United Nations were deliberate nonsense. As a boy, he recalled how the opening sentences in a new school book were always the most important, the first page was neat and then the whole thing gradually got scruffier. That first page, though, had to be perfect.

'Where are you from?' Laura asked.

'I'm French.'

'French and what?'

'French,' he said. 'Italian too, I suppose, but French.'

'Ah, Italian, yup, that's it, what I thought,' she smiled, satisfied with her assessment.

He was relieved that contact had been so simple and that Laura's French was excellent. She had none of the stilted words and hesitant vocabulary of the English-speaking tourists who visited the pottery. Laura talked about the aims of the conference, what translation work he might do. She was even more attractive close up. Her skin was a pale, unblemished colour that he had never seen before, like some rare fabric.

'So can we count you in on this conference?' Amani said, reappearing. 'Will you do an internship with us?'

'Yes,' Marco said. 'When should I start?'

'Right now!' Laura laughed, 'we'd be so happy for help, especially with all those tapes.'

'We should be able to get you a desk quite soon,' Amani added. 'We'll get a contract to you. Leave your address and telephone number.'

Marco realized his audience was over. He stood up and edged towards the door. Laura accompanied him to the lift.

'Call me if there's any problem with the work we send you,' she said. 'Amani is always in a rush, so you might need to get hold of me.'

She took a card from her pocket and wrote her phone number on it, leaning against a bookstand by the lift. He watched her careful, rounded handwriting, the fountain pen with the marbled effect. It was a bit incongruous with the rest of her, the long corduroy skirt, the loose hair, the big hoop earrings, the rubber-soled red shoes. The shoes, in particular, struck him as they had a small 'x' on the leather of each heel. Whether that was the label, or a decoration she had added herself, he didn't know. Seeing him staring, she turned and looked at the ground behind her. He smiled, and she pressed the down button on the lift. 'Right, thanks for coming in,' she said.

At his flat, Marco took the first Malian tape from its box, trying to absorb the fact that he now had the beginnings of a job, and for the UN. Some of the interviewees, he read on the box, were *sans-papiers,* as they were termed, immigrants without the necessary administrative papers to regularize their stay in the country; others were of people from different walks of life with permanent residency already. He listened intently, but the more he listened, the less he felt able to judge what needed to be written down or filtered out. The Malians talked, in accented French he wasn't accustomed to, as if by talking, the dilemmas they described would disappear into the machine with their voices.

'My name is Awa. I'm from Mopti in Mali. I'm twenty-six. When I travelled to France, I was searched at the border. I had sewn my most important possessions into the hem of my dress – photos, wallet, and my dead mother's necklace. A policewoman made me take off my clothes and tear open the hems. I ripped the skirt with my teeth and hung it upside down so that all that I had fell onto the floor. I can hardly remember anything from the journey here except the sound of my things hitting the concrete.

'I've been in France for eight years. When I first arrived I lived in Montreuil with my brother and his family. The area was full of Malians. I moved to the centre of Paris. I didn't want to live like I'd never left home. What I love doing the most is taking the night buses across Paris, seeing the monuments orange with floodlights, all that electricity. I've crossed Paris before just to look at the railway stations at night. My brother says life was better at home. I think he just brought his problems with him and now they're harder to sort out in this country because it will never be his. I've told him there's no point coming here if you don't want to change, turn yourself into someone new. Anyway, you change whether you like it or not. That's how I see it.'

The sound on the tape trembled and Marco banged the top of the machine. A new voice swung back in. He could hear people in the background talking and switching their microphones on and off, testing:

'My name is Adama. When I was a child, there was a man who lived near us, in Ségou, who left for Europe. He went to meet someone in Italy, but ended up in France for work. When he returned he told everyone that he had met the woman he was going to marry. This Frenchwoman was to arrive eight months later and he promised to organize a wedding to which the neighbourhood would be invited. He set about transforming his house. No-one had ever seen him so busy. The house was painted, the trees in the garden pruned, flowers and vegetables planted. The place was so different that people would stop and stare. The day of the Frenchwoman's arrival neared. Flower buds started to come out, the beginnings of leaves, blossom on the trees. The day of the woman's arrival came and went, and weeks passed after that and still she didn't come. People stopped asking about the wedding and the man spoke to no-one. Flowers were in full bloom in the garden, vegetables of all colours and sizes. Fruit appeared on the branches of the trees. As the season progressed, the melons and tomatoes grew larger and larger; plants became weighed down by their ripe produce. Lettuces collapsed. Trees bent backwards. Still the man didn't tend to his garden. The fruit rotted, the vegetables split open. Flowers wilted and fell. The whole garden began to stink, a terrible stench. A group of neighbours, including my father, went to the man and pleaded with him to do something. He barricaded the door. The smell lasted for weeks, wafting over the streets into the centre of the city. Since I've been in Paris, I think of our Ségou neighbour often, I don't know why. I can almost smell the rotting vegetables and see the branches of the trees breaking with unpicked fruit.'

As a new interview was starting, the telephone went. Marco hesitated to get up. He had his paper on his lap, ready to write. The answerphone came on. It was his mother: 'You didn't call last night. Are you all right? Nothing much to report here, it's suddenly hot though, March and it's hot already, I'll never get used to this place, it was cold last week. At home, we had real seasons, you knew where you were. Call me, please, bye.'

Marco turned off the tape machine. He looked down at his pad and saw he had jotted down the words, 'real seasons', in bigger letters than the rest.

28

Apart from the cassettes, Marco was baffled by the quantity of contradictory material he had been given. What exactly he was meant to translate, he wasn't sure. Were the policy papers and national education strategies from Tanzania and Costa Rica to be translated into French or should he be summarizing the publications from the Togolese and Gabonese organizations which were already in French? He decided to call Laura, happy, after only two days, to have a good reason to get in touch. To his delight, she said they could meet that evening in a café off boulevard Henri IV. He presumed that she lived nearby. She told him later, though, that her flat was near the Jardin du Luxembourg. He had already ordered a coffee when she arrived and, as she approached the table, she asked the waiter for a fruit juice. She shook Marco's hand vigorously and laid out her folders. There was a matter-of-fact, but warm professionalism to her which startled him.

Laura took a magazine from her bag. It was *Newsweek*. There was an article on Latin-American immigration to the United States. 'I think,' she said, 'we should put together several documents for the conference, but one should be on the whole legality of migration, migration as a basic human right, you know, the fine line between being a refugee and an economic migrant, that kind of thing.' She had long earrings this time, strings of crimson beads that looked like berries, dangling down above her shoulders. When she spoke, they wobbled from side to side. He tried to talk about other matters. She was uncomfortable answering questions about herself. She repeatedly drew him back to the magazine by asking him about his views on the European Union and its relationship with the developing world.

He sensed she was beginning to wonder what she was doing in the café with him. He would have to keep his questions for the next time.

'Can I read that article again?' he asked, pointing at the magazine.

Marco looked over it once more, stopping to ask a couple of language points. The absurdity of his suspiciously naive questions made Laura laugh.

'Sorry, but I can't believe you don't know that,' she smiled. 'I've got a nasty feeling your English is every bit as good as mine.'

She decided to test Marco on the meaning of a few words in the text. He tapped his fingers on the table, hesitated, hummed and came up with approximate answers. He sounded ridiculous, he knew. He rolled off a list of English proverbs he had learned as a teenager, convinced that would lighten the atmosphere.

'The fishermen's fish are always dead in the boat,' he finished by saying. 'That's my favourite.'

'What? Never heard of it. You made that up.'

'No, I didn't.'

'I can assure you that expression does not exist in English. Maybe there's room for improvement after all,' she said, relieved.

Marco picked a few UNESCO documents out from his bag and put them in front of Laura.

'Now, what am I meant to do with these?' he asked, flipping open the pages.

Laura was puzzled herself by certain passages. He took note of her quick assessments and put the documents away. She drank her juice and he watched her tip back her head, fine strands of fair hair breaking free, falling against her long, pale neck, her bead earrings spinning.

'They're showing one of my favourite films, *I Vitelloni*, this evening, near here. Would you like to see it?' Marco said, surprised by his own boldness.

Laura put down her glass and stood up. 'Sorry, sounds really interesting, I'm afraid I can't, I'm meeting friends round the corner. I'll catch up with you at work, OK?'

'Right,' Marco said, scrambling to his feet. 'Bye, then.'

'Bye.'

Several days later, worried that he hadn't heard back from Amani or been sent any new documents, he called Laura before she left work from a phone booth near the Jardin des Plantes. When he heard people talking in the background, he went straight into asking about his translations and possible dates to come and see her at her office. He still hadn't received his contract, he added.

'Oh! I can't think about any of that now, I'm rushing out of the door. I ought to be with some friends in the Marais right now. Can we speak tomorrow morning? Sorry.'

Marco held the phone to his ear, unsure of what to reply. 'Wait…' he said, but she had gone.

He decided to take the underground home rather than walk. The Metro was packed. It was stiflingly hot, the heating still on full blast despite it being April. A musician in an Andean-style hat stepped on and played the guitar, singing out-of-tune Spanish. A dog with pendulous raw gums squealed when its tail got caught between the closing doors. The owner shoved everyone aside until it was freed.

'Dogs aren't allowed on the Metro, *c'est interdit*,' a woman shouted from the back of the carriage.

Marco saw that he was more or less going through the Marais. Maybe he should try and see Laura? Wasn't that where she said she was going? The idea excited him instantly.

He got off at Filles du Calvaire and walked into the Marais through its dense, narrow streets. It wasn't an area he normally frequented. He went down a couple of roads, looking at the people crammed onto the pavements, holding glasses, squashed on chairs inside dimly lit bars. Shop windows displayed clothes and design furniture. He stopped at a corner. There were more bars along the roads opposite. He worked his way along them, peering inside, surveying the milling crowds, listening out for her voice above the din.

After half an hour, he had reluctantly made up his mind to go home when he felt a tap on his shoulder. He turned to see a young woman with a thin jade necklace and green eyes. Grabbing Marco by the arm, she pulled him across the street, talking in English. 'Hi, I'm Clare, a friend of Laura's. She saw you walk past. We're over here.' She waited for a response and, when an astonished Marco didn't reply, she guffawed. 'Well, actually, it was me who spotted you first. I'm always on the lookout for blokes! Hope you don't mind.' They reached a table with six people seated round it. 'This is Marco everyone.'

Laura stood up. 'It was you! What on earth are you doing here? How weird,' she said.

Laura moved back to her chair on the other side of the table and resumed her conversation with her neighbour. Everyone round the table was talking noisily in English.

From time to time, Laura turned and smiled at Marco, 'Are you all right? How are those tapes coming along?'

Clare offered him a cigarette. He refused. A circle of empty beer bottles stood in the middle of the table. 'Want a drink?' he motioned to Laura and, after she had shaken her head, he set off to the bar. The queue was three people thick all the way down the counter. A stressed, sweating barman strained to hear orders and avoid the glares of impatient customers. This had definitely been a mistake. He watched Laura through the open doors. She looked remarkable, a short denim skirt, hair pulled up in a chignon, her curved, smooth neck. She was touching the man next to her, slapping him on the thigh, laughing. Was he her boyfriend? He realized he knew nothing about her. Maybe she was as relaxed with everyone? He had no idea what English people were like.

Marco walked back outside.

'Laura, listen, I've actually got to go. I forgot I have to do something by tomorrow. I'll call you, bye,' and he left before she could say anything. He thought he heard her friends laughing behind him, especially Clare, a kind of muffled, English-sounding wave of mockery. He ran to the nearest Metro station. A homeless man, his soiled trousers round his knees, was stumbling towards a couple of girls on the platform, asking for money. He knew the man wouldn't come near him. He felt there was an invisible belt of anger protecting him, and he would carry it for days.

29

Marco was watching television with a bowl of hot couscous on his lap. The rising steam from the puffed-up grains was tickling his chin. The telephone rang.

'You didn't call! Did you receive the contract?' It was Laura.

Marco couldn't find the remote control for the television. He tried to explain that he didn't always have time to come in or that perhaps he needed to think about it anyway, maybe this UNESCO work wasn't going to give him time to fit in his other translations, he needed to earn money, but the noise from the screen kept on drowning out his voice.

'Let me turn the TV off.' He came back to the phone to hear Laura sniggering.

'You were watching that rubbish on channel two, like me, weren't you?' Marco had to admit he was and they fell into a discussion about how diabolical the acting was and the plot dreadful beyond belief.

'You know that film I mentioned before, *I Vitelloni*,' Marco said, encouraged by her friendliness, 'it's still showing at a small cinema near Beaubourg. It's part of some Fellini festival.'

'I've got the *Pariscope* film guide here, hang on. Let me look it up.' Marco heard Laura flick the pages. 'Shit! It's ending today.'

'Oh well, doesn't matter,' he said, disappointed.

'Yes it does! There's a last showing at seven fifteen. If we leave now we could make it!'

'Leave now? I'll never make it.'

'Of course you will.'

'Let's just meet for a drink instead, I'll never…'

'You're wasting time already, *allez*, get a move on! Last one there pays for the tickets.'

The line went dead. Marco gulped down two spoonfuls of his couscous and sped to the door. He managed to get a Metro easily. A short delay at the Gare du Nord got him worried. He ran from the underground exit to the cinema on rue Quicampoix. There was no sign of Laura. He bought the tickets and waited. He got himself a can of juice from the Turkish café opposite and watched the doner kebab grill turn, bits of meat occasionally dropping off into a sizzling groove of fat below. He thought about buying Laura a juice too, or even a beer, a coke perhaps, but would she want a straw or a cup? The film was due to start a couple of minutes later. A middle-aged couple entered the cinema. The ticket woman stood to count her money and gather her things. Laura appeared at the other end of the street, hobbling. He waved the tickets at her. She wanted to hurry, but kept on pointing to her shoes with an apologetic grimace. They were a pair of leather sandals and between the toes was a wide metal hook that looked more like a knife than part of a shoe.

'They're agony,' she winced, handing Marco the money for the tickets.

'No, no, I'll pay.'

'Don't be silly, we agreed whoever got here last would pay,' Laura raised her eyes to heaven and made for the seats.

She said nothing during the film. She sat perfectly still, like a spectacular bronze bust, magnificent and stately, and he a visitor to a museum, walking round her, sure that she might have blinked or wrinkled her nose, but not able to prove it. Marco had been expecting the odd word from her, an acknowledgement that she was enjoying herself, maybe an explanation of the plot. Every time he looked round, he found himself transfixed, in the half-light, by her profile, her slightly almond eyes with the grainy make-up powder that stuck to her eyelids, the straightness of her nose, her neck again. When the credits came up, she did eventually turn to him and say, 'Thank you. That was wonderful.'

'It was my seventh viewing,' Marco admitted.

'You're joking.'

'No.'

'Well, it's definitely a change from the usual Hollywood crap,' she said. 'Come on, I'm starving, let's have something to eat.' She nudged him in the back, 'Aren't you hungry?' The gesture startled Marco, yet reassured him at the same time.

They walked towards the rue Montorgueil and into a side street where Marco knew of a Lebanese place that served until midnight. Marco ordered the food, trying to remember the different starters from his only visit with Rémy. They ate an assortment of dishes. He observed the elegance with which Laura unrolled her vine leaves to eat only the rice, neatly picking up each grain between her fingers. Laura teased the young waiter about a misspelling on the menu. Maybe she was like this all the time, with everyone, spontaneous and open, supremely confident.

'Are you a starer?' Marco asked, lowering his voice, emboldened by Laura's ordering of a fourth glass of wine.

'A what?'

'I find it hard not to stare at people in restaurants like this, don't you?'

'I can't say it's something I do regularly.'

Marco pushed his chair backwards, as if to tie up his shoes, and tilted his head to the side, sneaking a look at the people behind them. He eyed up one couple while appearing to search the room for the waiter.

'What do you make of them? You've got a better view.'

Laura peered over Marco's shoulder, studying the conversing couple, the thickset, middle-aged man with big ears and thinning grey hair, the woman opposite him, petite, in a beige jacket, cropped dark hair crowned with a pair of raised glasses. 'Look like an ordinary, dull couple to me.'

Marco swung round and swivelled back quickly.

'I bet you she's called Solange.'

'Stop being ridiculous.'

'Wait,' he said, holding his hand up. He dropped his napkin and proceeded to carry out an elaborate, crouching manoeuvre to retrieve it from under his chair in order to get a better look. He sat up, his face flushed, and leaned towards Laura, 'No, actually, I think she's an Aurélie or a Judith. Anyway, they're not married; they're definitely having an affair.'

'Oh for goodness' sake,' Laura spluttered, pushing him away playfully. 'They're brother and sister.'

'No way,' Marco coughed, bending round again for a glimpse. 'Different noses, and lip types,' he said knowledgeably.

'I have this theory about the French,' she replied. 'They all have a slight overhanging top lip.' She opened her mouth and curled her top lip downwards, in a half-pout, to show him: 'Like this.'

'That doesn't make much sense, I'm afraid,' he said confidently, immediately yearning to reach out and brush her mouth, and the tiny gap between her front teeth. 'There's no such thing as a French person ethnically speaking. I mean they're a complete mishmash, especially in Paris. They all have Polish and Russian grandfathers, Italian and Spanish mothers, you name it, Jewish, Catholic, the lot. In the 1920s, I think, at some point, there were more immigrants to France than America.'

'Thank you for enlightening me, professor,' Laura bowed her head in mock veneration. 'I'll stick to my top-lip theory even so, thank you. Maybe there's some muscle that gets used more by speaking French. Bet you hadn't thought about that?'

'They're lovers, but they're not particularly happy together, bit of a rut, years of the same thing.'

'Who?'

'Them,' Marco nodded, gesturing behind him.

'Oh, we're back on them, are we?'

'Yup. She's got no kids, psychiatrist or something, possibly a speech therapist. He's got loads of kids, still married maybe, about four children I reckon. He can't relate to them.'

'And they're planning a weekend away,' Laura said, her eyes lighting up with feigned intrigue and complicity.

'No, they haven't got enough money for weekends away. Look at their clothes.'

'Oh,' Laura said, disappointed.

'They meet in his office after hours. He's a copy-editor at some lesser-known publishing house and he hates his job. Only the cleaning lady knows about their affair. They've been paying her off for years. They make love next to the hoover cupboard, same place each time, like a ritual, on a soft patch of carpet they roll up afterwards. Can't you just see it?' Marco said.

'No, actually, I can't, and I'd rather not!'

The door of the restaurant shot open and a broad, curly-haired brunette in her early twenties pushed her way through the tables. She waved excitedly and marched to the table behind Marco and Laura.

'Sorry Maman, hi Papa, I can't believe I'm so late,' she babbled, sending a waft of pungent cigarette smoke over the surrounding tables. She grabbed an empty chair from the nearest table and kissed the thickset man on the top of the head. 'I do hope you didn't wait for me.'

Laura looked across the table, shaking her head at Marco. 'You're crap at this. Stick to your translations!'

'What about him over there, the long-haired weirdo on his own, he looks like a criminal on the run, or a disgraced philosopher,' Marco started, determined not to give up.

'No! Enough.' Laura said, rising out of her chair. 'Let's get the bill.'

They strolled towards the Metro. 'Can I show you more of those documents I'm having problems with?' Marco asked to hold Laura back.

'No, please don't. I've got quite enough on my plate already!'

'But I'm really struggling. I don't know what Amani wants.'

'Hmm, she's not the easiest of people. You'll work her out in the end. I'm really busy next week, meetings all the time. The head of the Bangkok office is visiting.'

'Well I'm only a few stops from here. You could come back, have a coffee and look at the stuff quickly.'

She didn't answer. They descended the stairs together, Marco letting Laura go first. He touched the top of her head lightly as she went before him. She didn't look round. She turned the corner and stopped to tighten her hairgrip. To Marco's amazement she chose the

Metro line heading north. 'What's your stop?' she asked. A train was pulling in and they hopped on. A man with a scraggly white beard sat opposite them. He looked Laura up and down, and then Marco. As they jumped off, they turned to see the bearded man still watching them, expecting him to wave.

At the flat, Laura picked out some albums. She was impressed by the fact that she had only heard of two of the musicians in Marco's collection. She found the soundtrack to the *Time of the Gypsies*.

'I've been meaning to see that film for ages, is it good?'

Marco couldn't recommend it enough. He poured Laura a glass of wine. She went through his books, opening some, studying the covers.

'What are all these guidebooks for? Are you planning a trip round the world?'

'I collect them.'

'What, guidebooks?'

'Yup,'

'Really? Why?'

'I love them, the tips and information, the possibilities; reading about obscure museums and sights. They're like encyclopedias, but you find out more.'

'You're a very curious young man, Signor Marco,' she said, patting him on the shoulder with a look of authentic amusement. She saw the fridge door papered with photographs.

'Where's this?' she said, peeling one off.

'Romania.'

'Really?' she said, impressed. 'I'd love to go there.'

'Oh.'

'What's it like?'

'What?'

'Romania, of course!'

Marco stared at the photograph in her hand and back at her face.

'Amazing,' he said hesitantly. 'The towns aren't great, but the countryside is like here twenty or thirty years ago, really beautiful and unspoilt.'

'And this temple? Where's that?'

'Japan.'

'Japan, wow.'

'Have you been?' Marco asked quickly.

'No, doesn't really appeal to me to be honest. Should I go?'

'Oh you must go, if you get the chance.'

'Well maybe, who knows?'

'It's totally bewildering, and the food is fantastic. Start in Kyoto or Nara, somewhere small, not Tokyo, that would be my advice.'

'And this one?'

'Mexico,' he said, and turned to do something else.

Laura moved to the aquarium with the terrapins, tapping the sides with her nails.

'Are they OK?'

'Who?'

'These poor creatures, they look bored out of their tiny minds.'

'They're fine. This is their calm time, before bed.'

Laughing, she pulled a book from the shelf entitled *British Architecture*. She found a map of London and waved at a green patch.

'I used to go to Regent's Park every weekend as a child, bloody dull it was too.' She then leafed through to a section on Art Nouveau and Arts and Crafts Houses. 'That's extraordinary,' she said, thrilled. 'I can't believe it, this book must be ancient.'

She pushed it open, pressing down on the spine, to reveal two black-and-white photographs, one of a large house and the other of an elegant room with elaborate lamps and chairs.

'What is it?' asked Marco.

'It's a yoga centre now, sadly.'

'How do you know?'

'My grandparents lived here. This was their house in Belsize Park.' She turned to the beginning of the book. 'It was published in 1955, that's why.'

'Your grandparents lived there?' Marco said, astonished.

'It's a long story.'

'Tell me.'

'I won't bore you with it now.'

'No, do.'

'It's really rather mundane actually.'

'Please.'

'Well, if you really want to know, my grandfather, who owned the house, was an incredible guy, we all loved him. He was one of the first to climb Everest after Hillary, that kind of man. We'd go on holidays, and he'd take me round the sights, talking to the locals, while my family was holed up in the hotel. We got lost once in Zanzibar...' She looked at Marco. 'I can't believe you want to hear all this?'

'I do.'

'Oh, OK, don't blame me if I rabbit on. Anyway, he died, my grandfather, and my uncle, the eldest one, a very grumpy man, who'd never had a girlfriend, even a friend in fact, somehow inherited the house. My father loved the place, as did my aunt, but the grumpy brother put it up for sale.'

'Why?'

'Because he wasn't brave enough to fight for it, I suppose. There were loads of tax issues. No-one talks to him now anyway. My father tried to scrape the money together to buy it, but he couldn't manage it. In fact I think the grumpy uncle put the price up for him, and that was it. I know my parents would have been really happy there, we adored it as kids. I can't bear to think of the hall covered in yoga mats, smelling of incense.'

Laura lay on a cushion on the floor and spread her arms out. Marco asked if he could kiss her and she sat up, flustered. 'Let's have another look at those books. Do you have anything on Peru? I've always wanted to go there. '

Around one in the morning, they were still sitting on the floor, listening to music. Neither of them had spoken for a while.

'What are you thinking?' Marco asked, breaking the uncomfortable lack of conversation.

'You don't want to know.'

'I do.'

'Sure?'

'Positive.'

'You really want to hear all my rubbish tonight, don't you?' She scratched her forehead and smiled. 'I was thinking, if you can believe it, about a tramp who shouted at me in the Metro one day,' Laura pulled a face. 'Funny how these things pop up again unexpectedly. I think that guy on the Metro we saw tonight, the one with the beard, made me think of it.'

'What happened?'

'It was years ago, he singled me out on a crowded Metro and humiliated me when I didn't have any money to give him.'

'What did he say?'

'It was more the way he said it. He screamed, "*Dégage petite pute de merde*, out the way you filthy little whore, you think you're better than me don't you," at the top of his voice. I can still hear it. The train took forever to reach the next station and everyone was staring at me trying to imagine what I'd done wrong. He carried on insulting me, saying I'd held my nose when he walked past. I had to jump off the train to escape.'

'Poor you.'

'I'd just arrived in Paris and I pelted through the corridors of the

Metro, trying to find the way out, going the wrong way, rushing through some half-blocked exit into a part of the city I didn't know, nowhere I wanted to be. I had to walk miles till I found a place I recognized.' She looked at Marco, sighing, 'Sometimes it seems I've always been racing round Paris, trying to understand what I'm doing here.'

'But you're happy at UNESCO, aren't you?'

'The job's good, but I worry I wasn't adventurous enough. I could have gone to Mexico or Egypt, somewhere far away, you know, somewhere different, where I could have faced a few challenges. I had a boyfriend at university who was part Indian. We spent time working in Madhya Pradesh, with local village organizations. He introduced me to all that stuff. I would have stayed there if we hadn't split up, at least for a while; I loved it, but he was hard work, not very nice in fact.' She scratched her forehead again. 'Actually, I nearly ended up in Rome.'

'Rome?'

'Yes, I had an internship set up there, at a UN agency, but I stopped in Paris for a night on the way, and I've been here ever since, never got back on the train!'

'Are you serious?'

'Kind of moronic, isn't it, to decide one's life like that, on a whim?' She smiled to herself. 'The train to Rome still leaves every evening. One day, I should watch it leave, or get on it. I hate having niggling regrets, don't you, thoughts of what could have been and all that, those missed opportunities and chances you didn't seize, the way they nag you, even at our age.'

'Well, you could have stayed at home.'

'True. Horrendous thought.'

'Why?'

'You haven't met my parents! They just don't get why I find

London so difficult, but everything feels so mapped out there. They expect me to merge into their life, you know, get into a car like theirs, and drive up and down the same stretches of motorway as them, to the same houses, to the same gatherings, with the same people as in my childhood. That's what my two brothers do.'

Laura reached for Marco's arms, turned them and ran a finger delicately over his veins.

'Is that normal?' she said. 'How fantastic to have such bright blue veins.' Then she stood up and made for the door. 'I really must go. I've got an early start tomorrow. Sorry to have twittered on like that, we did nothing but talk about me. Did I bore you senseless?'

'Of course not! Hang on. I'll call you a taxi or walk you to the rank.'

'No, don't worry.' The door swung shut.

'What about the translations?' he shouted after her.

30

Each day, Marco received more and more documents from Amani at UNESCO without any explanation or news on the office space that was, supposedly, being prepared for him. Laura's visit to his flat, too, had left him more confused than ever as to what attitude to adopt towards her. He thought about her incessantly and yet there had been little on her part to justify that, on the contrary she had refused his advances. Then again, she had been open and talkative, but maybe she was like that with everyone she met.

Marco made up his mind to confront Laura and, at the same time, request further clarification on his job. He arranged to meet her at a bar on rue Saint André des Arts, a favourite haunt of hers. Waiters converged on her in a disorderly welcoming party. The barman gestured to an empty table near the front. The first drinks were on the house.

'So are you having doubts about UNESCO or the work itself, I don't quite understand?' Laura asked him when Marco tried to explain his problems in a rather circuitous, uncertain manner.

'It's just rather tricky,' Marco answered, already regretting his decision to discuss anything.

'What is?'

'I feel I've just been dumped with this important stuff without any clear instructions,' he said. 'Finding my way through it is rather difficult.'

'Welcome to the UN!' Laura laughed in sympathy. 'I'm afraid it's up to you to make something of it. Strange, but true.'

'Really?'

'Sure. I was in your shoes five years ago, but you just have to plough on regardless of all the crap.'

'But what if you don't feel you're getting anywhere?'

'The UN can be horribly political and inefficient and this and that. The point though is to believe in what you're doing, not to get bogged down in wondering where you are going. Otherwise you end up like all those bureaucrats. You've got to make a difference on your own, with the people you trust.'

'You believe that?'

'Sure, not so much with these big conferences, I suppose, but when you see how the projects you support on the ground are working, how they transform people's lives or that the publications you've written are being used by organizations round the world, it makes it all worthwhile.'

'OK.' Marco nodded, half-convinced.

'Just imagine what it's like when you arrive in Mozambique, or Sudan, or Ecuador, somewhere like that, and you see what you're helping nurture. It's such a boost.'

Laura, it appeared to Marco, was truly committed to improving the world, but it was also a career for her. Perhaps he was just a new pawn in her game plan, someone who was going to help her up the ladder, do all the background work for the conference. The films, the dinner, the visit to his flat were all aimed at making that possible.

Laura got out her diary. 'How about you bring in all your documents and stuff next Tuesday or Friday, round five o'clock? We'll sort it out then. Maybe I can get Amani to come along?'

'If you want,' Marco agreed, forlorn, realizing that he hadn't resolved any of his dilemmas.

'Come on,' Laura tapped the table. 'Do you want to wallow in that internship of yours or do you want to move on? We need people like you.' Marco looked at her startled. 'Don't you think a bright young man can do something more than translation?' she said, taking a swig of her beer. '*Désolée*, sorry to be so blunt, but you need to get a grip here, stop all these lame excuses.'

Marco shifted his chair backwards. All he wanted to do was run, run with her and forget about this talk and these work concerns that got between them. The only real issue was her and him, and his irrepressible yearning to be with her. Laura finished her beer. She turned and beckoned the barman over. They exchanged news, chuckled about a friend they had in common. Marco wanted to leave again. Why didn't he have the courage to tell her that her apparent ease with the world and her forcefulness could be hurtful, condescending, but that he found her unbelievably attractive, more than he could really explain? The barman was called away. Laura said nothing. She fiddled with her beer mat, ripping the sides into tags then folding them in two.

'Do you want to see a film or have a bite to eat?' she asked.

By way of reply, Marco leaned across the table and took one of Laura's hands. He turned it over and kissed her in the middle of her palm. She started on a new beer mat, tearing it to shreds.

'You're turning me into a nervous twit,' she said. 'See,' her hand shook a little. 'Why did you have to turn up in my life? I was getting along quite nicely in my job, I was in my own little world with my friends and, out of the blue, here you are, knocking everything upside down, and I don't know anything about you, apart from the fact that you're different and have ridiculously long eyelashes.' She threw shreds of her beer mat at him. 'I've been doing my best to resist you for weeks, guess I'm failing miserably,' she said, heaving a sigh. She made a mound of mat shreds on the table. 'I kept on thinking you'd realized. It was doing my head in.'

'Well, you had a strange way of showing it,' Marco answered, astonished and excited by his rapid change in fortune.

'I was freaked out, I wasn't expecting you!'

'Still, it was a bit weird, the way you ran from my flat.'

'What about you, fleeing from that bar in the Marais like a criminal? Clare hasn't got over it, she thinks you're a nutcase. By the way, it's not going to be easy at work I can tell you. Luckily we're in different buildings. Amani is not to know about this, promise?' Laura beamed mischievously, grabbing Marco and leading him out of the bar. 'This is all so unprofessional of me.'

On boulevard Saint Germain, Marco put his hands round Laura's waist and pulled her towards him. He kissed her, unabashedly, holding himself against her, to prevent her escape as much as to contain his emotions. She closed her eyes and he pressed his mouth against her eyelids, finally tasting the velvet texture of her make-up, then the softness of her lips. They walked to her flat nearby. They stopped again on the stairs leading to the apartment and any reticence that Marco might have sensed in her had evaporated. She found her key. They rushed towards the bedroom and sprung open the door to find two bodies in the bed already, draped over each other, fast asleep.

'*Merde*,' Laura exclaimed, 'damn, I forgot my brother's friends were staying tonight. I didn't realize he'd given them a key.' They tiptoed back to the sitting room only to find a girl in a sleeping bag on the floor. 'Damn, damn,' Laura repeated. They stood in the corridor, kissing, undressing. 'No, no. We'll wake them up,' she said laughing, disengaging herself from Marco's arms. He managed to remove her bra and she jumped backwards, two small breasts freed of their covering.

'How did you manage that?' she said, amazed. 'That's a rather well-rehearsed skill!'

Marco felt faint-headed, giddy with exhilaration. He grabbed her again.

'Stop it. We can't. We can't,' Laura squealed. She raced to the front door and opened it, 'Come on, off you go! I'm sure they've woken up already.'

'I can't go now. Not now, you can't do this to me, after all this…' He made another clumsy lunge for her. She propelled him out of the door.

'One kiss, one kiss,' he insisted, 'just one.'

Laura pushed him backwards onto the landing. 'OK, OK,' she agreed and bent forward, her lips ready. Marco ducked under her chin and kissed her on the right nipple, clamping his mouth round it. Then he was off, charging down the stairs, bursting into the street, weightless as a child. He paused and put a hand to his mouth, touching his tongue with the tips of his fingers. On the boulevard, he looked back up at Laura's flat and saw her standing at the window, waving, one arm firmly guarding her breasts from the night's eyes. Marco walked towards the river. He stopped by an underground air vent. The rancid warmth of it reminded him of the stifling summer wind in the Camargue, the dank scents coming off the waterways. He closed his eyes and, through the stench of Paris, he thought he could taste salt on his tongue.

Marco took to visiting Laura's flat in the evening, straight from his newly designated office. Her success at keeping their relationship a secret impressed him. They occasionally met by the drinking fountains at the end of the corridors, near the washrooms, or on the fourth floor stairwell, but, in meetings and in the main hall, she all but ignored him. She enjoyed the game of coldly walking past him without so much as a look.

Marco was amazed at Laura's flat. He regularly found mattresses in the corner of the main room and heaps of luggage. Laura explained that friends from her university in England, and friends of those friends, and even acquaintances of those friends, were somehow always on their way through Paris or just visiting for the weekend. He couldn't believe Laura didn't object to this stream of intruders, but perhaps, that's how things were done in England. He stumbled on sleeping bodies at night on his route to the bathroom and discovered uninvited guests at dinner. Once, having negotiated his way round a snoring mass in a double sleeping bag, he found Laura smiling into her pillow at the fact that she didn't know the names of the couple blocking the corridor. It was another world for Marco, a version of Paris he had never encountered. Many of Laura's friends met in the Bastille, or around Saint Germain, and found bars or replica pubs where everyone was American and Australian, Irish or British. Laura was pleased, she confessed, that Marco had rescued her from this English-speaking circle and its claustrophobic routines.

Laura's friends, Marco could see, had a code of their own, an intimidating way of assuming that everyone acted like them, or understood their mindset. He longed for moments alone with her, away from her clique, especially the male hangers-on who viewed him with suspicion. He wasn't used to the gatherings they organized, to their confident chatting and wealthy insouciance. He remembered the few teenage summer evenings he had managed to escape the pottery and make it into Aigues-Mortes, how he had climbed the ramparts and sat looking out across the marshes at the sea. That was the peace he sought, that and Laura.

At a dinner organized by Laura in a restaurant below her flat, Marco was placed next to the only native French-speaker in the group, a young Belgian working for his embassy in Paris. Conversation was stilted. He questioned Marco, with evident jealousy, on how he had met Laura and what he was doing as a job. When he asked him where he grew up, Marco heard himself saying that his parents lived in Italy and had a second house in the Camargue where he spent much of his youth. He had gone backwards and forwards between the two countries all his life as his father was a well-known sculptor who travelled a lot. This invented, improved life came out of its own accord, spontaneously.

Marco hadn't told Laura anything of his childhood, or the pottery, and any wish to discuss it was fading fast with every new discovery he made about her background. The few times she had asked him about his childhood he had changed the subject. Laura was open about her family. She told him about her two brothers, one who worked in advertising, and the other as a lawyer, and her restless, self-absorbed parents. Marco found a framed photo in her flat of the house from his book on British Architecture. He saw a wide lawn, children clustered on the grass and trees in the background. Laura pointed to different windows explaining which bedroom she stayed in as a child, the kitchen area, the dining room, and described the views that could be seen from the top floor across London. She confided that all her childhood memories were miles in the past, that she was better off away from her family, the house in the picture and all that it entailed. She held him and said she found him intelligent and graceful, unlike anyone she had seen or known before, unfathomable. She teased him about the length of his eyelashes, dabbing them with her fingertips, blowing across his face. Marco felt a deep elation inside him.

31

'That beer was rough,' Laura grimaced, grabbing her toothpaste in the bathroom.

'Is that why you had seven bottles?' Marco said. He prodded her in the stomach, 'you're drunk.'

'The food was so revolting I had to wash it down. Next time, I'm not listening to your great ideas about trying new restaurants. Who would go to a Madagascan restaurant run by a couple of Parisian hippies anyway?' Laura spat some toothpaste into the basin, hesitated and steadied herself on the edge, 'Ooh, I definitely feel a little queasy.'

Marco busied himself making the bed, 'Here, come and lie down.'

Laura collapsed onto the crumpled duvet, trying to find a comfortable position. 'Your terrapins are very unhappy,' she murmured, looking to the other side of the room. 'We've got to do something about them.'

Marco knew his terrapins were sad. They had grown too big for their aquarium. Two of them fought constantly and another looked rather sickly. It rarely raised its head, shuffling aimlessly along the glass bottom.

'Aren't they from Florida or somewhere like that?' Laura asked, getting out of bed, and giving the creatures a closer examination. 'It's really not fair, they're not meant to be stuck inside.'

'Well, not much I can do about that. I'll get them a bigger aquarium,' Marco said. 'Anyway, what's this got to do with anything, aren't we meant to be going to sleep?'

'I don't know if I can bear looking at them any more, they're pathetic. It's awful.'

'Forget it…'

'We have to find them a better home, outside, somewhere big.'

'I'm really fond of them! I've had them for ages.'

'I saw something like a turtle in the lake at the Buttes Chaumont park recently. They'd love it in there.'

Marco pulled the duvet over him. 'You can't just drop pet terrapins in a pond.'

'Yes, you can. We used to go to the park at Chiswick House as children with my aunt. People were always putting their terrapins in the pond. The place is overrun with them now.'

'Can we talk about it another time?' Marco whispered, kissing Laura enticingly on the neck.

'No time like the present,' she said, pulling on her long blue skirt again. 'Let's do it now! Come on, get a move on! It's either that or having another drink.'

'You are joking, aren't you?'

'No, of course not, come on. Get a move on! Those animals are going to die soon if we don't do something.'

'But it's midnight, the park will be closed. You've drunk far too much.'

'Precisely, the room spins every time I lie down. I'll never be able to sleep. '

Marco snatched Laura's shoes away from her, but she was set on her plan. She poured out half the water from the aquarium, fetched a strong plastic bag, and lowered it into it. The dozing creatures looked up at her startled, sloshing from side to side, skidding along the tipped glass.

Before he knew it, Marco was chasing after Laura down the steps towards the Metro. They caught the last train and emerged a while later onto a dim street a few minutes from the Buttes Chaumont park.

'This is ridiculous,' Marco said as they walked round trying to find a point of entry over the railings. 'I can't believe we're doing this.'

'Hush, keep quiet. Where's your sense of adventure?'

They found a gap near the gate on rue Botzaris where there were a few footholds. Checking behind them, they scaled the railings and jumped onto the grass the other side. They ran through the park, the street lights fading, tripping over each other on the sloping lawns and paths.

'I'm really not convinced this is a good idea.'

'Oh stop it Marco, don't be such an old woman! We should have brought a torch that's all.' Laura shot up some steps, onto a path, down further steps, towards the middle of the park. A jubilant cry followed and Marco found her pointing at the moonlit lake that formed the centre of the park with its landscaped craggy rocks and grottoes.

'Isn't it beautiful?' Laura proclaimed, opening her arms wide, breathing in. 'You could be in the country, or some hidden corner of ancient Rome.' She looked at Marco, 'Well, go on then, pop them in the water!'

'But they've no clue where they are.'

'Think how happy they'll be.'

'I don't know, look at them.'

She peeked into the bag. The four reptiles looked rather pathetic and battered from their ride across the park.

Marco found some sticks and started to snap and bend them in different directions.

'What are on earth are you doing?' Laura asked.

'Making a raft. We can put them on it and push them away from the edge, towards those rocks and plants. They'll get eaten here.'

Laura began to titter, but, noticing Marco's worried face, she said, 'Yup, of course, that's exactly what we should do.' She set to work too, binding sticks together with long wisps of grass. From time to time, she let out a whimper of laughter. They stood to admire their handi-work. A rough, uneven raft several centimetres wide lay on the ground, complete with old food scraped from the sides of the aquarium. Laura added an artistically placed flower at the stern which Marco instantly removed. They put the terrapins on the raft, herding them back into the middle each time they scuttled to the edges. Marco set it on the water and gave it a gentle shove towards the rocks. The creatures glided into the night, shrouded in mist.

'Like Géricault's *Radeau de la Méduse*,' Laura said theatrically, suppressing a smirk, 'the heroic survivors of the shipwreck set off towards an uncertain fate.'

'I can't believe you can joke about this.'

'Bye, bye, my little friends,' Laura waved, her voice crackling. '*Au revoir*.'

Marco held up a hand to silence her. 'Did you hear that?'

'What?'

'That plop,' he said. 'I think one of them fell off. Maybe the whole thing sank.'

'It was probably a duck.'

'A duck?'

'Gobble, gobble!' Laura snorted. 'It's survival of the fittest from now on.' She swallowed a violent hiccup. 'You know that over half the turtles that hatch on those South American beaches get eaten before they reach the ocean. It's a bit like that, isn't it? This is their introduction to the real world.'

'They could get eaten by fish.'

'I'm only joking. The fish are asleep,' Laura reassured him, hiccupping again.

'Fish don't sleep.'

'Really? They must do, no?'

'Don't think so. I used to have fish in my bedroom. They never slept.'

'Come on, they must. What are you saying; that they float around all night with their eyes open?'

'Have you ever seen a fish with its eyes closed?'

'Umm,' Laura wobbled, 'can't think about that right now. I need a pee.' She pushed Marco aside with obvious urgency and scampered up the bank of the lake towards a flower bed. She squatted over a circle of pansies, her blue skirt spread out wide. She closed her eyes and bit her top lip, as if she were about to give birth or enter into a trance. Evident relief soon spread across Laura's face as a trickle of liquid sneaked its way under the hem of her skirt. The trickle became a stream, then a torrent.

'Blimey,' Marco said, savouring the expression Laura had taught him at dinner, 'careful you don't kill the plants.'

'Shut up!' Laura shouted. 'Look the other way.'

'You sound like a horse!' he said, dismayed at the rivulets of pee rushing through the earth. Marco hopped from one foot to the other to avoid the channels coming towards him. 'Enough!'

'Shut up!' Laura beseeched him. 'Stop it, I'm going to pee all over myself. Don't look, turn round.' She clasped a large plant nearby so as not to topple over. Her whole body heaved with laughter. The jet emerging from under her skirt seemed never-ending, splashing the mud, splattering her shoes.

'I can't believe it, did you drink your bathwater or what?'

'No, seven bloody beers. Now shut up, please,' Laura shrieked and still more and more pee shot into the earth.

Marco stood watching, speechless. He walked up to Laura and held her face, marvelling at her. He kissed her on the lips so hard she couldn't breathe. He kissed her to the sound of her spraying pee, to her squatting, to her skirt spread like a tent over the dampening earth, to the wonder of her long neck, her almond eyes. He reached into her shirt and stroked the top of her breasts.

'Stop it, you pervert!' Laura squeaked, fighting for air, 'hold me up. I'm going to fall over, I'm slipping.'

A torch beam lit up a tree in the distance and a voice called out, '*Il y a quelqu'un?* Who's there, what's going on?'

'I haven't finished,' Laura said, appalled, 'I can't stop. Hold onto me.' They peered down at the drowned plants, pummelled into the earth, flattened and lopsided, in puddles and holes, and still Laura couldn't stop peeing. The torch bounced towards them, getting closer. Marco, cursing, dragged Laura away, towards the gate. 'Stop,' she squealed, bashing his arm. 'I haven't finished, it's going everywhere. I haven't finished. Leave me alone!'

'Get a move on, please, hurry.'

Marco lugged her through the grass as she fought to straighten her underwear.

They picked up speed and ran. They began hoisting themselves over the gate. Marco had his right foot on the lock when he heard Laura practically vomit with hysteria behind him. She had fallen over.

'Quick, help me. I can't get up.'

The man with the torch was gaining ground. Marco threw Laura over his shoulder. He grabbed hold of a railing but slipped backwards with Laura's weight onto the grass again. 'I'm going to throw up, I tell you I'm going to throw up,' Laura said, clutching Marco's collar, half-strangling him. They attempted a new escape. The nightwatchman was near the gate. '*Arrêtez*,' he shouted at the top of his voice. They cleared the railings, and tumbled onto the tarmac on the other side. The guard fiddled with his keys to open the lock. 'Come back at once. What have you taken?' They tore down the street ahead, shooting down a side road, the guard behind them. Breathless, they raced downhill towards Belleville.

'Hang on a minute!' Laura said to Marco, her voice rasping. She hitched up her skirt. 'This is too uncomfortable.' The nightwatchman was now at the top of the street. 'Heh, *revenez*, hold it,' he yelled again.

He stopped dead in his tracks as Laura raised her skirt over her naked bottom, up to her armpits, and yanked her sopping knickers off over her shoes. She kicked herself free of her pants, turned and hurled them at the man behind. Marco wrenched Laura down the road again. When they turned, they saw that the guard was no longer chasing them. He stood at the top of the street, her knickers in both hands.

They continued to walk, reaching a café where a couple of elderly men played backgammon at a table. They looked disdainfully at Laura's muddied legs and Marco's flushed face and turned back to their game. Marco bought a couple of pancakes and they stopped to eat and kiss between mouthfuls. They studied a rolled-up piece of carpet on the pavement, directing water down the gutter of a side street.

'Took me two years to work out why there were pieces of rolled-up carpet strewn around the streets of Paris!' Marco said.

'Like the pigeons,' Laura added. 'Have you ever noticed how many of them here only have one foot or just stumps they hobble around on? It must be agony when they get their feet stuck?' She paused, and cringed. 'Do they just fly off and leave their feet behind or what? Imagine finding two little pigeon feet on your balcony, yurgh!'

Marco wanted to ask why that was relevant. What did the carpet have to do with the pigeons? Did she really worry about pigeons' feet? He never knew what was going through her head or when the right moment was to say certain things, such as the fact that he loved her, loved her beyond words.

'Don't be sad!' Laura said, seeing Marco's pensive face.

'I'm not.'

'Yes you are, I can tell. It's your terrapins isn't it? You think they're dead.'

'No, it's not that.'

'What then?'

'I don't like the idea of that guy keeping your knickers.'

'Ooh, let's not think about that,' Laura frowned, moving on. 'I could give you a pair if that makes you feel better?'

Marco followed the sway of her walk, scratching mud from the back of her skirt, the pancake rising uncomfortably in his stomach. It was remarkable, he thought, that Laura hadn't thrown up yet.

32

At weekends, Marco and Laura slept late into the morning and went to the market on rue du Poteau, scrambling for the last produce on display as the stalls closed. They staggered back, weighed down by stretched plastic bags. In a grocery shop, round the corner from the flat, on rue Hermel, they bought thick butter biscuits from Brittany. This, apart from Marco, Laura announced, was her most significant find since her arrival in Paris. She promptly bought four packets. The Algerian owner of the shop, Karim, welcomed their custom. Marco and Laura became regular visitors to the store, stopping and chatting each time they bought anything. The place was chaotic. The aisles grew narrower and narrower with every successive delivery until customers had to squeeze past each other, chests touching, bags and baskets catching. '*Pardon, pardon*, excuse me,' were the most common words in the shop.

One Saturday, when Marco was out meeting one of his old university professors, Laura painted the kitchen walls pale green. Marco took up the task of painting the other rooms white. He pressed his thumb into the wet paint by the front door, leaving a tiny crescent from the half-circle of his nail. By this marking, he swore to himself, he would remember exactly how he was feeling: that joy had become part of his life.

Walking back from the cinema, they found a low table with three legs dumped by a bin. Marco carried it up the stairs to the flat and cobbled together an extra leg with wood from a fruit crate. He pinned a wedge of paper to the substitute leg to prevent it tilting. The 'sick' table Laura immediately named it and draped a tablecloth over it like a bandage.

Laura gave Marco a camera for his twenty-seventh birthday. They bought it near Odeon Metro station and then perched on the banks of the Seine putting in the first roll of film.

'This central part of Paris,' Laura said, 'is too used to photographs. Let's stick to where your flat is.'

So they walked together near his apartment, slipping down dented streets where *halal* butchers were open till late and African shops were adorned with swathes of waxed fabric hanging over their doors. Cheap shoe stores jostled with shops where second-hand clothes were sold by the batch in cardboard boxes on the floor. It wasn't a Paris Laura knew. She filled Marco's flat with her finds – Chinese tin bowls, the complete set for a few francs, Senegalese baskets made of recycled plastic, Vietnamese spoons with images of dragons.

Laura wanted Marco to take photos of people, track down faces that weren't aware they were watching. Near place de la République, photographing a demonstration, a man with a newspaper in his hand shouted something at Marco and they had to move on fast. He gesticulated violently at them. They fled into the tightness of people in front of the shops, joining the trudging of the crowd's forward move-ment, avoiding the furtive street-sellers offering watches and gold bracelets from under their coats. 'The photos will be great. I can feel it,' she said and they kissed outside a travel agency with pictures of Tunisian deserts in the window.

Marco wanted to tell her to stop dawdling, but he knew Laura put the highest value on spontaneity and impulse. It was like the non sequiturs he still wasn't used to. They would be mid-discussion about cooking or something as banal as the positioning of a chair in the flat, when she would say, 'Do you think that London is colder than Paris in the winter? Did Rita Hayworth have humungous breasts or was that Jean Harlow?' And that would be that, she would be off on a line of thought that he didn't understand, that bore no relevance to his previous comment.

PART SEVEN

Aigues-Mortes

33

The Carlevaris pottery received an order for fifty Tuscan-style urns from a golf club near Avignon. Elena prepared the paperwork, calculated the transportation costs and reminded Giacomo that customers preferred to get what they ordered. A recent delivery of garden vases had been returned by a swimming-pool salesroom because of the snails that had been grafted round the rims at the last minute.

Djamel had more sense and listened to her. His expertise, in fact, was injecting new vigour and purpose into the pottery, boosting sales more than Elena could have imagined. She encouraged him to branch out further, not to feel so intimidated by Giacomo's silent disapproval. Latching onto the upturn in income as if to a buoy Elena planned a mail-order catalogue and worked out ways to install another kiln for Djamel. She divided the showroom into two distinct areas with Djamel's tagine bowls, incense burners and bulbous ashtrays nearest the till. Opposite were Giacomo's paper-thin plates and vases displayed in front of a sparse plantation of sculptures, menacingly distended and frail. She revamped the flat above the showroom. A wooden table, ordered from a warehouse in Turin, its polished top still sheathed in protective coating, was put in the kitchen. A new sofa, also from Italy, was installed in the sitting room.

Elena had hoped to go and buy these items herself, on a visit to her family. A letter from her sister warned against such plans. Her father, she wrote, had lost none of his hostility in old age. He spoke as if he had only ever had one daughter. Teresa enclosed a photo of her unsmiling children and another of the flowers on her roof terrace.

Braving her dread of going out alone, Elena took the train into Nîmes. In a clothes boutique within sight of the coliseum she picked out a series of skirts and shirts and took them into a minuscule changing cubicle. She undressed and stood naked, her old gold chain her sole attire. She studied the way it rested on her skin, the trembling movement of it draped over her collarbone. The noises of the shop rebounded around her, behind the curtain, customers talking, shoes clicking on the tiled floor. She turned and turned, looked at herself from different angles. She stepped up to the mirror and swivelled the hot spotlight downwards. The glass shone, flaring and dazzling.

The light was brighter than anything she was used to at the pottery and she discovered burst veins across her cheeks, a knot of wrinkles on her chest that formed when she pressed her breasts together. She noted too a loosening of the muscles under her arms, a trail of dimples on her bottom, new prominent veins snaking their way across her left shin. The ridged pattern of creases on her forehead had worsened, and there was a slacking of the skin on her eyelids. Grey hairs had started growing on the crown of her head. She pulled them out, tilting her head inwards, close to the heat of the bulb, pinching her fingers together in a tweezers movement. She tore out a clump of black hairs by mistake, regretting it immediately. Who, she wondered, still knew what she had been like in Varanelle, the talk of the sawmill? Was it not her who used to wade into the river, skirt raised round her waist, hurling stones at the water, eyes watching her from behind each tree? To the people in the shop, no doubt, she was just another tubby farmer's wife squeezing into their fancy clothes.

As if guessing her thoughts, the shop assistant shouted, 'Are you all right in there, Madame, do you want to try a larger size?'

'I'm fine,' Elena muttered.

She straightened up, gathering her hair in one hand and holding it above her head. Through a slit between the wall and the curtain, she observed the people in the shop, the mother choosing clothes with her teenage daughter, the short-haired woman with the pink scarf, the assistant with tight trousers and a sun-tanned, taut stomach. Each of them dominated the shop with such purpose that she stepped back and felt the coldness of the mirror slap against her spine. She remained still, winding her gold chain round her fingers, the mirror frosting her back with its shining glass. She imagined the assistant drawing back the curtain and leaving it open for all the customers to see. They would crowd round and peer into the cubicle, run their eyes over her. 'See,' the woman with the brown muscular stomach would say, 'she didn't look like this twenty years ago!' In expectation of this scrutiny, Elena put on her shoes and waited defiantly, tears rising in her eyes. Her heart beat furiously, she was sweating. Footsteps and voices brushed the curtain. She watched it flutter and wave, the heel of a man's shoe appeared and, with it, a glimpse of patterned sock. She drew herself up, stood on her toes. She dabbed her eyes with the corner of a hanging shirt. New customers came and went. 'Are you all right, Madame?' the shop assistant asked again. She looked down at the pile of items she had amassed in the cubicle and meant to try on. She no longer felt like buying anything. She dressed and made her way to the front of the shop, onto the street outside.

Elena wandered through Nîmes aimlessly. Each time she ventured out of the pottery, it only confirmed to her why she was better off staying at home. All this noise was not for her. She found herself at the foot of the coliseum, but instead of walking directly to the station, she was drawn into the grid of old streets and alleyways again. She spotted a jewellery shop at the end of the road. There was a chair at the back where a man was sitting. He got up to greet her as she entered. '*Bonsoir*, Madame.'

Elena studied the contents of the display units, their sliding glass doors locked, shiny necklaces, earrings and bracelets laid out in rows.

She circled round a table where necklaces of semi-precious stones were kept alongside some watches. One necklace was multicoloured: beads and pieces of jade, lapis, amber, bronze, copper and polished glass jumbled up together in a heavy cluster. Between each bead was a small silver charm, a minute shoe, a spoon, a hat, sandwiched by colour. She called the man over. He unlocked the glass and handed her the necklace. The weight of it struck her as much as the price tag dangling from the side, but she carried it to the counter as if it were already hers. For some reason she couldn't identify, maybe it was the colours, it reminded her of finding the first tomato of the season in the garden, hiding behind a leaf, as if it had always been there waiting to be picked, green and red in the sun.

On the train back to Aigues-Mortes, she chose a seat in the end row of the carriage. She hid herself by the window. From time to time, she turned and examined the sturdy neck of the male passenger in front of her. It was a stubborn neck, she thought, a neck that could withstand anything, that belonged to someone with no doubts, like the women in the shop, or her own father. The people around her read books and newspapers. A girl was filling in a crossword. She searched the pocket in front of her for something to read. She looked under the seats in the hope of a stray piece of newspaper, a brochure, an advert dropped from a magazine. There was nothing. It was little gaps of inactivity like this that broke down her defences and got her thinking too much. She knew she always had to keep busy, constantly busy. She leant against the glass window of the train. She watched the side of the track outside, meandering through the marshes, her head lolling uncomfortably on the pane. She tried to remember the orders coming in at the pottery, and built up a list of things to do in her mind. She opened up her bag and ran her hand over the beads of her new necklace, stopping to squeeze each charm between her fingertips. The train whined to a halt at Aigues-Mortes.

At the pottery, Elena went straight to Marco's bedroom. She leafed through his schoolbooks and opened the drawers with his pencils and pens, looking at his birdcages and empty aquarium. She waited for the room to come alive, the way it usually reassured her. She took down the photo of Marco in his last year at school. Normally she could see a likeness of Riccardo surface from it, behind his son, but it remained resolutely flat. She wanted to ring Marco, but decided against it. More often than not now, she could hear him searching for things to say, little banalities to keep himself going, to fill the silences, until it was an acceptable time to say goodbye to her with a parting nicety.

She carried a chair to the bathroom, climbed on it and reached to the top of the mirrored medicine cabinet. She removed a small package and read the instructions on the side. She broke the seal and extracted a bottle. She took off her shirt. She released the clips holding up her hair and let it fall over her shoulders. She ran the tap in the basin and ducked her head under it. She rubbed the contents of the bottle into her hair. She stood, her head wound in a plastic cover. Her hair would be black again. That, if nothing else, would be the same, the blackness of crow feathers.

34

Nassima had been upgraded from cleaner to sales assistant, and kitted out with a purple outfit – the words 'Carlevaris Ceramica' adorning her lapels. However hard the young Algerian woman tried though, her skills in the showroom weren't always up to Elena's high standards. In a series of lessons, and gentle asides, Elena decided to teach her employee the secrets of the trade, starting with her number-one golden rule: friendliness always, always, has to be rewarded with a purchase. 'If you talk, smile and laugh, especially laugh,' she explained to Nassima, 'you make sure you're paid back with a sale, *capisci,* understand?' Elena's panoply of methods varied: she could take husbands to one side and convince them that their tired wives needed a gift; invent arguments about the value pots would take on over the years, or simply place vases in the hands of little children, ensuring they screamed if they were asked to let go. If this last ploy was used, she would follow it up with a bold and well-rehearsed line, delivered with a mischievous grin: 'Just think how much quieter your journey home would be if you let the poor child have it!' She could persuade wives and mothers too that their families would be healthier eating off natural materials. Once a British family, who had stopped off for a couple of mugs, bought ten plates because she successfully shamed them for the tatty plastic dishes she had spotted through the window of their camper van: 'baad, disgoustaing tings, cheramik betta, all natoural.'

Another method was to follow visitors tenaciously like a wasp, letting out gasps of delight every time they touched an object. 'Isn't that beautiful, *très beau, bello no*? You wouldn't believe how much time was spent on that, *molto tempo*! It's unique, *unico, eccezionale*.' Finally, as visitors stood laden at the cash desk, each item wrapped in newspaper, Elena had a last trump card, and advised Nassima to take note. She would delve into a box under the counter and pull out an ashtray or an eggcup. 'I can do you a good price on this,' she smiled, 'just fifteen francs, *quindici, quinze*.' When clients said they didn't smoke or already had enough, she simply popped the ashtray or eggcup on top of their purchased items with a 'never mind, *non importa*, ten francs then. I'll be generous, just for today.' To sweeten any lingering misunderstanding, Elena accompanied customers to their cars, carrying the purchases herself with obvious effort and picked a bunch of rosemary that grew like a weed by the gate. She placed it as gracefully as a bouquet of flowers in the hands of the tourists and smiled, looking for signs of gratitude on their troubled faces.

Nassima had started working the moment she set foot in France, first in people's houses, then at a hotel in the resort of La Grande Motte, ending up at the Carlevaris pottery. Before she was really aware of it, she confided in Elena, it felt as if everything was conspiring to prevent her returning to Algeria. The money she earned was needed by her parents, and one of her brothers developed a health problem that required expensive medication. Her husband didn't talk to her about home, but she knew he missed it as much as her. During their first weeks in France, they would meet at night by the kitchen window and stare together into the concrete yard below. And each time she felt her family was still waving at her from the quayside, the port of Algiers fading, roofs and daylight rising into sky.

It had taken her years, she told Elena, to get used to things in France. Nothing in the Camargue was like her home, nothing except the sea which she saw every day on her way to the pottery, the same, impatient sea. Everyone had permanently busy lives to get on with and, at times, even her children were like strangers who resembled her but who belonged to a new forbidding world out of her reach. She could see little pleasure in the lives of the people in her town of Vauvert, on the edge of the Camargue, a place where the French and the foreigners rarely talked, where mutual recriminations were part of everyday conversation. She had once heard Giacomo hint that some Arabs, and Africans, made little effort to fit in, that the young men, in particular, were always running into problems. European immigrants in the past, particularly the Italians, he told her with pride, had always abided by their adopted country's rules. Did she realize, for example, that Yves Montand or Jean-Paul Belmondo were actually Italian? Half the people in the nearby port town of Sète were part Italian. Nassima had heard this reasoning before and didn't like it. Edith Piaf's mother was part Algerian, she had said. What difference did that make to things? She told Elena and Giacomo instead about the terrifying graffiti she had seen on the walls of Vauvert, the things people said in the streets. There was trouble brewing between Arab youths and shopkeepers in Vauvert and Saint Gilles. Some cafés, she had heard, weren't letting in young people of North-African origin. Each day there were more and more posters from the extremist parties with their slogans splashed across the walls, posters filled with hateful words ordinary people read so often that they ended up becoming part of their thinking. One day, she warned, the place would go up in smoke.

After years of working at the pottery, it was the dust and sand that got to Nassima though. Her battles with it had grown to epic proportions. She saw piles of it in every nook and cranny of the pottery, inside the vases, under the beds, sticking to the carpets, pushed down into the grooves of the floorboards, everywhere. She watched helplessly as visitors traipsed into the pottery straight from the beaches, carrying their sand with them, rubbed onto their skin like a rough film. Children were the worst, Nassima said. They never banged out their shoes or shook their towels. Their buckets and parasols sprinkled their poisonous load in trails around the showroom. She had asked Elena for permission to put up a sign outside the pottery, but no-one took any notice. She had even got Marco to translate it into English, German and Italian, to no avail. The sign had yellowed uselessly by the doors. At best, the visitors stamped their shoes against the entrance, and the sand simply gathered for the next person to step into. She had tried putting out plastic bins. The wind sent them flying, and the sand with them, into the showroom, scattering it so wide it sparkled in the electrical lights. It was from the state of the floor each morning that Elena could anticipate Nassima's daily greeting. If the soles of Elena's shoes crunched against thousands of glittering grains, she knew to expect a more muted smile, a slight curbing of her usual generous salutation.

Once she had cleaned the workshop and showroom, Nassima made her way to the apartment above. It had large rooms that spanned the building. From time to time in the summer months, Elena called in extra help for Nassima, a local woman who complained day in, day out about her back and never locked the pottery behind her. Checking everything the woman did took so long that Nassima said she preferred to clean alone. Elena encouraged Nassima to switch to other tasks, but even the pipes in the bathrooms, she worried, had to be cleared of sand. Everything was clogged with it. Often the dirty water refused to drain away from the bath or shower. It sat stubbornly with the soap and grit in a circle round the plug. Then Nassima got out the plunger and pumped with all her might, singing to herself. She rummaged around the plughole with the handle and she could hear the sand grate against the wood, a terrible scratching sound.

Elena noticed that when Nassima ate her lunch, she discreetly ran her finger round her mouth and took regular sips of water, as if she could taste sand cracking in her teeth, embedded in her food. In the evenings, Nassima laughed, she would even find sand in her hair, in her shoes, in the lining of her underwear. She longed for the rare rainy days when the showroom visitors stayed off the beach and the sand was battered down by the weather into a compact, solid block. The holidaymakers then took off to Arles, or Nîmes, to the museums and restaurants, dressed in see-through, plastic anoraks. The pottery became quiet again, peaceful and clean. Nassima took advantage of the stillness to scrub the floors, polish the till in the showroom and bang out the brushes in the courtyard. Strands of Elena's hair then floated free from the brushes. Some were black and smooth, the length of her forearm, as strong as wire. Others were like threads of wool – grey and lifeless.

On those rainy days, Nassima prepared the rooms calmly and cleaned them with extra care. She used the sprays she bought from the supermarket and filled the sitting room with jasmine, lavender in Elena and Giacomo's room, cedarwood in Marco's. Elena often found her sitting on the chair at the top of the stairs, a knotted handkerchief sprayed with cedar scent on her lap. It was something in the spray, she confessed, that took her back to her parents' house, at the bottom of their village, something like wood, but smouldering fire and cooking too. From her chair by the stairs, Nassima looked up at the seagulls circling above the skylight. After the seagulls came the swallows, cutting into the blue of the air. After the swallows, Elena also understood, came a reverie that belonged to another home, landscapes and languages that would never die away.

The third summer after Marco's departure, Elena noticed that Nassima no longer threw out the sand she swept up. She stopped pouring it into the bin on the road or out of the rear windows into the grass. She kept back old plastic bags instead and filled them, brushing the sand in neatly with her hand. Some days she could collect enough to fill two bags, other days less, always enough to weigh her moped down.

One evening, in the Grau du Roi, Elena happened to see Nassima park her moped by the beach. She watched as she took off her shoes and walked steadily in a straight line towards the sea, her bare feet sinking with the weight of her bags. For a long time, Nassima observed the edge of the sea pushing and changing its boundaries. Then she tipped her plastic bags inside out. The sand fell through her fingers. An unsteady mound grew in front of her. The approaching foam ate at the pile, wearing it away, capsizing it into the water.

It was clear that Nassima often stood like this, staring out to sea, the wind against her face, counting the clouds as if they were the mountains of Algeria on the other side. The wind beat at her empty plastic bags, curling them upwards. The mound of sand slid away. As long as she lived in France, Elena knew, Nassima would carry on bringing sand to the beach, sweeping it up from the floors of the pottery. She would bridge the sea with it: her family on the quayside, a pile of sand at her feet.

35

It was hot the following months, the sort of heat and pressure that shoved the Camargue backwards, inland, away from the sea. Elena left several messages for Marco; all remained unanswered. For three nights in a row she went to bed without hearing his voice and her nights were sleepless as a result. She guessed he was busy with his job. She had never heard of UNESCO before Marco started working for the organization, but, by listening out for it on the news, she had been surprised to find it mentioned rather frequently. On a couple of occasions, during the news, she had even seen the headquarters fleetingly on television and eagerly searched for her son's face in the rows of dignitaries and ambassadors, or on the podiums of con-ferences and awards – it certainly wasn't a job that was going to bring him any closer to her or the pottery. Her own father had taken her out of school at the age of fourteen on the pretext that he would teach her himself. She had later heard him explaining that a child who knew too much ended up spurning its parents. It had been five months since Marco's last visit. She could hardly believe it.

Giacomo encouraged Elena to go out more. It wasn't good for her to work so hard, stuck in one place. Didn't she want to go to Nîmes again, or visit some new sights? He offered to take her across the border into Italy, to the market in Ventimiglia. There was no point, she thanked him, in going to Italy if she couldn't go home.

Returning from the supermarket in Aigues-Mortes, Elena noted that the pottery lacked proper advertising. All the hotels and restaurants of the area had flashy billboards and arrows, bits of wood and plastic nailed to trees. The supermarket had its own painted wall on the way out of the town. The pottery had just three placards in the grass. On Elena's instruction, Djamel whitewashed pieces of wood and painted 'Carlevaris Ceramica' in red letters. Nassima added the directions below. Elena and Nassima waited in the van as Djamel planted the signs at the side of roads, heading to Saintes Maries de la Mer to fix the final placard. Each time, Elena blocked her ears to the banging of the hammer on the wooden stakes. From where she was sitting it looked like Djamel was thrashing someone, beating them to a pulp.

They had lunch in a café, under the shade of a tree. Thanks to Djamel, Elena announced, restaurants as far away as Perpignan were buying Moroccan tableware and, only the week before, a platinum blonde from Marseilles had ordered a hundred sunny-yellow plates, dishes and bowls. And there were more such orders coming in daily.

Elena left a stack of the pottery's flyers at the tourist office in Saintes Maries. She studied the posters on the wall: gypsy caravans on marshland roads, fishing boats, shots of crucifixes being carried on jostling shoulders. One poster showed the statue of St Sarah held by penitents, her body black against white ceremonial robes. On the shelves were books celebrating the town's origins, how a holy group, made up of Mary-Jacoby, the Virgin's sister, and Mary-Salomé, mother of the Apostles James and John, Mary Magdalene, Martha, Lazarus, as well as the servant Sarah, had come adrift in the Mediterranean and miraculously floated ashore on the beaches of the Camargue. It was certainly, Elena thought, a happier omen than the images she had seen of Marie Durand locked in her cell. She took some brochures and magazines, eyeing the leaflets for other potteries with jealousy. By the time she had left the tourist office she had a stack of documents and free postcards in her arms.

On the way home, Djamel told Elena of his plans for a holiday in Morocco. He wanted to load up his car with gifts and drive all the way to Tetouan where his family lived. He had made the same journey five years before, driving through the night. He had taken gifts for every member of the family. Somewhere in Spain, between Valencia and Algeciras, a parcel containing an electric food mixer had fallen off the roof rack and he hadn't realized until he got to Morocco. He had handed out the presents to his family but had nothing for his younger sister. She had told him it didn't matter; she was only interested in seeing him. It was the one present, though, that Djamel had chosen with real care. He didn't stop thinking about it all holiday. He only hoped that the mixer hadn't broken when it fell, or been crushed by another car, and that someone had managed to salvage it for themselves. He liked to imagine it functioning in some kitchen of southern Spain, an unexpected roadside present for a penniless family.

Elena had an hour to fill before tackling the accounts and orders. She thought about putting on the television, allowing the skipping from channel to channel to distract her. She flicked through one of the magazines she had picked up instead. It was a special issue on the history of the Camargue. After an article describing Aigues-Mortes's place in the Crusades, she learned that, in 1893, rioting French workers had stormed the salt fields surrounding Aigues-Mortes and attacked rival Italian seasonal labourers there. Possibly up to fifty Italians, she read, had been killed. Some had died in the marshes, cowering and hiding from the local population the police could no longer contain.

She lay silently for a long while, dissecting the text, trying to understand whether she had read correctly.

She went down to the showroom and dropped the article in front of Giacomo. Was this true? Had he been aware of these things when he bought the pottery?

'What?' Giacomo said. 'What massacre? Are you talking about the Huguenots or the Crusaders? The history of this area is a series of massacres.'

'What's a Huguenot?' Elena asked. 'The Italians, I'm talking about the Italians.'

Giacomo read the magazine. From time to time, he peered up to check the expression on Elena's face. 'Maybe I did know, maybe I didn't, I can't remember, why's it important? People were hungry in those days. They fought for each other's food, that's all. It was the same everywhere.' He turned and dropped the magazine into the bin. 'It's all in the past now.'

Elena left the showroom and joined the road. Two drivers slowed down to offer her a lift. She waved the men on and made for the umbrella pine further down the road. An idea grew in her, becoming more insistent each time she dismissed it. She recalled how the steps up to the main door had been chipped when they had bought the pottery. Giacomo had filled the gaps in with cement. Had they been the marks of knives and axes used to hack at the door? The murdered had perhaps tried to hide there, in their house, besieged and hounded. From the shade of the pine tree, she looked out over the marshes and imagined groups of angry French workers prowling, complaining loudly about not being taken on by the salt mines, accusing the Italians of snatching food from their mouths in their own country. She could see the Italians, their hands held out in front of them, fumbling, fleeing, tripping into the marshes, spreading in all directions. 'There's one here! *Tue-le!* Get him. Over here!' The reeds, it seemed, still rasped to the sound of their slaughter, the chases to death spanning a century back into the soil. The police, she had read, tried to protect them, but they were attacked all the same. Some Italians even took refuge in the bakery at Aigues-Mortes, others in isolated houses in the marshes. They were hunted down till nightfall, the next day too. She visualized their faces, blood forming loose scarves in the sun, seeping into the freshly raked salt – their wives, at home, waiting for their return.

Elena was startled by the call of a bird in the branches above her. She looked up. The bird sung again, and its repetitive song became the sound of shots being fired across the marshes, the click of knives and rods. Twenty years or so after her arrival in the south of France, Elena had finally been proved right: the Camargue was not going to hold anything good for her, nothing at all. Not only had it been the waste-land of her own life, but the very area Giacomo had chosen was a cemetery for scores of Italian martyrs who had lost their way. She left the cover of the pine tree and walked back to the pottery. A group of visitors was talking in the car park and she slipped behind the show-room to avoid them.

She stopped when she saw Giacomo by the back door. He was sitting on the doorstep with a piece of wood on his lap. Two branches, like arms, spread outwards from the central part. She watched him bring the wood to his face and sniff the bark before peeling it away. As he chiselled round the cartilage of ringed knots she saw that it was more sculpted than she had realized. At one end was already an upturned head with a funnel-like mouth. Giacomo smoothed the rough cheeks of the face with sandpaper, marking in a chin. It emerged from behind deep cuts and he carried on gouging until lips appeared. The chest opened up in a burrow of tunnels, each connected to the other by arches, ridges of sinew that were mounted by minute creatures with fine wings. Like a pendant in the middle of the chest was a ram's head with curled horns. Where the legs of the sculpture should have been was an array of fibrous, shredded ligaments, ground-down strings with sawdust pushed into the grain. Djamel called Giacomo from the showroom and he disappeared inside. Elena squeezed past the sculpture to get to the door. The wood gave off a strong scent of stripped bark, tempting her to touch it. She brushed her hand over the incisions of the eyes and mouth, expecting to be stung or infected by the weeping resin of the freshly cut wounds.

'*Ça va*? Are you all right, Madame Carlevaris?' Nassima shook Elena from her contemplation. 'You shouldn't stay outside like that, it's getting very hot again.'

Elena noticed a new group of visitors making their way to the showroom. 'Will you get them to buy something?' she asked. 'I'm suddenly very tired.' She set off upstairs, mumbling, 'Thank you.'

Somewhere she had the number of Marco's desk at work. She searched for it on the kitchen table.

'Marco, *sono io*…'

'Oh, hi, hang on…'

'I haven't spoken to you for days…'

'Sorry, could you wait a few seconds. I'm in the middle of something…'

Elena shook the receiver. 'Marco! I need to speak to you.'

'One moment.'

'Marco!'

'Yes, yes, I'm here, sorry. Someone was asking me something. What is it? Are you all right?'

'I need to talk to you, I found this magazine, there was all this stuff in it…'

'I won't be able to talk long I warn you now…'

'You always say that.'

'That's not true…'

'There was this article…'

184

'What article?'

'Oh, doesn't matter… you're not interested. When are you coming to visit?'

'What's new at the pottery?'

'Busy, busy.'

'That's good.'

'We sold that big pot.'

'What big pot?'

'The pot!'

'What pot?'

'The pot I was telling you about last week, it was thanks to Nassima, you never listen. The big one Djamel made, the Anduze-style garden vase.'

'Ah, yes.'

'Four thousand francs, not bad, eh? And you know what?'

'What?'

'She was like you, a translator.'

'Who?'

'The woman who bought it, from Dusseldurg, Dosseindolfer, something like that, in Germany.'

'Düsseldorf.'

'You know her?'

'Who?'

'The German translator, Moller or Mueller, a name beginning with M…'

'Why would I know her?'

'Well, you knew where she lived.'

'I didn't…'

'So when are you coming down?'

'That's great about the pot.'

'She was no beauty your friend, that's for sure.'

'What friend?'

'The woman who bought the pot, you're not listening, she had see-through hair and the poor woman's scalp was all flaky. No ankles either, just thick legs all the way down. She bought the pot though, nice of her, don't you think, paid cash. She has a big garden, she told Nassima. I don't know why she chats so much to people, even after they've bought something, she won't learn. The things customers tell her, I can't believe it. There was this woman from Lyon who was listing her daughter's problems to her, she told her everything, I mean everything…'

'Can I call you back?'

'Those people are still bothering you, aren't they? They probably keep you nailed to your desk all day.'

'It's just that I'm expecting someone.'

'Who?'

'The director…'

'If you worked here, you'd be your own boss. You wouldn't have to put up with all that.'

'It's not like that.'

'You'd be free here. We're doing well. I think you'd love it, it's all different now. Djamel's got so many ideas…'

'I have to go.'

'Call me this evening.'

'I'm going out.'

'When can I call?'

'I don't have my diary right now.'

'Well, maybe I'll have to come and see you in Paris?'

'Paris!'

'Yes, why not?'

'You hate travelling. You hate Paris.'

'But I have to see you, Marco, I have to.'

Elena put the phone down and opened the balcony doors. The sunlight erupted into opaque heat as she stepped outside. She weeded the window-boxes, going over her botched conversation with Marco in her head. Why couldn't they talk to each other like before? The earth was dry and powdery. She crushed sickly pale roots between her fingertips and flicked them over the railings. She watched as they fell, catching on the drainpipe below.

PART EIGHT

Paris

36

'Marco.'

'Hmm.'

'Marco!'

'Yes, what? What is it?'

'Wake up, stop it, wake up.'

'What?'

'It's OK, I'm here.'

Marco sat upright, agitated and sweating. Laura turned the bedside lamp on and they both recoiled, shielding their eyes, staring downwards at the twisted sheets about them.

'Breathe deeply.' Laura took Marco by the hand. She massaged his shoulders, placing her palm on his forehead. 'You're baking hot. You were talking in your sleep, shouting.'

'Was I?'

'I couldn't understand what you were saying. You whacked me across the face,' Laura tried to laugh, stroking his sodden hair.

Marco got out of bed. He grasped the nearby table. His legs felt shaky. 'What time is it?'

'It's four-twenty.'

He filled a glass of water in the kitchen. 'It's so bloody hot in this flat.'

Laura straightened the sheets and tucked the corners back under the mattress. She shook the duvet a little before covering herself with it again. 'Come back to bed,' she said. Marco crossed the room and looked out onto the boulevard below. There was no sound from the street.

'Were you having a nightmare?' He sat on the edge of the mattress. He didn't say anything. 'Were you?' she asked again, pulling the duvet over his bare legs.

'I used to have the same nightmare as a child,' he said.

'What about?'

'I find a burglar clearing out the sculptures and pots at home and I don't stop him. In fact he's in the house because I let him in. He knows I'm there and he can see me. He even talks to me.'

'And then what?'

'That's it.'

'That doesn't sound too bad,' Laura said, 'here, give me a hug.' She turned the lamp off and the dark sucked the room closed again, leaving only hollows of light in the cornicing above the windows.

'I used to have a nightmare as a kid,' Laura said, 'that came back all the time. I was being chased by musical instruments, if you can believe it, trumpets, cellos, drums, flutes, guitars, the whole lot, an orchestra. They would corner me, playing the same ghastly tune over and over, like circus music, then pile onto me, poking at my skin, forcing their way into my mouth. I haven't had it for years, luckily.'

Marco wasn't listening. He turned and faced the wall, his head on the pillow. He hadn't had his dream for years either, and never as vividly as just then. How could he explain to Laura that his father's face was closer than it had ever been? He had put down the pots and plates he was carrying and come over to find Marco in his hiding place. His father had looked at him straight in the eyes, and Marco had stretched out his hand and felt tears on his face.

'Marco?' Laura said. 'Are you asleep yet?'

'No.'

She leant over and wrapped her arms round his waist, bringing her hands together at his navel. 'You seem very edgy at the moment.'

'I'm sorry, I don't mean to be.'

'What's up?'

'Nothing.'

'Something's wrong?'

'No, nothing really.'

'Something though.'

'My mother's coming to Paris next weekend.'

'Great. Is that the problem? I'd love to meet her.'

'It may not be that easy. We'll have quite a tight schedule. She's only here three days.'

'Well, perhaps we could meet up for a coffee or something.' Laura said. 'I could take her shopping if you're busy? She might want to visit some shows or shops. We could go to the theatre?'

'She's not really like that.'

'I could pop over here for a quick bite on Saturday evening, have a glass of wine with her?'

'No, I...'

'OK, got the point. You don't want me to meet her, is that it?'

'She's quite old-fashioned, she wouldn't understand.'

'Understand what?' Laura asked, confused.

'That you sometimes stay in this flat, that you sleep here and we're not married, you know.'

'Right...'

'In fact, if it doesn't bother you, I'm going to have to hide your stuff. Maybe, even,' Marco hesitated a long time. He rubbed the back of his head. Laura withdrew her hands from around him. He had repeated the sentence to himself countless times, 'We could say we're going to get engaged if you do meet her. What do you think?'

'It's four-thirty in the morning,' Laura laughed, kissing him on the back. 'You're completely crazy. Come on, let's get some sleep.'

37

In the morning, Laura began picking up her possessions from around the flat. She slid them into a rucksack at the bottom of the cupboard. She disappeared into the bathroom as Marco made breakfast. They had organized a visit to a squat near Marx Dormoy on the way to work, a short walk from Marco's flat. An immigration lawyer they hoped would chair some of the discussion groups at the forthcoming conference had agreed to meet them there. The squat, Laura explained, was a former post office depot. Some people from it, in protest at being refused residency papers, had recently tried to occupy the Church of St Ambroise, only to be thrown out a few days later.

The squat was a large building with tent-like structures in the courtyard. Inside, the walls were painted in glaring colours, the doors plastered with posters and graffiti. Groups of men hovered near the entrance. They looked at them suspiciously as they edged past.

'You go ahead and deal with her,' Laura said. 'She'll guess we're together. I don't want Amani finding out.'

'But you're the one who knows the most about this conference.'

'Rubbish, the whole thing would collapse if you left. You're brilliant at persuading people. Besides, she's a woman; you can flutter your eyelashes convincingly. It worked with me.'

'Really?' Marco said.

'You know it did.' She patted him on the backside. 'Just let me know what happens. I'll wait for you.' He sauntered off into the labyrinth of the squat. 'Hey,' she called after him. He stopped and came back towards her. 'If she's pretty, don't flirt.' She thought about this for a while, before adding, 'Actually, don't flirt if she's ugly either.'

Laura peered at the bumpy walls, covered in damp stains and dripping water. She started to head down a corridor, but was stopped by a barrage of wary glances. She found a bench alongside a row of metallic crates and sat behind a table instead. A young woman arrived out of nowhere and plonked herself down opposite her. She introduced herself as Fatoumata, from Mali. Ceremoniously, she handed Laura a printed form. Laura smiled back, politely, a little taken aback. The woman pointed at the top of the form, as if the officialdom of its title and insignia would spur her to read it. It was a French Government housing form. Each time Laura turned a page, Fatoumata's eyes fixed on her expectantly. When no reply was forthcoming, the Malian woman started talking, in the hope that Laura, a complete stranger, would, somehow, be able to help her. Laura explained that she was only waiting for someone, who was waiting for a certain Catherine Berthier, that she didn't know anything about these official forms, or housing, that she might mess things up. It wasn't really her job to be at the squat, not at all, she said feebly. She worked at UNESCO, a branch of the United Nations; she was from Britain, London. The woman carried on talking, insisting Laura help her. Surely she knew about these things. 'UNESCO, *Nations Unies*, United Nations, that's good, very good,' she repeated, '*Oui, oui, Nations Unies, c'est bien ça.*'

Laura spread out the sheets with some reluctance. She read through the boxes, fighting to understand the questions without letting on that it was the first time she had ever read anything like it. She filled in the bit for the surname with Fatoumata's help. She raced through the first questions, eager to get it over and done with, then the questions got progressively more complex. Laura read the blurb and sub-clauses in italics trying to understand. She listened to Fatoumata list her problems. She was from the border region between Mali and Côte d'Ivoire. Her whole family were back there, except her. She came to France because her husband had a job on a construction site. Two years after she got to Paris, he ran off with another woman, someone from their country. It was too late for her to go back home, to Africa, but now she was illegal, her visa had just expired, but perhaps she could still qualify for housing. She wanted to keep her job as a cleaner in the suburbs of Meudon and for her children to go to school in Paris. Her children were born in France, she said. Then the account of her life trailed off into a diatribe against a man at the town hall who said he would have her children taken away and her deported. She began to cry and banged her hand on the table. Laura jumped. She clutched the legs of the bench and looked down at her watch.

'I have a meeting at my office,' she said to the Malian woman. 'I have to find my boyfriend.' There was no answer. 'Listen,' she said in English, 'I don't know much about these things, someone else should help you properly,' then she checked herself, apologized in French, hesitated, and carried on with the form once more.

Now Fatoumata had started on her elder child's health problems. Laura could not grasp what condition the African woman was describing. She didn't understand the final clauses of the form either. She looked up in the hope that someone would walk by. She found a rubber in her handbag and cleaned up the form. She went over several letters with a pen. The form was more or less complete. There were two children playing in a kind of kitchen area with a large aluminium bowl on the floor. They reached inside and pulled out spoons. Fatoumata yelled at them. She called them over and they ran round the table, darting in and out of Laura's legs and falling into their mother's lap. She told Laura that where she was brought up in Mali, there weren't many people, it was empty land as far as the eye could see. As a child all she had done was watch her father draw water from the well for the cows, and swim with her brothers in the river. They had to travel miles to get to the nearest big town. When she arrived in Paris, she could not believe how many people there were, people in every corner and road, walking, talking, rushing. She had found work in Meudon, cleaning an office building at night. She had got used to things in Paris and that's the way it was, you always get used to things in the end, don't you? Every day, she had to cross the city and sit on the Metro and people shoved and barged past her, into her. When she managed to get a seat, she could feel their shoulders squeezing her, the odour of their skin, then their flesh, compressed inside their clothes, so close to her, although she knew nothing of them. 'Most of these people,' she continued, 'I'll never see again. I look at their faces, European faces, Asian faces, African faces and I don't know who they are. My body is just pushed and pressed from every side, like a fruit in the hands of a child.' She laughed, stood and took the form Laura was handing her. '*Au revoir Mademoiselle*, thank you.'

Laura left the squat, taking deep breaths. She stopped on the bridge above the railway line coming out of the Gare du Nord. She watched the wagons of a goods train trundling by underneath her, filled with gravel and sacks. Marco came chasing towards her.

'Why did you go off like that? I was looking for you everywhere.'

'It was stifling in there. I had to get out.'

'Are you OK?'

'I feel pretty crap actually. This woman wanted me to help her and I don't know if I did.'

'Help doing what?'

'Filling in a housing form. I mean it all sounds pretty hopeless, her husband ran off with another woman, she doesn't even have any official papers. She's been threatened with deportation already.'

'Sounds like you did your best.'

'No, I was useless.'

'Don't say that.'

'I was.'

Marco pulled her towards him and kissed her. 'How about we grab some lunch? There's a Vietnamese place near Chateau-Rouge, we could have soup and noodles.'

Laura looked despondent. 'What the hell is the point of organizing this huge conference if we can't even help some poor woman like her with two kids, right here in Paris? I'm always saying that I care about things, but I didn't do enough for that woman, what kind of rubbish is that?' She searched through her bag. She fished out a piece of paper and a pen. She started back towards the squat.

'What are you doing?'

'I'm going to give her my telephone number.'

'Wait!' Marco said. 'Are you sure that's wise? You can't just give out your number like that.'

'I'll see you at work.'

Marco passed a street of shops with fruit in boxes and crates on the pavements. He crossed the market at Chateau-Rouge. African stands were piled with plantains and trays of meat, gasping fish thrashed around in shallow bowls of water on the ground. On boulevard Barbes, he bought a postcard of the place de la Concorde in 1900. He addressed it to Elena and Giacomo. He wrote: 'Hardly have time to think, work going well, hope things good with you two, hello to everyone at the pottery. This is perhaps not the best time to visit me, Mamma, sorry, shall come down to you soon though, promise, much love, Marco.' He sat on a bench and searched for a stamp in his wallet. A police car drew up. Two gendarmes approached a group of young men and asked them for their papers. People walked round them, giving them a wide berth. The young men started talking in a language Marco couldn't identify. Another policeman got out of the car. Marco quickened his pace, as if he were about to be caught red-handed, his heart beating, sweating under his shirt. He had to stop himself from checking his pockets, imagining that they were bulging with stolen or illegal goods. An African woman in bright yellow clothes and red flip-flops strolled from the market eating a cob of grilled sweetcorn. She rotated it in her mouth, biting off bits, cleaning her teeth with her nails.

'Marco,' Amani Sedeq called out as he walked past her office. 'Can I have a word with you?'

'These tape transcriptions you've been doing,' she said as he sat down.

'Yes.'

'They're excellent.'

'Ah, thank you.'

'To be frank, though, they're not really that useful, are they?'

'But...'

'I thought they'd tell us more about the movement of peoples across the world.'

'If they were alongside interviews of Hispanics in America, and Turks in Germany, Asians in Australia and so on, they would give us a global picture, that's what you said?'

'Did I? I'm thinking that's all rather confusing now. It's not concrete enough. We need to compile statistics, school drop-out rates, health issues, life expectancy, that's going to give us a better overview of the situation.'

'The interviews give a human dimension though.'

'Yes, but it's an economic and class issue, that's all I could think reading through your stuff. I mean, I came to Paris twenty-five years ago. It was a little bit tough at first, mostly because of the climate, but I got used to it. I'd had a French governess in Cairo as a child; I went to a convent school and all that. A farmer from the Egyptian country-side would have had a very different experience. He'd probably end up in one of those tower blocks in the suburbs with his children hurling stones at the police, burning cars, don't you think?'

'But...'

'We need to talk about economics and lack of education, bad governance, the absence of opportunities, that's generally what it's about, that's why people can't improve their lives in their own countries, and why they don't necessarily get any better here either.'

'The Malian interviews give such a sense of what it's like to be living in a foreign country...'

'Yes, but, come on Marco, this is an international conference, we haven't got time for any fanciness. We need solid facts.'

'Right.'

'Besides, I think you're being wasted on all this. I'm not one for compliments, Marco, but I think we could do with your input researching papers – less translating, more direct action, you know.'

'Right.'

'I want you to go to the education department. Get some statistics together, then we can set about doing some graphs. Can you do graphs?'

'I've never tried.'

'Great, I'm sure you'll do them brilliantly. There are lots of people here who can help you. They're easy on a computer I'm told. Ask Laura, she's fantastic at all those kind of things. Where is she, by the way, have you seen her?'

'No.'

He stood up to leave.

'Marco.'

'Yes.'

'I hope you didn't spend too much time on those tape transcriptions.'

'I...'

'Good, don't feel you wasted your time. Maybe we will find a use for them somehow.'

Marco sat in his office. He could hear Amani on the other side of the corridor, talking loudly on the phone. He locked his door and plugged in the cassette player. Before he could turn the volume down, a woman's voice, clear and vibrant, shot out of the tape machine.

'Assiata, aged thirty. We came from Mali to France and stayed. My children are at school here now and this is all they know, so I suppose we're here for good. Now it's their turn to get on. We've had nothing but trouble with them though. They respect no-one, they're rude and disobedient. They wouldn't have been like this had we stayed at home. A year ago, I discovered they were catapulting rubber balls into the street below their bedroom. There was a call at the door and this woman stormed up here, screaming, her left eye watery and red. The children denied everything, said she was lying and she was shouting at me, insulting me, in my own home. She said she was going to call the police and I thought if my husband comes home to find the police here, he'll be furious. They would check all our papers, confiscate things and even deport my brother who lives with us, he has no papers. I begged the woman to forget the whole thing. I made her some tea, offered her biscuits. I made a cold compress for her eye. She calmed down, then she started crying and telling me that she'd never had children and that she worked at the local electricity board and it was the most terrible job because all she did all day was photocopy and sign papers. When she left, I went to my children's room and saw the catapults under their beds. I said nothing, but I told my husband. When I was preparing supper, he locked himself in the children's room and beat them. I wish I'd never told him. They cried and pulled at the door handle to get out.'

38

Marco made a last-ditch attempt to dissuade his mother from coming to visit. He reminded her that she had never previously shown any interest in travelling anywhere, especially not Paris, and that, according to her, the city was always grey and dirty. She was adamant that she needed to see him. He found a hotel room for her round the corner from his flat by the church at Jules Joffrin. It was conveniently near him and out of sight of the unkempt back streets. Elena was horrified. She was coming to Paris to see him, just to see him, she complained vehemently down the phone, not be stuck in some poky hotel on her own. Marco spent a day cleaning. Laura removed the last of her things from the bathroom and concealed them with the others in the rucksack at the back of the cupboard.

Marco picked his mother up from the Gare de Lyon. She waited for him on the train, standing in the doorway. She kissed him and stroked his face lovingly.

'That's all I wanted,' she said, 'that's all I needed to do, to hold you again.' She stared back into the empty carriage behind her as if she might have forgotten something on her seat, or wanted to leave again. Marco led her down the steps. She looked into the station, at the crowds and ticket booths, at the trains arriving from Italy, and froze.

'Well come on,' Marco urged her, 'no point staying here,' but she was rooted to the spot. Little had changed in the station, she thought, except now it was Marco leading her.

She stepped forward, her eyes closed, reaching for her son's arm as her sole support.

Laura had suggested a whole itinerary for Marco, but he knew that any attempt at organized activities would be met with resistance. Laura, besides, wouldn't be there to help out. She had wanted to meet Elena on her last night, and even recommended and booked a restaurant for them, but Marco thought he had made it clear that it wouldn't be appropriate if she came. He had again stressed his mother's traditional views and her possessive nature. He sensed Laura was annoyed by the issue.

Marco got the taxi from the station to take them directly to the Alma Bridge, where the tourist riverboats were moored. Laura had got them seats on the best boat thanks to a friend. Marco was happy to see his mother at the front, looking at the passing monuments, but she soon complained about the polluted wind and sought refuge inside, a scarf round her head. Later, walking behind the opera house, she stopped to look at some fridges with ice dispensers in a kitchen shop. She asked Marco to enquire about the possibility of having one delivered to Aigues-Mortes. When the sales assistant quoted a price, she held her son like a shield in front of her and bargained vociferously, complaining that she knew about deliveries and the sum they were suggesting was extortionate. She came away empty-handed from Galeries Lafayette, horrified by the cost of everything in the department store and the throngs of pushy shoppers. Paris, Marco saw, irritated his mother with its noise and crowds. She grew tired and wanted to go back to Marco's flat. She'd just stay there, she said, she only needed to see him anyway, not the city.

Elena found her son changed, nervous and twitchy. A couple of times, in the street, she had tried to hold his hand and he had shaken himself free with the excuse of having to carry some shopping or tie up his shoelaces. He was thinner and she worried that his eyes were weary, an unusual flatness to the pupils. His apartment was dirty, too, under the apparent order. In the fridge was a carton of soup, half a take-away, no proper food. She set about cleaning as much as she could. She took the mirror off the bathroom wall and washed it with warm soapy water. She pulled the rugs from the floor and hung them out of the windows, beating them with a wide wooden spoon. She scoured the saucepans and scrubbed the kitchen surfaces. When she talked, Marco ducked all questions about his work, friends and career prospects.

Elena felt guilty that her son was sleeping on cushions on the floor, but it was a comfort, once again, to be sharing a room with him. She slept well, her best night in years, listening to his breathing, his particular smell on the pillow, the outline of him in the dark nearby. It took her back to their room at Varanelle, to her cousin Rosa's, how they would sleep there, face to face, the warmth of their breath mingling. The following evening, before turning off the light, Elena went to hug Marco goodnight but he subtly extricated himself from her embrace. She didn't say anything. It felt as if the fingers he had used to repel her had branded her arms with burns that smouldered and smarted all night.

Marco was called into work on the Friday morning. Elena sat glumly on a chair, alone again. Even being in her son's flat wasn't enough to see him. She only had the dusting of the bookshelf left, and there was still room in the small freezer for a few more pots of fresh tomato sauce. She wandered to the window. She noticed the cassette player on the shelf beside her and the tapes leaning against it. She pressed the button down in the hope of hearing some music. A person coughed and started to speak.

'My name is Sidy, I am fifty-five. Since I've been here, I've been in hospital three times, pneumonia three times. My wife won't stop cleaning, she says I'm ill because of the germs. I say she needs to get out, but she points out of the window at the rows of tower blocks over the road, and the kids who linger in the doorways, and says why would she want to go out? So I go out instead, and I sit near the football stadium. The crowds shout words I don't understand. It frightens me that they are going to pour out of the stadium and run over me, stamping on my head. There is a telephone centre nearby with rows of booths where you can call abroad cheaply. It's full of people from all over Africa – Congo, Cameroon, Guinea, Benin, Gabon, everywhere. I sit near there too and watch people as they leave, smiling, or with red eyes, holding hands, taking in news.

On the way to our flat, I pass the women cooking in the corridors and landings, the rooms packed with families, the lights and electricity wires loose. I worry the building could go up in flames, but no-one does anything. They don't care about us Africans. When I open our door, my wife is asleep and I think of myself struggling down the flaming stairs with our possessions, not able to wake her. I know I won't be able to wake her because I never can. That's how she sleeps, with her hands either side of her body, like the dead.'

Elena switched off the machine. She plucked two feathers from her duster and wondered, for a moment, if there was a fire exit in Marco's building. Was that really what he did for work, listening to such things? She rewound the cassette a little in the hope that he wouldn't notice her tampering. She carried on brushing the top of the bookshelf, blowing on the spines of the publications. She surveyed the titles: *Experiments in community schooling in Upper Egypt, Literacy and non-formal education in the languages of West Africa.* Did he read these books too?

She opened a book and saw pictures of people dressed in elaborate clothes reading under a tree in Africa, another had two Egyptian children playing in an oasis. Between the books was a stack of postcards. They were from Giacomo to Marco, describing events at the pottery, exhibitions in Nîmes, visits to places. On the front were images of the statue of St Sarah, the Alyscamps tombs in Arles, Van Gogh's *The Yellow House.* Inside a plastic bag wound together with string was a handful of photographs. There was one of two girls standing outside a nightclub, short skirts, legs on display, with a young man she recognized as Rémy. Another was of Marco sitting on the steps of the house in Varanelle. She had often wondered where that had got to, as well as the next photo of Riccardo and Giacomo as boys. They were wearing white shirts, lent by the photographic studio in Tolmezzo, their legs were scratched and rough, their polished shoes obviously a loan too. They held hands; and Giacomo looked scrawny compared to his broad-shouldered dark brother, his hair the summer blondness of a young girl.

Inside an atlas was a wad of papers slotted vertically between two maps of Vietnam and China. She worked her way through the papers, drawings for the most part, designs for statues Giacomo had sent, or plans for garden pots and fountains, all with their dates, as usual, written in perfect letters on the back. Towards the middle of the pile, she found a series of ink portraits, on yellowing paper, curiously lifelike for Giacomo's drawings. There was a note pinned to them in one corner: 'Marco, I thought you should have these.' They were interiors she recognized, of the first house in Clichy, and studies of a man, eyes and torso in close detail. She placed her hand on the paper, pausing to feel the texture of the indented pen marks against her palm. She studied the Adam's apple in the neck, the cracked lips, the mole to the left of the nose; the shrunken topography of a face she slowly realized was Riccardo's. She felt her throat clam up. There was one of Riccardo with a beard, leaning back on a chair, his arms as stiff as the wood supporting them. She turned it over: 5 July 1969. She reached for the others: 10 July 1969, 13 July 1969. They had been drawn in the two weeks before Riccardo's death. She stared at the empty eyes, the inattentive, faraway face, the extinguished cigarette between the fingers. She slumped back against the wall. What right had Giacomo to give these drawings to Marco when she had never seen them herself? She placed the drawings on the shelf, in a line, forcing herself to look at them again. The look on Riccardo's face was one of such loneliness she wanted to scream. She had been so close to seeing him then, so close. His hair, his gaze, the beard, and his posture in the sequence of drawings, she couldn't say what exactly, but something wasn't right... it was as if part of him had already died. She ran her hands through her hair, pulling at strands. How could these have been hidden from her?

She reached for another pile of photographs wedged between books on the shelf. This time they were of Giacomo's sculptures and pots, with notes asking for advice from Marco. It was obvious that the two of them wrote to each other all the time. Only the week before, she had seen Giacomo quickly put down the phone as she entered the showroom. From his shifty gestures, and hasty retreat into the backroom, she had guessed it had been Marco. Was Giacomo's meddling ever going to end? What was this supposed love of his – what had it ever done for her other than saddle her with more disappointment?

Elena cleared up the remaining cooking utensils. It became obvious to her what she must do. She left the flat, briefly hesitating on the stairs, and then pushed on. Getting round Nîmes, let alone Paris, was an ordeal, but she managed to find her way to a bus stop on the square behind the boulevard. She knew that if she found the right bus she would be all right at the other end. She studied a plastic map, trying to distinguish the red lines from the pink ones, and the crossing and merging of the routes. A bus with 'Clichy' marked up on its side arrived. She climbed on and sat at the front, her stomach hurting all of a sudden, gripped by pain. The bus ploughed through Paris, and the landmarks of her memory. In Clichy, she found her bearings easily. The gates to the cemetery on rue Chance Milly were the same. She recognized a tree in the distance and beyond it a block of mausoleums and pollarded trees. She walked to the outer wall of the cemetery. From behind the wall came the sounds of a railway.

Where Elena had hoped to find a wooden cross, she found nothing but lines of weathered tombstones sticking out of the ground. She had always remembered a carved stone crucifix that had capped the grave next to Riccardo's. The head of Christ had been worn away, the nose dug hollow in the chalky face. She had touched it herself, pushed the small head into her palm, all those years ago. She turned to search for it in the rows behind. She spotted something. She edged past a stack of browning flowers, side-stepped a broken vase. The crucifix was there, with its Christ's head. So this was it. She stood still. She looked round her. There was no-one to help her? She needed to find an attendant, someone. 'Riccardo! Riccardo!' she shouted. Where had they put him? She had renewed the concession with Giacomo. Why had he been moved?

By her feet was a mass of weeds, thick brambles snaking upwards. She knelt down and pulled at the growth. Underneath the weeds and braided roots, she saw something solid. She ripped the grass away. A rotten wooden cross lay encrusted in the mud and dust before her. She rubbed at it, prising it from the ground. As she lifted it, a horizontal piece fell off, leaving a jagged edge of dry splinters. Strands of root clung to the base. She brushed them away, splitting the more stubborn shoots with her nails. A metallic plaque was stuck to the front. She cleaned it with her spit. The inscription, Riccardo Carlevaris 1941–1969, sparkled and instantly dulled. She pummelled the ground, her temples thudding. She tore at the remaining stalks, upturning clods of roots and severing thick blades of grass. She threw the weeds to one side, on and on, wiping her tears with the back of her hand as she went. She found stones at the sides of the path and delineated the area round the tomb where she had cleared. She pulled mud from under the clumps of grass next to her and sprinkled it over the ground, flattening the surface with her palms, flicking away woodlice and worms. The earth was a gloomy shade, an uninviting colour of dried blood and dirt. There was nothing pure and regenerating in this Paris earth, nothing resembling the airy brown of the fields of her childhood. She found some wire on a bunch of withered flowers and bound the cross together. She pushed it into the ground, steadying it with a large stone. The grave was cleaner, the way she had first seen it, a heavy blanket of earth. She got up, her hands stiff and muddied from her work. She hurried towards the gates, worried the cemetery would be shutting. The bus drove past the factory. The entrance had changed, and behind it was a modern housing development with glass and steel doors. Young poplar trees were planted in the car park. She looked away.

Elena rang the buzzer for Marco's flat. He answered in an anxious voice. 'Mamma, is that you?' He was waiting for her on the landing. 'Where have you been? I got back at three and you weren't here. You should have left me a note.'

'I went round the block to try and find some courgettes, have a little walk. *Niente di speciale,* don't worry. There's not much in the shops here, at least nothing I've ever seen before.'

She slipped past her son into the kitchen. She ran the warm tap over her hands. Water, coloured with earth, slid from her fingers, streaking the enamel of the sink.

As they ate, Marco asked his mother how her day had been.

'I'm tired,' she said, 'very tired.'

She cleared the plates and stacked them beside the oven. Marco washed the saucepans while she prepared for bed. A film of gritty mud was stuck to the sink. He splashed it away.

'Goodnight, Marco,' Elena said, leaving the bathroom. She didn't try to hug him. She lay on the bed and pulled the sheet over her head. She put her fingers into her mouth and sucked them until the last traces of soil dissolved into her.

The evening prior to her departure, Marco took his mother to the Chinese restaurant Laura had recommended. She started complaining the moment they got to the entrance.

'This is going to be expensive. I could have cooked us something at your place.'

Marco had planned the evening with care, making sure a taxi was organized, asking for a quiet table. As they crossed the dining room, led by the waiter, he spotted Laura seated and waiting at a corner table.

'What are you doing here?'

'I couldn't resist coming,' she said, 'I wanted to see you so badly. Why weren't you at the office this afternoon like you said? I can't go three days without seeing you.'

'There's someone I'd like you to meet, Mamma,' Marco said, stammering and flustered, trying to regain control of the situation. 'I invited her along specially.'

Laura stood to greet Elena, shaking her hand warmly. Laura was wearing loose trousers, a fitted jumper. Her hair was up; its pattern of blonde and auburn streaks formed a perfect, rounded shape.

Elena sat down. 'She's tall, very tall,' she muttered.

Marco ordered tea. He had rung ahead to check that the restaurant had a decent rosé, the wine his mother preferred, but they had run out.

Elena was getting worried, 'No, really, we must only choose the cheaper dishes. Look at the prices! Marco what got into you? See the price of this thing!'

'That's for a whole lobster, look at the starters first.'

'I don't know what any of this is. I mean what's wrong with our food. I've never eaten this stuff in my life. Why do we have to eat weird things all the way from China? It can't be healthy.'

Laura giggled. Elena broke into Italian without looking in her direction. 'Marco, *ma non è possible… cos'hai fatto*? What have you done? Let's go home now, take me back to your flat. *Non voglio mangiare queste cose*. I can't eat this muck. The restaurant is too crowded. I can't hear myself think.'

Noticing Laura staring at his mother, Marco tapped her gently under the table with his foot. She went back to studying the menu instead.

'Listen, Mamma, I'll order you some food. Simple things like chicken and rice. You like rice, don't you?'

'Rice. I could have made rice at home. I didn't have to come all the way to Paris to eat rice, the Camargue is full of it, that's all they eat down there.' Elena fiddled with her handbag, pulled out a tissue from inside and patted her brow. 'It's hot in here. I suppose the Chinese like it that way. Isn't it hot in China?'

Elena picked up the porcelain block by her plate. When Marco explained they were for resting your chopsticks between courses, she popped one in her bag to show Djamel. He could copy it easily. There was no telling what some people bought. The first courses arrived and Laura seized on the sculptured carrots for conversation. Marco took this brief lifting of the atmosphere as a cue to speak. He reached out and touched his mother with one hand and then with the other held onto Laura.

'Well, I've got something to announce. We're thinking of getting engaged.'

Elena thought she could make out a photograph of the Castello Sant'Angelo in Rome on one of the walls, or maybe it was some citadel in China. She had never been to Rome, but she was pretty sure that was it. What such a photograph was doing in a Chinese restaurant she didn't know. People were constantly stealing bits of Italy and plastering them on their walls – pictures of the leaning tower of Pisa, gondoliers' hats, Marcello Mastroanni, Sofia Loren. She knew they were waiting for some reaction from her. She couldn't speak. She touched her multicoloured necklace, knocking it against her chest, pressing its silver charms hard between her fingertips. She stared at a passing waiter in the hope that he would stop and ask them something.

'Mamma, *cosa c'è*? Aren't you going to say anything?' Marco was looking at her.

Why was he drawing attention to her? Did he not have the decency to keep quiet? He played with his chopsticks, knocking the side of his plate. What a ridiculous and inefficient way to eat food! Who'd have ever imagined her own son using bits of wood to feed himself?

'I've got to go to the bathroom,' Elena said, standing. Her napkin fell to the ground and she knew that if she bent down to pick it up she would either faint or vomit, or both.

Laura turned to Marco in astonishment when they were alone. 'What on earth are you playing at?' she demanded. 'Thanks for telling me.'

'I'm sorry. It just came out, you weren't supposed to turn up like that.'

'Well, you fucked up,' Laura snapped. 'You fucked up.'

In the ladies' bathroom, Elena held onto the hand-drying machine as she ran the cold water in the basin. This had to be a joke. Marco had only left home a few years before. He was a boy. No, no, it was too absurd. How could Marco get married? And to that blonde girl? Well, she was hardly a girl. She was already a woman who knew her way with men. Elena pushed open one of the cubicles and sat on the closed lavatory seat. The floor was filthy. The grooves between the tiles were brimming with grime. Marco and she should be thinking about getting back to his flat. She could cook him some proper food, make a warm drink and they could forget this ever happened. It was late. She had a train to catch the next morning.

There was a knock on the cubicle door.

'Mamma! What are you doing?'

There was no reply.

'I'm sorry, I didn't realize Laura was going to come. Is that it? She wanted to meet you.'

There was still no reply.

'At least you've met her now,' Marco said. He heard his mother lean her head against the cubicle wall.

'Mamma, please come out. What's got into you?' He tried the door, banged the lock. 'Don't do this to me, be reasonable,' he said in a firmer voice. 'Just come out.'

'Reasonable?' she mumbled, 'you were the one person I trusted, the only one I could rely on, the only person in the whole world, and now…'

'What are you talking about?'

'You, Marco, I'm talking about you! You spring that giant of a foreign girl on me without any warning, without any respect. You can't treat us like this, first your father and then me.'

'My father? What's he got to do with this?'

'Yes, Marco, your father. I saw the way you left his grave, the way you betrayed him.'

The main door into the restaurant opened. 'What's going on? Is everything all right?' It was Laura.

Elena froze. Now this stick of an Englishwoman had the gall to come hounding her in here, sticking her nose in things.

'It's nothing,' Marco reassured her quietly, 'we'll be with you in a minute.'

'Is she OK?'

'Please, just go and sit down, we'll be right with you.'

Elena yanked at the loo paper and watched the plastic dispensing roll detach and smack to the ground. She paused and stood, her faltering breathing filling the airless cubicle.

'Let me deal with this, Laura, please, just go,' Marco whispered. 'I'll see you back at the table, give me a minute.' He cleared his throat. 'Mamma,' he repeated, turning back to the closed door, 'you're being unfair. I don't know what you're talking about.'

'Shame on you, Marco, you forgot your father, your own parents!'

'I…'

'You couldn't care less about us, could you? Could you?'

Elena heard the main door into the restaurant slam. The timer on the light switch went off. She sat back down on the lavatory seat in the semi-darkness. From the kitchens, through the wall, she could hear people yelling in a sharp, incomprehensible language. A fly took off from the cistern and landed on the mauve air freshener hanging from the cubicle wall.

39

Marco put his mother on the train at the Gare de Lyon. He came back to his flat to find Laura grinning. She pointed at the fridge and freezer lined with little pots and Pyrex bowls of tomato sauce. The flat had been cleaned from top to bottom, the sheets folded neatly in the cupboard and Marco's shirts ironed.

'What's so funny?' Marco asked.

'Well, at your age. I mean,' Laura said, 'it's unbelievable. So is this what your poor mother did during her stay? I wish I had a mother like yours. You should see mine when she comes to Paris. She spends her whole time gorging herself on patisserie and shopping for clothes with friends, barely a moment to see her own daughter!'

'You don't understand.'

'Oh yeah, mummy's boy…'

'No, really, you don't.'

'Ah come on, I'm only teasing. I understand Mamma's worried about her *bambino*.'

'No, you don't understand!' Marco said loudly.

Laura retreated to the edge of the bed. She sat with her arms folded. Marco stood in the kitchen, surprised by the vehemence of his outburst. He had never answered Laura back, or expressed himself with such force in front of her. He came through and sat down on the bed.

'I'm sorry. I don't why I said that. It's just that it's quite complicated. My mother's completely lost in a place like Paris. She wanted to help, do something familiar, it makes her happy to cook.' Laura moved away from him and walked to the window. She scratched at the glass. 'I'm sorry, please don't be angry, Laura, please.'

'OK, OK,' she said, 'it was all a bit weird for me too I guess, seeing another side of you through her. I wasn't expecting her to look like that. I don't mean her face – she must have been quite something in her youth, the thick hair and the big eyes. She's still beautiful, amazing-looking, in fact, but those clothes with the brassy buttons and that loud, multicoloured, clanking necklace she kept on playing with. If she dressed differently she'd look quite sophisticated. Funny she doesn't care.'

'She does care. She cares a lot,' Marco said, embarrassed.

'Well, I admire what she did in the restaurant. She's not fake, she's kind of sweet really.'

'Sweet is definitely not a word I'd use to describe her. My mother has been through a hell of a lot.'

Marco thought he had made his point clear enough and quite calmly this time. He wanted to change the subject and, above all, take Laura in his arms. He hadn't been with her for three nights. He pulled her towards him and the bed, but she wriggled free.

'OK, you're right, sweet's maybe not the word,' she said, 'but you know what I mean. I suppose, deep down, I'm still tarred by all the dreadful snobbery I had to put up with as a child. It's unbelievable how hard it is to shake off years of family pressure even if you hate it in yourself. I just really wasn't expecting her to be so, you know, un-educated, in a way, and untouched, as if she'd just arrived from the mountains. She's still so much of a... what can I say, I mean, I don't know how to say it, a... villager, I suppose, you know what I'm saying, if that's the right word, in the true sense of the word, though not really, a kind of innocent. You're so cultured and refined in comparison. It hadn't really occurred to me that we were from such different backgrounds. It's a bit of a shock. That sounds so awful doesn't it? I don't mean it badly, don't take it the wrong way, but you understand what I'm trying to say, don't you?'

Marco lay down on the bed and glared at the ceiling. He felt stripped bare, exposed. He rubbed his eyes. There were too many words going round his brain now and, behind them all, was the way she had said 'You fucked up' in the restaurant. He could think of no way of bringing it up, of asking her what she had meant.

'So what happened last night anyway? What was that argument about in the loo at the restaurant?' Laura said.

'Nothing.'

'Ah come on, your mother looked pretty distraught. Do you think she's all right? Shouldn't you ring your father and check with him?'

Marco turned away.

'Marco.'

'What?'

'You heard what I said? Shouldn't you warn your dad or something?'

'My father's dead,' Marco said in an emotionless voice.

'Dead?'

'Yes, dead.'

'What are you talking about?'

'He died nearly three years after I was born. I never met him.'

'What?'

'You heard me, he's dead.'

'Why didn't you tell me?'

'It's never come up.' Marco picked up a magazine off the floor and put it on the bedside table, jigging his leg up and down.

'I can't believe you wouldn't mention something like that.'

'I didn't know him.'

'But Marco, it's kind of important. Isn't it?'

'To be honest, it's not something I really think about that much.'

'So who do you call Papa on the phone? I don't understand.'

'My uncle, he ended up marrying my mother.'

'Your uncle?'

'My father's brother. He was working with my father when he was killed. He took care of my mother afterwards.'

'Hang on, hang on. Your uncle married your mother, your father was killed? How?'

'In an accident, something to do with a faulty machine, it happened here in Paris.'

'And you never wanted to tell me.'

'I don't know much about it.'

'Don't you want to know?'

'Not particularly. What good would it do? I never knew the man. He never knew me.'

'I find that extraordinary.'

'What? Laura…'

She walked out of the room, squeezing past the bed. 'Sorry, I just don't know what to say.'

She made herself a coffee in the kitchen. She poured the boiling water through a paper filter, and watched the liquid drop into the cup below. From time to time, she knocked the filter with her fingers.

Marco pushed the door open behind her. 'What have I said? I don't understand.'

'Nothing, nothing, it must be terrible for you, but I'm just a little overwhelmed. I don't know, it's rather upsetting, and disappointing.'

'Why? I'm fine with it.'

'You're not; how can anyone be fine with that? Some people spend their whole lives trying to find out who their parents are and you just

217

brush this off as though it's nothing. He was your father, Marco, your father, for goodness' sake! That's kind of important, isn't it? I suppose it explains why there seems to be a gaping hole in you sometimes, like a part of you is missing...'

Laura caught sight of a big plastic bag propped up against the side of the bathroom wall. She bent down to look inside. A piece of Sellotape sealed the top. She slit it open and found a pile of her things gathered together by Elena, or taken from the rucksack: her nightshirt, two bras, a lipstick, some hairgrips and a fashion magazine. At the bottom were strands of her blonde hair collected from the carpet and others, thick and soapy, extricated from the bath plughole.

40

Elena settled into her train seat, relieved to have left Paris behind. Her visit had merely reinforced the sensations of her first stay, as though the intervening twenty years had never taken place. Walking along the river, she had felt the urge to scream at Marco's lack of awareness. Could he not remember how the two of them had been there before? She had reminded him of so many events they had shared, shown him parks where he used to run, all to no effect. These are the trees you charged with your wooden pirate sword! There were swings here in this playground! Was it possible that the past meant nothing to him, that he had deliberately cut it out of his existence?

It was the Englishwoman, without a doubt. She was encouraging Marco to break away from her. She was educated, wealthy, she could tell – the way she dressed and her fancy manners, how she dabbed her face with her napkin as if she hadn't really eaten anything. She had never seen high-heeled shoes like that on anyone before. Many people from the Val di Cena, in places beyond Varanelle, had emigrated to

England. There was money to be made there. They sent back photos of terraced brick houses with square green gardens, and a place for a car in front. What if she tempted Marco there? He was so fine-looking he could have ended up with anyone, but she had trapped him. She wanted a child too, that was obvious. That's why she was in such a rush to get married. Coming up to thirty years old, she guessed, maybe more. She didn't look particularly fertile though, all tall and spindly. Her skin was pale, far too pale, so translucent she almost wasn't there. Nothing you could hook your eyes onto, all whiteness, plastic whiteness, tiny fair hairs on her arms, too fine to be real, like they were stuck on for effect. She had little wrinkles round her eyes and above her top lip when she smiled. She had heard that happened to fair skins in the sun. The breasts worried her the most. The girl had no breasts, no hint of anything. The girls Marco had tried to see in Aigues-Mortes had been similarly flat-chested. What was wrong with him? Why did he have such an aversion to breasts? Hadn't she nourished him herself, with her own milk, proper, natural, full breasts, a real woman's breasts?

Elena got up and walked down the train. She came to the buffet car. She ordered a mineral water, then a coffee. It was disgusting. They would never make decent coffee in this country. She sat on a barstool, her feet not quite touching the ground. She watched the landscape alter through the window as they went further south. The train came to a halt at a deserted station with two cars parked on an empty road. It set off again through rolling foothills with mountains in the distance. The villages looked depleted. Clusters of houses with rough logs stacked at the front came into view. Maybe in a place like this, she thought, not unlike Varanelle, she might have fared better. Instead, she was heading back to the flatness of the Camargue, and Giacomo.

Somewhere inside her, she hoped, there was still a solid core of brightness that she could hold onto, something that had been hers long before all this began, this travelling, these lies, but she wasn't sure. All too often she was struggling with the same anguish as the day she learned of Riccardo's death, the hasty decisions of that period reawakened; an obsessive, unsolicited repetition in her thoughts. It didn't help that Giacomo's early fond talk of Riccardo had faded, as if his elder brother's name had become an inconvenience, a detail to be forgotten. The little he spoke of him, she did not even recognize as her husband. She had protected Marco as a child with Giacomo's borrowed fatherhood, but the result was the abandoned grave in Paris, the hidden portraits of Riccardo. She could see now that she had latched onto Giacomo without real judgement all those years ago. It had been an act of desperation when she was lost in Paris, then resignation, but it had become a lasting state. She had tried to believe she was happy, those first years at the pottery, which was easier with Marco around, but the emptiness of that pretence was all too obvious at present. Their marriage had always felt like a form of adultery. Giacomo had constantly rushed her forward with decisions, passing over her misgivings. How easy it was to counter every argument and doubt of hers by saying that he loved her more than anyone. No-one, he still said, would ever love her the way he did, even when she said she found that insulting to Riccardo, an affront to the life she had lived before him. All he had done was to take her son from her and offer his gangly sculptures in exchange. Perhaps, in fact, he had just had pity on her and called it love, stolen her grief and tried to make it fit his own incomprehension of life. It wasn't her that he had been after in Paris, but a woman, any woman, to fulfil the tasks of his life. He had inherited her.

The one thing she was still certain of was that she had loved Riccardo. Their three years together, their meetings in the forest, and their marriage, were the high point of her existence, as vital as a lung inside her. She would make Marco understand about the love that still wed her to his father. She would tell him how his father had followed her from the fields, how he'd waited weeks and weeks for the chance of approaching her alone. Marco was of an age now where he could understand these things. He might realize what it meant to her, understand where he came from, the sacrifices they had both made for him so that he could have a decent life, sacrifices that had led Riccardo to his lonely death. She would make Marco laugh about the way Riccardo had stood at the side of the road out of Bardi and just waited for her to walk by. As she passed him, he had simply started walking alongside her. She hadn't dared speak, just glanced sideways, noting his immaculately white teeth, the heavy hoods of his eyes, and then the strange accent she had never heard before. He was carrying a leather bag in one hand. She discovered later that he had been trying to get to his mother's funeral, but had been prevented by the snow on the railway tracks. The ground was still slippery and when they reached a steep stretch he grabbed her hand to help her over the ice. Before she knew it, they were holding onto each other for support, sliding over the rocks in the path. He had fallen over in a heap before the last hill to Varanelle, making her laugh. Maybe he had done it on purpose. That's when they had started talking properly, retreating behind a group of trees so as not to be seen. She had kept on looking at his teeth, and the prominent veins in his hands. His eyes were full of fire. She had never been alone with a stranger before, but it didn't seem awkward in the least. In fact, she had agreed to meet him that very evening, without hesitating, as if it were the only thing to do. And she had gone through with it. She had dared slip out to meet him despite the risks, running all the way to the sawmill. Yes, she would tell Marco all this, and how she had ached for him at night, in bed with her prying sister, unable to sleep or rest, her whole body sickened with a desperate longing for this stranger who had spoken to her of Argentina, of his desire to travel to worlds she had never dared imagine. She would have followed him anywhere. For him, she would have overcome all her fears.

She played with the handle of her coffee cup. All this thinking and rethinking wasn't helping, only making her ill. She drank the remains of her mineral water and felt a twinge in her gut. It was the same pain as she had felt on the bus in Paris. She was becoming bloated and uncomfortable after meals. She was certain it was an ulcer. She had read about these things, how worries burrow away at the lining of the stomach. No-one knew the extent to which her heart thumped with dread as soon as her work at the pottery was over, or how she feared moments alone with herself. She tried to consider the things she wanted to do back at the pottery. She could come up with nothing. She had only been deceiving herself by imagining that the new-found success of the pottery was going to change the fundamentals of her life. No increase in money was going to bring Marco back, or resolve this life and its battering of regrets and anxiety.

A man in a white shirt came and sat next to her in the buffet car. He ordered a glass of wine. She heard the jolt of his cufflinks on the metal bar and watched his starched sleeves crease as he drank from his glass. Elena cautiously twisted her seat round. The man was tanned with clean-shaven full cheeks. There was a smell of eau de cologne about him. He sprung open a briefcase, rearranging his business cards, aligning his pens. He found an old wrapper from a chocolate bar and flicked it onto the counter. She looked down at his polished black shoes, at the rounded steel base of the bar stool. There was a small rip in the hem of his right trouser leg. A voice came over the train's loudspeakers, announcing the next stop.

The train drew into a station, its platform a rush of people. The man got off, taking a large bag from the rack by the door. The train pulled away and gathered speed. Elena drank her last drop of water, tipping the bottle into her mouth. It was warmer already. She shoved the cap into the neck of the bottle and pushed it downwards with her finger. She rattled it noisily from side to side. The buffet attendant asked her if she wanted to order anything else. She shook her head. He brought out a dripping cloth and wiped the surface of the counter. He took the glass of wine and threw the remains of her coffee into the sink behind him. He scooped up her empty water bottle, along with the chocolate wrapper, and dropped them into the bin. He gestured for Elena to stand back, reached up for the metal shutter above him, and brought it crashing down onto the counter. Elena fought not to cry. Giacomo, she promised herself, I won't let you steal my life any more.

PART NINE

Aigues-Mortes

41

Elena made up Marco's bed with clean linen. She settled into it, pulling the sheet up to her chin, and stared at the ceiling, at the outlines of the stacked cages and boxes on the walls.

'What are you doing?' Giacomo said, opening the door.

'I'm sleeping here from now on.' She wrapped the sheet tighter around her.

Every evening from then on Giacomo came back to the doorway of Marco's room to try and talk to her. During the day, she found him following her, a drawn-out, formless shadow travelling through the pottery, turning up in the showroom unexpectedly. His restlessness made it impossible for her to sleep despite the corridor that separated them. If he crept into the room, she feigned sleep and felt him standing over her, his eyes on her nightdress and hip bones, fixed on her breasts. He didn't have a pen or paper with him, but she could hear him drawing her, transporting her from the bed onto his white notepad, her limbs messy squiggles and scrawls that he twisted and turned as much as he liked, playing with her body across the paper.

One night, the arch of her foot was poking out of the sheets and she knew he was there, a few centimetres away. She could feel his hand held out above her, tracing a line either side of her mouth, streaking a furrow down her neck towards her chest. She sat up and opened her eyes, certain he was about to get into the bed, but he had vanished. She was left clutching the pillow in expectation of an unknown pain.

Elena walked to the church in Aigues-Mortes in an attempt to stem the gathering turmoil inside her. She walked in the midday heat, the drier the better, to burn her thinking, parch her throat and tongue of their sounds. She had scarcely spoken to Marco since her visit to Paris. His calls were now briefer than ever. She just about had time to say hello before he came up with his excuses. And in every short conversation, she felt he was distancing himself from her, climbing a ladder with her firmly attached to the bottom rung. She was even intimidated by him now, his education, his job, by her own son.

At the church, Elena settled into a back pew. The building had become her one refuge. She liked its gentle humidity and thick walls; how she could breathe in the face on the crucifix, soak up the light from the windows. Two women at the front turned their rosaries. She took her Italian Bible from her bag. She read, smoothing the pages with her fingertips. Certain phrases jogged her memory, words she had once learned and practised as a child in catechism classes in Varanelle. How they had become tainted by false accents. At the pottery, talking to clients, or Nassima, she often repeated herself, got muddled over descriptions, found French words in Italian. It was even worse when she was thinking alone. The dialect of her family and mountains then came back in waves, but the sentences on her tongue were no longer her language. There had been a time when she had first arrived in France that she had held onto a few of her parents' sayings, her own little vocabulary, like a talisman. Now it was all inverted ideas and heavy expressions, coloured by foreign clumsiness, and the sound of the reeds in the marshes. She couldn't get back to her former self. It was as if the young woman she had once been in Varanelle had never existed, was just an invention of her own nostalgia. She had let herself become salt, salt that would not dissolve, the smell of the Camargue. And it was a smell that should never have been hers. By leaving home, she was sure, she had missed out on the person she should have been, who she was meant to be. She had ended up a stranger to herself, with a false life, her place in the world a charade.

She brought her bible to her mouth, opened the book and kissed the paper. She read at random, skimming the pages, eyes scanning. The print on the near-transparent pages came to a halt. She brought it closer to her face and read. Psalm 32: 'When I kept silence, my bones waxed old through my roaring all the day long. For day and night thy hand was heavy upon me: my moisture is turned into the drought of summer.' She stared at the page in her bible. She read and reread the sentence, not understanding, her voice rising from a whisper to a pitch that startled her. She shook her head. What was happening to her? Like unhealed wounds, her fears were reopening with alarming haste; pushing old anxieties and events to the surface once more. She couldn't stop herself from returning to the same place in her head, over and over. Was this punishment for her sins, her first couplings with Riccardo in the forest, and her life of betrayal with his brother? Her only hope, though, was that, in God's eyes, she had somehow kept herself pure, remained faithful to Riccardo by her second barren marriage. Its infertility had perhaps annulled the offence.

Why had she bothered leaving Varanelle for this life? Only a few hours from Italy, she felt she were marooned, silted up like the town of Aigues-Mortes, wedged in by the hateful waterlogged marshes around her. She might as well have been in Australia or even South America, the distance from home seemed just as great. At least in those countries, she knew, she would have truly travelled. She had calculated that if she left the pottery in the morning she could be back in Parma or La Spezia by evening. What had she gained? Any old labourer could walk across the border at Ventimiglia and do what she had done. In France, she was halfway between ocean and sea, nothing.

She leaned her head onto the wood of the pew in front, wound her fingers round her necklace and pulled till she felt the clasp was about to break. She slotted her bible into her bag and left the church. She walked down the pedestrian street, with its rows of tourist shops, to the local surgery near the Chapel of the White Penitents. Giacomo had made her an appointment with Dr Couret despite her objections. Indeed, to cover her resentment towards him, and disguise her growing bleakness, she had started telling him about the ulcer she thought she had. He would now corner her and ask about it, without mentioning anything else, and she preferred it that way. Her bloated stomach was somehow a separate being that solicited its own response, a decoy for him. Her bouts of nausea and indigestion were getting worse however. Some days she couldn't even face eating. But it was due to her anxiety, of that she was sure. The moment before sleep was the worst, when the most routine problems became insurmountable hurdles, when the repetition of her dilemmas made her feel like she had never experienced anything other than relentless disarray. It was then that she could feel the shards of the past just beneath the surface of her skin, working their way up through her body, only to emerge again, clean and transparent, out of her scars. She had one particular recollection that kept on coming back to her with increasing precision. It was of the Armenian who had lived opposite them in Paris. She had cried so much for that old woman dying alone. For herself too, she had cried.

She looked through the window of the surgery and saw a group of people in the waiting room, chatting, leafing through magazines. She hesitated before opening the door. '*Bonjour,* Madame,' the receptionist said. She waved her hand vaguely in her direction as a return greeting. The idea of undergoing the prodding and intrusion of a doctor's examination wasn't pleasant. She considered leaving, but settled down on a chair by the magazine table. A poster about the risks associated with drinking was pinned to the wall opposite. The corners were bent back and shiny from the heads that had rested against it.

The doctor came through and mispronounced her name loudly. Elena stood.

'*Entrez, entrez,*' Dr Couret said, ushering her into his room. 'You're having problems with your stomach? Is that right?' He patted the raised bed in the corner and laid out a paper sheet on top. 'Let's have a look, then.'

She lay back on the bed and let the doctor lift her shirt until the hem of it fell across her chin. His hands were surprisingly warm. He felt her sides, ran his fingers along the lower ridge of her ribcage. She wanted to laugh and cry from his tickling.

'I can't feel anything abnormal,' he reassured her after a while. 'No swelling or tenderness.'

She sat up and pulled her shirt back down, rearranging her hair.

'Do you have a good appetite, Madame Carlevaris?'

'Yes.'

'But you have problems digesting, is that it?'

'I feel bloated after eating.'

'Have you tried varying your diet?'

'Yes.'

'Do you think your stomach aches could be psychosomatic?' he said after some hesitation.

Elena looked down at the carpet, then the doctor. She wouldn't let herself be intimidated by this man with his long fingers and confident, learned words.

'What do you mean?' she said. 'I don't understand what you're saying.'

'Might they be brought on by stress, somehow be related to what you're thinking?'

'No,' she cut in. 'No.'

'Are you sure?'

She knew what he was trying to get at, hoping to catch her out. She fixed him in the eye, making sure he blinked first. 'I'm quite sure,' she repeated.

As if she hadn't said anything, the doctor carried on. 'Would you say you were a depressive, Madame Carlevaris?'

'No,' she mumbled. 'I'd say I was like everyone else actually, normal, you know, up and down. We all are, aren't we?'

'I remember all those fertility tests. That's a hard thing to live through, not being able to have another child, and now your son being far away.'

Sensing Elena's mood darken, the doctor smiled. 'And how is young Marco? I haven't seen him in years. Is he enjoying Paris?' She didn't reply. Dr Couret leaned towards her. 'These are just questions to help you, Madame, you mustn't be offended. I'm trying to understand, it's my role, it's why I'm here. Your husband is very concerned about you. He says you've had bleak periods in the past.'

So that was it, Giacomo had mentioned more than the ulcer, behind her back.

'What,' she said, scowling, 'would the medical profession make of his sculptures?'

'We're talking about you.'

'Well, please tell me, what would a doctor think of a man who spends whole days chipping at pieces of wood that end up looking like corpses or parts of the body that are best left hidden?'

'I think you should consider taking some antidepressants,' Dr Couret said in a calm voice. 'I can guarantee they work. They would be a great relief to you.'

Elena was already at the door and through the waiting room, bidding the doctor farewell. She was not some banal depressive, some pathetic weakling. The truth, she wanted to tell the doctor, is not what you think. You know nothing of me or what I've been through! What do you care if my head is a mess? What does anyone care?

She walked out of the city walls, alongside the car park and onto the road towards the pottery. She stopped by a ditch in the marshes. She watched egrets, buffeted by the swell of the wind, jerk and twist in an effort to land. She noticed an animal's skull in the grass and thought of the butchered Italians of 1893, as if under the shifting reeds of the Camargue, and broken vases of the pottery, the bones and souls of her countrymen were stirring, spreading out a path for her feet.

42

Giacomo undressed on the coldness of the bathroom tiles and climbed into the bath. He closed his eyes, pushing down into the water, anticipating its comforting, warm rise to his neck. He lay still, as the window steamed up, the walls flowering with clear droplets. He looked down at his body, the wet, sparse hairs flat on his chest, his pale legs, his near-extinguished genitals, the ghostly shadow of himself, submerged. He rubbed the tips of his fingers together with soap, kneading and boring little holes in the bar with his nails. The water round him became tinged with clouds of red and grey. He rubbed again, unable to rid the lines of his hands of their years of engrained clay.

Since Djamel's arrival at the pottery, Giacomo often retreated upstairs to be alone. After his bath, he would put on a dressing gown and sit in Marco's bedroom to draw, or read, before Elena came in to sleep in her son's bed. It was there, at the desk by the window, that he decided to write to his nephew.

Marco, he began, *I have imagined this letter, or something like it, hundreds and hundreds of times. In my mind, I have written to you over* and over again. I understood immediately on your mother's return from Paris that her visit had brought no good. And, indeed, things have got worse since. Whatever I do, she reacts negatively. I can only wait, as usual, for this new storm to pass, but it has never been this bad. It has made me think that I should write. Where to start, beloved Marco? How to explain the things that need to be explained?

Perhaps I should tell you something of our childhood. When we were children, your father and I, there was only one road to the village of Pieria below. It was the way we went every Sunday to church, down a narrow path that clung to the mountain edge. When the sun was too strong, or the wind blowing, we would cover our faces with our hats, or remove the shirts from our backs to hold them up like kites. There was always a point where we would stop and watch the crows circling beneath us. They turned like falling leaves, round and round. When winter came, and the cold trapped us in our house, our father made us pray at home and all we could hear were those crows flying in a black whirlwind. One day a man, who'd been imprisoned abroad during the war, chased up the mountainside and shot all the crows, firing wildly, hunting them down to the last one. He couldn't stand the noise, we were told.

In the forests, your father and I searched for birds' nests in spring and waited patiently for the eggs to hatch. A week or so later, we would return and collect the featherless fledglings and watch as our mother fried them in a pan. It was the only meat we would have for days. We ate everything but the beaks, legs and all. Your father and I would climb the mountains for hours, up into the distances where the clouds broke on the sloping earth, till the houses vanished beneath us. The Carnia Mountains were our domain, our own, vast world. I always fought to keep up with your father and he would slip off sometimes, leaving me straggling behind, lost in the forests, or on a mountain face, until he sprang up unexpectedly, out of nowhere, laughing at his tricks. He would skip on brittle ledges next to ravines, enticing me to copy him. He'd climb trees and tease me from the top until I battled to reach him, whereupon he would swing to the next tree and slide back to the ground. Only at swimming could I beat him and, in the summer when we visited the lake, he avoided any races. Behind the house, I had a buried cache from our outings. I had the leg bone of a wild cat, your father a ripped map, a compass and a pair of shoes. He never told me where he got them from. He always hid his possessions in a corner of the barn.

When our Papa was dying, I remember being led into the cramped room behind the fireplace and listening to our mother telling the doctor we couldn't afford any more medicine. Our father, with his patchy beard, was lying with his head up against a pillow, and we knew that meant he was going to die in pain. A priest was called and, while he was on his way, our father's half-closed eyes became fixed and the short, sharp wheezing stopped. The room smelt of burnt wood. It was early spring. When I see an open fire I still sometimes think of him and how, as child, I believed his soul had left with the smoke up the chimney. With Papa's death, your father took over the running of the house, watching the cattle and goats. He moved into our parents' bed and our mother slept next to me round the fireplace. I used to hear her talk to herself at night, sitting up by the gaslight stitching clothes. Your father spoke of moving to a smaller house down in Pieria where our mother could earn money mending garments and we could get work more easily. Mother wouldn't hear of moving. She had spent forty years high up in the mountains – for her the village was too closed, too full of people and talk. She liked to look out of the window and see nothing but peaks, unwatched, alone. One winter, the barn where the cattle were kept at night burnt down. We never knew if it was lightning or the straw catching fire. Your father and I picked our way through the burnt carcasses, trying to find something we could salvage, but there was nothing. One calf had fought its way out under the door, only to die coughing fire in the field. It was decided that your father should leave to find work. That was 1963. He had always wanted to go to far-off

235

places. He'd always imagined, he said, making his fortune in Argentina like our cousin. He used to collect photos of the country. We knew of someone, though, who had gone to work at a sawmill in the region round Parma. That sounded like a better choice.

Our mother cried for two weeks before his departure. I held the dangling strap of your father's bag all the way to the station with my mother's faltering steps behind me. When I breathe in deeply enough, even now, I like to think I can awaken the smell of that leather strap on my hand. He was going to come back soon, my mother told him at the station, but I already knew that everything was about to change. Our mother was only convincing herself. She gave him a spare key to the house, an iron key with a long handle like a tail. I have that key somewhere. I can show it to you. You should have it in fact. I suppose it is now yours, though the house has been sold. It may sound strange to you in Paris, with the money you're used to having, but we only just managed to scrape enough together for your father's ticket to Parma. My mother cheered him by saying that life for him would be better near Parma than in New York, Australia, London, Paris or Argentina, all those places where thousands of Italians worked as muratori, *builders and plasterers, but those were precisely the places your father wanted to visit.*

With the money your father sent home, we were able to stretch our food further, afford new things. Our mother fell ill that winter, complaining of chest pains. Your father had been working in the village of Varanelle some time. I tried to get word through to him that she had been taken sick. The doctor said her heart was giving out. I took her down to Udine for treatment, to the hospital. She asked me to open the windows to see the mountains in the distance, but there was nothing to see, only the backs of buildings, their angles and tiled roofs. The mountains are there, I told her as she died, the mountains are there, and Riccardo is on his way.

It was from Udine that I departed for Paris myself, at the age of eighteen, on my first train ride, my first trip beyond Friuli. I left one day early in 1965, nearly a year after our mother's death. Life had been lonely up in the house above the village. Looking back, I find it hard to understand why I didn't look for a solution nearer home, but I was being pressured by a nearby landowner into selling the remains of the barn and our house. I sold it to him for a pittance. I tried to stand up to his bargaining and veiled threats, but he had no time for my protests. The house, the man said, was barely worth the ground it stood on. That was perhaps true, but it was still a house, all that we had then. If your father had been there, things might have been different, but he hadn't even come home for our mother's funeral and I'd heard nothing from him in months. Besides, there was work to be had in Paris and I needed to buy a ticket. I went ahead with the price I'd been offered. I knew a man from Tolmezzo who'd settled in Paris and he was encouraging people to join him in his business. I sewed my money into the lining of my coat for the journey. I can still see that final day in Pieria as if it were today, how I took every-thing in for the last time: the houses, trees and fresh scented air. The faces of the people on the roads to the station were like masks. Initially, I stopped to say goodbye, then people became uncomfortable, with sadness or envy, I was never sure.

When I left Friuli, I felt I was leaving life itself behind. I reached Paris after a three-day trip. In my pocket I had an address. If I got lost, the man from Tolmezzo had written, I only had to ask for the main square in Clichy. It was a direct enough walk from there. If that didn't work, I could make my way to a church where the cleaner was Italian and ask again. I spent a day finding the house in Clichy. It was a run-down building split into several sleeping rooms. A basic kitchen and bathroom were on the ground floor. My room was at the top, under the eaves, next to a landing where electrical wires poked through the floorboards. The room was bare except for a bed with a mirror on the wall beside it and a cupboard. I waited for the man from Tolmezzo in that room, scarcely venturing onto the landing, not daring to leave the building in case I got lost. The man finally arrived, dressed in overalls, and greeted me with a loud 'Bonjour'. I can't tell you how that unknown French salutation shocked and threw me. I nodded back and he broke into Friulano dialect. I grasped at our language after my three-day trip, its familiar comforting sounds. I asked too many questions: where would we be working; how much did we get paid? Did he like Paris? The man said he'd explain all that later, he didn't have time then. If I wanted food, he told me, there was bread in the kitchen and I could buy basics in the shop three streets away. He put a French banknote on the bed and left. There was nothing rich about him, his overalls were as shabby as the clothes the men wore at home. My room was barely fit for animals.

I walked down to the washroom on the ground floor. A queue was forming outside the door. The other men said nothing, turning from my nervous smiles. When I introduced myself, they nodded as if they knew who I was already and had no wish to find out more. Back in my room, I tried to get comfortable on the bed, hoisting a blanket off the top of the cupboard, covering myself in it. It had the same rough feel as the cover my father used for his horse in winter. I tried to imagine the warmth of the stable, the cattle barn, the bittersweet pungent dung and behind it the mountains above Pieria. I couldn't sleep. I was so afraid Marco, so afraid. I started to cry. I hadn't cried that much since childhood. That was my first night in Paris.

Giacomo stopped writing. He turned the page over, studied what he had written, frowned and buried his head in his hands. He folded the sheet of paper neatly and put it inside a red-covered book. He took a new piece of paper. He exhaled, pushed the pen into his mouth and bit down on the plastic, scraping it along his teeth. He stood, walked round the room, pulled at his hair, rubbed the back of his neck. He went back to the table and sat down.

Marco, he wrote once more, *my old world began to crumble that very* first night in Paris. I realized that I had left home and no matter what I did I would never be able to go back. I mean I could have gone back, but I understood, even then, that I wouldn't be the same person again. I recall thinking that if I'd returned to Pieria, there would have been nothing left standing. The landscape would have been stripped, gaping holes in every place I'd known and been to. I lay wondering about this, on the bed on the far side of that room in Paris, and stared at the money the Friulano had lent me, rolling it between my fingers.

I worked a year with the man from Tolmezzo. I built up a life and had a little money coming in every month. I learned about masonry and mosaics. I enjoyed the mathematical precision with which colours were placed against each other, fitted into gaps like a puzzle, the way they revealed hidden shapes and figures. I soon had a good enough reputation to be able to decorate bathrooms and kitchens at weekends. People came and asked for me, but it was hard work and the money, I knew, wasn't good enough. A couple of co-workers put me in contact with a factory that needed people with my skills. It made bricks and fancy bits of masonry like cornicing. I was told I could do mosaics if the demand was created. Work at the factory was sometimes gruelling, but it was better paid. There were tough jobs, like carting building materials, roof tiles and breeze-blocks, but I stuck to it.

Out of the blue, I received news that your father was on his way from Varanelle to join me in Paris. He had sent a message via the man from Tolmezzo. I waited several days, nervous with anticipation. I didn't know why he was coming, or what he wanted from me. Things had always been complicated between us, but I was the only family he had left. In Friuli, he had tolerated me, viewed me as a young follower when it suited him, but the rest of the time he ignored me. I'd always treated him like my parents, giving in to his demands, in fact more than my parents as I was the youngest. Perhaps Paris, I thought, was going to be a chance for us to change all that. I cleaned out my room, installed a mattress in the corner, *organized work for him at the factory. He arrived late one evening. It was more than three years since we'd seen each other. He greeted me warmly. I expected to find the same brother I'd seen leave Friuli. I discovered a new person. He looked taller and the lines to the sides of his mouth were more marked. He was awkward, out of place in the city, edgy, both foreigner and newcomer. I was used to watching him master the rock faces of our mountains, stride across steep grassy terrain with the cattle, not sitting under the eaves of a Paris house. He told me about his new wife, his plans for settling in Argentina, and the forthcoming birth of his child. He kept on standing and looking out of the window and I thought of myself a couple of years or so earlier, overcome by the same unfamiliar noises and smells. I had since worked out a way of being in Paris. I could negotiate the confusion of it, the chaos, but, for him, it was all disorientating. I did my best to explain, but all he wanted to know was how much he would be paid at the factory. It wasn't long before he asked for his share of the money from the sale of the house. I said I had divided the money up fairly already. He insisted I give him more immediately. I had other money I had made from working. I reached into the back of the cupboard and lifted a loose plank with my penknife. I kept my money there. I said I could help him out if he wanted, but I'd got just as much as him from the house. I gave him a wad of notes. He counted them out. 'I'll be needing more than that,' he said. He was upset. 'How's it possible for a house to be worth so little?' he asked angrily. I said we had been foolish to think we could get much for it. His voice grew louder. He wouldn't have been cheated like a child he said. It was my fault for not fighting enough. I had messed things up, and thrown away the only opportunity he'd ever had. He would make more in Paris, I told him, but all I wanted to ask him was why he had never come back to see our mother or attended her funeral, and why was I only now discovering he was married? When had the wedding taken place? Who was his wife? I offered him my bed to sleep in and I made him supper. He lay on the bed in silence and went to sleep in his clothes. He didn't eat.*

Your father got a job on a building site where the factory delivered materials. He worked hard at the beginning, earning the respect of the foreman. I saw the way he observed his new environment. The city slowly caught him in its claws. I volunteered to show him areas I knew, the shops, the parks, or the way the Metro system worked. He didn't like the fact that his younger brother was more knowledgeable than him. We made several trips together, but he gradually shook off my offers of help, and made a point of finding things out on his own. He became acquainted with people I'd never seen. Within three months, I heard, with amazement, how he could have a basic conversation in French. Your gift for languages, Marco, definitely comes from him. He began to negotiate the city with skill. It was he, in fact, who showed me places I didn't know. He liked the bars and cobbled streets near Montmartre. He took me to a vineyard there and we ate bread and cheese together perched on a wall. In the place du Châtelet, he liked to sit and watch the crowds go by. He had never encountered so many different types of people and clothes. I was impressed by his ease with strangers, the way he could attract attention in the street, make shopkeepers laugh, ensuring he always got what he wanted. Sometimes I would find myself running behind him, fighting to catch up, watching him charge ahead, through Paris, a tall silhouette in the crowd, and it was as if we were back in Friuli all over again, just that the rocky ledges had turned to buildings. All the time, though, he was looking for ways to get to Argentina.

I often had an hour or two in the room before your father returned from work. I was hanging my jacket in the cupboard we shared when I came across a photograph of a young woman, more beautiful than anyone I'd ever seen. Her eyes and hair were the colour of coal, like a creature from the spirit world of my childhood, frail and strong at the same time. Her neck was slender and smooth. Her head was leaning to the side, two drop shapes, like tears, as earrings. The photograph had a stamp on the back from a studio in Bardi, Provincia di Parma. It was the first time I saw your mother and I removed the photo from the wardrobe and held it in my disbelieving hands. I carried it to the light and watched how the naked bulb made the young woman's face glow; her hair seemed to move, glistening with blackness. When your father came home, he changed out of his dirty clothes, shaved and put on a white shirt. He said he was going out for the evening. He had a meeting in a café with people who knew about Argentina. As he was leaving, he told me not to fiddle with his things in future. I asked him what he meant and he said, 'The photograph, don't touch it.' I stood in front of him, disconcerted. 'She's very beautiful,' I managed to say. 'Just don't touch my things,' he repeated. 'Get yourself your own woman if you can.' And he closed the door. Despite his warnings, I went back to the photograph in the cupboard, again and again, and stared at it endlessly. There were evenings when I put it up against the windowpane and watched the city's reflections adorn her head like a halo.

Weeks went by and your father showed no sign of returning to Italy for your birth. He had decided, with your mother, he told me, to go straight to Argentina. He had found a cheap ticket on a boat. It was an opportunity he couldn't miss. He had met a man who knew people selling land in Argentina, others who had found ways of importing goods. He gave me an address and told me to send his wife money from time to time until he had made enough himself in Argentina. It was money I still owed him, he made sure I understood. I watched your father pack to leave, and put Elena's picture into his wallet.

Letters arrived for him after his departure, more and more of them, in the same perfectly formed writing, neat and practised, like that of a child. I hesitated some time before opening them. In one was a photograph of you, just a few months old, alongside your mother, the same dark eyes. I placed you in my pocket and no-one in Paris, apart from me, knew of your existence. You were my secret child. So many letters came and with each one, I discovered more about your mother. I didn't know what to do. She hoped I would forward them to your father while he was at sea, but I *didn't yet have an address in Argentina. I did as my brother had asked. I put money in an envelope and sent it to Varanelle. A month later I sent some more, this time with a card. It took me days to choose it. It was of the vineyard in Montmartre at harvest time. Women and men in loose clothing held baskets of grapes and the white Basilica of the Sacré Coeur stood in the background. Elena never wrote again. I supposed your father had sent an address in Argentina for his post, possibly the garage where he had ended up working. I sent her another envelope of money and then another, but there were no replies. I went back to her first letters to your father. Between each of her carefully written and rehearsed words was a well of unspoken frustration. Yet the pages were filled with such messages of love that they were a wonder to read. To be loved by a woman such as her was beyond my reach, something, I knew, I could never have. I sensed though, that I could give that kind of love myself, to someone resembling her. Not being able to send letters, I invented replies instead, and wrote to Elena in imagined words. At night, I prayed to the Lord to protect her. She became the bearer of my fragile dreams. It was she who, despite myself, fired my longing for a better future. It was she who gave me the strength to live alone and so far from everything I knew.*

Giacomo tightened his dressing-gown cord. He stretched his limbs, shook his hand. He banged the pen on the desk, digging miniscule holes into the wood. He began to write again.

How can I tell you, Marco, about your father and all that it is going to mean to you, all the things that happened? Your father returned from Argentina three years later, without warning. He hammered on my door in the early hours of the morning. He was impeccably dressed; hair cropped short, hands clean and soft. He was tired, he said, very tired. The exhaustion on his face was obvious. I served him some food and gave him my bed. He needed money badly. He had run up debts. I gave him what

I could. I assured him the factory would take him on again, if he wanted. He said he had been cheated in Argentina. His investments had turned out to be a scam. The land he bought never belonged to him. He fell into a sinister mood as he spoke, lighting up cigarettes in quick succession, and I let him be for fear of upsetting him further. The next day he stayed in the room sleeping. I provided him with food, and warmer clothes which he didn't wear.

He accepted work at the factory straight away. I saw him eating lunch on his own, shunning the company of our co-workers. I set off to join him then decided against it. He acknowledged me, but it was as if he wasn't there. Those weeks after your father's return from Argentina are a memory of silence for me. I could see that my presence was a burden to him, his work at the factory a constant reminder of his failure in Argentina and our humble beginnings in Friuli; all the things he had once been. He hated the idea of being back with me, doing menial tasks. In his head, he was no longer a labourer. He had worn elegant suits, he said, listened to singers at pianos, danced and talked with rich people in Buenos Aires. I became even more unsure of what to say to him, inadequate in front of the foreigner my brother had become. When I mentioned you and your mother, he said he would only return to Italy when he had enough money to show Elena. He told me he missed you without knowing you, and thought about you constantly. Yet with the money I gave him, he went out in the evenings, bought new clothes, refused to accept that he was back at the factory. He was meticulous about hanging up all his clothes. He polished his shoes every morning and talked again of new business plans.

At weekends he would seek out old acquaintances and he came back to our room full of plans of how he would return to Argentina and reclaim his money. There was little communication between us most of the time. I had no choice but to watch this change in him and shelter myself in my work, because I understood then that the hostility and distrust he had felt towards me as a child hadn't gone away. Those very sentiments had flared up again, and he found them hard to hide. Now he hated me for helping him, for being there behind him all the time, watching his failure, offering advice. He hated me for witnessing his distress and broken pride, and for knowing, unlike everyone else, that he had a wife and child waiting for him. I saw the games we played as children in their true light, the way he used to dare me out onto mountain ledges, bet that I couldn't recover a stone he threw to the bottom of the lake. He knew that I would have done anything for him to like me; that was the way of our childhood, the way it had always been. When you were a boy, Marco, I told you about an occasion in a cave. I said your father put on a ram's skull to frighten me. What I didn't say is that he left me in that cave, in the labyrinth of tunnels, and returned home. I would have done anything for his admiration back then and I humiliated myself so many times to earn his esteem. In Paris, I wanted to talk to your father as an equal for the first time. He told me that I knew nothing, understood nothing. I hear those words over and over again, and I feel that he was right. I still don't understand.

I was woken one night by your father returning to our lodgings. New smells entered the room, the peppery hot breath of beer, scent and the smoke of cigarettes. Your father was talking. A woman stood by the door, wrapped in an overcoat. I slid under my cover shielding my eyes from the light on the landing. Your father motioned through the door and the young woman walked in. He invited her onto his bed. She kept on looking over towards the mattress in the corner, to my bed, and I pretended to be asleep, the blanket over my head. I watched your father kiss and cup her body, and I felt a rage and indignation that were chased by a more desperate, faster urge to see a woman undressed for the first time, to hear the sounds of her body revealed. They took off their clothes. They climbed onto the bed, warm, easy shapes of bucking and twisting. She pushed him against the pillow. From the floor where I lay, I could feel the room shift and shudder to the figure of their movements. The girl's brown hair covered my brother's face, obscuring him. She turned to the side and, I was sure, *she was looking at me, her eyes fixed on me. She spread her arms out, her hands dipping into the dimly lit space between us. I removed the blanket covering my face so I could look at her. She held my stare and it was as if she were pulling me towards her, as if my arms were gripping her nakedness, and the heat of her skin were cloaking me. Afterwards, as your father stood with the woman, their bare, sweat-covered bodies exposed, kissing, I felt myself trembling, fighting against a rising confusion inside me.*

I never mentioned your father's night visitors, never alluded to them in our rare conversations. Their number and frequency steadily increased after his return to Paris, as did his drinking. There was a fat man from Naples in our building called Gennaro. 'You know the girls love us here,' he joked during my first days in Paris, 'you only have to click your fingers if you're Italian, snap, snap and they come, boum, boum, bang, bang, and it's done. È vero, it's true, they come running, come le mosche, like flies on a dog turd! It's even better in London, you should see them there.' How many times in those few weeks did I listen to gasps and laughter under the sheets of my own bed? There was Micheline, a red-haired, slim girl, Diane, Pauline and others, countless names, too numerous to mean anything, names that were forgotten, names that were never asked, invented even. How many times did I wake my brother in the morning with cold water on his face, gently shaking the frightened shoulder of a sleeping partner? The girls were surprised to see me, another man, an awkward younger brother, rising from a bed in the corner, offering them coffee or a glass of water as they sat naked, struggling to get dressed with me standing beside them. Often your father would still be drunk in the mornings and shout angrily at me if I made too much noise or dared speak to the girls.

I was sometimes afraid, but, still, when I could, I protected him from the vicious remarks of our fellow workers who talked about him behind his back. I came up with excuses to the factory and continued to clean the room and provide food, working twice as hard as I ever had. Your father shrugged off my fussing, telling me I was obviously still stuck in my village ways. Did I want the same miserable life as our parents? he asked. Was I going to be a slave to others all my life, never free, never myself? Unlike me, he had seen fabulous cities and distant countries. The world, he said, was a bigger place than I thought. Why, he added, didn't I have a girlfriend? What was wrong with me? Was I not a man yet, or perhaps I was becoming the girl our mother always wanted? My sister, he called me more than once in those days, my little sister. Other times he was unexpectedly friendly, as if he regretted his previous moods, needed to confide in someone, or even ask my opinion. He told me there was an area of Buenos Aires that looked like Paris under the burning South American sun, the sea up the coast the colour of a bird's eggshell. He said things would have been different had I been able to come with him to Argentina or if I'd managed to sell our house for a decent amount of money in the first place. Together, we could have found a way of turning that sum into something that really worked, something that could have completely changed our lives. 'You'll never know what loneliness I felt there,' he said to me too, 'a terrible separation from the world.' I told I did know, I'd been in Paris, alone, long enough, but he shook his head. 'Over there, over the ocean, it's different. On the boat, looking at the empty seas you're nothing and it's the same when you arrive, and when you're lost you've got nothing to hold onto.' He had a wife and child to get back to, I said, that must have helped him. Again, he shook his head and I didn't understand. 'You think that helps,' he said, 'it only makes it worse.' Then, when I wasn't expecting it, he announced he was heading back to Varanelle.

There isn't a day when I don't go over these events, feel overcome by a rush of recollections and its chain of accompanying images that refuse to slip away. The only consolation of that period was that photograph of your mother that had returned with your father. When he slept, I took it from his wallet again and held it with all my might. It hadn't faded in three years. In fact the surfaces shone brighter than ever, as if the radiance

of the sea or the warmth of Argentina had made her features blaze.
Speak to me, Elena, I would say, speak, tell me what to do!

Marco, I've tried to extinguish this pain by loving your mother, your
father's wife, and loving you, his son. When I was at my lowest point, your
mother and you arrived in Paris. Your mother was so beautiful it took
everyone's breath away. She came from pristine mountains like me,
landscapes I thought I'd forgotten in the dirt of Paris. She spoke the
language of someone who'd never seen the world, my former, precious
tongue. She was broken and grieving, and so was I, for so many reasons I
couldn't admit to her. She loved your father. She loves him still. I will
always be second to him. I have had to accept that. Over the years, though,
her mounting bitterness has soured my attempts at mending her dreams. If
we'd managed to have children, things would have been different. I believe
life would have treated us less harshly. Since your leaving, she thinks that
amassing money through the pottery is the only way left to make her happy,
but it won't help her. She doesn't want to understand the beauty of the
world or the work I have tried to fill our home with, or even the love that
could have united us. It was the same with her naive wish to emigrate to
America that poisoned our early days together. I always knew, unlike
many Italians I met abroad, that I couldn't go back home. What was I
going to do in Pieria, up in the mountains, especially after our mother's
death? People, up there, aren't very tolerant of dreamers and wanderers,
but that didn't mean I was going to get lost in America or Argentina, all
those far-off places your mother pined for but was terrified of visiting
alone. I searched for a harbour for the three of us, a quiet, safe world, here
in the Camargue, somewhere to feel secure. France was perfect for us. It
feels more like my country now than Italy. It has served you well too,
embraced you, but that wasn't enough for Elena. She always had an eye
looking backwards into the past; it blinded her to the possibilities of the
future. She imprisoned herself in self-imposed limits. Sometimes I catch a
bitter grimace of resentment on her face and it travels through me,

consumes me. There are days when I feel crushed. What, I wonder, will it take for her to see me?

I must carry on though, because I love her, because I love you. I took to you immediately, my nephew, and longed to be the father you were missing. Your mother often tried to wrench you away, threatening to leave, or saying I had no rights over you, but it was as if you were mine from the moment we met. You looked nothing like your father as a child. In fact, straight away, people remarked on how much you looked like me and that was confirmation that you were always meant to be my son, that we were two of a kind. It was Elena who was sometimes the odd one out. Yes, it's true. It was like she had brought you to me. Our union was no coincidence. I know all these trials have existed to fulfil a life for you. This is why things have turned out the way they have. We could have been happy though, truly happy, us three, and I think at times at the beginning we were, on those picnics, travelling around in the van, but Elena chose not to stay that way. She clung to the dead, blaming me for her discontent.

Sometimes, at the bleakest of moments, however, I look back and fear that Elena is right, that this has all been my fault, that I hid behind my brother, used his love for her to disguise my own, and I can hardly bear the weight of it. Did I usurp my brother's place, was I too greedy for a family and a wife? Did I take something that wasn't mine to take, did I steal your lives for myself? Yes, I did covet my brother's wife, I did desire her well before your father died. I was jealous of him, in my very bones, of the effect he had on people, especially women, of his stature and sense of freedom. I wanted to rescue her, and you, for myself. These things won't leave me alone. And yet if I'd shaken off my brother's shadow, and said what I knew, I would have lost her, and you, for ever.

Please know, in the midst of all this, my dearest Marco, that you are my son, my only, beloved son. When I see your achievements, I know it's all been worthwhile. Your mother and I have tried to make you content in our different ways. You are all that we have, the sole future of our lives.

You are a remarkable boy, more intelligent than we could have ever hoped for. You are stronger than all of us put together. I love your knowledge. I couldn't begin to describe the world with such precision and detail. Your telephone calls and cards are like chapters of books for me. I try to find elegance in my words, ways to match my ideas, the bursts of emotions inside me, but it's only when hacking away at wood, or following the circular movement of the pottery wheel, that it all makes sense. Only then do I manage to forget, and become absorbed by other things.

Forgive me this outburst. If you were ever to reject me or stop loving me because of what I've told you, I wouldn't be able to bear it. I wouldn't survive. I say that very clearly. The fear that you would spurn me, love me less if you came to know your father's failings, and my connection to them, has followed me every day for the last twenty or so years, and prevented me from speaking. Forgive me, forgive your father. He loved your mother, he loved you, of that I'm sure, but he was running with the world, desiring things he couldn't have. All he wanted at heart was a different life than the miserable existence our parents had lived, but he wanted it all, and he wanted it without any concession, straight away. He could never stick at anything or see problems through. That was just the way he was.

I didn't need to say all this to you, I have managed to carry it on my own, often with great difficulty, but maybe it's better you know why things are the way they are, why they've always been so. I must warn you that your mother still has many brittle memories from that period of her life. She never talks about such things as her father's violence and awkward love for her, or your father's death, but I know they are always with her. Just as her father has never forgiven her, she won't forget. She would be devastated to be asked certain questions or to know that you've found out so much without her, through me. We have never spoken of these matters. To her, your father was the perfect husband, taken away from her, sacrificed for money, eternally young. To you, he was the character of your childhood stories, the name you attached to the heroes of your books and games.

What else could I have done than to encourage such things, to push life forward, again and again? Please promise me that your mother will be left out of this. She is filled with such uneasiness these days. I worry about what she might do. All my love, and more.

Giacomo sat up. He was cold despite the heat outside. He pulled his dressing-gown cord tighter. It was late. Elena would be waiting with the supper. He looked at the last sheets of paper he had just filled with such urgency. He read and reread them, crossing out and rewriting, scribbling new words in the margins. He stopped, rested his head in the palms of his hands and scratched his hair. He picked up the first sheet of paper tucked in the red book on the desk, describing his childhood and his early years in Friuli. He verified each line, signed his name at the bottom of the paper, surrounded his signature with a doodle of a bird landing, feet stretched downwards, folded it and placed it in an envelope which he addressed to Marco. He sealed it, rummaged through the desk until he found a stamp and stuck it on the front. He took the remaining papers, the passages about Riccardo in Paris, the women, the explanations he had stored up and repeated for years. He ran his eyes over the mass of lettering. He stared blankly at the desk, his head held low. His eyes filled with tears. He sat still for a while and then took the sheets and ripped them up into equal strips.

He gathered the pieces together and entered the bathroom. With the flame from the boiler, he set fire to each strip of paper and dropped them, one by one, into the lavatory and pulled the chain. He opened the window to get rid of the smoke. He hung up his dressing gown, pulled on his underpants, his socks, trousers and shirt. He went down the corridor towards the kitchen, hesitated and then hurried back to the bathroom. He lifted the lavatory seat again, peered inside to check it was clean. It was white, shining, except for a charred and weightless ribbon of paper which rose up out of the bowl, floating into the room. Giacomo caught it and crushed it, wiping the ash on his trousers. Elena was dishing out their supper with the television in the background. The sound of it was barely audible over the rush of the bathroom tank refilling.

43

A night insect with bow legs and folded wings crawled along the corridor ceiling. It reached the edge of a beam and dropped onto the floor. Giacomo padded into Marco's room and hovered by the bed. Elena was asleep. Her hair was bunched in thick circles over her shoulders. Strands fell across her forehead. He knelt down and contemplated the skin of her cheeks, her closed eyes. The nearer he knelt, the more her scent hit him. The warmth of her breathing prickled his face. He pulled the sheet from her chest, centimetre by centimetre, lifting it upwards between trembling fingers. Her neck gleamed with sweat. Her breasts were pressed into her nightdress. The shadows of her brown nipples coloured the thin fabric.

'What are you doing?' Elena sat up with a start, knocking Giacomo's chin backwards.

'I'm sorry,' he blurted, holding his arms out, 'sorry.'

'Get out!'

'You don't understand.' He clambered onto the bed. 'I want to be with you.'

'No.'

He searched for her hands under the sheets, caressing her legs. 'I can't bear this any longer, Elena, my Elena, please.' He kissed her and nudged her necklace to one side, leaning his face against the softness of her stomach, touching her shoulders. She held him back and he switched the bedside light on to talk to her. It shone yellow behind its shade, blinding Elena. She closed her eyes. The flickering imprint of the bulb stayed inside her pupils, then it dimmed and blurred and, the more she focused on it, the faster it slipped away, until it became indistinct from the warm sensation on her cheek.

'Don't kiss me,' she said, opening her eyes.

'Why are you turning me into something I'm not?'

'Leave me alone, Giacomo.'

'Please, can't we be together?'

'What do you want from me?'

'I'm your husband, for goodness' sake.'

'My husband,' she said, pushing him off the bed, 'died a long time ago.'

Giacomo stood up, his face reddening. 'And still you haven't understood a thing about him, have you? Nothing. You've no idea who he was!' he spat. He turned and rushed through the door, slamming it with all his might.

Elena tugged the sheet over her head and pressed it against her face, rubbing her ears, as if wiping away the words she had heard. She stumbled from the bed and down the corridor. She grappled for a coat by the front door and a pair of shoes. She made for the courtyard below. A troop of sculptures greeted her: shapes of defeated lovers, women and men, bodies of disproportionate limbs. She darted through them to the edge of the back garden. Clouds of insects gathered round the street lamps on the road. They collided in the sky, swirling in hazy circles, briefly connecting rings in the evening air. She stood at the side of the road, unsure which direction to take. She ran through a gate, towards the troughs where the horses came to drink. Her heart was pounding. A stitch pierced her side. She found an overturned trough and sat down on it. She regained her breath, got up and carried on. She followed a barely visible dirt path, on and on, past the rice fields. She no longer knew where she was. She spun round on herself and walked the other way.

The bouncing beam of a torch approached over the fields. She knew immediately it was Giacomo. Why was he always two steps behind her? She joined a new path towards the canal ahead and began to run as fast as she could along the towpath. She came to a narrow concrete ledge that turned into a mud track, knocking stones into the water as she went. She heard them drop, rippling the calm surface. She could hear cars on the road in the distance. A cow lowed in a nearby field, she couldn't tell from which angle. She saw the outline of the Tour de la Carbonnière, a tower on the road to Saint Laurent d'Aigouze. She advanced towards it, comforted by its familiarity, skirting the dips and mounds of the marsh. Her foot slipped down a hole. She bit her hand to muffle the pain. She pulled herself up onto a clump of reeds and rubbed her ankle. There were holes everywhere. She hobbled on, tripping and splashing into an expanse of shallow water. The ground was swampy beneath her. She tried to turn back and sank. She got up and fell again. Her hands grappled with the mud around her, skidded and slid. She crawled along onto a more solid bed of reeds. She had to keep calm. Mosquitoes filled her ears with noise, picking at her face.

Surrounded by obscurity, she found herself picturing the massacred Italians of 1893. She chased the idea from her, but she had built up the scenes all too clearly. The workers' clothes, she imagined, had been the same for days at a time, unwashed tastes, crusts of bitter salt on the skin. Their hair was thick with it, stiff and solidified; a soft cushion for the knives and bludgeons. She pushed on towards the Tour de la Carbonnière. She had only gone a few metres when she sank back into the earth. This time it pulled at her knees, dragged her down. The awkward lacework of one of Giacomo's sculptures passed through her head, her own skin the leathery tan of beaten bark. She had to get out of the water. Then more images of the Italians came with increasing urgency, pushing at her. Gangs of armed men chanted, swinging batons and tools to cut the air, to crush Italian heads. Giacomo's torch beam swept the fields behind her. The water was eating at her waist. She could feel it readying to welcome her. Her chest hurt, her breathing uncertain. She gagged, over and over, expelling the remnants of her supper, emptying her stomach of its bile. Her body sank into the reeds, she dug at the sandy earth and it filtered through her fingers; fibrous meshes of roots gave way under her. She took a deep breath. It was fleeing from her, the sense of order, of time; all blurring, the past, the smells and coughed-back feelings. Her body felt like a sapless stalk, her mouth pasty and thick. Water pushed into the pockets and lining of her coat, coming in waves of warmth and coldness. A bird was thrashing in the marsh next to her, dipping and rising, the smell of its wetness reached her. The mud pushed at her face and smeared her tongue with grit. A voice, shouts and more noises came. The mud burned. She could no longer feel anything. She tried to tug herself upwards, letting out a loud cry, pulling, crawling, but she was sucked back down. She clutched at sharp roots that lacerated her palms and wrists. These new wounds stung and bit, forcing her to let go. Her mouth filled with water, soaking into her eyes. The light of a torch stroked the reeds in front of her. Giacomo cleared a passage through the reeds, grabbed her hands and wrenched her out of the water.

'I'm here,' he said, tightening his grip on her.

At the pottery, Giacomo opened the shower and led her under it. He adjusted the nozzle and directed the jet of water against the fine grains of sand stuck to her back, rubbing her neck as he went. Streaks of dirt whirled round her feet, sliding down the plughole. Giacomo washed Elena's shoulders, splashing her stomach and chest with soap. He straightened her neck and, with cupped hands, poured water over her hair, lathering in squirts of shampoo. His fingers caught on knots of black hair and he unwound each one, his own clothes drenched. He worked traces of mud out of her ears, from the corners of her eyes. Elena bent her mouth upwards at the shower, opening it to receive the spray of warm water. She closed her eyes, her mouth and throat spilling with a gargling moan. Giacomo switched off the shower and fetched a towel. The last drops of water gathered under the showerhead and fell onto Elena's hair. He led her to their room and she dropped backwards onto the bed.

Elena looked at Giacomo unable to speak. Should she ask him to leave, or thank him for saving her? She didn't know. She had never known. She shivered; goose pimples forming on her arms and legs. Giacomo turned the television on and tucked a sheet over her. 'What do we do now?' she asked as he left the room, but he didn't hear. The screen lit up with a car being chased by another down a road that could have been America, France, Italy, anywhere.

Dr Couret arrived in the morning. Elena heard him ask Giacomo whether the cuts on her wrists were self-inflicted. He prescribed a combination of antidepressants and installed a chair for her on the balcony. As she weeded the window-boxes, she thought that her time in the Camargue had been one slow migration, a trajectory of a few metres from the showroom to this balcony, a platform of rusty railings and shrivelled plants ready to peel off the face of the building in expectation of her decline.

Plates were being stacked in the kitchen behind her. Water ran in the sink. 'Nassima,' she called. There was no reply. The radio came on and a plaintive woman's voice, in Arabic, floated into the corridor. Elena listened, the taste of her new pills in her mouth. The song cut at her, spreading its notes and incomprehensible words into a pattern of sorrow she recognized. The song was for her, and Nassima, for all women waiting on the wrong side of the past.

PART TEN

Paris, May 1996

44

The delegates walked through the hall by the main amphitheatre, underneath posters proclaiming: *International Conference, New Patterns of Migration: a Challenge for the World, UNESCO, 27–30 May 1996.* To the side of the hall was an exhibition room with stands displaying photos of refugee camps, next to shots of Tibetan children studying in crowded schools. The conference's final speeches came to an end. Several resolutions were voted. Publications were promised. Ambassadors and members of international non-governmental organizations mingled with UNESCO staff. A tea-lady with a trolley came out of a side door and a steady stream of people headed in her direction to scramble for the limited cups of coffee and tea on offer.

'I think we've done it,' Marco smiled at Laura. 'It's been a huge success.'

She shrugged. 'I don't know; it's always a bit of an anticlimax after these things isn't it? I'm never sure what good they do at the end of the day.'

'That's not what you said before. You heard all those ministers pledging a different approach to asylum seekers, more humane border controls. And those funds they promised from the European Union…'

'They say that at every conference. You believe all that?'

'Of course.'

'Um, you'll see, they want to look good in front of each other. Those funds won't materialize.'

'That's so cynical. I'm sorry; I really think we've achieved something.'

'Fatoumata called me this morning.'

'And?'

'She received an official letter asking her to come in for a meeting, but she thinks it's a trap and she'll get sent back home. Poor woman is beside herself. I gave her some money for the kids.'

'What's she going to do?'

'She's thinking of joining a protest group.'

'For what?'

'A large group of Africans are going to squat in the St Bernard Church. Some of them are even thinking of going on hunger strike.'

'But that's ridiculous.'

'Why?'

'Well, what good is that going to achieve?'

'It might make people wake up.'

'To what?'

'To the fact that other human beings in this city have absolutely no rights at all.'

'I hope you dissuaded Fatoumata.'

'Course not. I think she's at the end of her tether.'

'You want to get her into trouble?'

'Sometimes, I don't understand you, Marco. You seem to care, then you don't. It's all some kind of a game for you.'

'You're playing with fire. Fatoumata thinks you can help her, but you can't. This is a huge problem, not something you can solve.'

'Why? Why can't I help her? I have to try, don't I? Isn't that better than just leaving the poor woman to rot, without any papers, or a roof over her head…'

'Sorry, if you'll excuse me. I've got to talk to this guy.'

She looked up to see Amani approaching with the French education minister. 'I'll leave you to grease up to the people that count then,' Laura sneered. 'That's obviously more important to you.'

'Laura, wait!' Marco protested, but his hand was already being grasped and firmly shaken by the minister.

'I've been told of your efforts. You did an excellent job, Monsieur Carlevaris. Thank you.'

Laura stood in the photocopying room on the fourth floor, a stack of draft final resolutions from the conference in front of her. She finished a cup of water from the drinking fountain. Through the window, she could see the array of different national flags along the streets spearing the summer sky. She scrunched the plastic cup in her fist, and dropped it in the bin and returned to the photocopier. Milena, a secretary she knew, walked past.

'*Quelle tête d'enterrement!*' she said, 'You look miserable. Everything OK, Laura?'

Laura pressed the button on the machine, her face illuminated by a spray of flashing light. She waited for the secretary to leave. The woman carried on standing there, arms crossed, expecting an answer.

'I'm fine, thanks Milena,' she muttered.

'No, you're not, look at you. Didn't the conference go well?'

Before she knew it, Laura was flipping paper in and out of the machine, stabbing at the start button. Between jets of green light and noise, she explained to a woman the age of her mother, someone she saw once a week for a few minutes only, that she was beginning to feel as if she barely knew the man she loved, as if the past two or so years of their relationship had been some kind of illusion. It was upsetting her more than she could say. She was terrified.

'I never thought you could love someone without really knowing them. Maybe it's nothing,' Laura added, amazed by her own frankness. 'I don't know. Men, eh!'

There was no comment from the secretary. The paper drawer on the photocopier jammed, sending a heap of blurred and skewed sheets onto the ground. Laura banged the button repetitively. She turned the machine off and on at the wall and tugged furiously at the drawer, a red light beeping with a high-pitched squeal.

'Allow me,' the secretary said, prising open a plastic panel inside the photocopier. She withdrew shreds of eaten paper and tossed them aside. She clicked the panel closed again, pressed the button and turned to Laura. '*Bon courage*, I'm sure things will work out. Get some rest, and eat, always eat well, that's what we say in my country, eat.' She fished her keys out of her bag and marched off down the corridor.

Laura left a note for Amani, saying she was too tired to attend the delegates' dinner. She stopped to look in a bookshop as she walked to the Metro. She worked her way through the novels laid out on the central table. She examined an illustrated book on marine life before returning to the sounds of the warm street. She didn't get on the Metro. She carried on wandering, till she reached Sèvres-Babylone and then Saint Germain. She strolled down to the Seine. Evening was falling. The bright beams of passing *bâteaux mouches* filled the sky and rotated along the whitened facades of the buildings by the river. She found a telephone cabin further down the street. A bus drew in beside her, jangling the metal sides of the booth. A plastic map, dividing up the world into time zones, danced from side to side on a broken hook above the telephone. She strained to see the digits on the dial in the dusk. She held the phone to her ear.

'Hello, it's Laura.'

'Who there?'

'Laura, it's Laura,' she articulated clearly. 'Laura.'

'Who?'

'Who are you?'

'*Que?* What?'

'You, who are you?'

'No good English, *Español*, speak Spanish, I'm maid, new Colombia maid in London, Colombia. '

'My parents,' Laura said, surprised. 'Where are Mr and Mrs Roseborough?'

'Gone.'

'Sorry?'

'Yesterday gone. *En vacaciones*, on holiday, gone, *entiende*? You understand?'

'Where?'

'Hein?'

'Where?'

'Hong Kong.'

'Oh, right,' Laura said, 'thank you,' and replaced the receiver. She watched an approaching car. Music burst out of its open windows and then trailed off into a remote rumbling.

At her flat, Laura searched through the wicker basket by her bed for a hairgrip. She came across a 1920s black-and-white postcard Marco had bought her. It showed a grinning, moustached man in tails holding a birthday cake in one hand and a knife in the other. There was a caption below it: 'Happy Birthday! Some cake, Miss?' She placed the card on the table and pulled off her tights. She leant sideways and backwards, trying to unzip her red dress, wriggling and straining her arms over her shoulders, round her back, before giving up. The phone rang. She didn't pick it up. She put on some music. Through the glass lid of the hi-fi, inside the silver CD, she followed her reflection spinning in the constricting red of her dress.

45

Over the course of the dinner the conference delegates thanked Marco
for his work one by one. Amani was unusually warm, assuring him that
she would do her best to secure him a permanent post. There was still
work to do finishing the publications, but things were looking good for
him. Marco excused himself and walked back to the nearby UNESCO
building. The night watchman let him in. He sat at his desk, not
wanting to return home yet. He was in a state of high emotion. The
conference had gone exceptionally well. He had shaken hands and
talked with more ministers than he could remember, but Laura's
absence at dinner had disturbed him. He tried to ring her. There was
no reply at her flat. The corridors were empty except for the cleaning
ladies, slapping wet mops like dying fish against the linoleum, bumping
the wheels of their trolley bins into the skirting rail. Marco sorted the
piles of paper on his desk, reading the names of the conference
participants heading the faxes. The people he had spent months trying
to contact down unreliable African and Asian telephone lines were
preparing to leave Paris. He could now put a face to every name.

The delegates who had seen the transcribed interviews had been in
agreement with Amani. Publications needed facts not personal stories.
The final report, then, would be solely made up of analysis and
statistics. Marco had one last tape of Malian interviews left. He had put
off listening to it, out of superstition, as if it would mark the end of
something he couldn't define. He picked it up off his desk and plugged
in the cassette player.

'My name is Camara. My wife died thirty years ago. I left Mali with my
youngest son to join a cousin in Paris. I got employed by the Paris street-
cleaning service. I'm always finding things. I have hairgrips, photos,

shoehorns, necklaces, the whole lot. I have a key ring I found two years ago.
It's in the shape of a long country. A man told me it was Sweden, although
someone else said it was Italy. I like the feel of it in my pocket. I'm near
retiring age and I worry how my son will manage. He has something
wrong with his kidneys. I'm sure he could work, but he does nothing but
complain. He doesn't realize the chance I gave him by coming here. He's
been offered a job selling postcards on the steps of the Sacré Coeur
Basilica, those long strings of cards that you spread out like an accordion.

'I can't afford to go back to Mali. I'm a sort of a Parisian now, I
suppose. I'm not the person I was when I left, but that doesn't bother me.
You know, I don't even recognize the old photos of myself. It's as if they're
from a world I never knew. It's much easier to imagine that everything was
better in the past, but was it? I don't know. I do send things home, a group
of us clubbed together to send footballs for the local team and full kits and
shoes. I've got the photograph, all the young men of the village in our
clothes. On Saturdays, I walk to the supermarket. I see what items they're
selling off for less, food that's cheap because it's passed its sell-by date. On
the way back, if it's sunny, I stop in the garden square and watch the
children play. There's a boy who looks just like my son did when he was
little, before he became fat.'

Marco rewound and listened to the last sentence and fast-forwarded.
He straightened the edges of his paper and drew a circle which he filled
with more circles, and more circles inside them. He looked at the other
boxes of tapes on the floor. One was recordings of Mozambicans in
South Africa, another of Haitians in the US. He found some from Italy
and put one in the machine. The first interview was of a Kurdish man.
He spoke of his time in a remote rural area, cutting trees. He had
moved to Milan in search of better work, ending up in a welding
workshop. Marco stopped the cassette. He copied down some words
in the Kurdish man's broken Italian. He wrote *workshop, mountain, tree,*

trees, in a column, one on top of the other. Then he scrawled over each word. He started the cassette again. In his mind, on the edge of the recorded interview appeared an image of his father, a solitary figure on a mountain peeled of its grass. He guessed his father's voice had been similar to Giacomo's, less timid though, rough even, perhaps similar to that of this Kurdish man. And his face – was he the frozen portrait in his old bedroom photo, or the burglar who called his name?

It was one in the morning. Marco looked into the corridor. It was empty. There was no sign of the nightwatchman. He took the letter Giacomo had sent him out of his jacket pocket. He sat down and went through it again. He had probably read it ten or so times. The tape unwound, the Kurdish man's voice spewed out in coils.

46

The days following the conference were strangely flat and Marco left work early. He caught a Metro at La Motte Picquet Grenelle and sat on one of the push-down seats at the end of the carriage. He had a headache. He had spent three hours translating and, now that he had left the office, he couldn't stop. It had been similar when he had learnt to type. No matter what he did, even in bed, his fingers tapped away at imaginary keyboards, stringing out sentences into the dark. On the Metro, he had to stop himself from automatically translating billboards in the passing stations, even the safety instructions by the doors. His head had become a burrow of glossaries, interconnected passageways, ladders and wires joining up phrases and adjectives with verbs that were no longer simple abstract notions but sounds that always had to be real, flawless and natural. He was distracted by a couple reading from the same book, their eyes darting in perfect timing from page to page. An elderly man on the other side to him had a bent nose and a reddish bruise on his cheek. A sheet from a discarded newspaper lay on the floor. Marco scanned the titles. He arrived at Porte de Clichy and got off, racing up the stairs onto the square. He walked up the avenue de la Porte de Clichy, under the *périphérique*, and into the suburb beyond.

He found the address for the old factory without too much difficulty, but it was now a modern housing development. Marco observed the building from the pavement opposite. He had no recollection of the place whatsoever though the experience had to be somewhere inside him, inaccessible to his memory: the day he first met Giacomo, his mother's grip on him, the trip from Italy. Visualizing the street map he had studied at work, he turned and retraced his steps until he came to the cemetery. A few cars were parked by the entrance. One had a boot full of wreaths and flowers, strings of leaves hanging limply over the rear lights. He trod between the rows of tombs, joining paths, towards the furthest alley.

His father's grave was clean and simple. His mother, he guessed, had cleared away many of the weeds. Marco sat on the gravel. He thought of his father's body on the factory floor and of its remains, under the earth, close to him. On the other side of the path, ahead, he could see a couple standing over a grave. The woman watered some plants with a bottle while the man held onto her. Marco listened to their murmured conversation and the water sliding off the surface of the stone. He wanted to talk, to say something to the ground, but no sound came.

It was late when Marco arrived back on boulevard Ornano. He noted with disappointment that the lights in his flat weren't on. Laura had promised to be there. He sorted through the letters in the postbox. Laura, to his surprise, was in fact in bed, half-asleep. She greeted Marco with a drowsy hug. He raised the duvet and got in, beside her, fully-clothed. Laura's nightshirt lifted with the duvet, halfway up her back. She yanked it down and tucked it firmly between her legs. He laid his hand on her shoulder.

'How was work?' she asked. 'Has Amani lumped you with hundreds of new jobs?'

The shiny cover of a book beside the bed caught the light from the street, a bolt of colour in the dim room. Laura laid her head against Marco's chest, wrinkling her nose at the itchiness of his jacket. He picked a bag off the floor and put it ceremoniously in front of her on the bed, urging her to open it. She tore off the paper to discover a pebble painted like a tortoise.

'It's a paperweight,' he said, proudly. 'From Bolivia. Do you like it? I found it this evening.'

Laura put it on the bedside table that already contained three other gifts from Marco: a Chinese bowl, an Indian copper bell and a carved alabaster lion. He wandered over to the kitchen and came back with a glass of water to find Laura had gone into the bathroom. His eye caught a silver frame holding the photo of an old man. Laura had placed it on the mantelpiece. He turned it over, examined it, studying what he felt were the distinctly English features.

'My grandfather,' Laura said. 'I felt like putting up a few of my things, is that OK?'

'Sure, go ahead, I'm delighted.'

'Promise?'

'Absolutely.'

'Sorry I didn't come over to see you today. We had a visit from the Vietnamese national commission.'

Marco took a tape from the bookshelf. 'You've got to listen to this, you'll love it. I keep on forgetting to play it to you.'

'Hang on, we haven't talked properly for days.'

'Listen to this first, please. It's a Neapolitan song. I found a collection of old recordings in Aigues-Mortes of all places, last time I was there. You'll love it.'

'Marco…'

'This guy's voice is amazing, listen!'

He pressed 'Play' and slipped off to the kitchen. It was a tape from work instead of the music he hoped for.

'My name is Oumar Traore. Not having any papers is the hardest. I feel I don't exist, as if I'm no-one, a spirit, an invisible spirit.'

Marco ran over and stopped the interview. He put on the music, which he also stopped on Laura's insistence. He washed, got undressed and lay down next to Laura. He put his arms round her and kissed the back of her neck, curling her hair in his fingers.

'If you don't want to talk, I'm going to get some sleep,' she said. 'I'm exhausted.'

Marco kissed her anyway, linking his hands round her waist to lift her nightdress. She pushed him off her. He held onto the fine hem again, inching it upwards.

'Stop it,' Laura sat up, pulling her nightdress down once more. 'Can't you see I'm shattered?' Faced with Marco's surprise, she told him that they didn't need to make love every night. There were other ways of feeling close. They had been together long enough, surely their lovemaking didn't need to be the daily reassuring occurrence, and certainly not the twice-daily routine, that he often wanted.

'But we haven't seen each other all day…'

'Just not now, please, go to sleep, think about something else!'

'What's wrong?' Marco said.

'Nothing, nothing.' Then she hesitated and turned back towards him. 'It's just that you give me paperweights, play music and it's all so senseless. We can't even manage a proper conversation.'

'Don't you like the paperweight? I was sure you'd love it.'

'I mean it's beautiful, kind of, but what use is it to me? What use are any of these presents to me? You just float in here and plonk a present on the bed, as if that's enough to make sure I'm satisfied. Well, it's not enough and the funny part is you don't even know why.'

'Why?' Marco asked in a faltering voice.

'Why? Because not only do you not let me know who you are, you don't even let yourself. You spend your time filling your head with knowledge and distractions, accumulating and running. You just do more and more to hide from yourself.'

'That's unfair, I…'

'I'm sorry, Marco, I know it sounds harsh, but I worry that you're more foreign to me than all these Malians I'm meeting at the St Bernard Church at the moment, all those people from a country I've never even visited. I don't understand you, certainly not your mother and your background, the pottery or where you're coming from. I guess you had some pretty heavy crap when you were a child, or maybe you didn't, how would I know? You've never said anything. You tell me nothing, share nothing. It's as though I only exist in your imagination. I don't even know what you want out of life. I don't know who you are.'

'What are you on about?'

'You.'

'I love you, Laura, isn't that obvious?'

'Yes, you love me, I know that, I suppose, but sometimes, it feels so incredibly one-sided, like I'm doing all the hard work.'

'What does that mean?'

'I need to talk, I need to share things, argue a bit, you know, sound out your deepest emotions. I get the impression I'm just making conversation with you at times, just going through the motions, chatting politely – that can't be right, can it? We go to films, listen to all your music, laugh at your jokes, but all those things I've found out aren't you, they're just what you've chosen to show as you, they're intimations of what's inside you, hints that I can't decipher any more. Do you see?'

Marco stared up at the ceiling, his head on the pillow. So this is it, he thought. I must answer. The flow of words that could represent him couldn't be truncated or reduced any longer. What he feared, though, was that, increasingly, he spoke a language only he understood. His ideas didn't inhabit words that others comprehended. He rolled over towards the windows. He still hadn't fixed the corners of the blind in the bedroom. 'Think of something else,' she'd said. He was always thinking of something else, every day crowded with phrases and languages that he shuffled around and repositioned as many times as he swallowed and blinked. Yet speaking, just plain speaking, he couldn't do. Laura had closed her eyes.

'If you're not going to answer me I'm going to sleep, goodnight,' she muttered.

The awareness of Laura's body, next to him, was too much. It began to overpower him, smothering any possible words. She was right – sometimes he did want to make love to her again and again, over and over. It was never enough, as if he could crush her with his need, but why, he couldn't say. He was relieved that he hadn't had to tell her anything about his day. What was he going to tell her anyway? How his mother had rung him at work, sounding more inconsolable than ever. They had argued. Something in her voice had changed. Maybe it was the pills the doctor had prescribed. He could tell she had wanted to say more and she had been close to saying it, but he had invented an appointment to end their conversation. He had felt cowardly and unkind. Did Laura care about that? Would she want to know about the letter he had received from Giacomo, the new things he had had to take on, the visit to the cemetery that it had provoked?

Laura had taken most of the duvet. Marco got out of bed.

'Marco,' Laura whispered.

'Mmm. What?'

'Sorry. I didn't mean to sound harsh, I'm completely exhausted at the moment, I don't know what's wrong with me. I feel ill, kind of heavy. Maybe it's this business with Fatoumata. They could get thrown out of the church.' She repositioned her pillow. 'Put the music back on if you want,' she added. 'It was nice.'

Marco fetched an extra sheet from the cupboard and laid it on the bed. An articulated lorry thundered down the boulevard below. The walls rattled in its wake. He stood over Laura, her blonde hair fanning out across the pillow. She was all that he had, all that he wanted. He would cling onto her; weave himself to her so as not to drown. Through the window he could see that the traffic had died down to a few drips of red and yellow, small, regular shots of colour sent in all directions by an urgency he had no part of, but which felt as critical as his own.

Behind these thoughts, but disconnected from them, were the remote sensations of a child walking through grass – thick, fertile, velvet grass that brushed his knees, licked his skin, not the sore, bristly reeds of the Camargue. Maybe it was from Italy, he didn't know. Perhaps he had invented it from one of the few photographs he had seen of himself in Varanelle, leaping through a meadow with the mountains behind. Or was it how he imagined his own conception, his parents in the grass above the village, his father's mind already on the other side of the world, running with his dreams? The sounds and the smells escaped him, but his parents' entwined bodies, he was sure, were naked like roots pulled from the ground.

47

Laura put on a pair of tights, and asked Marco to help her zip up her dress at the back.

'Let's go,' she said, opening the door. Laura had heard Rémy's name mentioned many times and had badgered Marco into arranging a drink with him.

The Metro journey to place d'Italie seemed endless. Marco fended off curious stares, lingering eyes that stuck to Laura's legs, the tight red dress against her thighs.

'*Enti helloua,*' he said to her, '*helloua.*'

'What?'

'*Enti helloua.*'

'What?'

'It's Arabic,' he winked, 'I was saying you're beautiful. You're meant to say *shoukran,* thank you, or something like that.'

'What are you on about?' Laura got up and waited by the doors. 'How many more stops?' she asked.

'*Talata.*'

'How many?'

'*Talata.*'

'Sorry?'

'*Wahed, etneen, talata,* one, two, three!'

'Oh, honestly,' she spat in exasperation. 'You're a complete freak sometimes.'

Rémy was effervescent with enthusiasm. As he kissed Laura hello, he nudged Marco with a playful, reproachful look. 'He's not much of a friend,' he said. 'He's kept you hidden away for years. If you hadn't answered the phone I'd never even have known you existed.'

They settled round a table at the back of a café. Rémy lit up cigarette after cigarette, regaling them with stories of his recent upsets with women. Marco worried that Laura was getting bored – even if she was responding to his quips and accounts with bursts of laughter. He proposed they went to a restaurant, but they both ignored him. Rémy instead decided to launch into tales of their school years in Aigues-Mortes.

'Have you been to the pottery?' he asked Laura with evident relish. Her negative reply sent him into squeals of delight. 'Well that's a treat in store. You won't believe it, I tell you, it's quite something!'

Marco stood. 'We ought to get going.'

'And you should have seen what used to happen when he got off the school bus,' Rémy continued. 'All us adolescent boys would hurl ourselves at the window to watch him being hugged by his mother. We'd have done anything to have been in his shoes. It was extraordinary, she'd smother him in kisses, you know, proper kisses, and squeeze him in her arms. Sometimes there'd be a fight for the seats at that side of the bus, so we could all get a good look at her.' He lowered his voice a little, 'Sorry, Marco, but it's true.'

'Let's get a bite to eat further up the street,' Marco tried again. Did they fancy couscous or Chinese? There was even a Basque restaurant in the Butte aux Cailles if they wanted?

Laura waved him back to his seat, 'Oh, stop it you old fusspot, sit down, no, no, we're staying here. This is far too exciting. Carry on, Rémy!' The two of them shrieked with laughter as Rémy filled the next hour with anecdotes and snippets of Marco's childhood and their school pranks. Any idea of going to a restaurant was forgotten as Marco was left to remember the first time he had invited Rémy home from school and how his young guest had come across the discarded sculptures his mother had placed at the back of the house.

'Are those breasts?' twelve-year-old Rémy had asked without

hesitation, pointing at two engorged protuberances on a bent-over body.

Marco had done his best to explain, the way his mother had taught him to confront nosy customers: 'No, course not, they're just shapes, kind of landscapes.'

Rémy hadn't been convinced. 'Are those legs? What's that down there?' Straddling a seated figure with its head flung back in pleasure, Rémy fumbled between the stiff knees of a sculpture, his hand slipping down a deep crack in the wood, 'And that, I suppose,' he laughed, 'is a letter box.'

It had taken Marco hours to persuade his friend not to say anything to the other children at school. Rémy had held his promise for years and, now, just when it was vital he keep quiet, it was bursting out in the face of the only person who really mattered, the only person who had ever mattered. Marco got up, walked to the bar and ordered himself a coffee. Laura and Rémy's strident voices could be heard across the café. Snatches of excited conversation reached him; gusts of hysteria buffeting him backwards.

It was too late to contemplate going to a restaurant when they finally left. Rémy and Laura gave each other drunken embraces and pledged to meet up again soon.

'Why did you go off in a huff?' Laura asked, on the Metro home. Marco said nothing.

'Come on, it was only a bit of harmless fun. Rémy's great.'

Still he said nothing.

'You've really got to loosen up. I should be the one in a huff anyway. How much more lying am I going to have to put up with?'

'Why do you say that?'

'Why the hell do you think? Because, quite evidently, you didn't go to school in Italy or have a house there as you once said, and your father, who is your uncle anyway, doesn't sound like the kind of prestigious sculptor who travels the world, hopping from gallery to gallery.'

Laura thrust her head back against the seat and stared out of the window. He couldn't tell if she was really looking at the tunnel walls, but he longed for them to end, for the bright sparkling lights of a Metro station to flood the carriage. He began to formulate some kind of reply in his head, but all he could think was that it had been a mistake to take Laura to meet Rémy. Her encounter with his mother had been bad enough. Now, however, Laura was no longer going to be able to pretend or dare imagine a better home for him. It really was a dingy pottery off a dusty road and the reality of it, he feared, had been worse than she expected. Perhaps he was imperfect in Laura's eyes, but the missing pieces she was finding were not the ones she had been hoping for.

He had to talk to her. Yes, he had lied, he would say, no, not lied, no he hadn't lied, that was the wrong word, not really lied, just embellished, because he loved her too much, and he always fought to say things the right way to her. No words were ever right. Or was it that he didn't have his own words, just borrowed guidebook words, foreign languages that masked his own non-existent tongue? If he sought to justify what Rémy had said, she would find him weak, apologetic or just plain under-privileged. She was always so confident and assured that words petered out in his mouth, died on his breath as he started talking. He hated the way that he would begin discussing certain subjects and then feel ashamed of himself, as if she had some superiority over him. Months previously, prior to his mother's visit, he had thought the moment was right to tell Laura about his childhood. He had worried how he could admit to someone like her that as a child and teenager his life had often been intolerable, an anxious search for meaning. He had feared she would shrug it off with a 'That's OK. We've all had weird kids' stuff,' a familiar line of hers. It wasn't just kids' stuff though.

He laid his head on her shoulder, tickling her affectionately. He talked about a publication he had found at work. It was about the plundering of the rainforests by large drug companies – fascinating, enraging material. Laura sat up and pulled her diary from her bag, reading through her timetable for the following week.

At the flat, Marco found a message from his mother on the answerphone. 'I know it's one in the morning, but give me a call, please, as soon as you get in? Please my love, *ti prego amore*. I need to speak to you.'

'Bloody hell,' Laura groaned. 'Doesn't she ever leave you alone?'

Marco waited for Laura to go into the bathroom before he dialled the pottery number.

'What's wrong?'

'I needed to hear your voice,' Elena answered, immediately calmed by the sound of him. 'I got into a panic when there was no reply, I couldn't help it, I was worried. I couldn't sleep. Where have you been out so late?'

'Listen, you can't just leave messages like that. I was out, OK, nothing to worry about.'

'I'm sorry, I…'

'It's very late. Listen, you are taking those pills, aren't you? They do work, Dr Couret told me.'

'You spoke to the doctor?'

'Briefly.'

'Why couldn't you ask me yourself? What's wrong with everyone these days?'

'So, are you going to take them?'

'What difference are they going to make?'

'They'll work. You've got to keep at them.'

'When are you next coming down? That's all that matters to me, Marco.'

'I'm still working most weekends. There are things to clear up after the conference.'

'I saw something on your meeting on the TV the other night. Did you meet all those fancy people?'

'Some of them.'

'Why weren't you on TV too?'

'It's not like that. Listen, you'd better sleep.'

'With all the work you're doing for them, you'd have thought they could give you a bit of the limelight, put you on TV.' Elena laughed a little. 'Let me know if you're ever on, I'll get Nassima to come and watch it with me. She says she can tape it on a video cassette or something like that.'

The bathroom door opened and Laura emerged with a towel wrapped round her.

'Sure, I'll tell you,' Marco whispered. He looked at Laura, pointing at the receiver with an apologetic grimace.

'Will you come and see me?'

'I hope so, as I said I just never know how busy I'll be. I'm going to get some sleep, I'm really tired.'

'I bet you're not too busy to see that girl, Lara or Lola, whatever she's called.'

'Laura,' he corrected her, regretting it instantly. She turned round at the mention of her name. Marco forced out a feeble smile.

'Well, am I right or not?'

'Let's get some sleep.'

'I don't like to interfere, you know me, I'm not like that,' Elena started, 'but she's not for you. I know you like I know myself. My son needs a real woman, someone who's solid and reliable, do you see? She's all flighty, looking for excitement, all that enthusiasm wasted on herself... that's what rich people are like. You don't know, but I do. She's not one of us. Don't say I didn't warn you.'

'I don't want to hear this, I've had a long day,' Marco said, lowering his voice again.

'OK, you're right, sorry, let's not argue! I can't bear it when we do.'

'So, goodnight Mamma.'

'I know you're not interested in what I have to say, but it's not too late for you to get a job locally. You could work in Montpellier, I'm sure they're asking for translators down here. Shall I look in the papers for you? Things are better now with Djamel. We make money, quite a lot. We could get you a car, your own car, even build another room, a separate house at the back, how about that, your own house in the garden behind? Think how happy we could be! We could clear the sculptures and…'

'Listen, I'm fine in Paris. I'm staying here for the time being. I like it. You waste so much time fantasizing about this and that, wrapped up in your own head. You've got to move on a bit, stop kidding yourself about everything…' Marco could hear his mother's breathing momentarily stop. He waited. There was no reply. 'Are you still there?' he asked. 'Mamma?' There was still no reply. 'I'm sorry, I have to be here, in Paris, for my work, can you not see that?'

'Because of her?' Elena piped up feebly. 'Is that it?'

'Just make sure you sleep, please Mamma, you have to. The doctor said you had to sleep more.'

'As if it's that easy. If you were here, we could talk properly. We never talk. You know I only sleep well when you're around.'

'How many times do I have to tell you…'

'Don't go, don't get angry.'

'It's very late now.'

'What's that coughing?

'Promise me you'll take those pills, Mamma.'

'What's that coughing in the background?'

'I don't know, nothing.'

'I heard coughing.'

'It's the TV.'

'She's with you, isn't she? She's there.'

'Please…' Marco cringed, 'I'm going now.'

'She's living with you, isn't she?'

'Goodnight.'

Elena pulled the flex of the receiver until it was taut. 'Goodnight,' she said, and let the phone spring from her hand onto the floor.

Marco turned to see Laura in bed, asleep, one of her hands draped over the side of the mattress, an elaborate lapis ring on one of her fingers. He picked up a book, but was unable to concentrate. He had wanted to ask the local chemist about the pills his mother was taking, but the shop had been closed. He should have talked to her more about the medication anyway. He found it increasingly hard to get any point across, as if he had less and less to say to his mother. He found it deeply disturbing, abhorrent even.

Marco got into bed to hear the knock of the video shop postbox and the footsteps of someone running.

48

Marco and Laura returned from the market, their plastic bags bursting with an assortment of vegetables. 'We have to talk,' Laura said. Marco gripped the door handle in front of him. He watched the brutality of Laura's purposefully restrained gestures as the words burst out.

'I'm pregnant.'

Her voice flowed clear. It hung there for him to understand. He couldn't move. Laura carried on, and she almost shouted, 'There's no easy way of saying this and it isn't just because of you, but we're not ready for this, for all this.' Without looking up, she added, 'I never wanted this to happen, to be in this situation, especially at my age, ever. I'm going to have the pregnancy terminated, it's only a month or so old.'

Marco's hands were quivering. It was strange that it should be his hands shaking. They had never trembled before. They entered the flat. He spotted a patch on the wall in front of him where there was no paint. He concentrated on it, aware that it was absurd to be focusing on such a thing, but doing it all the same, more and more. It was only a small area, like a stain, not covered by white paint.

'Did you hear what I said? I can't have this baby.' Laura's voice splintered and the enormity of her statement swung back at her. 'Please answer me, Marco! Answer me.' He wandered about the apartment, not understanding, barely listening; the sound of his name buzzing at his temples. 'You've got to talk to me!'

'We'll keep it,' he said. 'We'll work out a way. You can't just decide something like that. You're talking about a baby.'

'I've already found a clinic where they do it. Please don't complicate this, Marco.'

He didn't have the strength to stand up. He sat on one of the chairs, his arms loose. He felt Laura touch his shoulder. 'We've got to be realistic,' she said. 'Try and understand. Neither of us is ready for this, least of all you.'

'I don't agree, Laura, I just don't agree,' he said. 'You make yourself ready, for your own child you do anything, that's what you do.'

He watched as Laura fell onto the sofa and began to cry. She put her head in her hands. 'Laura, Laura,' he repeated.

Then there it was, this thing lying there between them. How long had she known, or begun to make the connection between her tiredness and the pregnancy? How many nights had she imagined their child growing in the closeness of their own bedroom, waiting for the time to announce its end? A few wisps of Laura's hair were touching

281

Marco's face. She brushed them away as if that were a connection too intimate and threatening, an extension of the pregnancy.

Around nine in the evening, Laura switched on the television. It was a documentary on street children in Romania. In underground passages and manholes around the main railway station in Bucharest, a group of ten children lived sniffing glue and scavenging food from the dustbins. Marco felt a queasiness in the pit of his stomach. His hands still shook. The patch of bare wall had his attention again. How come he had never seen it before? He couldn't have been taking too much care on that part. He had removed the brush hairs that had got stuck in the paint, but never noticed the patch.

49

Marco didn't go to the UNESCO offices the following morning. He called in sick, spending the day at the flat. As he made himself some late supper, Laura reappeared. He was surprised she hadn't gone back to her apartment. He clung to it as a sign she was less decided than she made out. She undressed for bed.

'Thank you for coming,' Marco said.

'I need to be here, with you, but don't talk, not now.'

'Why?'

'You'll try and change my mind and I can't have my mind changed because…'

'Because what?'

'Because sometimes I want this child too.'

Marco couldn't sleep, and he knew Laura was also awake. What, he thought, happens when everything slips away, and washes off you like water?

The following days had a similar pattern. There were times when Marco found himself frozen, unstuck, oblivious of what he had been doing. He sat at his desk, holding a pen or even the phone, not remembering why he had picked them up in the first place. He left work early and went over her words, and more words, in his head, translated them, un-translated them. In the evenings, he ate out of tins or opened packets of dried foods, unable to prepare proper meals. Laura avoided the kitchen, working long hours, arriving at the flat late and leaving at dawn, and yet she still chose to return.

They went for a walk, to the St Bernard Church. The door was open. They explained who they were to a man standing guard. Groups of African men and women were seated on the flagstone floor on rugs and covers. Sleeping bags were slung over boxes. The pews had been pushed to one side. Someone had hung a colourful banner with large lettering from one column to another. '*Droits pour les sans-papiers,*' it proclaimed, 'Rights for asylum seekers'. Another said, '*Liberté, Egalité, Fraternité,*' on a faded ripped sheet, yet another, '*Non aux lois racistes.* No to racist laws.' Below the altar was a stack of mattresses. Laura approached a group of women and asked for Fatoumata. They pointed to the back of the church, near the entrance to the crypt. The building was cool despite the summer heat, a moist, musty smell hanging off the walls. Fatoumata, her hair wrapped in a bright green headdress, smiled when she saw Laura and led her off to show where she was sleeping. People had hung their clothes in the confessionals. Below a plaster statue of St Joseph were bottles of mineral water. A bunch of flowers had been left at the statue's feet.

Fatoumata was emaciated. 'You're eating a bit aren't you?' Laura asked. '*Tu manges un peu?*'

'I don't think I'll carry on with the hunger strike, not with the kids around.'

'How are they?'

'Not too bad, considering,' she said. 'We had a wedding in here today.' Fatoumata raised her eyebrows, 'Imagine that, with all of us looking on. They showered her with rice on the way out of the church.'

She told Laura and Marco too about the government official who had come round the church, how they had jeered and hissed at his presence. He had warned them that they would achieve nothing by their actions. The head of the *sans-papiers* protest thought differently. People in high places were worried by their movement. It was getting wide coverage. A television crew had been the day before. Fatoumata called to her children, told them to stay near her. They weren't to go off like that. A police car sped down the street outside and many people looked uneasy. Then all became calm again.

The answerphone was flashing when they returned to the flat, but no message had been left. Marco reached over and unplugged it at the wall. He knew it could only have been his mother calling at such a late hour. Laura fumbled around for a few coins at the bottom of her bag. She walked down to Karim's shop, knocking a carton of oranges with her elbow. The price sign fell to the floor. She bent down, twirled it in her hand, before sticking it forcefully into a gap in the corner of the box. Karim was serving an old woman, counting the change in her hand. His thick hands foraged in the woman's translucent smooth palms. He made stacks of money on the counter, explaining the transaction in detail. The woman nodded, asking him to go over it again and then looked confused. Laura walked round the shop, stopping at the frozen section. The cold air from the humming freezer didn't make her flinch. She slid open the plastic lid and peered at the rows of peas, fish fingers and slabs of meat sealed in cellophane. She only had thirty francs. Karim spotted her and waved. She edged her way back to the counter with a loaf of sliced bread and a tin of sardines. Karim enquired about Marco, and asked how her work was going, what they were up to for the weekend. 'Must hurry, *salut*,' Laura said, dropping the money on the counter. She made her way back up to the apartment. She ate quickly, leaving half the sardines in the tin for Marco. He tipped them onto a plate and cut a piece of bread, but the sight of the white fish spines poking out of the oil and the smell of their headless flesh put him off eating. He sliced a fish in half, then worked his way down the vertebrae with his knife, snapping each one in two.

Laura got into bed. When Marco came out of the bathroom he said, 'You can't keep putting this off. I need to know what decision you're making. I need to have my say.' He sat on the edge of the bed and she drew her knees towards her chest.

'I postponed the appointment at the clinic. I can't think straight.'

Marco's face lit up. He kissed her. 'You'll see. We'll manage with this child.'

'I only postponed it, Marco, I didn't cancel. My head's a mess. You're not ready Marco, I'm barely there, but you, you have no idea what it takes to have a child. You don't even know who you are, I don't know who you are, that's hardly a good start.'

React, react, Marco thought, speak out. It's now or never.

'You can't treat me like this. You can't just shut me out and take this decision alone. I want to keep my child. I have to keep my child.'

'Then what? You'll look after it, will you? You'll find the money, the patience, the new flat we need and the time, the years, the sleepless nights and all that? And what if you mean it now, but can't handle it when it comes to it? What then, eh? It's so easy to say you want to keep it, but you're not carrying it, feeling sick every day, you can just walk away from this if you want. You've lied to me in the past, who's to say you're not lying now? I can't work you out.'

'Laura!'

'What?'

'Listen to yourself.'

'It's true, I don't know anything any more. I've never felt so disorientated in my whole life.'

'Well what would make that better? Tell me,' he asked, beseeching her.

'Time,' Laura said. 'And we don't have it.'

50

Laura was steering Marco towards a decision. She believed that her sticking around in his flat wasn't helping to resolve anything for either of them. It was, if anything, only making matters worse. She wanted to go to England for two or three weeks. She still had a little time until a final decision had to be made. Everything in her head, she told him, was out of kilter, disordered. She needed to think of herself and find space to breathe. Marco tried to deflect the course of events, saying they could go on holiday together, ask for a break from their jobs, do anything they wanted. Laura was set on her idea: she needed to spend time in London, at home, talk to her family and friends.

She put a few of her clothes in a plastic bag. Marco insisted on accompanying her. They took a taxi together. It was dark with rain and muggy. The passing traffic added a background hum to the repetitive thump of the windscreen wipers, cutting into the stuffy air of the car.

'This is absurd, Marco, you don't need to come with me.'

He sat next to her, motionless even when they arrived at her flat. Laura opened the car door, one hand behind her back holding onto Marco's thigh, unable to turn round and face him.

'You won't have it done in England will you?' She didn't reply. 'Laura,' he said. 'Promise me you won't.'

'I'll call you.'

She let go of him and walked up to the building, stopping at the door to tap in the entry code. She didn't wave. Marco waited for the lights on the third floor to flicker on. The meter ticked away on the taxi dashboard. The driver coughed to catch Marco's attention, asking him if he wanted to go somewhere else. 'Back to where we came from,' he said, and saw that the man didn't immediately comprehend. 'To boulevard Ornano?' the driver asked, uncertain, and Marco nodded. On the journey home, he held his head in his hands and the crying he was expecting didn't come. It worked its way backwards into him, noiselessly, an internal sobbing. As he got out of the car, Marco slipped the driver a thirty-franc tip. 'Here,' he said, 'take it.' The man watched him get out his flat keys without driving off. Why won't he leave? Marco thought. Hadn't he bought enough of his respect? The car remained stationary behind him, engine chugging, as he crossed the road. The driver was on his radio telling all the taxi owners of Paris that he had seen a man being thrown back, alone, into his past.

Marco spent an hour, or more, in front of the mirror in the bathroom. He shaved, picking at cuts on his face until it was covered with welts. He brushed his teeth once, then again, three times, until his gums left tinges of blood in the water he spat out. He turned the tap on, hot water, boiling to touch, steam rising, misting over the mirror so that there was nothing of him to look at. Laura would be on her way to London now. The taxi's meter, he felt, was still running, ticking over in the bathroom with him. He thought back to that morning and how he had looked at Laura and immediately seen that something in her had been folded away, handed over. When would she make her final decision? He didn't know. She was the one who had urged him to break free, to be himself, and now she was walking away from the person she had so carefully helped to build and given the chance to hope. If she terminated the pregnancy, what was stopping her from leaving him too? Maybe Laura reckoned her role had been to accompany him to this point and then let go. She could not have been more mistaken. He needed her more than ever. She was racing straight back to London and her old life and he was left marooned in a future she had invented for him, where he didn't belong without her.

Marco couldn't think clearly, only a steady nausea in the mouth, a dud weight in the gut. He had had everything with Laura and not been able to secure it. The days of doing up the flat, scouring the streets for furniture, and just being with each other, belonged to another world. Nothing had any sense but Laura, nothing else mattered. His sole thought was her.

He revisited the memories of their last lovemaking, the sensations and nakedness of it alive in his brain, mingled with a yearning to know when the child was conceived, at which point had new life taken hold and started to grow in Laura. Did the child have stumps for hands already, did it have eyes? What form had it taken? He could sense its heart beating inside her, the two of them, father and child, their fates intertwined, enmeshed within the organs of her body. His chest restricted, his breathing difficult, just as he had felt as a child in Aigues-Mortes. He concentrated on the traffic turning off the boulevard below, trying to distinguish individual cars from each other in the rush and stream of lights. He studied his reflection in the smooth glass, imagined it breaking, inviting him towards its thousand falling pieces.

51

After work, rather than going home, Marco crossed Paris, sliding under the glare of the street lamps, exposed, speckled with dirty shadows. Often, he didn't know where he was heading – Paris was no longer a city, but a grid of remembering, tints of loss on the pavements, an impossible undergrowth to wade through.

Each day, he went a little further, slipping under the *périphérique* ring road into the suburbs, as he had done in his first year in the city. He returned regularly to Clichy, to his father's grave. His father had left him unborn. He had never waited to see him. Marco stood in the cemetery, caught up in a torment that unified the strands of his life into a single arc extending from Laura's womb deep down into the dried earth beneath him. The past was a mistake that had to be repaired, an error that reached back to his birth. His mother had been offered a second chance with Giacomo and failed to take it. The foetus in Laura was his second chance, a reincarnation of himself, of his own fatherless birth. His life now depended on it, that's all he could think.

Returning home, after work, Marco started visiting Karim's shop more frequently. It became a harbour before the seclusion of his apartment. One visit, he found Karim talking to a client at the till. Marco hung around the apples. Like Laura, he put down the blemished ones and chose from the bottom of the box. He circled round the shop waiting for the other customers to leave. When he heard the last '*Bonne soirée*, bye,' he made his way towards the till. He placed the apples on the weighing machine. They rolled forward. As Marco tried to stop them, Karim took hold of his wrist.

'You don't look well! Where's Laura? I haven't seen her for a while. Wait, I'll close the shop and we'll have a coffee.'

Marco poked at the paper bags in front of him. He heard the door locking. Karim swivelled the open/closed sign over. They moved into the back of the shop. Karim boiled some water to make coffee, pouring a thick, dense liquid into a cup. He didn't take any for himself. Marco drunk, a few sips only. He said Laura would be away for some time. Karim's red-rimmed eyes watched him. When he asked what for, Marco shook his head with an empty insistence. He didn't have any words to add. Karim told Marco about his monthly trips to a café near boulevard Poissonière. The owner had the cassette of a song from his childhood. 'I go and have two coffees, standing at the bar and, if there's no-one there, the barman winks at me and puts on this cassette he has. It's an old song from Algiers, sung by a blind woman. I grip the counter and, every time, I have the same images, the same feelings, as if I'm not in the bar at all. I plunge straight back into my childhood. The barman has offered to copy the cassette for me, but I don't want to own that song. I want to know it's there, in that café, somewhere in Paris. If I had it at home, I wouldn't know that once the song ended I could walk back into the street and this life.'

Karim lifted a cushion off a trunk and opened the wooden lid. He pulled out a photograph album fastened with a golden clasp. He laid it out on the table in front of them. He turned each page with a quiet determination. 'Some of these people,' he said, 'I haven't seen for over thirty years. This man is dead, this woman too.' His fingers floated over the photographs. Then he came to a page with a woman and children, the wife he saw in the summer, the children he missed. The last page was stuck with bits of paper: Karim's first boat ticket to France, his first Metro ticket, his old residency permit, two postcards from a friend. 'The other day, my family sent me a video of themselves walking, laughing and talking at the camera. I turned the volume down and just watched their faces. No, I couldn't have heard what they were saying. I wouldn't have been able to listen.'

There was a knock at the shop door. Karim handed Marco the album and left. He heard the open/closed sign being spun round again. He looked through the album, the Arabic and French words under the pictures, the spirals and hooks of letters, the neat lines. He studied the photos, expected smiles from faces he had never seen. No-one noticed him, hidden away behind the cartons and crates. A queue formed at the till. Customers came and went, and none of them was Laura.

Marco wrote to Laura after two frustrating telephone calls in which they hadn't been able to talk properly. He wrote:

Since our conversation two days ago, I can barely look at this flat which only reminds me of our life together. I've been walking instead, through Paris, crossing meaningless streets to fill this time without you. I feel so sad when I imagine you alone trying to choose between life and death – because that's what it is, however brutal it sounds. What can I do to prove to you that I'm here, that I was always here, and ready for this? You must believe me when I say I can be the person you want me to be, for us. What does it matter that we're different, that my history, as you say, is unresolved. I've changed more than you can imagine already. I used to inhabit a closed, strangled world, a million miles from the things you've introduced me to. If I hadn't broken away I would be a potter today, a very bad potter I'm sure, but a potter all the same. And you would have been one of those well-dressed women who visit the showroom in the summer. I wouldn't have been able to come near you, of course, just look up from my wheel in time to see you leave.

I only started to live when I reached Paris, and met you. My happiness at being with you was also intimidating. I think that's why I'd buy you those presents you believed were so useless, the paperweight, the carved lion and the bowl. They were a way of avoiding words. I felt I could slip up at any moment with words, forfeit your respect and belief, and that was near impossible to imagine as I loved you too much already. I felt foreign, and unformed, next to your confidence and family history. So I hid myself away, cloaked myself in reinvention, but only to make sure I never lost you. It's strange, but I'd never wasted time in Paris until this week, but now it no longer makes any sense for me to measure my days with achievements or learning. I have never dared remain still, you are right. I have lost precious opportunities to be myself with this eagerness to change and transform everything. Yet, as I write to you now I feel a new strength that comes from my love for you. It is also my child that is making me strong. In my head I talk to it and make a decision for you, like a waiting father.

I will ring you at your parents' tonight, but I wanted to put these things on paper, express myself without your interruptions on the other end of the line. I know this isn't easy, but I feel I'm being punished for things that no longer define me. What if my mother had had the possibility of having an abortion so as to travel with my father? What if in those days she'd had the choices that you say we have? I keep on thinking of that. It's as if you say my own life should never have been.

In an attempt to relax, one evening, Marco read a guidebook to Guatemala. As he copied down the names of the country's most interesting archaeological sites, he rebelled against his habits. What was he doing? Where was all this getting him? The bookshelf behind him was at breaking point, groaning under Arabic language courses, Spanish reading aids, English glossaries, brochures, magazines and periodicals of all kinds. He had recently had the feeling that its stacked shelves only needed a nudge and they would collapse. Something was tearing away at him, the uselessness of his years of camouflage. He had clothed himself in foreign voices and lost his tongue. His own version of the tower of Babel was teetering, breaking apart, and there would be nothing to replace it but him.

PART ELEVEN

August 1996

52

The day Elena finished her second course of medication, an article on the pottery was published in the regional newspaper, the *Midi Libre*. It immediately brought more visitors, but upset Giacomo with its description of him as 'an uprooted labourer with a dazzling touch of imaginative flair'. A wealthy German businessman from Bonn bought two sculptures and took them off in his estate car. Others that had been gathering dust in the workshop, or growing weeds in the garden, were uncovered and put on display. Elena went and stood on the balcony to face the sun alone. In her mind, she was as weak and small as an insect, her wings broken. Through the glistening heat, she stared at the sculptures below her, silvery and hazy, poised for escape.

The gate from the car park opened and she saw a well-dressed man with an orange tie and grey hair approaching the showroom. She went down to the courtyard to meet him. He introduced himself as a gallery owner and curator from Paris. He had visited a few months beforehand, he said, and come to an arrangement with her husband. He had a show starting the following week along the theme of 'Natural Artists and Art Brut'. Giacomo was included. It was sponsored by the Paris city council, he said, and the emphasis was on the untrained aspect of the contributing artists – farmers, road-sweepers, dustmen, people who had no education in formal art. It was a kind of marginal, raw art, inherent really. Elena found the man's explanations completely baffling. She hadn't understood a word.

'And where is Monsieur Carlevaris?' he asked.

'I think he's away for the day. He left this morning.'

'I haven't got long. I've got to pick up his piece.'

'What piece?'

'He's called it *Friulano*. Here, I have a photo of it in the catalogue.' He opened a booklet and passed it to Elena.

'Ah, that!' she said. 'It's at the back.'

She opened the door onto the dry grass behind the building. It was peppered with towering statues. The gallery owner weaved his way between sculptures. Some were over fifteen years old, others more recent. He paused to take photographs of various pieces. 'This is amazing,' he said. 'Absolutely amazing.' They both spotted the Friulano sculpture at the same time.

'It's even better in real life.'

'You think so?' Elena mumbled. She hauled a log from a nearby stack and placed it at the foot of the sculpture. She climbed on and looked into the mouth, scraped and blew again. 'It's not too dirty, at least.'

'It's superb. I love it.' He took a sheet of bubble wrap from the bag he was carrying. 'Could you help me?' he motioned. 'Here, take this end.'

They stretched the plastic between them and wound it round the midriff of the sculpture. Elena called Djamel and watched as the two men lugged the sculpture to the van. It was placed on the floor of the vehicle and chained down firmly. Before the gallery owner closed the doors, he turned to thank Elena.

'See you next week then,' he smiled.

'I don't think so.'

'That's a shame,' he said, genuinely disappointed. 'It'll be a great event, I'm trying to get some big names to come, pump it up. Your husband will be in good company. I've got great press coverage already.'

Elena didn't reply. She tapped her feet together, waiting for the man to drive off.

'I sent an invitation to your son. He wrote such a nice piece for me in the catalogue,' he added, slamming the van doors. He clambered into the front seat. 'Oh, I forgot,' he said, fishing his wallet out of his pocket. 'Here's the cheque for your husband.'

Elena shook it incredulously. 'Five thousand francs,' she said. 'What's this for?'

'For taking part in the show, the Paris council are covering the costs.'

'What if it sold?' she asked, astonishing herself at entertaining such a ludicrous possibility.

'Twenty thousand. That's what I've put on the price list.'

Elena looked at him again. 'Are you serious?'

The Parisian started up the van, unsure what to say. He began to lift his hand to wave, then gripped the wheel and drove off.

Elena turned towards the nearest sculpture in the parking lot. Through the barrel of its unfilled body, she could see the brown, bristling rug of the marshes in the distance. She hurried to the show-room and placed the cheque under the coin tray of the till. It was a little before two o'clock. She set about displaying Djamel's newly made bowls. She wrote out prices on a sheet of stickers in neat figures, peeling them off one by one. She found the orders dossier bound with metal clasps. She stacked papers on the top in order of importance. Clearing Giacomo's worktop, she found drawings mixed in with administrative papers, uncovered orders for pots that had never been honoured, letters that had been left without reply. On many pages was the same doodled motif, a lizard emerging from a circle, its tail forked in two, its front legs crooked. She came across a postcard of a Brancusi sculpture. On the back was a quick, scrawled line from Marco: 'Saw this and thought of your new work.' She put it to one side and took the medical file from the shelf. Dr Couret had asked her to bring in some papers before her next appointment. Next to her documents, she found Giacomo's blood-test results and a wad of forms from the hospital in Nîmes. They were the conclusions of his fertility tests more than fifteen years previously. They stated, in each case, that he had no problems. At the top of every sheet was a tiny drawing of her, probably done as he waited to see a doctor. She was standing in various poses. In one she was smiling and in another she was lifting a pot onto a shelf, and her raised hands had flowers and leaves budding from her fingertips. How could she be so important to him? What was this unrelenting devotion of his that clung to her like skin? She had never known what to make of it, but had he not been there – that was something she could no longer make sense of. She folded the documents away and heard herself say, 'Giacomo,' the way she used to repeat Riccardo's name.

She went to check the roll of tissue paper in the lavatory. She gave the room a spray of air freshener. A delivery man dropped off a new order of lampshades to fit onto the stands they sold. She walked up to the apartment, leaving Djamel in charge, and peeled some potatoes. She found her new box of antidepressants in the bathroom cabinet and took two immediately. She rang Nassima's number to try and persuade her to curtail her week's holiday, but there was no reply. No doubt she was busy with her children. She looked out at the car park again. There was no sign of Giacomo. In the sitting room, she switched on the television. There was very little of interest on. Even so, she kept on getting up and flicking from one channel to the other, in the hope of coming across something to grab her attention. She hesitated about getting a magazine. She walked down to the showroom and listened to the answerphone. There were no messages. Where was Giacomo? Why hadn't he told her he would be out all day? She wanted to talk to him, but to say what, and how? They had never spoken enough.

She returned to her room, swallowed hard and opened up her wardrobe. She knew what she had to do. She couldn't put off the inevitable any longer. She started to pack her clothes into a suitcase. She went into the bathroom and filled a leather pouch with some make-up and her pills. She pulled her suitcase down to the pottery and opened up the till. She worked her way through the notes of money, counting and placing them in the inside pocket of her jacket, dropping the coins into her purse. She called a taxi and waited.

53

Marco was heading through the main entrance at UNESCO when Raul Leccese greeted him. 'How are you? I hear you shone at the conference. Well done.'

'It wasn't really anything to do with me. The whole team was great,' Marco said, speeding on towards the lifts.

Leccese trotted behind him. 'Tell me, I keep on meaning to ask,' he said, 'are you any relation of someone called Giacomo Carlevaris?'

Marco stopped and looked at him. 'Why?'

'Oh, I saw the name mentioned in an exhibition on the rue de Seine. Something like, 'A new look at Art Brut, the imaginary world of the marginalized.' Marco pressed the ground-floor button on the lift. 'It was in the Paris *Time Out.*' The lift arrived, the doors began parting. Marco shot inside and banged on all the buttons at once. 'It said they were mostly builders and farmers. I thought I might go…' Raul Leccese laughed loudly as the sliding doors snapped together and the lift shot upwards with a lurch to the stomach.

Marco ran down the linoleum corridor to his office. He settled down at his desk. There was a knock at the door.

'What now?' he muttered to himself.

'Marco, your father called,' Amani said, popping her head round the corner. 'For some reason it was put through to me. He sounded pretty anxious to get hold of you.'

Marco got up and closed the door. He slid open the window. He looked down at the Japanese garden in the forecourt below, watching the surface of the ornamental pond breaking with the movement of a fish. He turned and picked up the phone, dialling the number of the pottery.

'It's me,' he said to Giacomo.

'She's gone… she just left.'

'Who?'

'Your mother. I came back and she'd gone. Djamel told me she waved at him, said something about going home. She had a suitcase.' Marco drew up a chair to sit down. 'What am I going to do?' Marco held his head in his hands, wedging the telephone between his neck and shoulder. 'What shall we do?' Giacomo insisted.

'Nothing. There's nothing to do.'

'But, shouldn't we tell the police?'

'Why?'

'Well, she's on medication. Where's she going?'

'To Varanelle, like she said. She knows what she's doing.'

It was Giacomo's turn not to say anything.

'Are you all right?' Marco asked. There was no reply other than his shallow breathing.

'So it's come to this,' he whispered, 'it's come to this,' and he put the phone down.

The train to Paris was full. Mountains of luggage blocked the doors on and off the train. Giacomo bought himself a travel magazine in the station, not moving from his seat for the duration of the journey. The main feature of the magazine was on Mali – the Dogon people,

Bogolan fabrics, the River Niger, the musicians and artists of the country. Adverts suggested hotels to stay in, and various tourist itineraries. Among photographs of sculpted doors and riverbanks with diving children, Giacomo found an image of a crowded market. He ripped it out and examined each face as if he might know them. He ran his fingers through the damp coffee stain on his folding table, tracing a loose circle that gradually broke and trickled across the plastic.

At the Gare de Lyon, he waited for the last passengers to get off the train, gripped his bag and followed the crowd down the platform. He looked ahead through the archways of the station into the grey light and bustle of Paris before disappearing into the Metro, the summer stench, the hurrying faces and noise descending with him underground. He re-emerged on boulevard Ornano. He found a café with a view of Marco's flat. He spent the best part of two hours there, opposite the entrance. He didn't move, fixed in a position of waiting and watching.

Marco wandered past at half past six and entered his building. Giacomo lingered another ten minutes, looking up at the windows under the eaves. He paid and walked over. There was an entry dial. A woman, returning from work, made to open the door and he introduced himself, explaining his predicament. She let him into the hallway, insisting that he ring on the intercom before the second door. Marco Carlevaris, she said, lived in flat 9, top buzzer. Giacomo waited until the woman had left and pressed the button.

'*Oui*, who is it?'

'Marco, it's me.'

'Who?'

'Me, it's me. I decided to come for the exhibition after all. There's no point me being at home without your mother, I can't stand it. I couldn't get hold of you and I thought…'

The intercom went dead and the door clicked open. Marco was standing on the landing when Giacomo reached the top of the stairs, out of breath. He panted, tried to smile, 'I couldn't miss the show. It's a really smart gallery, somewhere central.' He fumbled through his pocket for the invitation, handing his nephew a dog-eared, creased piece of card. Marco took it and read it quickly.

'Course it's tonight, sorry I forgot,' he said, passing back the invitation.

'May I come in?'

'It's a mess, I warn you.'

'Who cares?'

'Come in quickly. It says half past seven on the invitation. You'd better get a move on.'

'This is nice,' Giacomo said, peering into the rooms.

Marco looked thin and unkempt. His clothes were thrown across a rug by the bed. Books were in piles by an electric fan.

'You don't look great,' Giacomo said.

'Nor do you.'

'Have you had any news from your mother?'

'No.'

'What am I meant to do, I…'

'I know it's hard,' Marco stopped him with a raised hand, 'but I have problems of my own right now, I'm sorry. Laura and I haven't seen each other for over two weeks. She's pregnant. She was due back yesterday or today, I haven't heard a thing.'

'Laura's pregnant!'

'She's still not sure she wants to keep it.'

'Oh Marco!'

'Thanks for your letter by the way, I haven't had time to write back,' Marco added. He stared ahead blankly. 'Do you want a drink or something?' he offered. 'I didn't even think of that.'

'No, no, I'd better be off.' Giacomo patted him on the back. 'Will you come to the show with me, then?' he asked. 'Say no if you don't

302

want to, but it would be fantastic, it might give you a bit of a change of scene, looks like you need to get out. I'd love to introduce you to the organizers, show off a bit, you know, here's my Marco who works at the United Nations, speaks five languages and all that.'

'That's a very good reason for me not to come,' Marco sighed. 'I haven't been out that much recently. I'd prefer to see it on my own, next week, if that's OK. I know where the gallery is.'

There was nothing more Giacomo could say. He began backing out of the flat. As he was heading off down the stairs again, Marco called after him.

'You should take that jumper off and wear this jacket. It would look better, especially in this heat.' He handed him a linen jacket. 'I don't need it, keep it.'

Marco retreated into his flat. He listened to Giacomo's footsteps down the stairs, before unhooking another jacket from the wall.

'Wait,' he shouted. 'I'm coming.'

From boulevard Saint Germain, they could see a crowd on the pavement ahead, spilling from the exhibition space onto the pavement. They crossed the road and stood by a parked car. The gallery window was lit up by bright spotlights pointing upwards. On a ledge, placed against the glass, was a plastic bag bursting at the seams, stuffed with fluorescent coloured sharp sticks that made it look like a painted hedgehog or sea urchin. On top was a papier mâché doll's head with a wig of flowing hair that tumbled downwards, twirled and snared on the protruding sticks.

'That was made by a dustman from somewhere in the Alps,' Giacomo said as they entered the gallery. 'Look, mine is down there,' he nudged Marco and pointed to the back of the room.

On a pedestal, against the wall, was a human-like sculpture with a roughly hewn, ragged body, its head smooth and tipped back, mouth open.

'Shame they put it there. Oh well,' Giacomo said, disappointed.

He turned and squeezed through the crowd to look at the other exhibits until he was cornered by the curator. A cluster of people formed round him. He thrust a hand out to greet them before being drawn into a collective appraisal of his work.

Marco stood captivated by his uncle's carved figure, its aquiline nose and dented face. All around him, people held glasses of wine, flicking their cigarette ash into bowls of sand on the floor, a babble of greetings and studied laughter. The sculpture's chest burst open with burrows, around a ram's skull, a quarry of tunnels, each adorned with animals, lizards with broken mouths and damaged tails. The arms dangled down the side of the torso in injured submission, the legs were more like fibres of wood, fanning out in strings that resembled nerves and bone. Marco spotted Giacomo in the corner of the gallery. He was clutching a plastic cup of white wine, two women talking to him animatedly. Marco walked up to the sculpture and grasped its hand, tightening his hold until he could feel it cutting at him. The spotlight above the sculpture shone into his face, heating the wood until it felt alive.

A large man in a blue blazer with a badge gestured in his direction. 'Monsieur,' he said. 'Don't touch the exhibits!' Marco clung on, mesmerized. The man walked towards him. 'Hey, I said don't touch the stuff.' People turned round to look. Marco searched for Giacomo at the rear of the room, near the window, but could not see him in the milling crowd. He hung onto the sculpture, only pulling back when the man came right up to him. 'Don't let me catch you doing that again,' he said. He was so close that Marco could see the man's patchily shaved neck, the starched collar jutting into his blistered skin, his thick eyebrows with several wiry hairs that extended beyond the others. 'I know this sculpture,' Marco shouted at him. 'I'll do what I like.'

He pushed through the crowd, unable to locate Giacomo, hurrying down the road. Where was his uncle? He turned back and searched another street. He went down to the edge of the Seine. He came to an alcove in the wall above the river and buried his head in his arms. The anger he had expressed in the gallery continued to surge through him. So, was this the reply he needed to give to the world? Was this the voice Laura was waiting to hear, the language he should have spoken long ago, the words of refusal he had suppressed since childhood? Below him a mass of foamy debris floated at the edge of the Seine, slapping against a brick hollow in the embankment, the water breathing in and out.

He looked up to see Giacomo further down the road. He was leaning over the stone parapet, staring into the river.

'I was looking for you,' he said, walking towards him.

Giacomo glanced up, a meek smile of relief on his face. 'I hate these kinds of gatherings, not my world. All that talking.'

'Your sculpture's great, though.'

'Do you think?'

'I loved it.'

'The gallery owner said it probably won't sell, but he wanted to show it all the same. That dustman's doll sold in five minutes. I don't understand.'

'Oh well, you never know, it's good that you came. You might make some interesting contacts.' The two men remained side by side, watching the river. A plastic bag rotated in the currents of the water. It vanished below the surface then shot back up, a different contorted shape. It rushed headlong towards one of the pillars of the bridge.

'I'm not sure what to do about your mother,' Giacomo said. The plastic bag hit the pillar, mounted the base and briefly snagged on a stone before being sucked back into the water. 'It's as if I don't exist in her eyes, after all these years. I don't understand. Your father's the only one who counts.' Giacomo's face didn't flinch, but Marco sensed that his words were louder than he wanted them to be.

'I'm sorry.'

'These last months have been quite impossible.'

'Since she came here. It didn't go well. She hated Laura from the moment she saw her.'

'I wouldn't say that.'

'Well, I can think of no other way of saying it'

'The doctor says she has severe depression. It should have been dealt with years ago.'

'Perhaps.'

'No, she has, very bad, they've increased the dosage of pills again.'

'I've come to understand certain things.'

'Like what?' Giacomo followed the plastic bag in the water. His hands played absently with the edge of the parapet; his knuckles bumpy and pale, stained with clay powder.

'I mean,' Marco said, 'we put up with things, we accept things because it suits us, because we can't face up to who we are and our lies.'

'How's that?'

'It suits her to be the way she is, depressed and deluded, so she doesn't have to deal with her failures, and you let her be like that, for your own reasons.'

'I don't understand what you're saying Marco, your ideas are always so complicated. You know your mother...'

'Ah, come on!'

Giacomo stiffened. 'She hasn't been well. She has problems, you know that as well as I do. Dr Couret says...'

'That's what I mean. By protecting her, you let things fester.'

'I don't understand, Marco, I don't get what you're saying, what do you mean "fester"?'

'Yes, you do, you know exactly what I'm talking about.'

Giacomo brought his hands to his face and rubbed his eyes. 'I think we should be getting back to the exhibition. It looks rude to stay away...'

'Don't run off. Talk to me, I need to understand. It's my life too.'

'I'm listening, Marco, I'm…'

'I've spent my whole life trying to make sense of this, wanting to be someone else, wanting to reinvent myself because that's what I saw around me. What do you think it was like for me as a child, to hear the silence between you, to be the only one she came crying to in the night with things I didn't understand? And her telling me, day in day out, that I had to think of a father I never knew and who supposedly loved me and her, more than you, but who made our life a misery. And you agreed with it all, and took the blame without complaining – I don't understand.'

'I did my best, Marco. I love your mother. I don't think you realize how difficult it was for me.'

'I don't.' For the first time, to his own surprise, Marco felt his anger rise up against this uncle who had cushioned his world for so many years. 'How long is this going to go on?' he spat. 'I can't stand it any more.'

Giacomo stepped back from the parapet wall. He held out his hand towards Marco as if to repel his words.

'I'm sorry that you're going through a rough patch, but we have to be strong together. I'm telling you I don't know what we can do about your mother. You and I have to help her, like we used to, we've always agreed on that.'

'You never confronted her in case she rejected you. If you'd just stood up to her it all could have been different.'

'It wasn't that simple.'

'Course it was, but you sacrificed yourself, for no real reason I can see. Why did you do that? Why? I just don't get it. Why would anyone do that?'

Giacomo backed away. He turned and ran, darting into the traffic.

'Papa,' Marco screamed. 'Papa. Wait!'

He began to chase after him, waving at cars to stop and let him pass. They hooted and braked, shouted abuse. Marco reached the end of the road and raced down a side street. He looked round. His uncle had vanished.

54

Nassima sidestepped the edge of the sea and emptied her plastic bags onto the beach. She pushed her bare feet into the sinking pile, scrunching her toes over the sand, letting the waves splash her knees. The wind filled the bags and shook them violently. The sun warmed her face. She watched her shoes and handbag next to her, the sea sucking them into its froth. She walked back to the road, and climbed onto her moped.

'Madame Carlevaris!' she called out as she entered the pottery courtyard, 'Madame Carlevaris!' She went from door to door. She peered inside the showroom. Everything was tidily put away, each object in its place, clean. On a bench outside, in the shade, she saw Djamel sitting alone.

Elena sat on the train. The road to the side of the track was pulsing with cars. She watched the suburbs of towns spread alongside the railway line, rows of buildings rushing over the slopes, scarring the land. Her thoughts were full of the absurdity of this short distance that had separated her from her family. Four measly hours to the neighbouring border with Italy, yet that distance was her, all that she had been over the last twenty or so years. She felt strangely empty at the sight of the frontier with its overhead board marked ITALIA. Maybe she had expected more fuss, more differentiation and contrast. She didn't know. A guard climbed on the train and gave her passport a cursory check. The train lurched on. Now she was in Italy, and France was behind, dissolving backwards into the track. Soon, too, she would have to speak the dialect of the village, the language that had remained in her mouth all these years. The withered sentences would come back to proper life and carry her forward once more.

She stared at the people around her, looking into them as if they should recognize her and know what she was going through. She bought herself some juice from the attendant with the trolley. She found she was unable to talk, merely point. She couldn't say anything as banal as please or thank you, not yet. She had to save up for the right moment to enter back into her country. She had prepared this homecoming for too long, perhaps even from the moment she had left. She couldn't spoil it with dull, everyday words. She watched the landscapes build up and melt away around her, the houses, the church towers and adverts. Nothing was how she'd imagined it, and yet it was all there, unchanged, unaffected by her, by the insignificance of her presence. She was surprised by her lack of emotion; she'd expected something to give inside her, reveal itself. She thought of Marco and Laura. The girl, she knew, was above all this. She had been born of firm decisions and experience, from privileged loves and unbroken lines. Yet Marco had emerged from here, from this uncertainty. He had no abroad, only an impossible return.

In Parma, she got off the train and found a hotel near the station. She took her suitcase into the foyer and waited by the reception desk. A woman hobbled through a back door. She looked at her as she spoke, each sentence of her Italian vibrantly clear. For a brief second, she felt a tinge of the sensation she was hoping for. Then it went as the woman placed a heavy key on the desk and gestured down the hall. Her room was simple with a bathroom off the side. There was a phone directory by the bed. She opened it and looked through the entries for Varanelle. She couldn't see anyone with the name of Varsi.

In the morning, she left the hotel, counted her money discreetly inside her bag, placed some of it in her pocket and walked towards the taxi rank. The driver's, '*Dove*? Where to?' woke her. 'Varanelle, near Bardi,' she said, and the names took on a resonance they had lacked for years, as though she were finally pronouncing them correctly again. Varanelle. Yes, Varanelle. The sound of it was inebriating.

She sat back in the taxi. Parma and its outskirts ended and they broke into the countryside, trees bending over the road. The taxi driver tried to initiate a conversation, but Elena wasn't able to listen. 'Sorry,' she said, 'I can't talk, not today.' She pushed her hands deep into her bag. They turned into Castell'Arquato and drove into the main square. Two hotels stood on one side of the piazza, opposite the town hall. People were congregating outside a bakery. The car swept out of the town. They snaked up roads towards the mountains. The lushness, the green orchards and fields struck her after the aridity of the south of France. They passed through Bardi and carried on. Soon thicker forests shaded the road, the tarmac punctured by sprouts of grass, cracks with moss and ferns growing in them. They arrived at the edge of Varanelle. A group of houses with pots of plants stuck to their stone fronts hemmed in the road as it became the main street of a village. Elena asked the taxi driver to leave her in the square. She got out and sat on the steps of the church, the sun bleaching the paving stones.

She looked up the road towards the top of Monte Barigazzo. A plaque with the inscription 'Via Garibaldi' had been nailed to the corner house. She saw that each street out of the square now had a name. The houses too had numbers, ceramic squares pinned next to the doors. She started to walk, her suitcase knocking into her shin. A bar and a small supermarket occupied the end of the road by the fountain. Inside each house, as she walked on, she pictured faces in the darkness, furtive looks through the shutters and creaking doors. 'Is that Elena Varsi, the foreman's daughter?' She fancied she could hear the murmur of it, the spread of her name up the street. Or perhaps there was nothing. She thought of all those who had once left this place and never returned – ancient women stranded in the British rain, old men dragging their rheumatic bones across America, the great-grand-children of those who had emigrated to Australia, people who had no idea this place existed. As she passed in front of Stefano Zanelli's house, she wondered whether this was how it was for actors in films, made-up and invented characters in actual landscapes. Varanelle was real, but she was some sort of visitation, who could vanish and rematerialize, insubstantial.

She took the road that led to Morfasso. Long grass crowded the ditches. The village street came to an end and the road wound upwards through clumps of trees and haystacks. Mountains came into view and faded as the road curled on. A large farmhouse with stone steps stood back from the road down a short track. She climbed up the steps and knocked on the door. There was no answer. A blue estate car with a Parma number plate was stationed down the side of the house where the chicken coop used to be. The vegetable patch had been covered in tarmac. She knocked again. The door opened. A small, gaunt woman poked her head outside.

'I'm looking for the Varsi family,' Elena said.

'Who?'

'The Varsi, they used to live here.'

'We've had this house for five years. We come here every weekend,' the woman answered suspiciously.

'Did they sell it to you?'

'Who?'

Varsi family.'

The woman slipped inside again. 'Franco, Franco,' she called. An expensively dressed man popped his head out. 'What do you want?' he asked.

'Nothing,' Elena answered. 'Nothing.'

She descended the steps. She walked back down to the village. From time to time, she stopped and took it all in, the roofs of the houses, the mountains, the sound of her footsteps on the road. She walked into the field opposite the cemetery. She swapped her suitcase from hand to hand. A corner of Monte Barigazzo came into view again. She hurried through the field onto a dust path. Meadows, dotted with trees, sloped down to a river. The now-disused sawmill rusted above her, the road to it overgrown and pot-holed. A wood caged by beams of sunlight spread across the hillside ahead, bracken tipping onto the path. A bitter-sweet smell of undergrowth hit her. The trees grew sparser again and she came to a new field. The grass lashed at her thighs as she walked. With one hand she plucked at the heads of seeds.

She paused, looking at the crown of a mountain rising stiffly above the treetops. The rock pool was hidden by branches, the stream had run dry. She lay down and she could feel her whole body sinking back into the warmth of the earth, the feel of it on the bare skin of her legs. She remembered the photograph of Marco as a boy leaping through the fields, his hair almost orange in the evening sun, this grass, this same grass. She wrapped blades of it round a fist and tugged, pulling a net of roots from the ground. She saw the caved-in roof of a house in the distance and a clear image of Silvana Fontani came to her. Were all those white widows dead now? How many of them had lost their lives wed to the past and permanent guessing, stuck to the shadows of men they had met in their youth? Everywhere across Italy, she thought, there must still be houses, with their doors sealed and windows closed, the dried mud of former lives filling the holes in the floors. Elena felt the sun on her, visualized it slowly working on her complexion, forking wrinkles round her eyes, opening up furrows in her face. Was she to become one of the old women of her childhood? The sun faded behind a drifting raft of clouds, emerging further down on the mountain face. She made her way back to the village.

She decided to consult the café owner and stepped over a sleeping dog in the doorway. A short old man was seated at the bar smoking a cigarette. The place was empty.

'Could you tell me where the Varsi family live now?' she asked.

'Varsi?' the owner said.

'Varsi, yes Varsi.'

'There are none of them left up here.'

'Roberto Varsi died. There's still Anna Varsi,' the old man at the bar piped up. 'She moved to a flat on the other side of the village, one of those new blocks on the road to Bardi.'

The dog had woken and was sniffing her shoes. She looked at the man, his cigarette and the vacant tables. 'Which one?' she asked.

'They'll tell you there. I think it's the newest one with the pavement still unfinished,' the old man at the bar answered. 'Why do you want her?'

She didn't answer and he looked at her. 'Elena?' he said softly, but she was gone.

She approached the new block of flats on the edge of the village. It was built on a steep road, windows shaded by orange striped awnings, towering over the old stone houses next to it. Below the new apartment block was a car park with different lots marked out with white lines. Pots of clipped and pruned plants filled the stairways to the flats. A doormat and a few wooden crates were stacked up against a wall. Elena heard a discordant, jarring voice. She followed the sound to find her mother, white-haired, thinner and stony-faced, on a cement balcony, two floors above her. 'Mamma,' she wanted to call, but the name she had once used no longer seemed appropriate. Elena waved. Her mother's eyes didn't register anything. She hoped that if she concentrated she might make sense of the words her mother was mumbling to herself, a prayer perhaps, or a song, but they petered out, unintelligible and dried. She shouted to get her attention, but in the loud syllables of her voice, Elena sensed that she was only hearing herself – an empty echo in the back of her mother's mouth.

She climbed the granite steps, past the other apartments, and rang a bell. Her mother came to the door. She looked at her. They didn't talk. 'Is that you?' she eventually said, 'Is it really you?' Elena leant her head on her mother's shoulder. They remained like this for a long while. Her mother kissed her hair and pulled her inside. She shuffled ahead in her slippers, her stockings slacking at the knees, down a corridor with shining tiled flooring. Elena noted her lined hands curved inwards, her fingers stubbed and blunt. Her mother turned and stared again, hands on her haunches. 'Elena,' she repeated, 'Elena.' She took her hand and led her into the main room. A simple plastic-topped table stood in the middle of a room with a couple of armchairs. On the wall was a clock with the pendulum swinging noisily. The ticking of it coaxed Elena forward with its familiar noise. She recognized nothing else but that noise.

Her mother rummaged around in the kitchen for a box of biscuits. She placed it on the table and returned to the kitchen, ferrying fruit juice, glasses and a jug of water. 'I have rheumatism,' the old woman said. She helped herself to a soft biscuit and pushed the box to Elena. She opened her mouth and pointed to her four remaining teeth: 'Can't eat much either.' They sat round the table, listened to the clock and looked at each other, holding hands. Elena placed a photograph of Marco in front of her mother alongside another of the pottery showroom with its display cabinets and shelves. She fought to stop herself from weeping. She swallowed and smiled, smiled and swallowed, and watched her mother eating her biscuit with one side of her mouth.

§ §

Laura dialled Marco's number. She heard his voice and slammed the receiver down. Her own phone rang a few seconds later. The answerphone came on. She switched it off at the wall.

She picked up a few things and ran out of her flat. She caught the Metro to Simplon and went straight to Marco's. She typed in the code, opened the second door with a key and dashed up the six flights of stairs. She re-tightened her hairgrip and walked into the flat. There was no-one in the bedroom, no-one in the kitchen. The bathroom door was shut and she flung it open. He wasn't in there either. 'Marco! Hey Marco, it's me,' she called out, confused. She went into the bedroom and sat on the only chair. An eerie feeling was beginning to come over her when the bed stirred, the duvet shifting in a slow crumple. Marco sprung back the covers and stood up. His eyes were puffy, his face tired.

'What the hell are you doing under there?' Laura shrieked.

'And what are you doing?'

'I wanted to surprise you!'

Marco confessed that when he rang back and discovered she wasn't answering he had collapsed on the bed, convinced she had dialled his number by mistake. He joked that he had just been contemplating various options, from self-harm to suicide, under his duvet.

'It could have been like Romeo and Juliet.'

He pulled Laura onto the bed and hugged her with all his might, almost winding her in the process.

'Hang on!' Laura said, fighting for breath. 'I'm carrying something rather precious.'

'You are?'

'I am.' Marco pushed his head against Laura's belly, raising her shirt till he felt her skin on his face. She stroked his hair, lightly at first, then more forcefully. 'I shouldn't have gone off like that, leaving you here, I know, but I was so confused by you, by everything. It's still not that clear in my head, we…'

Marco sat up, 'I can't tell you how many times I've thought of this, you being here again.' He beamed at her. 'You're here,' he shouted in an elated voice. 'This calls for a bit of a tidy-up.' He ran about the flat, flinging dirty clothes into one corner, slipping into the kitchen, stacking up plates and encrusted saucepans. He kept on returning and staring at her in disbelief. 'You're back,' he repeated, 'you're back!'

'Where are all your books?' Laura asked.

Marco opened the cupboard and pointed at a row of boxes beneath the hanging clothes. 'I'm going to take them to a second-hand store.'

'Why?'

'They've been getting in the way for too long.' He knelt down beside her. 'You know, I never went to Japan or Romania, or any of those places.'

'Don't worry, I guessed as much.'

'You did?'

'Wasn't difficult.'

'And you still love me?'

'Why do you think I'm here, you fool.' She kissed Marco's hand and held it to her mouth. He ran a finger across her lips, retreating backwards to kick a shirt into the cupboard. He picked up a newspaper and folded it in half. He passed it to Laura, pointing at a photograph he had circled in biro.

'Look at this apartment, in the fifth arrondissement, near the Jardin des Plantes. It has two bedrooms and a sitting room. If we both gave up our flats, we could afford it. It would be good to be near a park for the baby.'

'Hang on! Hang on!' Laura said, reading the details. 'Sounds nice, but we're a long way off all that, aren't we? We need to work a few things out still, Marco. Promise me that? Don't let's brush this under the carpet. I want things to be clear.' She opened the windows as wide as she could. 'It's much hotter here.' She rubbed a flake of paint off the railings and looked at it. 'I read this wonderful article in London on ants. It's extraordinary how organized their lives are, how an ant nest is structured. There's a kind of clockwork precision to it all.'

'At least you haven't changed!' Marco said with a laugh.

'I bloody well have. I had the most terrible time in London. I've never felt so lonely in my whole life. I felt completely disconnected from my family, like some stranger.'

'I meant…'

'My mother was a joke. I could have done with one like yours. She was totally uninterested. Maybe she was embarrassed by it all, I don't know. We couldn't even talk about it. It was like a slap in the face.'

'I meant your comments a propos of nothing, talking about ants.'

'Oh.'

The telephone rang. The answerphone clicked on. 'Marco, *t'es là?* It's me, Nassima. There's a driver here who's come to collect something. I have been left no instructions, no telephone numbers. I don't know what to do. I haven't heard from your mother or Monsieur Carlevaris. Will you call me?'

Marco frowned. 'I had a go at my poor uncle, here in Paris,' he said. 'It didn't come out as I wanted, I was so angry all of a sudden. I called the gallery where he's exhibiting this morning. He hasn't been in.'

'And where's your mother…' Laura asked, but he put a hand over her mouth and held her instead, in an embrace neither could break.

Late that evening, they decided to drop in on Fatoumata at the St Bernard Church. She had ended her hunger strike for her children's sake, but was determined to stay on in the church. Laura was anxious to find out what had gone on in her absence. They went the long route round, walking up to Montmartre and down the other side to La Goutte d'Or. They saw that the vineyard behind the Basilica was parched and brown in the evening heat. The flats and houses surrounding the vines had their windows pushed open. On one of the walls of the vineyard, alongside the stone steps of rue des Saules, up towards the Basilica, they saw a seated man, his hands deep in his jacket pockets. He was contemplating the rows of vines lit up by streetlamps.

'Papa?' Marco shouted out.

Laura stopped, not sure whether to stay or not, but Marco caught hold of her hand and led her forward. Giacomo didn't notice them until they were right beneath him.

'What are you doing here?' Marco said. 'I've been trying to find you all day.'

Without replying, he climbed down from the wall. They walked together to the nearest café. Marco ordered water and a sandwich for Giacomo. 'Sorry,' he said. 'This is Laura.'

'Hello,' Giacomo said, avoiding eye contact.

'Why don't you meet me at the church?' Laura turned to Marco, beginning to feel uncomfortable, 'I'm sure you've got things to say to each other.'

She stood up. Marco jumped up after her.

'You'll be careful, won't you? It's already very late.'

'It's fine, don't worry.'

'No, seriously, there'll be crowds there and, you know,' he pointed at her belly.

'Yes.' She kissed him.

She let go of his hand and soon she was on the other side of the vineyard, tall and slender, her fair hair a remote dash of colour.

Marco pushed his chair next to Giacomo. 'I'm sorry for what happened last night, I really am,' he said. 'It all got to me.' There was no reply. The sandwich sat uneaten. 'Do you want to come back to my flat to wash or rest?'

'I should get the last train home tonight. There's one around midnight I think,' Giacomo said after a while.

'Not tonight, go tomorrow, there's no rush, we can spend some time together.'

They sat without exchanging a word. Giacomo stared at the pavement. Marco noticed he had the beginnings of stubble on his cheeks and that it was grey.

'Maybe we should go and find Laura,' he said, standing. 'I don't feel too happy about her being there without me.'

They walked to the St Bernard Church in brisk strides. Giacomo began to lag behind, unaware of his nephew's urgency. 'Could we hurry?' he said encouragingly.

As they came into the area of the Goutte d'Or, they saw more and more people. The front of the church was frantic with activity.

'How am I going to find Laura in all this?' Marco became twitchy. The two men searched around them, looking for her among the people coming and going.

'I hope she hasn't gone in already.'

A broad-shouldered man Marco had once seen with Fatoumata walked past them.

'Excuse me, have you seen Laura, a tall Englishwoman, blonde?' he asked.

'She's inside, I think,' the man said. 'Things are looking ugly. The police are coming.'

'We've got to find her,' Marco said, hurrying to the entrance of the church.

They squeezed past the men on the door. Visitors were being checked, but they got through unnoticed.

They took some time to adjust to the dimmer light of the church. There was no coolness coming off the stone floors. The air was thick with trapped human closeness. Around three hundred people, mostly Africans, Marco had heard on the radio that morning, had now congregated inside. A sound of talking filled the heights of the vaulted ceiling. Clusters of people massed in different parts, behind pillars, against the walls. In side chapels, women sat huddled together, their babies breastfeeding, children on laps, bright rugs and bags under statues and paintings. Some held small radios to their ears, waiting for news. Blankets were thrown across the backs of pews. A pile of mattresses rested against a confessional. A priest walked from group to group, stopping in front of the few hunger strikers. There were journalists and photographers snapping with bright flashes. Candles were lit, rows of holders with their flames flickering. The area under the pulpit was filled with plastic bags of belongings. Some people were trying to sleep despite the cacophony. Pews were being stacked up against the door to reinforce it and prevent the police from forcing an entry. Men passed pews to each other. One tried to say something, clapping to catch the attention of the people around him. They looked up for a while before turning away.

Giacomo thought he spotted Laura, but it wasn't her. Marco saw a woman in a bright green headdress instead. Fatoumata looked surprised to see them coming towards her.

'Laura's just gone to find you outside.'

'Outside?'

'Yes.'

'This is Fatoumata,' Marco said, turning to his uncle.

'Everyone says they're going to come tonight,' she said, sucking in her cheeks. 'I can feel it.' The three of them watched men carrying pews up to the front door. 'I better go and help the women prepare,' she added and slipped off with a determined face. 'Catch you later.'

They walked towards the front door, edging past people, apologizing as they went.

'We're not letting anyone out now. We've locked it,' one of the men at the entrance told them immediately. He placed a pew against the door, then another.

'When are you going to open it?'

'We'll keep it locked all night if we need to, till we know what's happening.'

'Damn it,' Marco said, turning to his uncle. 'What are we going to do?'

'Laura will go home, won't she? It's past midnight already.'

They faced each other. 'Well, we've got no choice but to wait here I suppose.' Marco's voice was tense.

'Let's go over there,' Giacomo pointed. 'It's too noisy here.' They wandered towards the back of the church, behind the altar. Some leaflets littered the ground. Marco bent down and took one. They stood alongside each other, close enough to touch. They found themselves at the base of the pulpit. They tried to find somewhere to sit, but everywhere was taken. The noise of the church was intense. They finally came upon an empty stretch of step at the entrance of an alcove. They sat down, pressed and pinched by the throngs of people round them. Marco looked at his uncle. Giacomo had closed his eyes.

'Are you all right?' Marco shook him. 'You should have eaten that sandwich I bought you.'

Giacomo held his head in his hands. Marco did the same, in an attempt to rest. It was obvious they would be there for hours.

Giacomo picked a piece of silver foil off the floor. He twisted and fashioned it into a small figurine, before scrunching it up and starting again. He changed the foil into a beetle with square legs and a wasp with rolled wings. Marco only hoped that Laura had had the good sense to go home. He saw that the front doors were now totally barricaded with pews. He tried to close his eyes, but couldn't help but notice the twirling and bending of foil in his uncle's fingers, new shapes and creatures destroyed and remoulded in a matter of minutes.

They had been there several hours when Giacomo began to talk.

'I can still hear him, all the time,' he said. 'I can.' He dropped the silver foil and clenched his fists.

'Sorry?' Marco said, 'Who?'

'Your father.'

'What?' Marco asked, but Giacomo was already speaking, quietly at first, then faster and faster, his hands falling still by his sides.

'After Argentina, he came to Paris. Things had gone badly for him over there. He hadn't made the money he wanted. He said he'd been swindled. One night, I found him blind drunk, sobbing. His wife and child, I said, would make things clearer when he returned to Italy.' Giacomo leant against the side of the carved pulpit staircase.

'You don't have to tell me any of this,' Marco said, putting his hand on his uncle's shoulder, 'I...'

'Things got worse,' Giacomo carried on, not hearing, 'he continued to drink. He met women, a lot of women, and men who promised him riches in Argentina again. Then, he announced that he was returning to Varanelle. I had bought a scarf with red circles like flowers, and a toy for you. I don't know what got into me. I saw the scarf in a window, walked in and bought it without thinking. I gave it to your father to take to your mother. I had never met Elena, but it didn't matter, it didn't matter at all. I had it put in a gift box by the shop assistant, in tissue paper with ribbons. Your father was very angry with me. "Stay out of my life," that's what he said. I can still hear the way he said it.' A group of shrieking children skipped over Giacomo's legs nearly knocking him onto the flagstone floor. A woman lying in a sleeping bag complained, shooing them away to other games. They held Giacomo's attention for a while. Marco had fallen silent.

'He was gone ten days. As I worked at the factory, I imagined your father reunited with Elena, meeting you. I was happy for him, and jealous too, intensely jealous. I hated myself for it. The idea of him being with her, your mother, tortured me. I thought, though, that a new sense of calm would come back to him, that he might even return via Paris with Elena and you. Your father would be himself again I hoped, and I would shake myself out of my fascination with her. Instead he arrived back, with the beginnings of a beard, in the early hours of one morning. He sat in the corner of the room and ate a hunk of bread. I got out of bed to talk to him. He didn't move. He told me he was leaving again. He'd find a way to get back to Argentina. That was where he wanted to be, in Buenos Aires, where he now belonged. He needed money for a ticket. I said he should work night shifts at the factory. They were better paid. In a month he could earn enough. I asked him how his wife and son were going to get there.

'His mood blackened immediately and he spat out the bread he was eating. His eyes blinked and he began to shiver. I didn't understand. I sat down next to him. Without looking at me, he said he had been to Varanelle. He had walked from Bardi, up the road to the village and, with every step, he said he'd felt the desire to turn round and run away. It wasn't a new feeling, anything unexpected. It was something that had been tearing away at him in Argentina. Each day, in Buenos Aires, he had tried to imagine Elena surrounded by the smells of the port, and him with her, under the vast skies, listening to the music and language of the streets, but it didn't fit. It was totally foreign to her, to all that she was. He couldn't picture her in the houses he visited. Even out in the countryside, on the edges of Buenos Aires, the plants and birds were strange, the heat a different burning. There was no place for her and the more he saw this, the more she seemed to slip from his grasp. It had put him off returning, made him repeatedly delay his trip back, but in Varanelle it was so strong as to be unbearable. Instead of heading for the farmhouse, he'd taken the steep path up to the sawmill, through the thickness of the forest, to be alone. It was there, cornered by his doubts, that he understood that it really had all broken apart inside him, beyond repair. His life back with your mother was another empty dream, as doomed as his money-making in Argentina. His past desire for her was that of a man who hadn't yet seen the world, who knew nothing. He had discovered an independence in Argentina that he couldn't lose, a total release from the conventions and hardship that had always held him back. He waited for hours under those trees, fighting this pitiless emotion inside him. The more he went over it in his head, the more he saw that he wanted nothing to do with his old life, and that the decisions he had once taken in Varanelle came from a man who no longer existed, who had disappeared the day he left. Too much had happened, he said, too much had changed. He and Elena no longer knew each other. The person he had once been at her side was a ghost he now didn't understand, a stranger. He had thought of her continually, but it had been an illusion, she was no longer real, like our native Friuli, a hollow image he had outgrown. The scent of different women stuck to him, the dirt of money, the sounds of new experiences, the salt of the seas he had crossed. All these were boundaries he had stepped over and he couldn't retreat from or cancel out. How could he respond now, he said, to the innocent expectations of a woman who had never been beyond Parma, who thought the next valley was a foreign land? He went back up the hillside, furiously pulling bark from the trees as he went, still trying to dismiss the thoughts that had lodged themselves in him so firmly. He came to the point above a barn, he said, and walked round the side. He cut across to the path towards Morfasso. Below him, the farmhouse came into clear view. He sat on the stump of a felled tree and waited. He hoped by seeing Elena, and you, that he'd change his mind.'

Marco closed his eyes. Despite the din of the church, he could only hear his uncle's subdued voice inside his head.

'After a while, your mother and you came out into the field beside the house. There was a dog with you, and you chased it up and down. Elena was more beautiful than he had remembered, her hair longer than it had been, her skin dark from the summer. He wanted to touch her without being felt, call her without being heard. You were big for your age, and you spoke well. The sound of your voice reached him, but he couldn't hear the words clearly. He watched you on and off for the rest of the day, as you both emerged from the house, hanging out the washing, feeding the chickens. He saw your aunt too, and your grandfather who scooped you up in his arms and carried you on his shoulders. Seeing this, your father wandered up to the forest again. He found a stream and washed in a rock pool, drank from it. At one point, the dog found his tracks and he heard it barking wildly. He ran further into the forests. He slept the night at the base of a tree, the warmth of its bark against him. In the morning, he returned to the sawmill and climbed over the fence. He broke into the workshop, ripping the lock off the door. He turned the place upside down, trying to remember where your mother had said the wages were kept. When he found the hidden box, he took a bundle of wages. It was money, he told me, which your grandfather had cheated him out of three years before. He ran downhill and headed to the copse of trees by the farm. He saw you standing alone by the chicken pen, gathering up stones in a wooden box which you carried to the side of the house.

'He watched you. His stomach ached with hunger. His hands were dirty from his night outside. He waited and waited. He whistled. You looked up and he called your name, slipping behind the trees afterwards. You turned round, searching the woods for the noise. He whistled louder, and you began approaching hesitantly, curious but wary. He called your name again, over and over, backing away from the farm each time into the trees. You walked through the woods, checking around you, unsure. Your father was huddled in a tiny clearing. "Marco," he said to you, "Marco." You looked up. He could see you wanted to run at the sight of him, but you didn't. Your father knelt down. "Marco," he said again. He touched your head, and you let him. He studied your face and you stared at him. You didn't move, you looked at each other a long while, then you ran, without turning round, sprinting out of the woods towards the farm. Your father ran too, retracing his footsteps up the hillside towards Bardi. He looked at Varanelle once more, in the distance. "Elena, Marco," he yelled at the top of his voice, and he continued to flee through the undergrowth.'

Marco leant on Giacomo's shoulder. He straightened the collar on his uncle's linen jacket. Two men carrying another pew stormed past, elbowing their way through people.

'Marco, I can't console you, I'm not worthy of that.' Giacomo turned his eyes from his nephew, but held onto his shirt, his long fingers on his sleeve. It was around seven in the morning. There was a commotion at the front of the church then it died down. Giacomo carried on talking, as though the noises of the church didn't exist, as if he weren't there himself.

'The morning he came back to Paris from Italy,' he said, 'I saw your father close down. He had said too much to me. He had opened his heart in a way he had never done and he hated me all the more for having been a witness to it. I tried to talk to him again, but he got drunk often. He was as fragile as he was aggressive. I didn't know how to deal with it. Each night he returned with a new woman, as if asking her to propel him into a different future. He worked at the factory in the evenings, counting out his money before he left. I joined him on the odd shift, doing extra hours. One evening, he was more restless than usual. I knew I shouldn't mention Elena, but I did. He was unsteady on his feet. I said he should reconsider his decision. How were his wife and child going to survive without his money or him? I would take him to Italy personally, and sort it out, I had decided. It would do me good to go back. He told me I was an idiot, who knew nothing, understood nothing. "You still don't get it, do you? After all that I've told you." I sat down beside him. I said things weren't as desperate as he thought. I would help him put it all right. He laughed. He told me he didn't need my help. What good had it done him in the past? None at all. I was like our cousin in Buenos Aires who had been nothing but a toothless old man, unable to do anything for him, another person who had crossed the world for nothing.

"'But you still have her," I said, "you have Elena." A brutal frustration darkened his face and it was all directed at me. "I'm telling you it's all gone. It's all lies now." "She loves you," I repeated, "I know she loves you." "You think it helps to be loved like that? It doesn't. It makes it all impossible." I persevered; I told him he didn't realize how lucky he was to have a wife like Elena. Maybe he didn't see that now, but he would later, when he was calmer. She was every man's hope. I'd do anything, I said, to be in his position. He went mad. He lashed out at me and pushed me to the ground. I was shouting, trying to protect my face and he threw me against the metal bed. I stood up, and he shoved me down again, my leg was slashed against the edge of the bed. I put my arms up to protect my face from his blows, trying to fend him off with my feet. "She wouldn't even look at a loser like you," he screamed. I fell to the ground. My leg was bleeding badly.'

Giacomo realized he was holding Marco's jacket and let go. 'Don't look at me, don't,' he said. His eyes were full of distress and fatigue. He ran a hand through his hair. 'I made my way to the factory although I could barely walk. I had bandaged up my leg as best I could. We were both meant to be working a night shift that evening. He was there, in the hangar. He had drunk more.' Giacomo carried on talking, as emptily as an automaton. 'He was driving a vehicle loaded with bricks. The factory was deserted, lit by dim strips high up in the hangar. When he saw me, he hoisted the nets of bricks off the truck and left them dangling on the pulley so that he could shout at me. "Riccardo," I shouted back at him. I wanted to show him my injured leg and ask him whether he realized what he had done, that he needed help. I could see he hadn't fastened the pulley properly. When I came up to him, he fought me off again, pushing me to one side. I told him to watch out; he was too drunk to work. He carried on manoeuvring the pulley. As I spoke again, the wires holding the bricks above him snapped and broke away, dropping in a cloud of red powder, smothering his screams.'

Giacomo rubbed the side of his neck and looked down at the flagstones of the church. 'When I got to him under the bricks,' he continued in a quieter voice, 'all I saw were his legs convulsing; the fabric of his trousers and his skin were meshed together. The rest of him was covered in rubble. I told him to hang on. I threw the bricks to one side, scrabbled desperately, yanked and pulled to get to his muffled breathing underneath. I told him I would get him water, look after him, he wasn't to worry. I told him we should never argue again. When I reached his chest, I found it pierced with wounds, his shirt covered with rings of red. "I'll get you out of there," I said. I had to unfold his arms shielding his face. Most of his face was untouched, his mouth filled with blood. His tongue had been partly severed and split. He was gasping, pointing, trying to raise his hand towards a door. I knew I had to call someone, get help, but I had to stay with him too. I was going to save him. That's all I could think. I wanted him to know I was going to save him. He was my brother, my only family left. He needed me. We should forget about everything else. I got water and poured it into his mouth. It foamed and frothed with blood. I had to fetch someone, I knew I had to. I tried to carry him, but he kept on pointing at the telephone, his voice rasping in his throat. He began to retch. I held his neck up, wiped his forehead. I said I'd run and get help, find the watchman, call, telephone, anything. Still, I knelt there, holding him, looking after him. I was looking after him. I didn't act quickly enough. I was going to save him. He was nothing without me, lying there. I would save him, only I would save him. I was going to get him back, I would do it. Then I said sorry for talking to him about Elena. I didn't go fast enough. I stayed there, his head in my hands, his blood on me. I carried him a few metres. I knew I was going to save him. He would owe his life to me. He would never treat me badly again. I saw Elena in my mind and wanted her recognition too. I thought that, I did, and about how he had hated me at times and how I had hated him, many times, how beautiful she was too, always so beautiful, yes, even that. And that I wasn't a loser, he couldn't call me a loser.' Giacomo rubbed his neck again. He pulled at the hair of his temples, fingering his earlobes. 'I worried about who to call, I didn't go fast enough, I watched him, I waited too long, I stalled and panicked, and then the moaning stopped. By the time the nightwatchman came I'd wiped his face with water and swept back his hair. His face was calm. That's what the nightwatchman said to me: "His face is calm." The rest of him was broken.'

Giacomo drew his jacket together, shifted from foot to foot. A hard thudding, a hacking, rose from the front of the church drowning out all other noise.

'*Ils sont là*, the police are here, they're here!'

The point of an axe split the door and bits of wood flew onto the floor. Another swing of the axe ripped into the door again. It started to give. The stack of pews was shunted back and held against the hammering. Shouts came from outside the church, louder and louder; soon policemen with truncheons and protective clothing shoved their arms through the destroyed door. The pews came crashing down. Swarms of police officers rounded up the nearest Africans, leading them away. A tang of tear gas began to rise. Marco saw a policeman grab Fatoumata and bundle her towards the exit, her hands yanked up behind her back. He darted through the crowds towards her.

'Be careful with her, she hasn't done anything,' he yelled. He pulled Fatoumata away, only to find a truncheon raised above him.

'Marco,' Giacomo shouted. He hurled his nephew out of the way. A truncheon, then another, flew into Giacomo's stomach. He stumbled and fell.

56

Elena cooked and cleaned. With soapy water, she washed the tiles of her mother's main room and the windows, occasionally pausing to look at the view. In the corner of her eye, she could see the cemetery with its newly rebuilt walls and ranks of crosses. Her grandparents, she remembered, were to the left of the gate. She had an aunt by the only tree at the back, a cousin in the end row. Somewhere was her father.

Giacomo had once told her that, as a young child in Friuli, people always used to stare at him as if he should say something, as if he had just arrived to speak. Yet he had never wanted to talk. He had always looked up into the forested mountains and sun and all that he could see had been enough. She surveyed the hills and peaks on the horizon and knew for a moment what he had meant. This is all there is, she agreed. What more is there? What more should I want now?

She went into the room where she was sleeping. She took off her apron and searched through her suitcase. She undressed and chose new clothes from her pile of possessions. She put on her multi-coloured necklace with the silver charms. She had a heavy flask of Parisian scent and she sprayed it over her wrists and dabbed her temples. Her sister was coming with her husband and three children. She combed her hair, pleased that she had dyed it again prior to leaving. She pulled on a pair of tights, a skirt and high heels. She straightened the creases out of her top. She found her pills in her sponge bag. She pushed one out of its tiny silver foil pouch and held it in her hand. She wasn't sure she wanted anything to muddy or colour this day. She slipped it into the back pocket of her skirt all the same. She opened the sitting-room door. Her mother looked up at her and said nothing.

She heard a car parking in the forecourt below, and three noisy teenagers chased up the stairs, bursting into the room. Behind them came a middle-aged woman. Teresa had grown dumpy: her hair was straight. Her neck was thick, that's what struck Elena the most. She was dressed simply. Her husband was small. That's all she could think of him, he was small. They all stood facing her. She kissed them each, in turn. She saw one of the young boys wipe his cheek afterwards. Was it the scent, the lipstick or because of what he had been told about her on the way? Her niece, a slight girl with jet-black hair and bushy eyebrows smiled at her.

She went to the kitchen to fetch the juices and food. Teresa followed her. They didn't talk. They busied themselves. The two of them put dishes on a wooden tray. Elena took a flat plate and dropped biscuits onto it. She looked round her for napkins. She found nothing and tore pieces of kitchen paper from a roll. Her brother-in-law was smoking. The smell of it filled the flat. Teresa reached for her hand by the sink.

'I never thought you would come,' she said. 'How long will you stay?'

Elena noticed that everyone and everything had fallen silent. She hadn't yet spoken. She was expected to speak. She felt for the pill in her back pocket, traced its contours with her finger.

'I'm not sure,' she said, 'depends.'

More questions followed, the children shouted and jostled each other, and the husband puffed on his cigarette. A biscuit fell from the plate onto the floor. Some juice was spilt on the tablecloth. Elena turned to her mother. She wasn't paying attention. She was looking at the clock.

'I have a business to run,' Elena struggled to say above the gathering noise. 'I can't stay too long. I have two employees, but I need to be there really.'

'Two employees,' the room repeated, 'two employees.'

'And what about Marco?'

'He works for the United Nations,' Elena said.

'The United Nations!' The room swelled with her words again.

'And your husband? Why didn't he come?'

'He has an exhibition in Paris at the moment.'

'Is he famous?' one of the children asked. The clock began to chime.

'If you don't mind,' Elena said, 'can we open the windows?' She grabbed the handles and wrenched them open. She pushed open the door onto the balcony and stepped out. She breathed in, clearing her lungs. She turned to see the young girl with bushy eyebrows next to her.

'*Ciao*, hi,' she said, staring.

'Hello,' Elena smiled. 'And what's your name?'

'The same as yours.'

'Really? I thought Teresa was joking.'

'No.' The girl looked uncomfortable.

Elena fixed her eyes on the mountains. 'Tell me what you do?'

'I'm at school in Genoa. I hate it.'

'So what are you going to do when you leave?'

'Dunno, I don't want to work at the post office like mum.'

Elena placed a hand on the girl's head. 'I'm sure you'll find something.' Her hair was thick and lustrous, her skin pure. 'You're beautiful,' she said.

'Is it true, Auntie, that you ran away because of your husband?'

'That's all a long time ago now,' she replied. 'We don't have to think about that.'

'Don't bother your aunt,' Teresa called from inside. 'Come inside.'

More questions greeted Elena as she left the balcony. She stooped to pick up crumbs and replenish glasses. She handed out pieces of kitchen paper to the children.

'Stop it. You shouldn't be doing anything. You'll get your lovely clothes dirty,' her mother said. 'Let your sister do it. Teresa get the broom.'

Elena apologized and disappeared into the bathroom, removing the pill from her back pocket. She swallowed it, pushing her face under the cold tap. She looked in the mirror and wiped drops from her face with a towel that smelled of mothballs. She pulled her hair back. She removed a piece of biscuit from her teeth with the end of one of her nails. She could hear them talking on the other side of the door.

'She looks beautiful, doesn't she?'

'See her clothes, and that necklace,' Teresa answered, or maybe it was her mother. 'She must have money.'

'Have you found out if we can stay in the south of France yet?' the husband asked.

'Sssh,' Teresa said. 'That kind of thing takes time.'

The clock ticked. One of the boys had put on his walkman. It hummed in the background. 'Turn that dreadful thing off,' the husband said.

Elena went from the bathroom to her room. She found her flask of scent and sprayed more on her wrists. The niece with the bushy eyebrows entered without knocking.

'Want some?' Elena asked.

'Yeah, please,' the girl beamed.

She sprayed her niece's wrists and showed her how to wave her hands afterwards.

'Time to go,' her brother-in-law shouted down the corridor.

'Why don't you visit us in Genoa this weekend?' Teresa asked Elena at the front door. 'Or we can come back here on Saturday.'

Elena felt a tug at her hand and saw that her young namesake was hanging onto her. She bent down. 'Bye.' She kissed the girl on the forehead. 'Wait,' she said before hurrying to her room. She opened up her wallet and took out two banknotes. As everyone piled down the stairs, she held her niece back and slipped the folded notes into her hand. 'Sssh,' she winked, a finger on her lips, 'don't tell anyone.'

Dusk descended and, after supper, Elena's mother fell asleep in her chair in front of her favourite quiz show. Elena removed the remote control from her bent hands and the glasses from her face. She continued to watch the show, listening to the questions from the host. She was surprised at how good she was at firing back answers. She was on a winning streak, not that anyone knew, least of all her sleeping mother. She punched down her fists on imaginary buzzers on the arms of her chair in response to the questions. What would Marco make of this, she wondered? He was sometimes so clever and made her feel stupid despite himself. She didn't know what she could hope from him now. He had moved into another realm, beyond her reach. She tried to picture him with her in Varanelle and realized that it was impossible. He didn't belong here at all. He had become a Parisian, a sophisticated young man. No-one would have ever known that his young feet had touched these mountain fields.

She got two more quiz questions right. By coincidence, they were related to pottery terms and places in France, even something about the Crusades. The programme ended with its catchy music. Elena watched the final sum of ten million lira flash up on the screen. That money could have been hers, practically. She couldn't believe it. Her mother murmured something in her sleep, snuffled and shifted, and she lowered the volume. Is this what her mother had done every evening since her father died? Was this the solitary life that she would have ended up living had she stayed? Her days were filled with such questions, and the loneliness of their permanent reiteration. Twice her mother had asked her how long she was going to stay and she hadn't known what to say. She hadn't mentioned Giacomo at all. When she thought about her sudden departure, she felt she hadn't just run away from him or Aigues-Mortes, but from herself and all that she had become, all that she had believed over the years. She quickly flicked channels.

She tuned into the story of a detective with a drug-addict son. The detective hadn't a clue about his son's double life until he was caught stealing by a fellow officer. The colleague, however, turned out to be a dealer himself who was aiming to supply the son with drugs. The adverts came on. Elena clicked to another channel. It was the news. Throngs of riot police were camped outside a church. Sirens were screaming, flashing. She couldn't immediately work out where it was. It was familiar, definitely somewhere in France. Then the newsreader spoke of the St Bernard Church in Paris that had been squatted and occupied by three hundred immigrants, mostly Malians. Fears had mounted for the condition of ten immigrants who had started a hunger strike forty days previously, and the place had been evacuated the night before. Policemen were shown clearing demonstrators from in front of the church, truncheons in hand, guns in their belts. She zapped to another channel. She couldn't face seeing such things. Yet the image of the church swept through to the next programme, latched onto her. Elena tried to focus in on a comedy. It was about a young couple setting up their first home. Elena switched back to the drug-addict drama. Was this really the kind of stuff her mother watched all day long? She got up and opened the window.

She turned to see the policeman and his son in the midst of a confrontation. The colleague burst in and threatened them with a gun. Without waiting to see what would happen, Elena changed back to the news. Scenes from the previous night in Paris were being replayed. A police spokesman was talking. He was appealing for calm with a loudspeaker outside the church. Then a group of riot police charged, their axes ready, and started hacking down the church door, wrenching it from its hinges, splintering the wood in two. There were screams from inside the building; more police officers rushed in, entered the church and pulled women and men out. Africans, in flourishes of colourful dresses and tunics, were dragged by the arms, handcuffed and bustled violently into police vans. More and more policemen went in, joined by reinforcements. The Africans struggled, women yelling, twisting free and escaping a few metres before being floored by officers. Elena quickly pressed the button back to the channel with the comedy. The builder was trying to kiss the wife, who ran round the kitchen screeching with laughter before giving in. He pushed her down onto the table and it collapsed beneath them. She thought of the Africans and the church. Elena switched the television off. She sat there, sombre. She wanted to scream, 'Please God, no, no, not in church.' She thumped down on the edges of the chair. Her mother stirred and went back to sleep. No, no, she repeated at the screen. She pushed her hair back from her forehead.

Another version of the news began after the comedy. The newsreader went over the situation in Paris. Somewhere, somehow, she recalled Marco mentioning the church and its squatters. Maybe she was mistaken. She watched an emaciated young African woman with a bright green headdress writhing on the floor of the church, her children screaming beside her. She was lifted up by one policeman while another grabbed her hands and cuffed them together. Her skirt, covered in dust, unravelled from her waist. She looked at the camera. Elena watched and blinked. Even the cameraman couldn't hold her panicked stare. The camera swept away, across the inside of the church, the altar strewn with clothes and broken objects, the mess on the ground, the pews pushed aside. Elena turned, following the lines of plaster in her mother's room. Everywhere she looked the African woman with the bright green headdress got there first.

She felt restless. Her throat was dry. She undid her shirt at the neck. New scenes of devastation were being presented on television. The newscaster drummed out figures, the number of injured, the police deployed. Policemen from other areas of Paris were seen preparing to leave for the area round the church and possible riots. People huddled round the cameramen recounting their stories, describing the sequence of events. Others, silent, hung back, unable to speak, unwilling. Then, there she was again, the woman with the headdress and hollow face. She was being hustled into a waiting police van, her children tripping over themselves to hold onto her. A panel of experts and politicians popped up out of the blue beside the newscaster's desk in the studio. They talked about the possibility of such protests taking place in Italy. The discussion turned to a heated argument about expelling illegal immigrants or providing them with papers. A man with an upturned nose warned of future invasions, raising his voice and Elena punched the remote control, trying to find something else to watch. The image went hazy. She got up and banged the top of the television, twiddled the tuning. The adverts clicked in, with an even more blurred screen. She turned the television off. New sounds rose up in the room: axes hacking, van doors slamming and the knock of overturned wooden pews on a desecrated stone aisle.

Elena's mother was staring at her, bleary-eyed. 'Why did you bang the TV like that? You're going to break it.'

'It didn't work.'

'What are you talking about? It always works.'

Elena switched on the light, 'I have to go and make a call from the café. I'll help you to bed.'

Her mother got to her feet. 'What do you think I do every night on my own? I don't need any help,' she said, shaking off the hand on her arm.

'Well, I'll go to the café then. I'm not sure how long I can stay. I'm sure there's stuff to do back at the pottery.'

'What do you mean, Elena? You only arrived last week. Your sister is coming to see you again next weekend.'

'I'm sorry. Giacomo, my husband, will be needing me, I'm sure'

Her mother puffed out her cheeks and sighed. She slid down the corridor to her room. Before she closed the door, she examined her daughter in the bright light. 'You never did know what you wanted,' she said. 'Why can't you just get on with things like everyone else?'

Elena found her purse in her handbag and left the apartment. The cooler air outside was a welcome relief. The café was emptying of its last customers; a group of middle-aged men in shirts stood beside two teenage boys pushing their scooters. They stopped and let her pass between them. She spoke briefly with the café owner and was shown to a telephone in the corner on a ledge. She dialled Marco's number in Paris and left a message. She rang the pottery, both the home number and the showroom. There was no answer. When she looked over her shoulder she saw that the men had returned inside and were standing watching her. She turned round again and faced the stack of tattered telephone directories against the wall. An ashtray was placed next to the telephone. It had a picture of Bardi Castle imprinted in its bowl, smeared with streaks of grey powder. She tried to remember Nassima's home number, writing out several possibilities on the spines of the directories. She rang two wrong numbers and then got through.

'Is that you, Nassima? I'm sorry to disturb you at home, it was all a bit of a rush when I left. I was wondering if you'd seen Monsieur Carlevaris today?'

'What?' Nassima asked, confused.

'Is he all right on his own? How did his trip to Paris go? I can't seem to get hold of him.'

'You don't know…'

'Know what?'

'He's in hospital, in Paris, he got beaten by the police, they say it was an accident, he was caught up in some demonstration… or something, I'm not sure what he was doing there, he was with Marco and his girlfriend, at that church thing.'

'What hospital?' she said, frightened.

'I'm sorry, Madame Carlevaris, I shouldn't be the one telling you this. You should call Marco.' There was a prolonged silence. 'I'll get you the number at the hospital.'

Elena wrote down a shaky number on the open page of a directory. She hung up and held onto the side of the telephone ledge. She found it hard to keep her grip. She picked up the phone again and dialled the hospital number. She was put through to one ward after another until she found a compassionate nurse. She was put on hold again. She opened the directories and straightened their folded-back page corners. She tapped the ashtray, knocking the powder of the sides into the bowl.

Marco was on the other end, his voice unexpectedly clear. 'Mamma?' he said.

She began to cry at the sound of his voice.

339

'What happened?'

'His arm was broken and one of his ribs…'

'What?'

'We're here. Laura's been brilliant. He'll be fine.'

'Can he talk, can I talk to him?'

'No, he's sleeping, they operated on his arm.'

'I don't understand. What was he doing there?'

'It's a long story… I'm sure he'll tell you.'

'When can I call back? I need to talk to him.'

'I think we should let him sleep for now. I'll let him know you called.'

'Tell him to hang on, tell him I'm coming for him. You have to.'

'I will, don't worry. The doctor has arrived, I have to go.' He paused. 'Are you all right there?'

'Me?'

'Yes.'

'I'm fine.'

'I must go now.'

'Call the café in Varanelle if there's anything new, it's the only one here.'

'OK.'

She read out the number taped to the receiver.

'Marco,' she said, 'I can be in Paris tomorrow evening if I leave first thing in the morning. Tell him to wait for me, you will won't you? He'll be OK won't he, he'll be fine? Tell him…'

'Yes, don't worry. The doctors are calling me, I'd better go.'

Elena put the phone down. There was quite a crowd behind her now and they gave no sign of dispersing. One of the men was erroneously relaying her conversation in half-whispers to the others. They pretended to be ordering another round of drinks as she looked in their direction. She rolled her thumbs along the ledge and battled to focus on something solid. Nothing came. She noticed a corridor ahead that led to the lavatory and walked to the end. There was a door that gave way to a courtyard stacked high with crates of empty bottles. Beyond it was a steep gravel path towards a gate. She stumbled up to it and heaved it open. The road curled round the back of the village. The church loomed in front of her. She climbed the steps and tried the front door. It was locked. She tested the other entrances. The sacristy door sprung open when pushed. She penetrated into a damp-smelling room that led to the main church. She found the stand for burning candles, dropped some coins into the tin box and took the pack of matches resting at the side. She lit the wick of a candle and stuck it into an iron holder. She sat on a pew and followed the flickering of the flame. She prayed for Giacomo and repeated his name until it was carried with wisps of clear smoke up into the church. Drips slid from the candle. The flagstones beneath the holder were a mound of wax, as they always had been, regularly scraped and cleared, but always the same. Years of hopes and fears, the prayers of her own lifetime molten together and dried.

Before dawn, Elena laid her clothes in her open suitcase and came out of the bathroom with her sponge bag. She tucked it between the folds of her clothes.

'Still leaving?' her mother said in the darkness of the corridor.

'I told you, Giacomo's not well, I wish I could stay longer, but I can't.' She checked the make-up on her face, extra layers to cover her sleepless night. 'I'll be back,' she repeated.

'If you wanted to come back, you wouldn't leave. That's what I said to your sister before she went off.'

'I have no choice. Why don't you come and visit me in France?'

'At my age? No, no, I'm not going to start travelling now.'

Elena zipped up her suitcase and took her silk scarf out of her handbag. She tied it round her neck.

'Look at you,' her mother said with a dry cackle, 'you've become such a Frenchwoman.'

'You've never even seen one!' Elena protested. She picked up her bag and went down the corridor to the door. She heard her mother behind her, the soles of her slippers slapping the tiles.

'Will you give me that photograph of Marco,' the old woman asked. 'I would like to look at it from time to time.'

Elena handed her the photograph and held out her arms. 'You're all right, aren't you, Mamma? I just can't stay.'

Elena walked down to the parking lot below. She didn't hear her mother close the front door. She looked back, but couldn't see her at top of the stairs. The taxi met her in the village square by the café. Its shutters were thrown open and she was glad no-one came out to give her news of any phone call. As she got in the car, she thought of Giacomo in the hospital ward. She was leaning down and holding him and the longer she did so, the less awkward it felt, both of them again, in each other's arms for renewed solace, two brothers and their wife.

Acknowledgements:

This book would not have been possible without the support of my family: my mother, Dominic, Piers, Lavinia and Carla, Michael and Marcia; and the insight and time of some extremely generous and astute people: Laurence Laluyaux, Christopher and Koukla MacLehose, Deborah Rogers; and the reading and knowledge of other exceptional friends: Cesca Beard, Kate Brooke, Petra Cramsie, Julie Démeocq, Hanifa Dobson, Cécile Gavazzi, Raphaelle Liebaert, Pippa McGuinness, Beatrice Monti della Corte, Faith Mowbray, Emma Richler, Alejandra Riera, Carmela Uranga and Romilly Walton-Masters.

Thank you, too, Francesco and Delfina.

For news about current and forthcoming titles
from Portobello Books and for a sense of purpose
visit the website **www.portobellobooks.com**

encouraging voices,
supporting writers,
challenging readers

Portobello
BOOKS